Br
Christmas

A Christmas gift…in a small velvet box

Three passionate novels!

In December 2007 Mills & Boon bring
back two of their classic collections,
each featuring three favourite
romances by our bestselling authors…

BRIDES FOR CHRISTMAS

Claiming His Christmas Bride
by Carole Mortimer
Christmas Eve Marriage by Jessica Hart
A Surprise Christmas Proposal
by Liz Fielding

IN BED WITH THE BOSS

Bedded by the Boss by Miranda Lee
The Boss's Proposal
by Cathy Williams
In Her Boss's Bed by Maggie Cox

Brides for Christmas

CLAIMING HIS CHRISTMAS BRIDE
by
Carole Mortimer

CHRISTMAS EVE MARRIAGE
by
Jessica Hart

A SURPRISE CHRISTMAS PROPOSAL
by
Liz Fielding

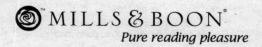

MILLS & BOON®
Pure reading pleasure

Harlequin Mills & Boon Limited,
Eton House, 18-24 Paradise Road, Richmond, Surrey TW9 1SR

BRIDES FOR CHRISTMAS
© by Harlequin Enterprises II B.V./S.à.r.l 2007

Claiming His Christmas Bride, Christmas Eve Marriage and A
Surprise Christmas Proposal were first published in Great Britain
by Harlequin Mills & Boon Limited in separate, single volumes.

Claiming His Christmas Bride © Carole Mortimer 2004
Christmas Eve Marriage © Jessica Hart 2004
A Surprise Christmas Proposal © Liz Fielding 2003

ISBN: 978 0 263 85529 6

05-1207

Printed and bound in Spain
by Litografia Rosés S.A., Barcelona

CLAIMING HIS
CHRISTMAS BRIDE

by

Carole Mortimer

Carole Mortimer was born in England, the youngest of three children. She began writing in 1978, and has now written over one hundred and fifty books for Mills & Boon. Carole has four sons, Matthew, Joshua, Timothy and Peter, and a bearded collie called Merlyn. She says, 'I'm happily married to Peter senior; we're best friends as well as lovers, which is probably the best recipe for a successful relationship. We live in a lovely part of England.'

Don't miss Carole Mortimer's exciting new novel, *The Sicilian's Ruthless Marriage Revenge*, out in February 2008 from Mills & Boon® Modern™.

CHAPTER ONE

'I REALIZE this is a christening, but isn't it a little early in the day's proceedings to be wetting the baby's head?'

Caught in the act of raising the glass of champagne to her lips, Molly froze. Unfortunately, the bubbly wine in the glass didn't freeze, too, slopping over the side to splash over her hand and down her wrist, instantly soaking into the sleeve of her jacket.

'Even for you,' that taunting voice added derisively.

Molly looked up indignantly, glaring across at the man who stood in the doorway watching her with hooded eyes so dark a blue they were almost the same colour as the iris.

Gideon Webber...!

She closed her eyes briefly. It had to be *him* who caught her guzzling a glass of champagne, didn't it? It just had to be!

He was the reason she had sneaked in here for this illicit glass of champagne in the first place, knowing she was going to need every bit of help she could find to face him later on this morning.

Except it wasn't later. It was now. And as she glanced back across at Gideon Webber she could see that same look of contempt on his arrogant face as had been there the last time she had seen him. The first as well as the last!

Not that the man looked any less lethally attractive than he had just over three years ago, when they had last met; his hair was that strange but attractive mixture

5

of golden blond and molasses, his eyes that deep cobalt-blue, his nose long and arrogant, over a finely chiselled mouth, his chin square and determined. The last time Molly had seen him he had been wearing casual denims and a tee shirt, but today he looked even more arrogantly attractive in the formal dark suit and snowy white shirt, the latter complementing his golden tan.

Which he had no doubt recently acquired at some expensive ski resort—it was all right for some! Molly thought uncharitably.

'And what's that supposed to mean?' she snapped, even as she put the glass down on the table. She reached into her bag to look for the tissue she had put in there earlier for emergencies, having decided she had to be ready for any eventuality today! The last thing she wanted was to start sniffing in the middle of her nephew's christening.

Gideon Webber shrugged broad shoulders, the slightly contemptuous smile still curving that arrogant mouth. 'You seem to be rather—fond of—the odd glass or six, shall we say?' He arched mocking brows.

'No, we will not say!' Molly returned waspishly, stuffing the ineffectual tissue back in her bag. The sleeve of her jacket was still soaking wet. She just hoped it wouldn't stain when it dried; she had paid a lot of money for the new suit she was wearing in honour of the day.

Gideon Webber grimaced unrepentantly. 'We've only met twice—and both times you've had a glass in your hand!'

'The last time it was Alka-Seltzer,' she defended with another resentful glare.

'So it was,' he acknowledged with hard mockery. 'I remember commenting at the time that you would probably have been better downing another glass of whatever had put you in that state in the first place!'

Molly drew in a sharp breath as he made no effort to hide his deliberately insulting tone.

She had been dreading today anyway, ever since Crystal had told her who Peter's two godfathers were to be. But she had finally convinced herself that surely Gideon Webber was too polite to make any reference to their last memorable meeting. Obviously, in light of their present conversation, it was a totally erroneous assumption for her to have made about this—this—

This what? she questioned herself heavily.

Under any other circumstances she would have considered this man lethally attractive, 'drop-dead gorgeous', as some of her more colourful friends might have said. And he *was* gorgeous, no doubt about that— over six feet of lethal attraction. He just also happened to be one of the few people who had ever seen her the worse for wear because of too much alcohol…!

Time to take a bit more control of this conversation, she decided firmly. 'Those were exceptional circumstances,' she told him decisively.

He raised blond brows over enigmatic blue eyes. 'And today?'

'Oh, for goodness' sake,' Molly snapped impatiently. 'At most, I've had two sips of champagne.' She picked up the glass to take another assertive swallow. 'That makes three now.' She looked across at him challengingly.

He gave an acknowledging inclination of his head. 'If you say so,' he drawled.

Molly felt the colour enter her cheeks at this obvious scepticism as to the amount of champagne she had actually imbibed—a colour that didn't exactly go with her blaze of rich Titian hair. But, damn it, the man was making it sound as if she were some sort of alcoholic who sneaked around swigging alcohol whenever there was no one else around—

Wasn't that exactly what she had just been doing?

Well…yes. But—

She gave an irritable sigh. 'I do say so.' She nodded curtly. 'I was just—it was only—' Oh, give up, Molly, she advised herself self-disgustedly— While you're not ahead! 'Shouldn't we all be leaving for the church?' she prompted briskly.

'Crys sent me in search of you for just that reason,' Gideon Webber confirmed dryly.

Crys had sent this man to find her? But why not? Crys, of all people, could have no idea how much Molly had dreaded seeing him again. And that was the way she wanted it to stay!

She put the champagne glass down on the table. 'I'm ready if you are.'

He gave a mocking inclination of his head before turning to open the door for her. 'After you,' he invited smoothly.

Molly straightened her shoulders, aware of that hooded gaze following every inch of her progress, knowing what he would see, too: a small redhead with warm brown eyes—eyes usually full of fun and laughter!—dressed formally today, in a dress and matching jacket, her legs shapely, the heels on her shoes a little high for comfort, but their colour exactly matching that of her suit.

'Just one more thing,' Gideon Webber murmured softly as she would have passed him in the doorway.

She raised wary eyes, suddenly tense. 'Yes…?' she prompted cautiously, wondering what the 'one more thing' he wanted to say to her could possibly be. Apart from mentioning their unforgettable first meeting, of course!

He gave a humourless smile, that gleam of white teeth looking almost feral. 'Has anyone ever mentioned to you that women with red hair shouldn't wear certain shades of pink?'

His remark was so unexpected, so insulting in view of the fact that she did have red hair, and that the suit she was wearing was pink, that for several seconds all Molly could do was open and shut her mouth like a goldfish in a bowl, with no actual sound passing her lips.

She had loved the style of the dress and jacket as soon as she'd seen them in the shop, but although she often did wear pink, had been a little unsure about this particular pale shade, debating long and hard while in the shop and trying the suit on whether or not it was actually the right colour for her. The shop assistant, probably sensing her uncertainty, and, in retrospect, probably feeling in danger of losing her commission on a sale, had assured Molly that she looked wonderful in it.

So much for wonderful!

Her eyes sparkled angrily as she turned to give Gideon Webber a haughty glare. 'Most men would be too polite to say such a thing,' she bit out scathingly.

Humour glinted in his eyes now. 'Most men couldn't tell you what any woman was wearing yesterday—let alone whether or not it suited her!'

He had a point there, Molly acknowledged ruefully, thinking affectionately of her stepfather. As long as her mother wasn't actually walking around in something indecent, she was sure Matthew wouldn't notice what Caroline was actually wearing.

'I—'

'Molly!' Crys cried thankfully as she spotted them at the end of the hallway. 'And Gideon,' she added with even more relief, strolling down the hallway to link her arm with Molly's. 'We thought the two of you must have decided you didn't want to be Peter's godparents after all and run away together!'

Molly gave a disbelieving snort at this possible scenario, not even daring to look at Gideon Webber for his own reaction to the remark. She was easily able to guess at the derision that would be curling those arrogant lips.

Especially as she was wearing a shade of pink that clashed with her red hair!

Damn him for telling her that; she now felt decidedly uncomfortable in the suit, what little confidence the champagne had given her evaporating like mist.

But she still had the christening and the rest of the day to get through yet. After that she could scream and stamp her feet in the privacy of the guest bedroom on the third floor above them!

She and Crystal had been friends since schooldays, going their separate ways careerwise after that. Crys had become a first-class chef before opening and running a successful restaurant, as well as appearing in her own cookery programme, and Molly had chosen to go into acting.

Crys had also married three and a half years ago, that marriage tragically coming to an end when her husband, James, died of cancer only months later. But to Molly's delight Crys had met and married Molly's stepbrother Sam almost two years ago, and the couple now had three-month-old Peter James. Hence this christening, three days before Christmas.

The only fly in the ointment—in fact the only cloud on Molly's present horizon!—was that Sam and Crys had asked her previous brother-in-law, James's older brother Gideon, to be one of Peter's godfathers. An honour, Crys had informed Molly happily, he had been only too pleased to accept.

Which had put Molly in something of a quandary. She didn't have happy memories of her one and only meeting with Gideon Webber, and she was sure his own feelings towards her were somewhat less than cordial. But as she had already been asked by Sam and Crys to be Peter's godmother, and had readily accepted, she could hardly turn round and tell them she had changed her mind because Gideon Webber was one of the god-fathers, now, could she?

Of course she couldn't, and so she had armed herself with every feminine weapon she could think of to give her the self-confidence she needed to face the man: new hairstyle, professional make-up, new clothes and shoes. Even a surreptitious glass of champagne to give her an extra boost! She just hadn't taken into account the fact that Gideon Webber, like his younger brother, was an interior designer. And that he would instinctively know she was wearing a shade of pink that didn't go with her red hair!

But at least Crys had interrupted the exchange, and spared her any further insults from the man.

In the rush that followed their mass departure, Molly found herself in a car with her stepfather on the way to the church in this ruggedly beautiful part of Yorkshire where Crys and Sam lived most of the time now. Her mother and the second godfather had elected to travel with Gideon Webber in his dark green Jaguar, and Sam and Crys were travelling separately with Peter James.

Merlin, Sam's Irish Wolfhound and Peter James's guardian from the very first day the baby had arrived home from the hospital where he had been born, sat forlornly on the driveway, watching their departure with the obvious intention of waiting there until they returned with his precious charge.

'Matthew, what is Mum wearing today?' Molly prompted casually.

'Wearing?' Matthew repeated frowningly as he concentrated on following Sam's car the short distance to the church.

'Yes—wearing,' Molly confirmed dryly. 'As in colour?' she added helpfully.

Her stepfather's frown deepened as he obviously gave the question some thought. 'Well,' he finally said consideringly, 'it's a sort of blue thing. Or possibly green. A dress, I think. Or it might be a jacket and skirt. In any case, I'm almost certain it's blue or green,' he added, with a decisive nod of his head.

Molly had already seen her mother on her arrival a little over an hour ago, and knew for a fact that the 'blue or green' suit, of whatever description, was actually a dress and long jacket in a beautiful shade of turquoise. Which, to most men, probably could be described as 'blue or green'…!

And that, in Molly's estimation, just went to prove that Gideon Webber wasn't like other men!

Well, she already knew that, Molly acknowledged with a sigh as she turned to look out of the car window at the Yorkshire Moors.

How she wished today were already over. Then she could get on with enjoying Christmas with Crys, Sam

and baby Peter James. Her parents were leaving tomorrow on an extended cruise to somewhere warmer than
England—which was probably just about anywhere in
December—and so wouldn't be here for the holidays,
which was why they were having the christening today,
before the parents' departure for warmer climes.

After all, what was it? Molly reasoned with herself.
One day. Not even that, really. Just a few hours. And
then Gideon Webber would depart and the four of them
could get on with anticipating Christmas.

But those next few hours, spent in Gideon Webber's
acerbic company, could feel like a lifetime if he continued with the insults!

'Glass of champagne?'

Molly turned frowningly towards the sound of that
voice, her frown dissipating as she recognised David
Strong, an actor who starred in a television series written by her stepbrother, Sam. David was Peter's other
godfather.

Tall, dark and ruggedly handsome, aged in his early
forties, David brought his own brand of charm to the
television series *Bailey*. But he had been widowed several months ago, when his wife had been killed in a car
accident, and the sadness in his eyes and the lines beside
his mouth, despite the warmth of his smile, were tes-
tament to his recent grief.

'Thanks.' Molly accepted the glass he held out to her.
Having met David socially several times before, she
was perfectly relaxed in his company.

Though she couldn't repress her furtive glance
around the room to check whether or not Gideon
Webber was watching her accept the glass of champagne, and she frowned her irritation as he raised his

own glass of what appeared to be sparkling water to her across Crys and Sam's crowded sitting-room.

Molly turned quickly away from the easily discernible mocking humour in those dark blue eyes, the unbecoming colour once again flooding her freckle-covered cheeks. Damn the man. What was he? A one-man vigilante on the consumption of alcohol? Or was it just her consumption...?

Probably, she accepted heavily, wishing once again it had been anyone else but him who had seen her condition on that morning just over three years ago.

Although the world of acting was very often awash with the stuff, Molly very rarely drank alcohol herself—had found that it didn't mix with early set calls or late-night theatre appearances. Which was probably why the downing of that bottle of wine just over three years ago had completely knocked her off her feet!

But there had been good reason for that, she reminded herself defensively. Knowing yourself in love with a married man—a married man who assured you he had every intention of remaining that way—would induce any sane woman to turn to the bottle. Besides, it had only been one measly bottle of white wine—not the whole crateful Gideon Webber seemed to be implying!

Did wine come in a crate? she wondered illogically, or—?

Get a grip, Barton, she instructed herself severely, determinedly turning her attention to David Strong. After all, he was almost as good-looking as Gideon Webber—and much nicer to boot!

'It's good to see you again, David,' she told him warmly.

'And you.' He nodded, brown eyes crinkling at the

corners as he smiled. 'Although from what I hear we should be seeing a lot more of each other in the near future...?' He raised dark brows questioningly.

Ah. Obviously someone had told him. Possibly Sam, as a courtesy to the leading man in his award-winning television series? Or had the secret leaked out in some other way? Probably the latter, she accepted ruefully; the supposed secrecy of the acting world had more holes in it than a sieve!

She gave David a quizzical smile. 'Do you mind?'

'Not at all,' he answered easily, giving her the famous grin that had made him such a hit with female television viewers. 'I think it's past time Bailey had a more permanent love-interest in his life,' he added reassuringly.

That wasn't quite what Molly had meant by her question. It was one thing having the writer of a television series pop up in the studio whenever he felt like it—as Sam often did—it was quite another to have that writer's stepsister appearing in the series with you. As the main character's permanent but definitely whacky girlfriend!

Molly had been working mainly in American theatre the last few years, with the occasional television role thrown in, and until recently had had every intention of remaining out there. But a couple of months ago Sam had sent her the first script he had written for the new *Bailey* series, due to begin filming in the New Year, along with a cryptic message. 'As I wrote the Daisy role based on you, only you could possible play her! Come home. I need you.' Enough to evoke anyone's curiosity.

Although Molly hadn't been quite so sure after reading the script of that one episode!

The character of Daisy was an outgoing, dangerously inquisitive private detective, endearingly naive when it came to the vagaries of human nature, and most of all accident-prone—to the point where objects—usually bodies—seemed literally to throw themselves in her path for her to fall over.

Based on her? she had wondered, slightly dazed. She was outgoing, yes, and could be slightly eccentric, yes. But she wasn't too sure that any of the other character traits fitted her, no matter what Sam might think to the contrary...

But the director of the programme had seemed happy enough with her audition when she'd returned to England a couple of weeks ago, and hadn't hesitated about offering her a contract to cover the next *Bailey* series.

She had thought that particular snippet of information hadn't yet been leaked, but obviously she was wrong; it was one of those well-guarded secrets that everyone knew about!

'I actually meant, do you mind that I'm going to appear in the *Bailey* series with you?' Molly corrected ruefully.

David raised dark brows. 'The director assures me you were brilliant at your audition; why should I mind?'

She gave an awkward shrug. 'Well...Sam is my brother.' She pointed out the obvious. 'And I wouldn't like you to think—some people might think that had something to do with my getting the part.' She grimaced.

'The word you're looking for is nepotism,' drawled an insulting voice.

Gideon Webber's voice. Of course. He seemed to lose no opportunity to insult her.

Was it acceptable for the godmother to hit one of the godfathers at a christening party? Molly wondered angrily.

Probably not.

Pity.

'Gideon!' David greeted the other man warmly—giving Molly the necessary time to clasp her hands tightly together in order not to give in to her initial impulse, after all. 'It's really good to see you again,' the actor added smilingly.

Again? Molly wondered frowningly. Since when did television actors' and interior designers' paths ever cross? Never, or so she had hoped when she had decided on this move back to England. Although it now appeared she might have been wrong about that...

'You can forget nepotism,' David added with a grin. 'From all accounts, this little lady can act her socks off.'

'And any other part of her clothing. Or so I'm led to believe,' Gideon Webber returned dryly.

Molly's gasp of indignation was lost in David's roar of laughter. Obviously he thought the other man was just joking. Molly knew better.

She looked up at Gideon Webber with narrowed eyes. His expression was openly scathing, and the colour slowly crept up into her cheeks. Exactly what had he meant by that remark?

'How did you know she has to take her clothes off in episode four?' David prompted the other man humorously.

Gideon's gaze didn't waver from Molly's as he answered the other man. 'Just an educated guess.'

Molly had no privacy to digest what David had just said. She had to take her clothes off?

Having only returned from America a couple of

weeks ago, and been busy since then moving into the flat she had found in London, there hadn't been time yet for her to read any of the other episodes in the new *Bailey* series.

She didn't have a bad figure, definitely had curves in all the right places, but nevertheless Molly wasn't sure she wanted to take all her clothes off for public display. Even with someone as nice as David.

And, if the derisive look on Gideon Webber's face was anything to go by, he didn't think her body was good enough for public display, either…

CHAPTER TWO

DAMNED cheek!

There was nothing wrong with her body—no excess bulges, her breasts pert, her waist narrow, hips slender, legs shapely—so why didn't Gideon Webber think she was up to playing a nude scene?

Molly angled her chin challengingly at Gideon before turning to smile at David. 'I think it might be rather fun,' she assured him airily, hoping that none of her inner trepidation showed.

Until this moment there had been no mention of the fact that she had to appear nude in episode four or anywhere else. And she had signed the contract now!

Just wait until she got hold of Sam!

'So do I.' David grinned boyishly. 'I have to say that Sam's happy marriage to Crys has certainly livened the series up!'

So it would appear. She really did need to talk to Sam—if only to see if there were any other surprises that he hadn't told her about.

'They are happy together, aren't they?' Gideon murmured ruefully, looking across now to where Sam and Crys were talking softly together, their eyes glowing with the love they felt for each other, which had only deepened on the birth of their son.

'Of course they are,' Molly said waspishly, frowning. Surely this man, just because Crys had once been married to his younger brother, didn't begrudge her the happiness she had now found with Sam?

Molly knew that Crys had loved James very much, but she was only twenty-nine now—the same age as Molly herself. Surely Gideon didn't think Crys should have remained faithful to his brother's memory for the rest of her life? If he did, then he should never have agreed to be Peter's godfather.

Gideon turned back to her, blue eyes hard as sapphires. 'Then let's hope they stay that way,' he bit out harshly.

Molly's frown deepened. 'Why shouldn't they?'

'I think those two have already had their fair share of bad luck where love is concerned.' David was the one to put this in quietly.

Molly knew exactly what bad luck David was referring to: Crys's past loss was obvious enough, and Sam hadn't looked at a woman until Crys after being publicly persecuted by his ex-fiancée twelve years before.

But, after David's own recent loss, it was insensitive of Molly and Gideon to be carrying out this conversation in front of him at all. Even if the antagonism between the two of them was so intense it could be cut with a knife.

'You're right, David,' Molly soothed, putting an apologetic hand on his arm. 'Isn't he, Gideon?' she prompted hardly.

'I think so—yes,' Gideon agreed lightly, but a much stronger emotion burned briefly in the darkness of his gaze as he continued to look down at Molly.

And just what did he mean by that remark? And that look?

This man was too deep for her, too enigmatic; in fact, she could definitely feel a headache coming on!

She drew in a sharp breath as she deliberately turned away from that compelling gaze. 'If you'll both excuse me...? I just want to go and spend a few minutes with my parents before they leave,' she added apologetically, knowing her parents had to go shortly.

'Don't let me stop you,' Gideon Webber assured her abruptly.

If he so wanted to avoid her company, then why had he come over here and joined in this conversation at all? Molly wondered bad-temperedly.

'See you later.' David had recovered enough from the reminder of his recent loss to smile at her.

'Of course,' Molly said gently, not even sparing Gideon Webber a second glance before walking away to join her parents as they stood together across the room.

Damn the man. Damn. Damn. Damn!

Today's christening should have been a wonderful family occasion, full of warmth and love, with all of them doting on Peter James. Instead, because of Gideon Webber's presence, it had become something of a nightmare for Molly. But it was a nightmare she intended putting an end to at the earliest opportunity.

'You!' Molly gasped her dismay the following morning as she entered the kitchen to get herself a cup of coffee and found herself confronted by Gideon Webber, obviously doing exactly the same thing.

She had managed to excuse herself from the christening party the day before as soon as her parents had left, her claim of a headache completely genuine by that time.

She had certainly had no idea that Gideon Webber had spent the night here, too.

'Me,' he confirmed, his smile taunting her obvious

displeasure at finding him here. 'Coffee?' He held up the coffee-pot in his hand.

A brandy would have been preferable after the shock she had just received. But that would only confirm for this man that she was some sort of dipsomaniac!

'Thank you,' Molly managed to squeak, through a throat that suddenly seemed extremely dry and lips that had gone numb.

What was he still doing here? she wondered wildly.

Unusually for December, the sun was actually shining, and the birds had been singing, too, as Molly made her way lightly down the stairs, filling her with pleasurable anticipation for the day ahead.

Anticipation that had just taken a definite nosedive!

'Here—drink some of this.' Gideon pushed a mug of steaming coffee into her unresisting hand. 'Headache still bad?' he prompted mockingly.

He was the headache! And, yes, it was bad—a terrible pounding had started behind her eyes and it hadn't been there seconds ago.

'I wasn't sure whether or not you took sugar,' he drawled as she sat down to take a much-needed swallow of the coffee—and almost choked on it. Not only was it unsweetened, it was also strong enough to strip the enamel from her teeth.

'It's fine,' she managed to gasp, her eyes watering from the resounding slap Gideon had given her on her back. The thin green jumper she wore with denims was no barrier against the force of that hand.

Why hadn't he just asked her how she liked her coffee? Or would that have been too easy?

Probably, Molly instantly answered herself irritably. It might also have deprived him of the pleasure of hitting her as well as choking her.

Okay, so he had stayed the night, for whatever reason. She accepted that, but that didn't answer the question: what was he still doing here?

'Crys and Sam have taken the baby and Merlin for a walk on the moors,' he supplied economically, before sitting down in the chair opposite hers across the kitchen table.

As she had been rather late coming down it didn't in the least surprise her that her stepbrother and Crys had already gone out for their usual morning walk with the dog. What she did find unsettling was the fact that she was left alone here for some time with a man who obviously despised her.

'Don't let me keep you from anything,' she invited stiffly as Gideon still sat across from her, calmly drinking his own strong coffee.

He raised mocking brows. 'What did you have in mind?'

She shrugged. 'Having your breakfast? Packing?' Leaving!

The sooner he made his departure, the sooner she could get on with relaxing—something she certainly couldn't do around this man, either physically or mentally. Every remark he made to her, it seemed, had some sort of double meaning.

'I don't fancy breakfast,' he answered her evenly. 'But you go ahead.'

'I'll pass, thanks.' She didn't fancy breakfast, either.

But what about his packing? He was dressed casually today, in fitted black denims and a deep blue tee shirt, which meant he had his suit from yesterday to pack, at least...

'It was a pity you left the party so early yesterday evening,' Gideon drawled lightly.

Surely he hadn't missed having her there? Or was it just that he hadn't had anyone to sharpen his rapier tongue on once she had gone upstairs to bed? That was probably nearer the truth.

'David had us all in hysterics with some of his more risqué stories of the acting profession,' Gideon enlightened her dryly.

She would just bet that he had. In her experience, there was always more action going on behind the scenes than in front of the camera. Although, thankfully, she had never worked with David before, so none of those stories could have been about her.

She gave a grimace of a smile. 'I'm sure we all have some of those we could relate.'

'Even you?'

Why had that sounded like *especially* you? Or was she just ultra-sensitive where this man was concerned? In the circumstances, was that so surprising?

She moistened dry lips. The strong coffee might have woken her up, but it had done very little to quench her morning thirst. 'Gideon, I think the two of us need to talk—'

'Morning, you two,' David greeted them heartily as he breezed into the kitchen, also dressed casually in denims and a tee shirt, his feet bare of socks and shoes, his dark hair still ruffled from sleep.

Molly stared up at him in stunned surprise; had David spent the night here, too? Obviously. It seemed she had missed more than risqué stories by going to bed early the evening before.

'I don't know whether it's the bracing Yorkshire air or the champagne I drank yesterday,' David said lightly as he moved to pour himself a mug of coffee, sipping at the strong brew with obvious enjoyment, 'but I slept better last night than I have for months,' he went on with satisfaction as he sat down at the table to join them. 'So, where's our godson this morning?' he prompted interestedly.

Their godson... For the first time Molly realised that the three of them were forever linked by this connection to Peter James. That wasn't so bad when it came to David, but Gideon Webber was another prospect altogether!

'Out for a walk with his parents and Merlin.' Gideon was the one to answer the other man. 'You'll have to excuse Molly, David; I don't think she's a morning person,' he told the other man dryly, before turning to look at her mockingly.

She wasn't at her best this morning, no, having so far received one surprise after another, but ordinarily she woke bright and ready for the new day.

Although somehow she didn't think Gideon was necessarily referring to *this* morning...

Her gaze narrowed as she glared at him. 'I'm not used to company in the morning,' she bit out tersely.

'Really?' He raised sceptical brows.

He *did* mean something else.

This man had judged and sentenced her on the evidence of that one morning just over three years ago— just one morning, when... When what?

When she had been tousle-haired and heavy-eyed from lack of sleep. When she had obviously been suffering from the effect of too much wine. When he had seen her dressed only in another man's shirt...

Yes, but...

Yes, but what? There was an explanation for all that Gideon had seen—or thought he had seen—but she very much doubted that this man wanted to hear it. Or whether he would believe it!

She stood up abruptly. 'I think I'll go for a walk outside and wait for Crys and Sam to come back,' she said tautly.

And she would hope that Gideon might have taken his leave before she came back. Although somehow she doubted he would leave without saying goodbye to Crys and Sam.

'If you hang on a minute while I put on some shoes I'll join you,' David told her as he stood up. 'Gideon?' he prompted brightly.

'You two go ahead.' He shook his head. 'I have a couple of calls I need to make this morning.'

'See you later, then.' David nodded, confirming that he, at least, expected to see more of Gideon today.

Which was no consolation to Molly at all as she waited outside for David to join her. If he was now making calls, exactly how long did Gideon Webber intend remaining here?

'What is it between you two?' David prompted a few minutes later as the two of them strolled across the gravel driveway. 'You and Gideon?' he enlightened her as she looked puzzled.

'Me and...? Nothing,' she scoffed forcefully. 'Absolutely nothing,' she repeated firmly as David didn't look convinced.

David quirked teasing brows. 'That wasn't the impression I got either yesterday or today. Come on, Molly, the two of us are going to be working together for months. I'm sure to find out if you're involved with anyone.' He grinned boyishly.

'Well, it certainly isn't Gideon Webber!' she snapped, two bright spots of angry colour in her cheeks now. 'The man does nothing but insult me every time he opens his mouth,' she added disgustedly, knowing it was the truth, and also well aware of the reason for it.

But what could she do about it? If she protested her innocence too strongly Gideon Webber was the sort of man who would only see her vehemence as an admission of guilt on her part. But not to protest was just as unacceptable—and more damning. It seemed that with this particular man she couldn't win.

Not that she hadn't had her share of romantic entanglements in the past, because she had. Gideon Webber just happened to have been a witness to the one time she had made a complete idiot of herself.

David chuckled. 'If we were all teenagers that would be a sure sign that Gideon likes you.'

'Well, we aren't,' Molly said disgruntledly. From the evidence she had seen so far Gideon Webber had never been a teenager—had just gone straight from babyhood to the acerbic man he now was. 'And I can assure you he doesn't.' She sighed heavily, knowing that Gideon's feelings towards her were much more complicated than that.

'More's the pity, hmm?' David teased.

'No, thanks.' Molly grimaced. 'The strong, silent type has never appealed to me,' she added derisively.

Although she had a definite feeling that as far as she was concerned Gideon wasn't going to remain 'silent' for long. At the moment his antagonism towards her was just bubbling below the surface, giving her the distinct feeling that it wouldn't stay that way for much longer, that he was going to have his say concerning their first meeting.

'If you say so,' David accepted teasingly, giving the

clear impression that he didn't believe her lack of interest in Gideon was genuine.

Well, David certainly wasn't in the minority when it came to that; Gideon obviously didn't believe a word she said, either.

'This is a great spot, isn't it?' David enthused happily as they strolled around the extensive grounds. 'I thought Sam was insane when he first decided to bury himself up here, but I can see the attraction now. Even more so now that he's married to Crys. You and she have been friends a long time, haven't you?' he prompted interestedly.

'Since school,' Molly confirmed.

'So you must have known James Webber, too.' David nodded.

Molly frowned at this mention of Gideon's younger brother, Crys's first husband. Her gaze narrowed and she looked sideways at David in search of any hidden meaning in his words. But he was totally engrossed in the rugged beauty that surrounded Falcon House, and was apparently just making conversation as they walked.

'Yes, I met James at university,' she said evenly. 'In fact, I introduced him to Crys,' she added wistfully. The guilt she felt at having ultimately caused Crys such unhappiness when James had died only months into their marriage had never been completely erased, despite Crys's now happy marriage to Sam.

David turned to her with raised brows. 'So you must have known Gideon, too? After all, the two brothers worked together.'

Thankfully, Gideon Webber, ten years older than his younger brother, had never been included in their group of friends. In fact, Molly had only met him the once. But that once had been quite enough, thank you!

She gave David a reproachful grimace. 'You really are wasting your time fishing in that particular direction, David—Gideon Webber and I dislike each other intensely.'

He made a face. 'Does Crys know that?'

She frowned. 'Of course not,' she dismissed abruptly. 'Why should she?'

David shrugged. 'Oh, it's only that… Ah, here they all are.' He nodded in the direction of the battered Land Rover coming up the driveway. 'Excuse me, won't you?' he added hastily as he turned back towards the house. 'But I don't think Merlin has made his mind up yet as to whether I'm friend or foe!'

Molly chuckled appreciatively as David beat a hasty retreat to the house; Merlin could appear quite intimidating until you got to know him. Or, more precisely, until he got to know you.

Having known the dog from when he was a puppy, Molly felt no such hesitation in waiting for her step-brother and Crys to get out of the car. Baby Peter was lifted from the back of the vehicle by his father, and Merlin followed quickly behind him.

'I thought I saw David with you.' Crys looked around frowningly after taking her son into her arms. She was ethereally lovely, with her silver-blond hair loose down her back, and the beauty of her face dominated by misty grey eyes. She was boyishly slender, in spite of having given birth to Peter James only months ago.

'You did.' Molly nodded, grinning. 'He seems to think Merlin needs a little more time to get used to him.'

Sam gave a rueful shake of his head as he absently stroked the huge dog behind the ears. 'I've assured him that Merlin won't bite him as long as he doesn't bite Merlin!'

'I'm sure that helped to convince him of Merlin's tameness.' Crys chuckled huskily. 'Time for breakfast, I think,' she announced briskly, placing the sleeping baby in Molly's arms. 'Pancakes all round!' she decided brightly as she walked towards the house.

Molly followed slowly behind Crys and Sam. Ordinarily she would have been one of the first to appreciate Crys's pancakes—they were to die for, light and fluffy, delicious with maple syrup or sugar. But not today. Not when the dark green Jaguar parked in the front driveway clearly told of Gideon Webber's presence inside the house still.

'Perhaps he'll choke on one of Mummy's pancakes,' Molly suggested hopefully to baby Peter as he opened his lids to look up at her with alert blue eyes. 'I know, I know, he's your godfather,' she accepted apologetically. 'But you do have another one—and I can hope, can't I?'

'Talking to yourself?' drawled a mockingly recognisable voice.

Molly looked up sharply to find Gideon Webber approaching the kitchen door from the front of the house, having moved so quietly she hadn't heard his footsteps on the gravel. Merlin obviously had, and was walking at the man's side, the two of them obviously happy in each other's company.

He raised dark brows derisively, obviously aware of her surprise at seeing him there. 'I had to get something from my car.'

Perhaps it was too much to hope that he had been putting his suitcase in the boot at the same time.

'I was talking to baby Peter, not myself,' she told him stiffly.

Gideon gave a mocking smile. 'Well, I suppose talking to a three-month-old baby has its pluses; at least he can't answer you back!'

Unlike this man, who seemed to have an answer to everything!

Molly eyed him scathingly. 'Unusual in a man,' she acknowledged dryly.

'In my experience, even more unusual in a woman,' Gideon murmured softly, before opening the door for her to enter the kitchen ahead of him, effectively cutting off any sharp retort she might have liked to make at this arrogantly sexist remark. And there were several she would have liked to make.

But the laughter and warmth in the kitchen, with Crys busy mixing pancakes, Sam and David helping to lay the table, the three of them talking as they worked, made her desire to snap a reply seem churlish.

Falcon House was a large, three-storey-high building, but Crys and Sam both loved their privacy, and they preferred to do most things in the house themselves. A woman came in from the village three afternoons a week to take care of any heavy housework that might need doing, but Crys did all the cooking herself.

Despite its obvious size, it was definitely a family home, full of warmth, love, and laughter, and Molly usually enjoyed her visits here enormously. Usually...

Why did Gideon Webber have to be here to ruin it all?

Although she had a feeling she was in the minority in feeling that way. David and Sam were obviously enjoying the other man's company, and Crys and Gideon were standing close together as he helped in the cooking of the pancakes, the two of them moving with an easy familiarity that spoke of a long friendship.

But was it just friendship, or did it go deeper than that? Molly wondered as she sat slightly apart from everyone else, still holding baby Peter as she silently watched them all. Certainly there was nothing more than that on Crys's side—Crys's love for Sam was absolute—but Gideon was definitely more at ease with Crys than Molly had seen him with anyone else. The two of them were talking softly together, Gideon smiling openly, his gaze warm as it rested on Crys—

Now what was she imagining? That perhaps Gideon was secretly in love with Crys? A man she had previously believed wasn't capable of feeling love for anyone?

Ridiculous, she admonished herself impatiently. Gideon had known Crys for years, he was her ex-brother-in-law—of course he had feelings for her; it was only Molly's own resentment towards the man that saw it as possibly being anything else.

'All right?' Sam prompted softly, having come to stand beside her without Molly even being aware of it.

She pushed her troubling thoughts firmly to the back of her mind, looking up to smile at her stepbrother. As well as being a highly successful screenwriter, Sam was the epitome of tall, dark and handsome, and Molly had adored him from the moment she'd known her mother was to marry his father seventeen years ago.

'Of course,' she assured him brightly. 'How could I not be when I'm holding my favourite nephew?' she added teasingly.

Sam came down on his haunches beside her, briefly touching his son's cheek in wonder. 'Your only nephew—unless you know something I don't?' He looked lovingly across the room to where Crys was laughingly serving pancakes.

'Not at all,' Molly chucklingly assured him as he turned back to her.

'Does it make you feel in the least broody yourself?' Sam asked shrewdly.

That was a little harder to answer. She wasn't even involved with anyone at the moment, had severed what had only been a casual relationship with a fellow actor before leaving New York. But she was twenty-nine now, the same age as Crys, and, if she were honest with herself, she envied her friend her loving husband and beautiful baby.

For all the good that would do her, Molly reproved herself ruefully. Without a man in her life, loving or otherwise, there would be no family of her own, either.

She grimaced. 'Sam, I doubt it's escaped your notice that I'm not involved with anyone just now.'

He shrugged. 'What do you think of David and Gideon?'

Molly frowned her puzzlement at this abrupt turn in the conversation. 'What do I think of them as what?'

It was Sam's turn to grimace. 'Well, I think Crys has one of them in mind as your future husband and father of your children.'

'She *what*?' Molly gasped her bewilderment, sitting rigidly in her chair now, unable to hide her horror at what Sam was suggesting.

'Don't tell her I said anything,' Sam told her hastily. 'I think it's all this domesticity that's gone to her head and infused her with this desire to matchmake for you,' he added affectionately. 'She wants everyone to be as happy as we are.'

Molly blinked dazedly. 'Yes, but—'

'Crys assures me that David and Gideon are both extremely eligible men,' her stepbrother teased.

'They may be—' her voice rose slightly '—but David was only recently widowed. And as for Gideon—I don't happen to—'

'Not a word to Crys about any of this, Molly,' Sam warned softly as plates were put on the table. 'She won't be very happy with me if she knows I've said anything to you.'

'But—'

'I'll put Peter in his cradle and then we can all have breakfast.' He spoke normally as he bent to take Peter and crossed the room to put him in the cradle that stood in the corner of the kitchen.

Molly stared after him, totally bewildered by their conversation.

What did he mean, Crys was matchmaking between her and David or Gideon? She wasn't due to start working with David until the end of January, and after today she hoped never to meet Gideon Webber ever again, so exactly when was this matchmaking supposed to take place?

She had a definite feeling she wasn't going to like the answer to that question.

CHAPTER THREE

'EVERYONE had enough to eat?' Crys prompted happily half an hour later.

Half an hour during which Molly's bewilderment hadn't lessened in the least. She knew that Crys was happier now than she had ever been, and that this second marriage to Sam was her whole life, but it certainly hadn't occurred to Molly that her best friend might decide it was high time that *she* found such happiness—to the point that she had already picked out two eligible men for her to look over as prospective husband material.

David Strong and Gideon Webber, of all people...

David was one of the nicest men Molly had ever met, and instantly put one at ease, but he was still suffering badly from the unexpected death of his wife. Molly was very much looking forward to working with him, but she knew he certainly wasn't on the look-out for another woman in his life in the near future.

As for Gideon Webber...!

The only consolation to her own aversion to such an idea was that, much as he obviously loved Crys, Molly knew Gideon Webber would be furious at the very idea of being matched with her.

'There's a good reason behind my wife's desire to make sure you're all well fed,' Sam remarked dryly after they had all assured Crys they couldn't eat another thing.

Crys grinned unrepentantly. 'With all the excitement

and preparation for the christening we haven't had time to put up our Christmas decorations yet,' she explained. 'Sam has some telephone calls to return in his study this morning and so I thought the four of us might have some fun putting up the decorations.'

'No problem,' David assured instantly.

'Glad to help,' Gideon added lightly.

Molly was so disturbed by this added delay to the two men leaving that she didn't say anything.

'You haven't heard where the decorations are yet,' Sam warned them wryly.

David chuckled, shaking his head as he looked at Crys. 'Your wife has the ability to charm the birds out of the trees, Sam,' he drawled affectionately.

'Or the decorations out of the attic?' Sam suggested ruefully.

'That, too,' Gideon acknowledged dryly as he joined in the teasing conversation.

It made Molly feel more out of things than ever; this Christmas holiday simply wasn't working out in the way that she had thought it would.

'How about you, Molly?' Sam turned to her as he, not unusually, seemed to sense some of her confusion. The two of them had always been closer than blood brother and sister. 'I was going to take Peter in with me this morning, but if you would rather look after him than help with the decorations…?'

She would rather do anything else other than spend the morning in Gideon Webber's company.

But even as she opened her mouth to accept Sam's let-out she found her gaze caught and held by Gideon's taunting one. Delicate colour rose in her cheeks and she knew he was aware, and obviously enjoying, her discomfort in his presence.

Her mouth set stubbornly and her eyes flashed before she turned to smile at Sam. 'Thanks for the offer, but you know how I've always loved putting up Christmas decorations.' And how little chance she had had to do so during her years in America.

It simply hadn't seemed worth the effort to put up Christmas decorations in her apartment these last few years, when there had been only herself to see them. She had been looking forward to being involved in all aspects of this family Christmas, including putting up the decorations, and she wasn't going to let Gideon Webber's presence ruin that for her.

'I certainly do.' Sam ruffled her hair affectionately. 'When she was younger she used to insist the decorations went up in November and didn't come down until February!' he confided in the others.

The colour deepened in Molly's cheeks, and she carefully avoided looking in Gideon's direction this time, sure those dark blue eyes would be filled with mockery. 'I'm not quite that bad any more.' She grimaced self-consciously. 'But I have always loved Christmas,' she admitted ruefully.

'Nothing wrong with that,' David assured her approvingly.

'Nothing at all,' Gideon agreed huskily.

Molly looked up at him sharply, expecting to see the normal derision in his gaze, but instead she found him looking at her quizzically, his thoughts unreadable. What now? she wondered frowningly.

Gideon gave a mocking inclination of his head. 'I've always thought that anyone who likes Christmas can't be all bad,' he drawled challengingly.

Brown eyes warred with dark blue for several long seconds before Molly broke the gaze to look at the other three people in the room; Crys still smiled warmly, David and Sam were busy clearing the table of the debris from breakfast.

Was she, Molly, the only one who could hear the deliberate insult behind Gideon's words? Probably, she acknowledged—no one else seemed aware of Gideon's antagonism towards her.

She turned back to him, chin raised as she met that challenge. 'What are your own feelings towards Christmas?'

They might have been the only two people in the room as they faced each other tensely.

Gideon's mouth quirked humourlessly. 'What do you think?'

He really didn't want to know what she was thinking about him right now.

'I have no idea,' she answered honestly. Trying to fathom the workings of Gideon could take a lifetime—and she really didn't have two minutes of her time to waste on the hateful man.

He grinned at her. 'I've always loved Christmas, too,' he told her mockingly.

It wasn't his words that disarmed her, but that grin. It transformed his whole face until he was boyish and charming. Two things she had never before associated with the arrogantly haughty Gideon Webber.

'Good,' she finally managed to answer inadequately.

The grin spread to the warmth of his dark blue eyes. 'Not what you expected to hear, was it?' he guessed shrewdly.

If there was one thing she had learnt about this man in the last twenty-four hours, it was never to expect the expected from him; he had so many facets to his nature it was impossible to second-guess anything he might do or say.

She gave a dismissive shrug. 'What I do or don't expect from you isn't really important, is it?' she dismissed heavily.

'Not to me, no,' he confirmed hardly.

Well, that definitely told you, didn't it, Molly? she acknowledged to herself ruefully. Just as well she felt the same way about him, wasn't it?

Brown eyes sparkled with sudden humour and she easily met his gaze this time. 'Well, I'm glad we got that out of the way, aren't you?' she taunted.

Was it her imagination or did she briefly see admiration flare in those dark blue eyes? Maybe, but it was so quickly masked by his usual mockery that even if she had seen it she knew Gideon wasn't happy with the emotion.

Well, that was just too bad. She was who she was, and she was pretty sure that wasn't the person Gideon thought she was. In fact, she was certain it wasn't!

Gideon glared down at her wordlessly for several seconds, eyes narrowing before he slowly turned away, an enigmatic smile curving those sculptured lips.

Now what? Molly found herself wondering for the second time in almost as many minutes. Why was it, she wondered, that this man always looked as if he knew something she didn't—like a cat that had lapped up all the cream?

And just as quickly she remonstrated with herself for such a fanciful thought; the only cat that Gideon Webber resembled was the feral kind—a hunting tiger, perhaps.

With her as his prey...

'We can all go out this afternoon and choose a fir

tree,' Sam was saying now. 'There's a place not far from here where you can pick and chop down your own,' he added with satisfaction.

'Excellent,' David said with obvious pleasure.

'A real traditional Christmas,' Gideon agreed, before once again looking at Molly, dark brows raised mockingly. 'Aren't you glad that Crys and Sam invited us all to stay over the holiday period?' he added softly.

Molly could feel all the colour draining from her face as the truth finally hit her with the force of an actual blow to the body. Neither David nor Gideon was leaving today. Or tomorrow. Or the day after. Or the day after that. These two men, as well as herself, were invited to spend Christmas at Falcon House, with Sam, Crys and Peter.

Why hadn't she guessed before? It had been there in front of her face all the time—the fact that David and Gideon had stayed the previous night, that neither man seemed in any hurry to leave this morning. Because they weren't leaving any time soon. In fact, it sounded as if the six of them were going to be cosily ensconced here together for the next four days at least!

'Still love Christmas?' a familiarly taunting voice murmured softly in the vicinity of her ear.

Her faith in the goodwill of Christmas had definitely been sorely tested in the last few minutes, but, yes, she still loved Christmas—in spite of whom she might be forced into sharing it with.

She turned sharply to tell Gideon as much, only to find that he was much closer than she had thought he was. His head bent towards hers, their breath intermingling as Molly's abrupt rejoinder died on her lips, and her gaze was held captive by Gideon's as her breathing seemed to stop altogether.

He really was the most attractive-looking man, that honey-blond hair falling endearingly over his forehead, his eyes a dark, fathomless blue over high cheekbones, the patrician nose and that firmly sculptured mouth.

'Will you be on the ''naughty'' or ''nice'' list this year, do you think?' he taunted softly.

Attractive-looking maybe. But as soon as he opened his mocking mouth the whole image was quickly dispelled.

Perhaps just as well…considering she had actually felt herself being drawn to that attraction for a few—mad—minutes.

She drew in a sharp breath. 'I…'

'Come on, you two,' David called over to them cheerily. 'We have decorations to get down from the attic,' he reminded them lightly.

Molly moved gratefully away from Gideon to join David as he followed Crys from the kitchen. But she was aware of Gideon's gaze following her every step of the way…

She was still muttering to herself as she tied the belt on her dressing gown later that evening, after taking a shower before going to bed.

Not that it had been an altogether bad day; the decorations had gone up without too much trouble, their evening meal had been prepared and eaten in companionably good humour, and conversation had flowed freely. Even after dinner, when they had all played a game of Monopoly, it hadn't been as bad as she had thought it was going to be—despite the fact that Gideon had easily been the winner.

No, on the surface it had been a successful day. Only

Molly, it seemed, had been aware of the barb behind every comment Gideon had made to her...

It had started with the naughty or nice remark, and continued unabated throughout the day—to such an extent that Molly had been relieved to excuse herself with the intention of taking a shower before going to bed.

'I'll give him naughty or nice,' she muttered to herself as she hurried down the hallway back to her bedroom. The last thing she wanted was to bump into Gideon when she was wearing only her dressing gown. No doubt he would find some sarcastic remark to make about that, too.

'I've always been nice,' she grumbled irritably as she opened her bedroom door.

Only to let out a loud scream as she saw someone silhouetted against the moonlight shining through her uncurtained window.

'I'm glad to hear it,' Gideon murmured dryly as he turned from gazing out of the window. 'But did you have to scream like that?' He gave a pained wince as he stepped forward into the glow of light given off by the bedside lamp she had left on for her return, still dressed in the casual shirt and trousers he had changed into earlier this evening.

'Yes, I had to scream like that!' Molly assured him furiously. 'What on earth do you think you're doing in my bedroom?' She glared across the room at him, her heart still beating double time, her legs feeling slightly shaky from the shock she had just received.

'Waiting for you, obviously,' he drawled dismissively. 'Do you think you could shut the bedroom door? If I'm staying, there's no point in drawing more attention to ourselves than necessary.'

No point in...! She had thought her torment was over

for at least today, and now he had the cheek to just appear in her bedroom like this!

Molly made no effort to close the door behind her. 'But you aren't staying,' she told him forcefully. 'In fact, I don't know what gave you the impression you could just come in here—'

'You said earlier we had to talk.' He shrugged.

Molly gave him an exasperated look. She *had* said they needed to talk—knew that he needed to be put right concerning several ideas he had conceived about her. But this was hardly the time—or the place—for such a discussion.

'Not now. And certainly not here,' she added impatiently. 'Do you have any idea what people are going to think if they find you in my bedroom?'

Crys, for one, would probably start picking out wedding-dress patterns.

'That was the reason I suggested you close the door,' Gideon reasoned dryly.

On second thought, maybe that wasn't such a bad idea, Molly decided, and she moved to close the door quietly. Anyone walking by to one of the bathrooms down the hallway would hear the two of them talking.

Gideon's brows were raised when she turned back to glare at him. 'Did you have a specific person in mind when you made that suggestion?' he taunted. 'I haven't interrupted an assignation, have I?'

Considering David was the only other eligible male in the household, Molly thought his remark in particularly bad taste. 'Don't judge everyone else by your own behaviour,' she snapped scornfully.

Gideon's eyes narrowed. 'Exactly what do you mean by that remark?' he demanded icily.

'Oh, it's different when it's made about you, isn't it?'

she derided exasperatedly, not really having any idea what she meant; it had just sounded like a good thing to say. It had also obviously touched a raw nerve...

'You—' She broke off abruptly as a knock sounded on the bedroom door, looking from the closed door to Gideon, her expression stricken.

'Molly?' Sam called concernedly through the door. 'I'm sorry to bother you, but Crys said she was sure she heard you scream a few minutes ago?'

Molly gave Gideon an accusing glare, having no idea what she should do now. If she opened the bedroom door then she would have no choice but to try to explain Gideon's presence here to Sam. And if she didn't open the door Sam was going to think it very odd.

'I think you had better open the door and reassure him of your safety,' Gideon murmured softly.

'Oh, you think, do you?' Molly muttered furiously. 'None of this would have happened at all if you had *thought* a little harder about the possible repercussions of a late-night visit to my bedroom!'

He gave a humourless smile. 'The only repercussion I could think of was if you thought I had come here with some idea of seduction in mind—'

'In your dreams, buster,' she cut in disgustedly.

'Molly...?' Sam sounded worried as he knocked a second time.

'It's okay, Sam.' Molly raised her voice so that he could hear her as she moved to open the door, deliberately keeping it only slightly ajar in the hope that he wouldn't be able to see Gideon in the room behind her. 'I'm fine, Sam,' she reassured brightly. 'I—it was just...I saw a spider.'

'And we all know how you love spiders,' her stepbrother sympathised affectionately. 'I'll come in and get rid of it for you,' he instantly offered.

Not with Gideon in her bedroom, he wouldn't! 'No, it's all right, Sam.' She firmly stood her ground in the doorway. 'I—you see...'

'The fact is, Sam—' Gideon spoke purposefully as he moved to stand visibly beside Molly '—I heard Molly scream, too, and I have already disposed of the spider by putting it out of the window.'

Molly closed her eyes briefly, wishing for this to simply be a nightmare, but knowing that it wasn't; it was possible to wake up from a nightmare! She opened her eyes again, to find Sam looking down at her speculatively, dark brows raised over knowing green eyes. After what Sam had told her earlier, concerning Crys's efforts at matchmaking, it wasn't too difficult to guess what he was thinking—or whose fault that was.

'That was kind of you, Gideon.' Sam turned his speculative gaze on the other man. 'I know from past experience how Molly hates to deal with spiders herself.'

'Didn't you know? Gideon is well known for his kindness.' Molly felt stung into snapping; the man wouldn't know 'kind' if it jumped up and bit him on the nose!

Her obvious sarcasm was completely wasted on Gideon. His expression was one of total unconcern.

'Well, if you're sure you're okay...?' Sam prompted lightly.

'I'm fine,' Molly assured him.

'I'll say good night, then.' Her stepbrother smiled, that knowing look still in his laughing green eyes.

'Again,' Gideon acknowledged dryly. 'I'll just have one last check for any more spiders before I leave,' he added dismissively.

And as there hadn't been a spider in the first place...

Molly found herself forcing a strained smile as Sam turned and walked back down the hallway to the bedroom he shared with Crys, giving him a half-hearted wave before closing her bedroom door and turning on Gideon.

'Now look what you've done!' she burst out furiously, eyes blazing deeply brown. 'Sam no more believes you were in my bedroom searching for non-existent spiders than I do!' she added accusingly.

He looked nonplussed and raised blond brows. 'He doesn't?'

'No,' she snapped, colour warming her cheeks as she remembered that earlier conversation with Sam. A conversation she had no intention of giving this man even a hint of!

Gideon shrugged unconcernedly. 'It sounded quite plausible to me. Especially as it turns out you really don't like spiders,' he added mockingly.

Molly's gaze narrowed dangerously. She had disliked spiders all her life, no matter what size they were. She had no explanation for it—knew there was no logic to the fear—she just couldn't stand them in the same room with her.

'So what do you imagine Sam *does* think I'm doing in your bedroom?' Gideon prompted softly, his expression deliberately guileless.

'I'm sure you can work that out for yourself!' she breathed agitatedly, knowing exactly what Sam would be thinking—saying—right now.

Gideon raised dark blond brows. 'As far as anyone else is concerned, we were introduced for the first time yesterday morning at the christening. Do you usually invite men into your bedroom on such short acquaintance?'

'Do I...? You're the one who invaded my bedroom, not the other way round!' she reminded accusingly.

It was bad enough that Sam and now Crys were aware that Gideon was in her bedroom, without having to take the responsibility for it, too. In fact, if she had to put up with any more of his insults this evening she was going to hit him.

'I didn't "invade" anywhere, Molly,' he came back evenly. 'I simply waited in here for you to come back from taking your shower.'

'And you had no right thinking you could do that,' she returned exasperatedly. 'I may have said the two of us need to talk, but I'm certainly in no mood to talk to you at the moment,' she added disgustedly.

There was a moment's silence, and Gideon's gaze was speculative now. 'Then what are you in the mood for?' he finally murmured softly.

Her eyes widened furiously at his obvious meaning. 'Why, you arrogant—'

'I don't think so.' Gideon reached out and easily caught her wrist as her hand would have made contact with one of his cheeks. 'In fact...' he muttered grimly, and his head lowered and his mouth took possession of hers.

Molly was so stunned by the unexpected kiss that for several long seconds she merely stood transfixed in his arms, his body hard against the softness of hers as his mouth explored hers with complete thoroughness.

Cold thoroughness...

That was what brought her to her senses, what stopped her from responding. Because, to her intense dismay, she actually wanted to respond.

Somewhere in the course of the last twenty-four hours—and she couldn't for the life of her imagine when it could have been—she had become attracted to Gideon Webber!

It couldn't have been when he was tormenting her. Nor when he was being sarcastic. After all, despite her earlier unfortunate love affair, she wasn't a complete masochist, and certainly hadn't deliberately allowed herself to become attracted to such an arrogantly impossible man. But for some reason she had done so anyway...

Which was why he had to stop kissing her!

'No!' She pulled sharply away to object, pushing away from him as his arms momentarily tightened about her.

Gideon looked down at her with hooded blue eyes. 'No?'

'No,' she repeated firmly, glaring up at him. 'I'm well aware of what you think of me, Gideon—'

'Are you?' he taunted, his arms dropping back to his sides as he slowly stepped away from her. 'Somehow I doubt that very much,' he added harshly.

Molly easily met that contemptuous gaze. 'I would have to be a complete idiot not to know,' she snapped. 'And, no matter what you may think to the contrary, I am not an idiot! For some reason you have decided I'm some sort of *femme fatale*—'

'For some reason?' he repeated scathingly, shaking his head disgustedly. 'I didn't imagine you that morning at James's apartment. Or the fact that you were completely naked underneath the shirt you were wearing— James's shirt,' he added pointedly. 'Two pretty good reasons for deciding something, wouldn't you say?' He eyed her contemptuously.

Molly gasped, could feel the flush in her cheeks. 'If taken at face value, yes. But—'

'What other way is there to take them?' Gideon cut in scornfully. 'You aren't trying to tell me that it was just coincidental that Crys was away at the time on a promotional tour for the publication of her newest cookery book?'

Molly looked at him wordlessly for several long seconds. He really did think...

She dropped down abruptly onto the bed, staring up at him disbelievingly. She knew he had a bad opinion of her, but...

She shook her head dazedly. 'Didn't you ever talk to James about that morning? Didn't you ask him?'

'No, I never spoke to James about it,' Gideon cut in harshly. 'And I didn't ask him anything, either. What I did do was tell him what an idiot he was for risking his marriage to Crys over a brief affair with someone like you,' he concluded grimly.

Molly felt numb—couldn't think, couldn't speak, could only stare at Gideon Webber in stunned disbelief. It had never occurred to her...

'So there you have it,' Gideon continued when she made no reply. 'Was this what you wanted when you suggested the two of us talk—all of this out in the open, with no more need for even cursory politeness between the two of us?'

'I wasn't aware that there had been much of that anyway,' Molly felt stung into replying, still stunned at what this man was accusing her of. He believed she'd had an affair with his brother James!

His mouth twisted humourlessly. 'There is in front of Crys and Sam,' he snapped. 'Crys obviously knows nothing about you and James—'

'There *was* no me and James!' she cried protestingly, at the same time knowing that on the evidence this man had, her protest sounded hollow, to say the least. Even if it *was* the truth.

His top lip curled contemptuously. 'Obviously nothing James felt important enough to need to make any deathbed confession to Crys.' Gideon gave a disgusted shake of his head. 'That's something to be grateful for, at least!'

'But...'

'But I know. And you know,' Gideon continued hardly. 'Let's just leave it at that, hmm?'

Molly's eyes widened disbelievingly. 'You surely don't think that I would ever—'

'Who knows what you're capable of?' he cut in disgustedly. 'From what I can gather, Crys is your best friend—and yet you felt no compunction about taking advantage of her absence from the marital home to jump into bed with her husband.'

This was incredible. Unbelievable. Oh, it certainly went a long way towards explaining Gideon's behaviour towards her—it was just totally inaccurate as to what had really happened just over three years ago.

'There's only one positive thing that I can see about this situation,' Gideon continued hardly.

'There's a positive to all this?' Molly echoed dazedly.

'Oh, yes.' Gideon nodded with grim satisfaction.

She blinked. 'And that would be...?'

Those dark blue eyes gleamed with that same satisfaction. 'Crys is now married to your stepbrother. A situation that would certainly alter if you were ever to feel the need to clear your own conscience. Crys would find it very difficult to stay married to the brother of the woman who had an affair with her first husband.'

'Now just a minute—'

'I've wasted all the time that I'm going to tonight,' Gideon rasped with a dismissive shake of his head.

On her, that was, Molly acknowledged numbly. This was worse, so much worse than she could ever have imagined. Oh, she had known there had to be a reason behind Gideon's complete contempt for her, had guessed that it probably had something to do with finding her in James's apartment that morning just over three years ago, but she had never imagined...

'Be warned, Molly,' Gideon added harshly. 'I won't ever let you do or say anything that will hurt Crys. Is that understood?' he prompted determinedly.

She swallowed hard. 'Perfectly.' She nodded, wondering if he weren't being just a little hypocritical. His protectiveness of Crys—erroneous as it might be in her own case—seemed to indicate more than just ex-brother-in-law affection on his own part.

Not that she was particularly interested in that; it was his belief of her own behaviour that was so disturbing.

Crys had been, and still was, Molly's best friend. And Molly had known James for some time before introducing Crys to him; James had been one of her best friends, too. But that was all he had ever been: her friend.

Not that she thought this man was about to believe that for a moment. He had formed an opinion of her on one brief meeting. A bad opinion. And the only way to even try to explain herself was to give him an explanation of a time in her life she would rather forget. An explanation he was unlikely to believe in any case.

'Good,' Gideon bit out with satisfaction. 'In that case, I have nothing further to say to you. Except—'

'Please,' Molly protested weakly, putting up a shaking hand to the temple that had started to throb painfully. 'I've already heard enough of your insults for one evening.' She sighed heavily.

Gideon paused on his way to the bedroom door. 'Oh, I wasn't about to insult you again, Molly,' he assured her lightly.

'No?' she said disbelievingly.

'No,' he said derisively. 'I was about to tell you that I'd lied about dealing with the spider. It's on the ceiling directly above your head. Have a good night!' he added tauntingly, before letting himself out of the bedroom.

Molly didn't see him leave. One glance at the ceiling above her head revealed that there was indeed a spider. A huge one!

She shot off the bed so fast she almost fell over, staring in horrified fascination at the long-legged, fat-bodied insect.

Swine!

Rotter!

Sadist!

And she wasn't referring to the spider!

CHAPTER FOUR

THE phrase 'you look like hell' came to mind as Molly looked at herself in the dressing-table mirror the following morning. Her hair stood out in a wild tumble of curls and her face pale, with dark shadows beneath her eyes.

It wasn't just any morning, either; it was Christmas Eve.

But she had never felt less like Christmas than she did at this moment. She had spent a sleepless night, alternately looking at the spider or thinking of the things Gideon had said to her the previous evening.

He really believed she'd had an affair with his brother James behind Crys's back.

For one thing, she hadn't felt that way about James— had only ever looked on him as a friend. For another, Crys was her best friend; there was no way Molly could ever have betrayed that friendship, even if she had been in love with James, by sneaking behind Crys's back and having an affair with him.

But if Gideon ever chose to tell Crys of that morning when he had arrived at the apartment Crys had shared with James, and found Molly in residence, her only clothing one of James's shirts, would her friend be able to believe in her complete innocence?

Molly would assure her that James had only ever been her friend. But in light of that night Molly had once spent at the married couple's apartment, while

Crys had been away, the night Gideon was aware of, too, would Crys still believe in her innocence?

Gideon had contemptuously assured her he had no intention of ever telling Crys about that night, that he had no desire to hurt her or to ever see her hurt, but would he continue to feel that way if it no longer suited his own plans?

Unhappily, the conclusion Molly had come to during the long sleepless night had been that she simply didn't know the answer to that question. Despite her aversion to going anywhere near the man ever again, she would have to speak to Gideon on the subject.

But not until she had done something about the way she looked.

And she did try. She washed her hair and styled it until it was silkily gleaming on her shoulders, applied make-up to hide her paleness and those dark shadows beneath her eyes, even chose her clothes carefully: a burnt-orange-coloured blouse teamed with fitted black denims. It was just that none of those things could hide the fact that she looked and felt thoroughly exhausted from all the thinking she had done during the night.

Oh, damn the man—and his suspicious mind. If it weren't for both those things she would be enjoying a warm family Christmas with Crys, Sam and the baby, just as she had envisaged when she'd accepted their invitation to stay.

'Last again?' Gideon taunted the moment she entered the kitchen, shortly after nine o'clock.

He *would* have to be the first person she saw this morning—and he wasn't alone, either. Crys was sitting at the kitchen table with him.

The latter turned to smile warmly at Molly as she walked over to pour herself some coffee from the pot.

'Sam and David have taken Peter and Merlin for a walk to give me a few minutes' break; Peter was cranky all night—didn't seem to want to settle.' She grimaced affectionately.

'I know the feeling.' Molly nodded, sipping her hot coffee, her brooding gaze daring Gideon to come back with another one of his barbed comments after the total inaccuracy of his initial statement; they both knew that David had been the last down the previous morning.

Crys at once looked concerned. 'Sam said there was a spider in your bedroom last night,' she sympathised.

Molly looked coldly at Gideon now. 'There was,' she confirmed flatly. And that sadistic swine had left her alone in her bedroom with it all night.

He returned her gaze steadily, the blandness of his expression giving away none of his emotions or thoughts.

In Molly's opinion he didn't have any of the former, and far too much of the latter.

'Lucky that Gideon was able to deal with it for you.' Crys nodded happily.

The only thing Gideon had dealt with was his own need to tell Molly exactly what he thought of her—before leaving her alone with that monster spider!

'Wasn't it?' she returned noncommittally, no longer even looking at Gideon, just too tired to cope with any more of his scorn, even in a look. 'Could I borrow your car to go into town this morning?' She turned to Crys. 'I still have a little last-minute shopping to do.'

It had also occurred to her some time during the sleepless night that, as she hadn't known they were going to be here over the holiday period, she didn't have presents to give to either David or Gideon tomorrow morning.

Not that she particularly wanted to get Gideon a Christmas present, unless it was a bottle of arsenic, but it would certainly look odd if she bought something for everyone else and deliberately excluded him.

There was no help for it; she would have to buy him a present, too. Something completely impersonal, she had finally decided—like a one-way ticket to the North Pole. He would certainly feel at home there, amongst all that ice and snow.

'I'm driving into town myself this morning.' Gideon was the one to answer her. 'So you may as well come in with me.'

Molly's eyes widened in horror at the thought of spending any more time alone with this man while she felt so tired and vulnerable. And she made no effort to hide the emotion when he looked at her mockingly.

'What a wonderful idea!' Thankfully Crys had turned to look at Gideon and didn't see Molly's response to the suggestion. 'Perhaps you wouldn't mind picking up a newspaper and my order from the butcher's while you're there?'

'Glad to,' Gideon assured her smoothly.

'Great.' Crys grinned as she stood up. 'I'll just go and get the list.' She hurried from the room.

Oh, yes, just great, Molly echoed heavily in her thoughts, knowing it had been taken for granted that she would accept Gideon's offer to drive her into town.

And why not? Ordinarily it would be the normal thing to do. It was just that there was nothing in the least 'ordinary' about the emotions that passed like electric volts between Gideon and herself.

'You look tired this morning.'

It was a statement, not a question, and a totally unwelcome one as far as Molly was concerned. Once again she looked up to glare at Gideon. 'And whose fault is that, do you think?' she challenged tartly.

He grimaced. 'From the accusation in your tone, I gather that it's mine...?'

Her eyes flashed deeply brown. 'You gather correctly. You—'

'Here we are.' Crys bustled back into the room with the appropriate list. 'It's the shop in the square—not the one down the street,' she added lightly, not seeming in the least aware of the tension in the kitchen between Molly and Gideon.

And why should she be? Molly reasoned ruefully. As Gideon had already pointed out, as far as any of the family were concerned the two of them had only met for the first time at the christening.

'I'm sure that between the two of us we'll manage to find it,' Gideon assured her as he stood up. 'Hmm, Molly?' he prompted pointedly.

Molly felt a small shock run through her body as he called her by her first name, sure that it was the first time he had done so in the last two days. Not that it had sounded in the least warm or familiar—just slightly alien coming from this particular man.

'I'm sure we will,' she confirmed flatly. 'I'll just go and get my coat and meet you at the car.' She turned to leave without waiting for any response to this remark, just needing to get away for a few minutes on her own.

To regroup.

Also to make sure she removed all sharp instruments from her handbag—just in case she was goaded into sticking any of them into Gideon as he drove. After all, it was him she felt like doing harm to, not herself.

The green Jaguar saloon was comfortable, she would give him that, Molly allowed grudgingly a few minutes later when she sat beside Gideon as he drove the car down the long driveway out onto the public road. Warm and comfortable. But that was only the car. The owner was anything but those things.

Perhaps it was too warm and comfortable, she decided a few minutes later as her eyes began to close and her head to nod tiredly.

'You really are tired, aren't you?' Gideon said slowly as Molly made a concerted effort to stay awake.

'Why would I say I was if I wasn't?' she snapped back testily.

There was complete silence in the car for several long seconds, and then Gideon gave a sigh. 'Perhaps I was a little hard on you last night,' he said grudgingly.

Molly turned to give him a sharply suspicious look. Surely he couldn't be apologising for the things he had accused her of yesterday evening?

He glanced at her, dark blond brows rising as she warily returned his brief gaze before it returned to the road ahead. 'I was referring to my omission to dispose of the spider,' he drawled derisively.

No, she had been right the first time; he wasn't apologising for the accusations he had made.

'Did you spend all night keeping a wary eye on it?' he added with some amusement—completely nullifying the previous apology.

'Don't give it another thought,' Molly dismissed hardly, determined not to give him the satisfaction of knowing she had done just that.

'I wouldn't have done—' he shrugged '—if it weren't for the fact that you look so exhausted this morning.'

'By "exhausted" I presume you mean awful?' she bit out resentfully; so much for the washed hair and make-up.

He gave another shrug of those broad shoulders. 'Well...'

Molly felt the angry colour warm her cheeks as she glared at him. 'Do you ever say anything nice?' she snapped caustically.

'Frequently.' He nodded, completely unabashed. 'For instance, in contrast to what you were wearing on Sunday, the blouse you're wearing this morning suits your colouring perfectly.'

The compliment was so unexpected that it left Molly speechless. And slightly tearful, she realised with dismay.

Overtired.

Overwrought.

Just over-everything...

Gideon gave her another glance, frowning slightly. 'Wasn't that a nice thing to say?'

Molly gave a deep sigh, aware even as she did so of just how tensely she had been sitting as she relaxed back against the seat. The problem was, even 'nice' sounded suspect coming from this man.

'Thank you,' she accepted huskily.

'You're welcome.' He nodded. 'I'll go and hunt down the spider when we get back, if you like,' he added huskily.

She shook her head wearily. 'There's no need for that.'

His eyes widened. 'You managed to deal with it yourself?'

'No,' she acknowledged ruefully. 'I meant that to my certain knowledge it hasn't moved an inch from its balancing act above the bed—so there will be no need to hunt it down.'

A frown appeared between those dark blue eyes. 'I'm not usually a deliberately vindictive man,' he rasped.

Molly grimaced. 'You're just happy to make me the exception, hmm?'

The frown deepened. 'Not happy, exactly...'

'Oh, just go for it, Gideon.' Molly gave a tiredly rueful laugh.

The frown remained. 'You really spent all night watching that spider?'

'I really did.' She nodded self-derisively. 'After all, I could hardly go along and ask Sam for help after you had assured him so emphatically that you had already dealt with it.'

Gideon's mouth thinned. 'I feel really bad now,' he rasped self-disgustedly.

Molly eyed him questioningly. 'How bad?'

'Bad,' he accepted slowly.

'Bad enough to listen to my side of what happened three years ago?' Molly came back, more decisively than she would have believed herself capable of this particular morning.

He stiffened. 'No,' he rasped harshly. 'I feel guilty for leaving that spider in your room when you obviously are an arachnophobic. That doesn't mean I'm about to let you try to convince me that I didn't see that morning what I definitely did see.'

Hard. Unyielding. Judgemental, Molly decided frustratedly. How could she reason with a man like that?

She couldn't, came the unpleasant answer. Although that wasn't going to stop her from trying.

'However,' Gideon continued hardly before she could formulate a reply, 'what I am willing to do is call a truce on the subject over the Christmas period.'

'Big of you!' she snapped impatiently.

His mouth tightened ominously. 'It's the best offer you're going to get,' he bit out harshly. 'In fact,' he continued grimly, 'as far as I'm concerned it's the only offer you're going to get.'

In other words, take it or leave it! And in the circumstances—not wanting to spoil Christmas for the others, if any of them should pick up on the barbed warfare between herself and Gideon—Molly knew she would have to take it.'

Her mouth twisted humourlessly. 'I take it this "truce" will cease being in effect the moment midnight strikes on Boxing Night?'

His own smile was just as humourless. 'Actually, I'm staying until the morning of the twenty-eighth—think you can manage to be polite for that long?' He quirked dark blond brows at her.

'I'm not the one being impolite!' she returned waspishly.

Gideon gave a shrug of broad shoulders. 'I'm willing to give the alternative a try.'

Molly bit back the angry retort she would have liked to make, on the basis that it wasn't a very good way to begin a truce—but that didn't mean she didn't still have murderous tendencies towards this arrogant man.

'Fine,' she bit out between gritted teeth.

He turned to give her a mocking glance. 'So, what are you going to buy me for Christmas?' he taunted.

Molly's eyes widened at his astuteness in guessing what her 'last-minute shopping' actually was, and then she gave a rueful shake of her head. 'I did have a bottle of arsenic in mind—but then I decided that might be a little too obvious!'

To her surprise. Gideon gave an appreciative chuckle. And once again it transformed his whole face, giving him a boyish look, turning his blue gaze warm rather than arctic.

Which, considering Molly's total awareness of him probably wasn't a good idea...

'Maybe a little,' he finally conceded, still smiling.

'What would you like me to get you?' she prompted interestedly, having no idea what this man's interests or preferences were.

In any subject!

He was here alone, so he obviously wasn't involved in a relationship at the moment; he would be spending Christmas with whoever it was if that were the case. But that posed the question: what sort of woman was he attracted to? Obviously not petite redheads who happened to be frightened of spiders.

Now why on earth had she had that thought? Molly wondered crossly. It was bad enough that she should have allowed herself to be attracted to him, without wishing he might find some redeeming attraction in her.

Besides, she already had an idea that Gideon's attraction lay towards fragile silver-blonds with haunting grey eyes. Crys...

'Well, I don't like chocolate, and I have enough aftershave already,' Gideon answered her slowly. 'Would a book be impersonal enough, do you think?' he prompted softly.

Molly felt her cheeks flush; did this man know everything? 'I'm sure that it would,' she bit out tersely. 'What sort of book did you have in mind?' Something erudite and learned, no doubt, Molly reasoned wryly.

Gideon shrugged. 'There is a book I've been meaning to buy for some time. I was waiting for it to come out in paperback, and then I just forgot to buy it...'

'Yes?' Molly prompted dryly, wondering if her bank

account had enough in it to cover the cost of a book this man hadn't yet got around to buying for himself.

The move from America back to England had worked out quite expensive, what with shipping her few personal belongings back here and finding herself a flat to live in. But, on the bright side, at least she was one of the ten per cent of actors who were in work at any one time.

Gideon eyed her frowningly. 'Perhaps you already had something in mind? Besides the arsenic, that is,' he taunted.

She gave a shake of her head. 'Not a thing.' She doubted the one-way ticket to the North Pole would have been any better received. 'In fact, I would more than welcome any useful advice you could give me in that direction,' she assured him briskly, knowing she had no idea what to get for David, either.

She was also wondering what Gideon had got *her* for Christmas...

Obviously he had already known he would be staying for Christmas, and who the other guests were to be, so he would have purchased something for each of them before coming up to Yorkshire. Knowing how he felt about her, she dreaded to think what he would have as a gift for her.

Gideon nodded. 'Okay, then. One of my favourite comedians is Billy Connolly, and—'

'I don't believe it!' Molly protested incredulously, and colour flooded her cheeks as she realised what she had said. 'I mean—well...Billy Connolly is—' Whatever she had been trying to say, she gave it up as a bad job to stare at Gideon dazedly.

Billy Connolly? He was her absolute all-time favourite comedian, and had proved himself to be an exceptional actor in recent years, too. She would just never, ever have thought that Gideon Webber would like him, too...

'An acquired taste,' Gideon acknowledged dryly, obviously mistaking her surprise for censure. 'One that I acquired during my university days and have never lost,' he added ruefully.

Molly had already read the book Gideon was referring to, written by the comedian's wife, and had found it to be moving, tragic. But ultimately the often outrageous Scottish comedian's gift of humour had shone through all the hardships suffered in his childhood. She was just having difficulty coming to terms with having that like shared by Gideon Webber, of all people.

'One that I acquired years ago, too,' Molly told him evenly, deliberately masking her surprise at his preference. If asked, she would have sworn that she and Gideon had absolutely nothing in common. 'And it's a great book,' she assured him. 'What do you think I should get David?' She deliberately changed the subject, still slightly rattled by discovering that she and Gideon had the same sense of humour.

'That's easy,' Gideon answered smilingly. 'We discussed the book last night, and David hasn't read it yet, either.'

David sharing her slightly offbeat sense of humour she could more readily understand...

Although wasn't it just a little too impersonal to buy both men the same gift? It might look as if she had been out and bought a job lot to attain a discount.

Gideon glanced at her. 'I can assure you that we will both be more than pleased with the gift.'

'Fine with me,' Molly accepted briskly, deciding that impersonal was definitely the way to go with both these men when taking into account Sam's warning of Crys's attempts at matchmaking.

Something to keep constantly in mind, considering Crys's satisfied look as she'd stood in the driveway and watched the two of them drive off together earlier.

CHAPTER FIVE

'THERE we are,' Gideon told Molly with satisfaction as
he turned from putting the huge spider out of her bedroom window.

'Thank you,' she accepted awkwardly, finding his
presence in her bedroom for the second time in twenty-
four hours more than a little disconcerting.

Their trip into town together hadn't turned out quite
as she had expected. She had thought that Gideon would
go off and do his own chores while she wandered
around doing her own. But that hadn't happened at all—
Gideon seeming quite happy to stroll around with her.
Even when she'd gone into the bookshop to buy the
two books Gideon had simply waited outside for her,
and then they had recommenced their stroll up the
street.

It had been a little disconcerting, to say the least. The
shoppers around them had obviously been infused with
the happiness of the Christmas spirit, and there had been
none of the mad rush and bustle in this little country
town that Molly had left behind her in London. People
had seemed to have time to stop and chat with each
other, even though most of them were laden down with
gaily wrapped parcels, and the coloured lights and decorated windows had all added to the relaxed atmosphere
of warmth and cheer.

Surrounded by such obvious good humour and goodwill, it had been impossible not to become caught up in

it—even Gideon had seemed more relaxed, if not exactly friendly.

That was probably a little too much to hope for, Molly accepted ruefully.

But his slightly softened attitude certainly gave her hope that the Christmas holiday wasn't going to be as unpleasant as she had thought it would—but not enough to introduce the subject of that night just over three years ago; that would be sure to reintroduce a complete dampener on the whole thing.

'Where do you suppose everyone is?' Molly frowned now, anxious to get Gideon out of her bedroom, but also concerned that there had seemed to be no one else at home when they'd arrived back a short time ago, having picked up the requested newspaper and meat from the butcher's.

Gideon shrugged. 'Maybe they've all gone out for lunch on the assumption we would probably do the same?'

Oh, yes, she could just see Gideon and herself sitting down to eat lunch alone together—something guaranteed to give them both indigestion, she would have thought.

Although, bearing in mind Crys's newly acquired matchmaking tendencies, Molly wouldn't put it past her friend to have deliberately left her alone here with Gideon in an effort to further their friendship.

'Maybe.' She grimaced. 'In that case—'

'Hi, you two!' David greeted them from the hallway just outside Molly's bedroom. 'Do you happen to know whether or not you've had chickenpox?'

'I beg your pardon?' Gideon frowned uncomprehendingly.

'Sorry?' Molly felt just as puzzled—although that

didn't stop the colour entering her cheeks at Gideon once again being found in her bedroom.

David stepped into the doorway. 'Apparently the reason Peter has been feeling less than his usual cheerful self is due to a rash on his face and chest. The doctor is with him now, deciding whether or not it's chickenpox,' he explained with a grimace.

'Oh, no,' Molly groaned sympathetically.

'Chickenpox?' Gideon's frown deepened. 'Isn't he a little young to get something like that?'

Too young, Molly acknowledged worriedly. Peter was only three months old...

'That's what the doctor said,' David acknowledged lightly.

'I'll go and see Crys now...'

David put out a hand to stop Molly as she would have hurried from the bedroom. 'Not if you haven't already had chickenpox,' he warned.

'I have,' she assured him. 'According to my mother I had every childhood disease going before I was a year old,' she added ruefully.

'Why am I not surprised?' Gideon muttered dryly.

Her eyes flashed deeply brown as she shot him a look across the room. 'Have *you* had chickenpox?'

He drew his breath in with a heavy sigh. 'As it happens, no,' he admitted with a grimace.

'Oops,' David sympathised. 'If it actually is chickenpox, it seems that Peter will have been at his most infectious from the christening onwards,' he explained at Gideon's questioningly raised brows.

It was all Molly could do to hold back her smile. Oh, it would be awful if a baby as young as Peter had contracted the infection, but the thought of the arrogantly confident Gideon Webber struck down with the unsightly rash was enough to make anyone smile.

'Perhaps you should leave now?' she suggested lightly—hope still sprang eternal that this man might not be here to ruin Christmas.

'That wouldn't be allowed, I'm afraid,' David was the one to answer her. 'The doctor has already said that if it is chickenpox, if we've all been in contact with Peter during the last forty-eight hours, that we would have to remain a self-contained unit for at least the next five days or so to see if any of us develop the infection.'

Five days? When Molly had been expecting to rid herself of Gideon within a couple of days!

But the look of mockery that had replaced Gideon's frown was enough for her to immediately hide her dismay. 'I'll go and see if there's any news,' she offered briskly, deliberately turning away from Gideon—and his knowingly taunting look.

Poor Peter did look very disgruntled when Molly entered the nursery a few seconds later, his face all red and blotchy from crying. Crys's face was pale and anxious as she held him in her arms.

'How is he?' Molly asked a grey-faced Sam as he stood beside Crys, looking down worriedly at his young son.

'It's what's commonly called milk rash.' It was the young female doctor who answered her lightly. 'Uncomfortable for Peter, but fortunately he doesn't have a temperature or anything like that,' she added reassuringly. 'Poor little love is just feeling a trifle fed up with the world—aren't you, Peter?' She touched him comfortingly. 'And his first Christmas, too.'

In actual fact, apart from the slight rash on his face and chest, and his cheeks blotchy from crying, Peter looked in better health than either of his parents, Molly decided, after taking in Crys's ashen face and Sam's anxious gaze as he continued to look at his wife and son.

'Well, that's really good news.' Molly smiled at the pretty doctor.

The doctor grinned back. 'Isn't it?' She nodded, obviously relieved to have someone other than worried parents to talk to. 'I'm sure the rash will fade very soon, and Peter will be back to his normal placid self,' she added dismissively, 'but if you have any more worries about him at all over Christmas, please don't hesitate to call me. I shall be on call all over the holiday period,' she said ruefully.

'Poor you,' Molly sympathised as she escorted the doctor out of the nursery and down the wide staircase to the front door.

The lights on the Christmas tree they had dressed the previous evening blinked on and off warmly as they passed the sitting-room.

The doctor shrugged. 'It seems only fair, as my partners all have families they would like to be with.'

The doctor was probably aged in her mid-thirties, and was extremely pretty in a blond, blue-eyed, no-nonsense sort of way; it seemed unfair that she was to spend Christmas alone.

'Everything okay?' David prompted as he came out of the sitting-room. He was obviously the one responsible for putting on the Christmas lights; neither Crys nor Sam was in any mood to think of anything to do with Christmas at the moment.

Molly drifted off into the kitchen as the doctor and the actor fell into easy conversation and David took over the task of escorting the doctor to her car.

From the looks of things, what with Peter's obvious discomfort and the doctor's visit, no one had yet had any lunch, and now certainly wasn't the time to ask Crys what she'd had in mind for the meal. But a quick look in the fridge revealed a huge bowl of freshly made chicken soup, and Molly had already seen there were three French sticks on the table to accompany it.

'Oh!' She gasped as she straightened from the fridge to find Gideon standing behind her; he moved with the silence of a feline.

'Steady.' He reached out and took the heavy bowl from her as it wobbled precariously. 'Where shall I put this?'

Those raised blond brows dared her to make the answer that had sprung so readily to her lips, but Molly clamped those lips together for several seconds before answering. 'Just on the table, thanks,' she said briskly. 'I think Crys and Sam need to eat something after all that worry,' she added ruefully.

Gideon nodded. 'Nothing ever looks as bad on a full stomach.'

Molly wasn't so sure that a bowl of soup and some French bread would work the same magic with her, concerning spending Christmas with this man.

Gideon grinned as he seemed to guess her thoughts. 'Well…usually not,' he drawled mockingly.

She glared up at him. 'Why don't you lay the table and make yourself useful, instead of standing there tormenting me?' she bit out crossly, having transferred the soup to a large saucepan and put it on top of the Aga to warm while she cut the bread up into more manageable pieces.

Gideon didn't move, still standing far too close to her

than was comfortable. 'Am I tormenting you?' he murmured huskily.

Molly swallowed hard. 'You know that you are!' she snapped, at the same time knowing that her voice lacked conviction.

What was it about this man that made her so aware of him? So physically aware of him—totally aware of the muscled tautness of his body, of the clean, male smell of him, of the arrogant curve to that sculptured mouth. In fact, she was so much aware of him at the moment that she could hardly breathe, let alone force her limbs to move away from him.

That dark blue gaze easily held her captive. 'In what way am I tormenting you?' he prompted softly, the warmth of his breath stirring the silky tendrils of hair at her temple, his mouth only inches away from her own now as he bent his head towards hers.

In what way was he tormenting her? In *every* way. Verbally, he more often than not left her self-confidence in shreds. Emotionally, he reduced her to a jibbering wreck. And as for physically...

She didn't want to think about what Gideon did to her physically.

'I must say it's good that Peter doesn't have chickenpox after all,' David said with relief as he strolled into the kitchen.

Molly looked up wordlessly at Gideon for several more long seconds, unable to break the pull of that darkly compelling gaze. She felt her cheeks pale as the seconds passed, knowing Gideon was the last man she should ever have allowed to affect her in this way.

Why did he?

He was rude to her. Insulted her at every opportunity.

Believed her capable of practising deceit on her best friend. Added to which, she didn't even like him.

But as he continued to look at her she could barely breathe, let alone think straight. Not a good combination.

'Oh, good—lunch,' David murmured with satisfaction as he gazed in at the warming soup.

Molly dragged her gaze away from Gideon's with effort, turning to smile at the other man. 'Perhaps one of you would like to tell Crys and Sam that lunch will be ready soon?' she suggested lightly, able to step away from Gideon now that she wasn't held captive by that compelling gaze. 'I know Peter isn't feeling so good, but they still need to eat,' she added ruefully.

'I'll go,' Gideon offered. 'I can always stay upstairs with Peter while they come down and eat, if they have a problem with leaving him alone.'

Molly looked across at him. 'That's kind of you,' she murmured slowly.

He paused in the doorway. 'I can be kind,' he assured her hardly, before striding purposefully from the room.

Molly grimaced her dismay, knowing she had once again said the wrong thing. But she knew, in their present circumstances, she would be hard-pressed to say the right thing where Gideon was concerned.

'Lovers' tiff?'

She turned sharply to frown at David as he stood watching her, a teasing smile curving his lips, dark brows raised mockingly.

He shrugged at her obvious displeasure. 'Sam said something this morning about Gideon coming to your rescue last night concerning a spider in your bedroom. Then the two of you went off shopping together earlier. And he was in your bedroom a few minutes ago,' he reasoned, his smile widening at her look of obvious displeasure. 'What else am I supposed to think?'

'Not what you *are* thinking,' she snapped disgruntledly.

'No?' David speculated.

'No!' she bit out frustratedly, a rueful smile starting to curve her lips now. 'Last night. This morning. In my bedroom just now. This is all just some silly idea of Crys's... I suppose you do realise that this is all some mistaken matchmaking on Crys's part? And you're another prime candidate?' She turned the tables on him, knowing she had scored a point when he looked totally stunned.

'Me?' David was visibly dumbfounded. 'But I thought Gideon...? Who does Crys have picked out for me, then?' he said dazedly.

'Me,' Molly drawled. 'According to Sam, she isn't too bothered as to whether it's Gideon or you I become involved with, so long as it's someone!'

'Thanks!' David grimaced.

'You're welcome.' She grinned, enjoying his discomfort after his having teased her so mercilessly.

He frowned. 'And I thought Crys was just being kind by inviting me to stay for Christmas!'

'Oh, she was,' Molly instantly assured him. 'She is. Crys is one of the nicest people you could ever hope to meet.'

'I'm glad we're all agreed on that point at least,' Gideon rasped as he returned to the kitchen, dark gaze narrowed questioningly as he looked stonily at Molly.

She held that gaze for several long seconds, and then she looked away, knowing from Gideon's accusing look exactly what he was thinking. But it was impossible to defend herself against such ingrained prejudice. And with David in the room she had no intention of even trying to do so.

Besides, Gideon, at least, was unaware of Crys's attempts at matchmaking. And Molly wanted him to remain that way.

'Are they coming down to join us?' she prompted distantly.

'Sam is,' Gideon confirmed. 'Crys will have something later; she's going to stay upstairs and have a nap with Peter. After her disturbed night, and with the relief of knowing it's nothing serious, she probably needs sleep more than food at the moment,' he added affectionately.

Molly knew how Crys felt. Her own night had been far from restful. Although she didn't have the added worry over Peter to contend with, too.

She nodded. 'I'll go and take over from her later, so she can have something to eat.'

Gideon eyed her for several seconds. 'That's kind of you,' he finally murmured dryly.

Deliberately. Mockingly. Tauntingly.

Okay, so neither of them had a particularly good opinion of the other. But if they continued like this it was going to make this time more difficult for the others than it already was.

'My mother always told me that kindness is a virtue,' she dismissed lightly, beginning to serve soup into four bowls.

'So is loyalty,' Gideon rasped harshly.

Molly stiffened, knowing exactly where that remark was directed. 'And honesty,' she bit out tautly, brown gaze challenging his now.

'Hey, can anyone join in this conversation? Or is this just some private thing between the two of you?' David interjected dryly, drawing their attention to the fact that he was still in the room.

It was a fact both of them seemed to have momentarily forgotten in their antagonism towards each other, Molly acknowledged, and she shot David a rueful smile.

'Luncheon is served,' she announced decisively, turning to smile at Sam as he came into the room. 'Are they okay?' she prompted gently.

He grimaced. 'Fine.' He nodded. 'But this was the very last thing we needed on top of... Well, we could definitely have done without this at the moment,' he muttered tensely.

Molly frowned at him. 'On top of what...?' she prompted, hoping the discord between herself and Gideon wasn't becoming a problem for the others.

'Nothing,' Sam dismissed abruptly. 'Just forget I said anything,' he muttered, sitting down to eat his soup distractedly.

'But Diana—Dr Chisholm,' David corrected ruefully at their puzzled looks. 'She told me that she doesn't foresee any complications with Peter.'

'I'm sure there won't be.' Sam nodded. 'I'm just worried about Crys, that's all.' He shrugged. 'She looks on our marriage, and Peter's birth, as her second chance. I don't want anything to spoil that. Not that it will,' he added hurriedly.

'What could possibly happen to spoil it for you?' Molly looked at her stepbrother dazedly.

'Exactly—what could?' Gideon was the one to answer hardly.

Molly didn't look up from her soup, but nevertheless she sensed his censorious gaze on her. And the reason for it.

So shopping this morning, even getting rid of that

spider from her bedroom earlier, had just been a temporary respite after all; Gideon obviously still totally distrusted her where Crys's happiness was concerned.

And not only was his distrust totally unwarranted, it was also highly insulting.

It also brought into question—once again—Gideon's own feelings towards Crys…

CHAPTER SIX

'I'M JUST going into town to pick up a few things Crys forgot to get.' David told them shortly after lunch. 'Anyone fancy coming for a drive with me?'

Sam had gone back upstairs to sit with Crys and Peter, taking some soup and bread up on a tray for his wife, leaving Molly with very little to do this afternoon apart from wrapping those two extra Christmas presents—which certainly wasn't going to take very long— and, of course, providing Gideon with a convenient target to vent his sarcastic humour on.

'You go ahead, Molly,' he invited now, barely glancing up from the newspaper he was reading as he sat at the kitchen table. 'I'll stay here in case Sam and Crys need anything.'

Her cheeks flushed angrily; as if she needed his permission to do anything. Or to be made to feel guilty because she felt the need to get outside in the fresh air— away from him—for a while.

'What the...?' Gideon rasped before Molly could think of a suitably cutting reply to his sarcasm, his attention suddenly riveted on the newspaper he had merely been glancing through before.

'What is it?' Molly frowned at him worriedly.

'Hmm,' David murmured distractedly, having glanced over Gideon's shoulder at the newspaper. 'It's a good photograph of us all, but...'

'Exactly—but!' Gideon muttered angrily, standing up, with the newspaper now tightly gripped between his hands. 'I don't think either Sam or Crys are going to like this.' He frowned darkly.

'What is it?' Molly repeated agitatedly, moving to look at the newspaper herself now.

What she saw there made her breath catch in her throat.

The christening on Sunday had been a completely private family and friends affair, but the photograph in this newspaper meant that at least one member of the press had found out about it. Not only had they found out about it, they had obviously hidden somewhere and taken a photograph of them all as they were leaving the church. The proud parents stood in the midst of Gideon, David and Molly, and all of them were named in the caption beneath the photograph...

'Oh, no!' Molly gasped her dismay, knowing exactly how much Sam was going to hate this.

Twelve years ago his life had been made a living hell because of his ex-fiancée and the lies she had told the press about him, to the extent that he had chosen to hide himself away here in the wilds of Yorkshire. His marriage to Crys almost two years ago had helped to soften his attitude, but certainly not to the extent that he would be happy to have his photograph plastered all over the newspapers. Or that of his newborn son...

'Damn it,' Gideon muttered grimly. 'Why the hell can't they leave them alone?'

'Because it's news.' David shrugged philosophically. 'I had the same problem when—when Cathy died six months ago.' He shook his head. 'If it's news, they'll print it; good or bad.'

'This is definitely bad,' Molly said heavily. 'Especially now, when Crys and Sam are already so distracted over Peter.' She frowned. 'I think perhaps you had better lose that newspaper, Gideon,' she advised worriedly. 'Tell Crys, if she asks, that we weren't able to find one.'

'Don't worry, I intend to,' he assured her grimly. 'I also intend finding out who gave them this story in the first place.' He threw the newspaper down on the table in disgust.

'Who gave it to them…?' Molly repeated frowningly. 'You think someone actually told them about the christening?'

'Well, of course someone told them,' he rasped disgustedly. 'And after years of Sam keeping his whereabouts a secret, that damned newspaper has also stated if not the actual address then the exact location of this house.'

Molly could only stare at him, her cheeks white with dismay. After his experience with his ex-fiancée, Sam had good reason to value his privacy. Even more so since he had married Crys and they had baby Peter. As Molly had already said, this newspaper article could only be bad news.

'But who would do such a thing?' She shook her head dazedly.

'Yes—who *would* do such a thing?' Gideon grated coldly.

Molly looked up sharply, finding herself caught in the sudden glitter of that dark blue gaze.

He didn't think—? Surely he didn't believe that she had had anything to do with this outrage?

'The new *Bailey* series, and the people starring in it, is mentioned several times in the accompanying article,' Gideon bit out tersely.

Accusingly…?

But she would never… Could never…

Gideon could have no idea of the disruption that had

occurred in her own and their parents' lives twelve years ago, because of the vindictiveness of Sam's ex-fiancée. The constant hounding by the press, her parents actually having to move house, Molly having to change schools in an attempt to shield her from all the adverse publicity. The new school was where she had met Crys and the two of them had become such good friends...

But that was Gideon's real problem, wasn't it? Crys... Molly was very fond of Crys herself, but Gideon seemed to care only about her, about protecting her...

'I think I will come for that drive with you after all, David,' she told him woodenly, deliberately keeping her gaze averted from Gideon. She sensed he was still looking at her. But she had to get out of here, or this time she really would have to hit him!

'Great.' David grinned his satisfaction with the arrangement. 'And I shouldn't worry too much about that newspaper, Gideon,' he advised ruefully. 'It's Christmas; by the time the holidays are over everyone will have forgotten all about it.'

Molly wasn't so sure about that, and she could see by the continued grimness of his expression that Gideon wasn't convinced, either. But with it being Christmas Day tomorrow there really was nothing they could do about it now. And Gideon throwing out wild accusations—completely erroneous ones—certainly wasn't going to help the situation! But, by the same token, neither was her reacting angrily to them...

Which was why it was better if Molly removed herself from his company for the moment. Better for Gideon, that was. For herself, Molly would have liked to set him straight over several matters. For Crys and

Sam's sake she would keep her own counsel. For the moment…

'I certainly hope so.' Gideon nodded abruptly.

'Ready, Molly?' David prompted lightly.

She was more than ready to remove herself from the odious Gideon's company, not even bothering to say goodbye to him as she followed David out of the house.

Really, Gideon seemed to think she was to blame for everything that happened. Everything bad, that was.

But who could it have been who'd told the press about the christening? Because it certainly hadn't been her!

'Cheer up,' David advised lightly after they had driven in silence for several minutes. 'It may never happen!'

'It already has happened,' she returned gloomily. 'Surely you must realise Gideon thinks I told the press about the christening?'

'He doesn't think that really,' David assured her with a grin. 'He's only off with you because he likes you.'

'You have to be joking!' Molly spluttered.

'I didn't say he was happy about it,' David accepted slowly. 'But he does like you.' He nodded with certainty. 'And a little jealousy because you've come out with me this afternoon can't be a bad thing!'

Molly shook her head in disbelief. 'You're being as ridiculous as Crys now,' she dismissed disgustedly. 'I don't like Gideon.' Even less so now. 'And he doesn't like me. End of story,' she told David firmly.

'Sure,' he accepted unconvincingly.

'I mean it, David.' She gave him a warning glare. 'The sooner Christmas is over and I can get as far away from Gideon as it's possible to be, the better I shall like it.'

He gave her a brief narrow-eyed glance. 'Methinks the lady doth protest too much...'

'Will you just stop it?' Molly's hands were clenched tightly in her lap. 'The man is absolutely loathsome!' she stated determinedly, clearly remembering the accusation in his gaze earlier.

Except she couldn't quite deny—to herself, at least—her completely nerve-tingling awareness of Gideon.

But just because she was physically aware of him that didn't mean she had to like the man.

Of course it didn't.

Except now she *was* protesting too much. Damn it. And most of all damn Gideon Webber.

'I quite like him myself,' David said slowly. 'And he's obviously very fond of Crys.'

'Perhaps too fond,' Molly snapped before she had time to guard her words, and at once felt stricken at having spoken quite so bluntly.

She liked David, would be working very closely with him in future months, but that was no reason to have voiced her inner suspicions concerning Gideon's feelings towards Crys.

Her cheeks felt warm with embarrassed colour. 'What I meant to say was—'

'Forget it, Molly.' David reached over and briefly squeezed her arm. 'It's an interesting concept, I grant you that,' he added thoughtfully. 'But not one I should put too much credence in, if I were you,' he dismissed.

'No,' she accepted gratefully. She really would have to be more careful about making unguarded comments about Gideon. To anyone.

'I mean it, Molly.' David gave her a warm glance. 'Try thinking about it from Gideon's point of view—'

'Do I have to?' She grimaced.

He chuckled softly, shaking his head in gentle reproof. 'From what I can gather, Crys is the only family Gideon has left. She *is* family, Molly,' he insisted softly as she looked sceptical. 'His parents both died years ago, and Crys was married to Gideon's younger brother. That brother is now dead, too. All Gideon has left of that relationship is Crys.' He shrugged. 'That's how I see it, anyway. I'm still extremely close to Cathy's parents,' he added huskily.

It was one way of looking at things, granted. But Molly wasn't convinced it was the right way as far as Gideon's feelings towards Crys were concerned...

Although it was definitely preferable to believing the man she was so attracted to was in love with another woman. Been there, done that.

'Before you start again, I did not tell any member of the press about the christening on Sunday,' Molly told Gideon defensively when she turned to find him standing grim-faced behind her as she set about preparing their evening meal. Crys was still totally occupied upstairs with the less-than-happy Peter.

His gaze narrowed. 'I—' He broke off as the telephone on the kitchen wall began to ring. 'Would you mind answering that?' he said slowly.

Molly looked from him down to her wet hands, where she was peeling potatoes, and then back at Gideon. 'It may have escaped your notice, but I'm a little busy at the moment!' she snapped irritably; in fact up to her arms in it was the description that readily came to mind.

Not that she at all minded preparing an evening meal in Crys's absence. In fact, she was more than pleased to have something to do. But at the same time she did not intend being harassed by Gideon. And the still-ringing telephone, like Gideon himself, was starting to grate on her nerves.

Gideon drew in a sharp breath. 'If I say please...?' he suggested tightly.

Molly blinked; that would certainly be a novelty. 'Well?' she pushed dryly when he made no effort to do so.

His eyes flared deeply blue. 'Please,' he finally bit out, through gritted teeth.

'Testy, testy,' Molly taunted as she moved to dry her hands before snatching up the receiver. 'Yes?' she prompted lightly.

Her query was met by silence. Not the silence of a call ended, but that slightly static silence that said the line was still open.

'Hello?' she said more strongly. 'Is there anyone there?' Her voice was sharp now. She was more and more convinced that there was someone on the end of the line. She could almost hear their breathing...

In answer to her last query there was a faint click on the line, the dialling tone immediately following.

Molly slowly put down the receiver before turning sharply to look at Gideon. 'What's going on?' she demanded to know.

'I have no idea.' He shrugged abruptly. 'But that's the third call like that since you left with David this afternoon. I wanted you to answer it this time to see if you got the same response I did when I answered the last two.'

'Hanging up?' Molly said slowly.

'Exactly,' Gideon confirmed grimly, thrusting his hands into his trouser pockets. 'Obviously the call wasn't meant for you, either,' he added frowningly.

Molly shook her head. 'Maybe it was just a wrong number?'

'Three times in as many hours?' Gideon said sceptically.

'It could be.' She shrugged dismissively, more interested in cooking dinner for them all than worrying about hang-up calls.

'Don't be ridiculous, Molly,' he snapped.

Her eyes widened indignantly. '*I'm* being ridiculous?' she repeated incredulously. 'Every time something bad happens around here you automatically assume I have to somehow be involved. No doubt you think I'm somehow responsible for these calls, too?' she challenged scathingly.

'Hardly, when you're standing right here beside me,' he returned harshly.

She shook her head disgustedly. 'I suppose that's one thing in my favour.'

Gideon drew in a harsh breath, obviously controlling his temper with effort. 'Look, I'm sorry if I was wrong earlier, concerning that article in the newspaper...'

'Are you?' Molly's eyes flashed disbelievingly. 'Are you really?' she repeated.

'Yes,' he hissed, his jaw tightly clenched, eyes darkly blue in his pale, strained face.

Molly frowned as a thought suddenly occurred to her. 'Do you think those calls could be from another reporter after a story? Or possibly even the same one?' she added hardly.

'They could be, I suppose,' Gideon said slowly. 'Although why would they keep hanging up in that way?'

Molly shrugged. 'Because it isn't Crys or Sam answering the calls?'

'But how would they know that?' Gideon didn't look convinced by this theory.

Neither was Molly, if the truth were known, but she couldn't think of any other explanation for them. Unless they really were just wrong numbers...

'I've disposed of the newspaper, by the way,' he added harshly.

'I never had any doubts that you would,' Molly returned with obvious sarcasm.

'Molly—'

'Gideon,' she interrupted firmly. 'It may have escaped your notice, but I'm trying to cook dinner for all of us.' She indicated the potatoes she had been peeling, and the duck sitting in the baking tray waiting to go in the Aga.

He frowned for several seconds, and then his attention shifted to the partly prepared food. Amusement glittered in those dark blue eyes when his gaze finally returned to hers. 'Do you actually know how to cook?' That amusement was reflected in his mocking tone.

Christmas is a time of 'peace and goodwill to all men', Molly, she reminded herself firmly. And one thing she had learnt about Gideon Webber these last few days—he was definitely a man.

She drew in a controlling breath. 'More than you do, I'm sure,' she told him with determined control; the duck would be much better cooked and then enjoyed by them all than aimed at this man's arrogant head.

'I'm sure, too,' he conceded with an acknowledging tilt of his head. 'The only thing I know about cooking is that one should keep the chef readily supplied with wine. Red or white?' he offered lightly.

Molly stared at him incredulously. Just when she

thought she really detested this man, he did something nice. Throwing her into complete confusion.

As if she wasn't confused enough already. She had every reason to loathe and detest this man, and yet every time he walked into a room she was physically totally aware of him.

Like now!

'Red, thanks,' she accepted stiltedly, before turning sharply away to bend down and put the duck in the oven. 'And, just to put your mind at rest about the cooking,' she told him, 'when I was "resting" about five years ago...' her tone was dry, as she knew that Gideon would be as aware as anyone else that the term 'resting', when applied to an actor, actually meant 'out of work' '...I helped Crys out in the kitchen of her restaurant. I'm sure it won't be up to her standard, but— Oh!' She had turned to find Gideon standing only inches away from her, and was suddenly breathless as she stared up into eyes the colour of a clear midnight sky.

'Oh, indeed,' Gideon murmured huskily, making no effort to give her the glass of wine he held in his hand.

Time seemed to stand still. The house was unusually quiet, with only the ticking of the kitchen clock on the wall beside them to tell them of the passing of time. Even Merlin was quiet as he dozed in front of the Aga.

Molly's mouth had gone dry, and colour warmed her cheeks as she saw Gideon's dark gaze follow the movement of her tongue across her lips.

She could barely breathe, was aware of Gideon with every sense and nerve of her body—aware of him in a way she had never been aware of any man before.

What would he say, this man who believed she had been his brother James's mistress, if the two of them were ever to make love and he discovered that she had never had a lover—that, at twenty-nine, she was still a virgin?

Well, that particular solution might be a little drastic—but at least he would know that his suspicions concerning herself and James were completely unfounded.

'Why are you smiling in that "I know something you don't" way?' Gideon prompted huskily, his dark gaze once again warily guarded.

It completely broke the moment of shared intimacy...

Thank goodness.

Molly sighed as she stepped thankfully away. 'I was merely wondering when you were going to give me my glass of wine,' she invented pointedly, at the same time drawing in deeply controlling breaths, completely flustered by these moments of intense intimacy she seemed to be sharing with Gideon more and more.

In the future—for the next three days, in fact—the less time she spent alone with Gideon, the better she would like it.

He looked down frowningly at the glass he still held, as if surprised to see it there in his hand. 'What can I do to help?' he offered abruptly, at the same time putting the glass of wine down on the worktop beside her.

Leave the kitchen and give her a few moments' respite from his totally evocative company seemed like a good idea to Molly right now.

Although, from the efficient way he picked up the vegetable knife and looked at her expectantly, she didn't think that suggestion was going to work. 'Finish the potatoes for me, if you will,' she dismissed airily, determinedly turning her own attention to preparing Brussels sprouts with almonds.

Molly wasn't under any illusions that the silence between them was in the least comfortable. She knew that just one word—the wrong word—could trigger hostilities between them once again.

Peace and goodwill—ha!

CHAPTER SEVEN

'WELL, isn't this a nice scene of domestic harmony?' David murmured approvingly a short time later.

Molly turned to give him a narrow-eyed warning look. Domesticity, my foot; Gideon was as domesticated as a feral cat. And, in view of the fact that they had been working together in tense silence for the last ten minutes or so, she doubted that he even knew what the word harmony meant as far as she was concerned.

'All you need is a pinafore, Gideon, and you'll completely look the part,' David added with teasing challenge, having given a hasty look round the kitchen to make sure they had put Merlin safely outside before coming completely into the room himself.

Gideon looked at the other man from under raised blond brows. 'And what part would that be, David?' he drawled softly.

The actor grinned unabashedly. 'Why, Assistant Chef, of course,' he said mockingly.

'Of course,' Gideon echoed derisively. 'Why don't you make yourself useful and pour us all some more wine?'

'I won't, if you don't mind.' David replenished their two glasses. 'Someone has to drive us all to church later tonight,' he reasoned. 'As you two seem to have done all the hard work towards dinner, it may as well be me.' He shrugged.

Molly had completely forgotten their plans to go to the late service that evening. 'Do you think Crys and

Sam will still want to go?' She frowned, having seen nothing of the other two since delivering Peter's medicine to them a couple of hours ago.

'Maybe not.' David grimaced. 'But that's no reason why we shouldn't.'

'Why you shouldn't what?' Crys asked as she came into the kitchen. 'Oh, thank you, Molly.' She hugged Molly when she saw that dinner was already well in hand. 'I feel awful for deserting you all like this today.'

'How is the little chap?' David was the one to ask gently.

'Much better, thank you.' Crys sighed her relief, looking less strained than she had earlier this afternoon. The colour was back in her cheeks, too. 'He's sleeping quietly at the moment, so Sam should be down in a minute or two. What were you talking about when I came in?' she prompted interestedly, smiling her thanks as she sat down and accepted the glass of red wine Gideon poured for her.

'Church later tonight,' David explained.

'Oh, yes—you must all go,' Crys insisted warmly. 'Sam and I went last year and it was very beautiful, with all the candles alight and decorated with holly. You—' She broke off as the telephone began to ring.

Molly froze at the sound, turning sharply to Gideon and finding her look returned frowningly as he, too, obviously wondered if this was yet another of those hang-up calls.

'I'll get it,' Sam told them as he came into the kitchen, and plucked the receiver from the wall. 'Yes? Speaking. Oh, fine thanks,' he answered warmly seconds later.

Much to Molly's relief, and Gideon's, too, if his

smile was anything to go by, this obviously wasn't another of those calls.

'Much better,' Sam continued. 'No, I'm sure there's no need for you to do that. Although…' He put his hand over the mouthpiece. 'Is there enough dinner for one extra?' he prompted softly.

'Molly?' Crys turned to her.

'I'm sure there is,' she confirmed lightly, wondering exactly who the 'one extra' was going to be; Sam's tone was extremely warm and cordial, so it certainly wasn't a reporter.

Sam removed his hand from the mouthpiece. 'Why don't you come over anyway and join us for dinner? No, of course you wouldn't be intruding,' he added firmly. 'We're eating about eight, so come about seven-thirtyish. I believe several of us are going to church later, if you would like to join us for that, too…? Fine, we'll see you later, then.' He rang off. 'Diana Chisholm is going to join us for dinner,' he announced happily.

'Oh, that's wonderful.' Crys smiled her pleasure. 'I didn't like the idea of her spending Christmas on her own.'

'You may as well open this house up for all waifs and strays!' David remarked caustically, scowling. Then he seemed to realise what he had just said. 'Sorry,' he muttered harshly. 'If you'll all excuse me?' He turned and strode purposefully from the kitchen.

'What's wrong with him?' Sam looked as dazed by the other man's abrupt departure as they had all been by the remark that had preceded it.

'My insensitivity, I think.' Crys gave a grimacing sigh. 'After all, it's David's first Christmas without Cathy, which can't be easy after all those years of marriage.' She stood up. 'I'll go and talk to him.'

'No, I'll go,' Gideon offered, putting down his wine-glass. 'It's a man thing,' he assured Crys gently as she would have protested. 'Less embarrassing all round if I go, and especially for David,' he added ruefully.

It might be less embarrassing for David, but Molly had serious doubts about Gideon being the one to deal with such a sensitive subject.

'Unless you would like to go?' Gideon paused beside Molly, obviously guessing at least some of her thoughts.

Although the mockery in his gaze seemed to imply he had completely misconstrued the reason for her expression of doubt. As usual.

'Not at all,' she assured him lightly. 'As you say, it's a man thing.' She looked up at him challengingly.

She was not in the least interested in David in the way this man seemed to be implying she was, but if he wanted to go on thinking that, that was his problem.

Gideon continued to look at her for several long seconds, then with an abrupt nod of his head he followed the other man from the room.

'Phew,' Sam breathed ruefully. 'Exactly what's been going on here today while Crys and I have been otherwise occupied?' He looked questioningly at Molly.

Apart from Gideon insulting her at every opportunity, then almost kissing her, and a photograph of them all being spread all over the newspaper—giving yet another excuse for Gideon to be insulting to her—and then being inundated with strange hang-up calls, absolutely nothing had been happening today!

All of which she had no intention of so much as mentioning to either Sam or Crys.

'Just normal Christmas Eve tensions,' she dismissed lightly. 'Now, tell me, Crys.' She turned to her friend and sister-in-law. 'Do you want me to serve an orange or an apple sauce with the duck this evening?'

Anything to do with cooking was guaranteed to distract Crys, and the two women discussed the merits of both sauces before deciding on apple. All the time Molly was aware of Sam watching her with amused green eyes, as if completely aware of her distracting tactics—and not fooled by them for a moment.

But then she and Sam had always been as close, if not closer, than real brother and sister. Sam was often able to tell what she was thinking before she was aware of it herself. She only hoped he didn't pick up on some of the things she had been thinking about Gideon Webber today. They were too contrary for her to make any sense of, let alone anyone else.

Think of the devil...

Molly felt herself stiffen defensively as Gideon strode back into the room, his good humour restored if his grin was anything to go by. Hopefully he had had the same success with David.

'Everything okay?' Crys prompted concernedly.

'He'll be down shortly,' Gideon reassured her. 'He's decided to shower and change before dinner.'

'Well, at least he is joining us.' Sam grimaced.

'Of course he is.' Gideon's grin widened. 'I only had to point out the advantages of having such a lovely and accomplished woman join us for dinner for him to agree to that.'

Oh, and what was she? Molly wondered disgruntledly. Chopped liver?

Probably, as far as Gideon was concerned, she accepted heavily.

Sam's actress sister—at the moment splattered with grease from basting the duck, her face flushed from the

Aga, her hair frizzed up from the heat—couldn't really compare to someone as coolly beautiful and caring as the doctor she had met earlier today.

Rather depressing, really, she acknowledged ruefully. Even if it was true.

'You two lovely ladies apart, of course,' Gideon added dryly. Rather too tardily, as far as Molly was concerned.

'Too late, I'm afraid, Gideon,' Crys told him laughingly, turning to link her arm with Molly's. 'Let's all have a bit of fun and dress up for dinner. After all, it is Christmas. Molly, what say you and I leave these two men to lay the table while we go upstairs and change before dinner?'

'Sounds good to me!' Molly grinned conspiratorially, deliberately putting her nose in the air as the two of them swept out of the room.

Crys gave a rueful shake of her head as they climbed the wide staircase together. 'So tell me, what's really been happening today while Sam and I have been upstairs with Peter?' she prompted dryly.

'Not a lot,' Molly said lightly, deliberately keeping her expression deadpan.

'Liar!' Her friend laughed softly. 'You and Gideon seem to be getting along together?'

'If by that you mean I haven't actually hit him over the head with one of your saucepans yet, then, yes, I suppose that we are,' Molly answered disgustedly.

Crys's chuckle deepened. 'Gideon is a love.'

Molly almost stumbled up the last stair in surprise at this statement. A love? Gideon?

'Well, I think he is,' Crys added with a frown of consternation at Molly's reaction to this statement.

'Probably because he is, as far as you're concerned,'

she dismissed. 'I'm a completely different matter, I'm afraid. Perhaps it's just that he doesn't approve of actresses,' she added, as Crys looked less than happy.

'But he did come and dispose of that spider for you last night,' Crys reminded her cajolingly.

'Crys, it's a mistake for you to try to matchmake between Gideon and me.' Molly didn't even attempt to correct her friend concerning Gideon's 'disposal' of the spider. What was the point? Probably she and Gideon would never meet again after this Christmas holiday. There was no point in upsetting Crys's friendship with Gideon just because she found him a sadistic swine.

'Sam's been talking to you,' Crys guessed indignantly.

'Not at all,' Molly said easily, having no intention of implicating Sam in any of this. 'I would have to be blind not to see what you're up to,' she told her friend affectionately. 'But just stop, hmm? I'm not Gideon's type. And he certainly isn't mine,' she added more forcefully. 'I've never been attracted to that arrogant, macho type.'

'But—'

'Excuse me, ladies,' cut in an icy-cold voice from behind them. 'But you appear to be blocking the stairway,' Gideon added pointedly as he stood on the step behind them.

Molly closed her eyes briefly before looking up at the ceiling above them, all other thoughts fleeing as she saw the yellow rose painted in the dome above. James's trade mark...

She became completely still. She had forgotten that she had recommended James's work to Sam when he'd been looking for an interior designer to come here four years ago, but that yellow rose above them in the domed ceiling reminded her all too forcefully of the friend, husband and brother the three of them had all lost.

For a few seconds everything seemed to stop, including time and sound, and a mellow calm settled over her before she once again became aware of exactly where she was. And whom she was with.

She turned sharply, hoping that Crys hadn't seen her brief distraction, or the reason for it; the last thing she wanted to do at this time was to remind Crys of the husband she had loved and lost. But she needn't have worried; Crys had been distracted herself by one of the Christmas decorations on the stair banister that had come loose, and she was attempting to fix it back in place.

Not so Gideon, Molly saw with dismay. His jaw was set rigidly, blue eyes glittering with fury as he glanced up at the domed ceiling and then back at her.

Molly stepped away. 'I'll see you both later,' she managed to murmur before hurrying up another set of stairs to her bedroom on the third floor.

She closed the door thankfully behind her, knowing it was pointless even trying to explain to Gideon what had happened just now; he didn't seem to believe a word she said anyway. And especially when it came to the subject of his brother James...

She was almost knocked off her feet as the door was pushed open behind her, and regained her balance to turn and see Gideon silhouetted in the doorway.

'What the hell do you think you're doing?' he snapped furiously, moving into the room to close the door behind him with barely suppressed violence, his eyes glittering dangerously as he looked across at her with unconcealed contempt.

Molly swallowed hard. She could try pretending she

had no idea what he was talking about, but she had a feeling that would just make him angrier still. If that were possible! But at the same time she knew he wasn't going to believe her if she told him the truth—that just for a moment, for a very brief moment, she had felt a closeness with James, an emotional affinity, and had mentally assured him that Crys was happy again now, that Sam would take care of her always.

If she even tried to put that into words she knew how stupid it would sound.

And to someone like Gideon, who seemed to enjoy thinking the worst of her, it would sound so much worse than stupid…

'Well?' he bit out harshly, a nerve pulsing in his jaw, hands clenched at his sides.

Molly drew in a deep breath. What could she say? How could she explain?

'How dare you moon about like some lovesick idiot?' Gideon rasped before she could formulate any sort of reply. 'James is dead,' he snapped viciously, before stepping forward to grasp her arms painfully in his hands and shake her slightly. 'Dead—don't you understand? When are you all going to accept that!'

Molly felt the colour drain from her cheeks at the stark brutality of his words. She knew James was dead, they all did, but that was no reason not to think of him sometimes. Especially now. Christmas was like that—a time of warmth and joy, but also a time to think of loved ones who were no longer here.

She shook her head. 'I have accepted it—'

'No,' he rasped forcefully, shaking her again. 'I don't think you have.'

Molly's breath caught sharply in her throat. 'I don't give a damn what you think—'

'In that case…' Without any warning, any indication of what was coming, Gideon's mouth came crashing down on hers.

Molly was too stunned by the assault to respond at first, her breath lodged somewhere in her chest as Gideon crushed her against the hardness of his body, his arms like steel bands, his mouth ruthlessly plundering her own.

But that blinding numbness only lasted for a matter of seconds, and then Molly started fighting against him in earnest, her hands pushing at his chest as she wrenched her mouth away from the punishing determination of his.

'Stop it!' she gasped, glaring up at him with pained brown eyes. 'Gideon, stop this!' she cried again as his eyes glittered fiercely down at her.

He became very still, his face pale, set in grim lines as he stared down at her with narrowed eyes, his hands still tightly gripping her arms.

Probably as well; she wasn't sure she wouldn't collapse completely if Gideon weren't holding her upright.

'Please—stop,' she groaned emotionally.

She simply couldn't take any more today. The last twenty-four hours seemed more like a hundred. And it wasn't over yet.

'It's Christmas,' she added huskily.

Gideon blinked, still frowning darkly, although the glitter seemed to be fading from his eyes.

He shook his head. 'What the hell am I doing?' he finally muttered self-disgustedly, releasing her abruptly to step away.

Molly swallowed hard. 'I have no idea. But I have a feeling you're going to regret having done it once you have time to think about it,' she added shakily.

One thing she was absolutely sure of was that the last thing Gideon really wanted to do was kiss her—at the time it had probably just seemed preferable to any other method of silencing her.

Gideon continued to stare at her for several long, breath-stopping moments, and Molly wasn't sure quite what he was going to do next. In the circumstances, he probably wasn't too sure himself.

He gave another shake of his head, frowning darkly now. 'I apologise for…for whatever that was,' he bit out abruptly, turning sharply away, seeming dazed by his own actions.

Molly felt her heart sink as she watched him walk heavily across the room. 'Gideon…!' she cried out as he opened the bedroom door.

'Yes?' He turned back to her, his expression bleak.

She bit her bottom lip, not quite sure what to say to him now that she had his attention, only aware that she couldn't let him leave like this, with so many things left unsaid between them. 'About James. I—we all still miss him,' she breathed huskily.

If anything he looked even bleaker. 'Some of us more than others, it would seem,' he rasped, not waiting for her answer, but letting himself quietly out of the room.

Molly sat down heavily on the bed to bury her face in her hands as tears fell hotly down her cheeks.

CHAPTER EIGHT

'YOU look gorgeous!' David told her admiringly as she entered the sitting-room a short time later to join the others for a pre-dinner drink. 'Like Mrs Christmas, in fact,' he added teasingly, obviously having got over his upset of earlier.

Or else he was just hiding it well...

Molly understood what he meant about the knee-length, figure-hugging Chinese-style red dress she was wearing this evening; it was a bright poppy-red that someone was sure to say didn't go with her copper-red hair.

Although Gideon seemed unusually quiet this evening, standing broodingly beside the fireplace, looking elegantly attractive in his black dinner suit and snowy white shirt. And as remote and cold as a statue as his gaze briefly met hers.

Molly quickly averted her own gaze, turning to smile at Sam as he handed her a glass of champagne. 'What are we celebrating?' she teased.

'The slightly late start of Christmas,' he returned ruefully. 'Diana is upstairs with Crys right now, checking on Peter, but she assured us that Peter really doesn't have chickenpox, and that he is much better already,' he added with satisfaction.

'That's wonderful,' Molly said with relief. 'Definitely worth drinking to.' She took a sip of the bubbly wine, without looking at Gideon this time to see if he was watching her. She had a feeling that looking at Gideon was going to be quite hard to do after that earlier scene in her bedroom.

'Where's Merlin?' she prompted, with nothing better to say.

Sam arched a mocking brow. 'Where do you think?'

She smiled. 'Upstairs, keeping watch over Peter.'

'Right first time!' Sam grinned. 'I—' He broke off as they heard the telephone ring in the kitchen. 'Now, who could that be—telephoning on Christmas Eve?' He frowned.

'I'll go; it could be the parents,' Molly told him quickly, putting down her wineglass to hurry across the room, not wanting anything to spoil this time for Sam and Crys now that the worry over Peter was apparently at an end. Something she couldn't guarantee if it should be another one of those hang-up calls.

'I'll answer it,' Gideon told her gruffly, and the two of them reached the sitting-room door at the same time.

Molly felt the colour warm her cheeks, not quite able to meet that piercing blue gaze as she looked up at him. 'Fine,' she accepted huskily, turning quickly away so that he shouldn't see how even being near him like this affected her after what had happened between them earlier.

Because, despite Gideon's anger, his forcefulness, Molly knew that part of her had wanted to respond to his kisses, that she had wanted to kiss away his anger, to know the deeply sensual man she sensed below that surface of fury.

Ridiculous when everything Gideon said, everything he did, told her of his contempt for her. He—

'Penny for them…?' David prompted as he moved to stand beside her, putting her glass of champagne back in her hand.

She gave a sad shake of her head. 'I can't make any sense of them, so why should you?'

David gave a rueful shrug. 'We're a strange collection of people, aren't we?' he murmured ruefully as Diana Chisholm and Crys entered the sitting-room. Both women smiled at Sam as he turned to them enquiringly. 'There's Crys and Sam, obviously the centre of this motley crew—'

'Speak for yourself,' Molly cut in teasingly.

He gave a nod of acknowledgement. 'And there's baby Peter, too, of course. Then there's Dr Chisholm: beautiful, probably only in her thirties, but obviously dedicated to her career. Then there's you: Sam's sister, Crys's friend, the only one of us who's really entitled to share this family Christmas. And there's me, of course, recently widowed, fighting shy of being anywhere that's going to remind me of Cathy and the Christmases we spent together.' He smiled self-derisively.

'Don't.' She put a sympathetic hand on his arm. 'Don't do this to yourself, David,' she urged. Though at the same time she was curious as to what his explanation would be for Gideon's presence here...

But as Crys brought Diana Chisholm over to formally introduce her to the two of them Molly knew she wasn't going to hear David's opinion of Gideon being there. Pity. That might have been worth hearing.

Where *was* Gideon? It had been some time since he went to answer the telephone call, so what was keeping him?

'Excuse me,' she murmured before slipping away, confident she could leave the slightly melancholy David in Crys's more than capable hands.

She found Gideon in the kitchen, standing in front of

the window, staring out, supposedly, up at the starlit sky. She came to a halt in the doorway, not sure whether or not she should intrude on what was obviously a moment of privacy. She decided not.

'Makes you realise how insignificant we all are, doesn't it?' Gideon murmured just as she would have turned and walked quietly away. He turned to face her, his face partly in shadow. 'The stars,' he explained at her puzzled look. 'Did you know that some of them have died, completely disappeared, before their glow is even apparent to the human eye? Quite—'

'Have you and David both forgotten to take your happy pills this evening?' Molly cut in pragmatically. 'You're both so introspective I think you must have done!' she explained as his eyes widened. Inwardly, she wondered how he had known she was standing in the doorway, sure that her high-heeled shoes hadn't made any noise as she walked down the thickly carpeted hallway. Eyes in the back of his head, probably; he certainly didn't seem to miss much.

Gideon continued to look at her for several seconds, and then his mouth began to twitch, his eyes to glow with suppressed laughter. 'If it happens again we can always rely on you to bring us back down to earth, can't we?' He was openly chuckling now.

She shrugged dismissively, not sure it was actually a compliment, but deciding to accept it as such. 'Who was on the telephone just now?' she prompted lightly; at least they weren't arguing for once.

'My assistant.' He grimaced. 'A client wants me to fly to Vienna the day after Christmas.'

'"All work and no play",' Molly quoted dismissively, suddenly wondering if his assistant was female, and also if their relationship was just business orientated. Surely it was a little unusual for an assistant to track you down at someone else's house on Christmas Eve, of all days, just to tell you about a commission?

Just as quickly she admonished herself for even thinking such a thing. What difference could it possibly make to her whether or not Gideon's relationship with his assistant was purely business—or his relationship with any other woman, for that matter?

'Not this time.' Gideon shook his head firmly. 'I'm fully booked until at least Easter; this client will just have to take a number.'

James, she knew, had been an extremely popular interior designer, but the name Gideon Webber had been in vogue long before James had come on the scene. Obviously his designs were still sought after.

'Come on,' Gideon said firmly, crossing the room in three strides. 'Let's go and join the others.' He took a firm hold of her elbow. 'And David was right, by the way,' he murmured as they approached the sitting-room. 'You do look gorgeous in that dress,' he enlarged at her questioning look.

Molly was so stunned at the unexpectedness of the compliment that she stopped dead in the hallway, looking up at him with widely surprised eyes.

She had taken great care with her appearance after a glance in the wardrobe mirror in her bedroom had confirmed her earlier suspicions that she looked a mess. She had showered and washed and styled her hair so that it fell in soft russet waves past her shoulders. Her make-up was golden, with the merest hint of green shadow on her lids, the lipgloss a perfect match in shade for the dress.

But the last thing she had expected was that Gideon would be complimentary about her appearance.

He was looking at her quizzically now, and Molly spoke quickly to bridge the awkwardness. 'You're looking pretty good yourself,' she said bluntly, at once cringing inwardly at her less-than-sophisticated answer.

He gave another grin, suddenly looking roguish. 'Well, at least you and I have taken our polite pills this evening,' he murmured dryly, before his expression darkened. 'Molly, I'm afraid things got rather out of hand earlier, and—'

'Please,' she cut in abruptly, no longer able to meet his gaze. 'Let's just forget about it.'

His head tilted towards her, his face only inches away from her own now, his hand beneath her chin so that she had no choice but to look at him. 'Can we do that?' he prompted huskily.

Well, she certainly couldn't—not when a part of her still burned to know where those kisses might have led if she hadn't stopped them so abruptly.

'Of course we can,' she assured him brittlely. 'It's Christmas,' she announced, with the same determination she had earlier. 'And we should all try to be nice to each other at Christmas.'

His mouth twisted derisively. 'I admire your sentiments—even if I think them somewhat ambitious.'

Especially where the two of them were concerned...

'Yes. Well.' She gave a rueful shrug. '"Go for it" has always been my motto. Now, I suggest we do join the others,' she added briskly, stepping away from him, her chin tingling from his touch. 'Before our polite pills wear off.'

To her surprise Gideon laughed out loud this time. Looking so attractive when he did so that Molly's breath caught in her throat.

'You know...' he sobered slightly, shaking his head

'…you aren't quite what I thought you were going to be.' This last came out in a slightly puzzled voice, as if he was surprised at the admission.

'I'm not?' Molly said warily.

He grimaced. 'No.'

She shrugged. 'Actually, I don't think I'm what you thought I was at all. But that's just my personal opinion, you understand?' she added dryly.

Gideon looked at her frowningly for several long seconds before once more taking a firm hold of her arm and opening the sitting-room door. 'Let's, as we've both already suggested, join the others,' he said grimly.

Molly wasn't sure what the state of play was between herself and Gideon after this latest exchange, but at least it helped to make the Christmas Eve dinner more enjoyable for all of them. The two of them were no longer snapping at each other, and even David seemed to have shaken off his mood of despondency as he conversed with Diana Chisholm about her work.

In fact, the dinner passed off quite enjoyably, with everyone complimenting her on her cooking. Molly was pleased by their compliments, while at the same time assuring them that Crys would have done a better job of it.

Even Peter joined them for a while when they reached the cheese and port stage of the meal, seeming much happier now, despite the sprinkling of spots on his delicate baby skin.

It certainly wasn't the time for the telephone to ring intrusively for the sixth time today.

'I'll go this time,' Molly said determinedly, even as she stood up, having already sensed Gideon's sudden tension as he sat beside her at the table. 'At this time of night it's sure to be a wrong number,' she added, after a dismissive glance at her wristwatch.

'I'll come with you,' Gideon put in abruptly, also standing up.

'There's no need,' Molly assured him with a warning glare; someone was going to suspect something if the two of them kept jumping up like this every time the telephone rang.

Especially as she wasn't really sure herself that there was any need for them to do so...

'I need to make a call myself,' he insisted firmly, following her from the room.

Molly turned to glare at him as she hurried to the kitchen to answer the telephone. 'You do realise that everyone is going to start speculating about the way we keep disappearing off together like this,' she snapped impatiently.

'Let them,' he came back harshly, lifting the receiver from the wall before Molly could even reach for it. 'Hello? No, this isn't Sam,' he answered slowly, giving Molly a raised eyebrow at actually receiving a response this time. 'Would you like me to—? Damn it,' he rasped, holding the receiver away from his ear before slamming it back on the wall. 'She rang off,' he muttered impatiently.

'She?' Molly prompted frowningly.

'She.' Gideon nodded grimly.

Molly eyed him warily. 'Why are you looking at me like that?' she asked slowly, very much afraid that the temporary truce between them was about to come to an end.

'Because Sam isn't here for me to look at *him* like that,' Gideon snapped, moving abruptly away from her to start pacing up and down the kitchen.

Molly watched him for several seconds, not at all sure she knew what was going on—she certainly had no idea what Gideon was thinking behind that grimly set mask.

She frowned. 'Gideon—'

'What does your brother think he's playing at?' Gideon bit out angrily, his eyes glittering deeply blue. 'Isn't a beautiful wife like Crys and a newborn son enough for him?'

'Well, of course it's... Gideon, what are you implying?' Molly stiffened indignantly as she began to get an inkling of exactly what Gideon was saying.

He continued his pacing. 'It's the usual scenario, isn't it? The mistress telephoning her lover over Christmas because he's spending time with his family and she feels left out—'

'Now, hold on just a minute,' Molly exploded incredulously. He couldn't really think that Sam...?

'Do you have another explanation for the way this woman keeps ringing off when it obviously isn't Sam answering her calls?' Gideon paused in his pacing to challenge her scathingly.

She glared at him. 'I don't have any sort of explanation for the telephone calls, or any reason for a woman to keep hanging up like that. But the one thing I do know is that Sam does not have a mistress.' She shook her head disgustedly. 'Having seen how happy he and Crys are, I don't know how you can even suggest such at thing. Unless you're just looking for an excuse to cause trouble between them because of the way you feel about Crys,' she added accusingly, her cheeks flushed with anger, her eyes glittering deeply brown.

Gideon became very still, every muscle and sinew of his body stiff with resentment. 'And exactly what do you mean by that remark?' His voice was dangerously quiet.

Molly raised her chin defiantly. 'Anyone with eyes in their head can see that you're in love with Crys yourself,' she felt stung into accusing.

And then she wondered at her temerity. Had she really just voiced what had until this moment been only suspicions?

Yes, she had! But in her own defence it had only been because of the things he was saying about Sam.

How dare he say those things about Sam?

After Sam's bad experience with his unbalanced ex-fiancée twelve years ago, he hadn't so much as looked at another woman until he'd met Crys. And, okay, it hadn't exactly been love at first sight between the two of them, she remembered with affection, but it was obvious to anyone that the two of them now loved each other very much, that neither of them had eyes for anyone else.

To anyone except Gideon, it would appear...

From the dangerous glitter in his eyes at the moment, she had a feeling that the only emotion he was feeling right now was murderous anger—towards her.

CHAPTER NINE

MOLLY eyed Gideon warily, unsure what was going to happen next—those 'polite pills' had most definitely worn off.

'How dare you say something like that to me?' Gideon demanded coldly.

'How dare you say something like that about Sam to me?' she returned heatedly, her hands clenched at her sides as she met his gaze unflinchingly.

He gave an impatient shake of his head. 'Forget about that for the moment. Let's concentrate on—'

'No. Let's not forget about it!' Molly cut in determinedly. 'Your accusations...your suspicions about Sam and some other woman are totally unfounded,' she insisted firmly. 'Just something nasty and trumped-up because—'

'I would advise you not to repeat what you just said about my feelings towards Crys,' Gideon put in softly, a nerve pulsing in his tightly clenched jaw.

Molly faced him unblinkingly. 'Why not?' she scorned. 'Because, no matter what accusations you may make about other people, you are above such things? Or because it strikes a little too close to home? What—? Oh!' She had time only to gasp before his mouth took fierce possession of hers.

And yet somehow it wasn't a kiss of anger as before...

Gideon held her captive merely with his lips, plundering hers, and a light cupping of a hand on each of her cheeks. He held her face up to his, the kiss gentling after that first assault, sipping and tasting.

Heat coursed through her as she responded to those kisses, an aching need engulfing her. Her body curved into the hard length of his as if by instinct, and every hard contour told of his own rising desire.

His lips left hers to travel down the scented column of her throat, and the heat of his breath, the moist warmth of his lips against her skin ignited a fire wherever they touched.

She wanted this man.

Oh, how she wanted him!

His tongue probed the hollows at the base of her throat, dipping and tasting, and Molly shook with desire as she clung mindlessly to the width of his shoulders, the heat of his body matching hers.

She gasped as his teeth bit the lobe of her ear, the gasp turning to a throaty groan as that bite turned to a sensuous nibbling that raised her temperature even higher.

Finally those lips returned to hers, easily transmitting Gideon's passion and desire, and Molly returned those emotions as she pressed closer against him.

'Hmm-hmm,' interrupted a softly teasing voice. 'When you have quite finished seducing my little sister, Gideon...' Sam drawled as the two of them sprang abruptly apart, 'Diana has received a call on her mobile and won't be able to join us in going to church, after all; I thought the two of you might want to come and say your goodbyes,' he told them pointedly.

For a few moments Molly had trouble remembering who Diana was, and from the frown on Gideon's face he wasn't faring much better.

Although he recovered more quickly than she did,

straightening purposefully before nodding abruptly. 'I'll go through now,' he bit out tersely, giving a brief, dismissive nod that included both Molly and Sam before striding from the room.

Molly let out a shaky breath, momentarily closing her eyes, sure she must have imagined what had passed between herself and Gideon just now. Because it hadn't been anger. And it hadn't been disgust. To her, at least, it had felt like something else entirely.

She needed time to think, time to analyse what she thought had happened—

Sam was eyeing her mockingly when she opened her eyes, his smile one of teasing affection. 'Anything I should know about, little sister?' he asked softly.

Not until she had worked out for herself what just now had been all about. If she ever did.

And Sam certainly didn't need to know that one of his guests believed he was having an affair with another woman, Molly recalled frowningly, the rosy haze that had briefly surrounded her disappearing completely at this recollection.

No matter how it might have felt to her at the time, Gideon had kissed her initially because of the accusations she had made concerning his own feelings towards Crys. And she mustn't forget that fact.

'Not a thing,' she assured Sam lightly, moving forward to link her arm with his. 'Let's go and say good night to Diana.'

'Fine with me.' Her stepbrother nodded. 'But don't think you can avoid answering me forever,' he warned teasingly. 'Something is definitely going on between you and Gideon,' he stated with certainty.

'Something' definitely was—she just had no idea what.

*   *   *

Neither did she have any clearer an idea once she was alone in the house with only Peter a couple of hours later, having insisted on being the one who stayed behind with the baby while the others all went to the late church service.

'You're my idea of the ideal male companion,' she told the baby ruefully as he slept in the cot in his nursery. 'Totally uncomplicated.' She smiled. 'You cry when you're hungry, and sleep when you aren't.'

Peter gave a brief smile in his sleep, as if in sympathy with her, although Crys had assured Molly that those smiles were of the windy type.

'What am I going to do, hmm?' she mused as she stood up and moved to the window, staring out at the starlit sky much as Gideon had done earlier this evening in the kitchen.

Gideon.

Every thought, everything she said, all seemed to come back to Gideon just recently. Which wasn't surprising, considering the circumstances, but she could do with a little respite now and again. Like ten years or so.

'He kisses me, Peter,' she continued slowly, 'and yet I'm not even sure that he likes me. If you had asked me yesterday I would have been absolutely sure that he didn't!' She grimaced.

Earlier today she had been sure of the same thing. And yet this evening...

There had been none of his earlier contempt in the way he had kissed her this evening, none of the anger, either. Just... Just what?

She really didn't know.

She did know that she was becoming far too attracted to him. Possibly more than attracted.

What did that mean?

She couldn't be falling in love with Gideon! Could she...?

Molly gave a pained groan as she realised that she already had, that every word Gideon said, every gesture he made, affected her more deeply than any other man she had known.

Great!

Another Molly blunder. She had fallen in love with the one man guaranteed to hate her.

She—

She frowned slightly as she saw car headlights at the top of the driveway, and glanced down at her watch. The others couldn't be coming back from church yet; it was only just after midnight, and the service hadn't started until eleven-thirty.

But there were no other houses down this stretch of road, so the car had to be coming here. Unless it was some late-night revellers who had lost their way?

Even as she thought this she saw the car turn in the driveway and disappear back down the road.

'Too much Christmas spirit,' she told Peter, though the baby was sleeping on unconcernedly, she discovered as she glanced back into his cot. Great; she was talking to herself now.

She had never realised how creepy it was being alone here late at night. She had always had Sam here in the past, and latterly Crys and Sam. But it definitely wasn't a place she would want to spend too much time in alone. She wondered how Sam had stood it all those years before he and Crys were married.

'I know he had you.' She grimaced apologetically at Merlin as he lifted his huge head to look at her, almost as if he had guessed her thoughts. 'But it's still a little creepy. Come on,' she prompted the dog, deciding it was probably best if she kept herself busy. 'Let's go down and prepare mulled wine and mince pies for the returning carollers.'

Nevertheless, she pulled down all the blinds at the kitchen windows before preparing the wine and putting the mince pies in the warming oven. 'Just in case,' she told Merlin ruefully.

To say she was more than a little relieved when she heard the crunch of gravel outside to announce the return of Gideon's Jaguar—the car the others had elected to go to church in—would be putting it mildly. Every creak of a tree branch outside, the rustle of fallen leaves on the driveway, even the whoosh of the central heating as it went into action, had seemed intensified in the stillness of the house, making her slightly jumpy.

'Oh, wonderful!' Crys enthused as she came in the kitchen door first and smelt the wine and mince pies, her cheeks rosy from the chill night air, her eyes bright with happiness. 'Has Peter been okay?' she added anxiously.

'Of course,' Molly reassured her, smiling at Sam and David as they came into the kitchen, but quickly averting her gaze before Gideon entered, obviously having lingered to lock up the car. 'Go up and check on him if you want to,' she told Crys affectionately, turning to pour mulled wine for them all as her friend hurried off up the stairs to check on the baby.

But all the time Molly was aware of Gideon's brooding presence where he stood next to the Aga, warming his hands. Even more so now that she had realised she had stupidly fallen in love with the man. It made her other ill-fated love of over three years ago seem quite sane in comparison.

She took the plate from the warming oven. 'Mince pie, anyone?' she offered stiltedly, her gaze still lowered so that she didn't actually have to look at Gideon.

'Thanks.' David put down his mulled wine and helped himself to one. 'I don't know about the rest of you, but I intend going up to bed as soon as I've had these; I'm absolutely bushed.'

'So am I,' Molly agreed quickly, having no intention of lingering down here and possibly being drawn into a late-night conversation that would include Gideon.

'I'm just going to take Merlin out for a last stroll,' Sam told them. 'Crys spent hours making those mince pies, so you had better keep me one, Molly.' He grinned.

'Will do,' she assured him lightly. 'Mince pie, Gideon?' she offered abruptly, still not quite looking at him.

'Thanks,' he murmured huskily, his hand briefly coming into Molly's lowered line of vision.

It was a strong-looking hand, the fingers long and artistic, the nails kept short, his wrists wide, covered in soft blond hair, making Molly wonder if he had that same downy hair on the rest of his body. It was a thought guaranteed to make her completely lose her appetite—for mince pies, anyway.

'Aren't you having one?' Gideon prompted softly.

'Er—no.' Her mouth had gone so dry she would probably choke on what she knew was mouthwatering pastry. 'I had one earlier, while you were out,' she dismissed, turning away.

Her hand shook slightly as she took a much-needed sip of her mulled wine. She recognized that the situation between Gideon and herself was becoming intolerable if she could no longer even look at him.

'As it's after midnight—Happy Christmas, Molly.' David moved to kiss her on both cheeks. 'And many of them,' he told her warmly as he stepped back.

'You, too.' She smiled, her heart suddenly fluttering as she wondered if Gideon might decide to do the same; she wasn't sure how she would respond if he did.

But she was saved from answering that question by the kitchen door opening. Sam stood in the doorway, his expression one of impatient exasperation.

'Merlin has run off and isn't responding when I call him,' he bit out irritably. 'Would the two of you mind coming out and helping me look for him?' He looked at Gideon and David.

'I'll come,' Molly offered, having taken one look at David's face and realised he still wasn't too sure of the Irish Wolfhound's temperament. 'David is exhausted, and I could do with a walk in the fresh air anyway,' she added as she put down her glass and collected her coat and scarf from the back of the door.

'I owe you one,' David told her ruefully as she followed Sam and Gideon outside.

She paused to grin at him. 'Don't worry, I'm sure I'll be able to think of some way in which you can repay me.'

'Think away,' he invited. 'After all, I have to keep my leading lady happy, don't I?' he added teasingly.

Molly was still grinning as she closed the kitchen door behind her. Although her smile faded as she turned and found herself face to face with Gideon.

Hie mouth twisted derisively as he looked down at her. 'How touching.'

Molly opened her mouth to give a sharp reply to his obvious sarcasm. And then closed it again. What was the point? Gideon was never going to have a good opinion of her, so why bother to even try?

'We're supposed to be looking for Merlin,' she reminded him abruptly.

'Of course.' He gave a mocking inclination of his head, putting his hand out in a gesture for her to precede him.

Molly was glad to move away from the light given out by the kitchen window, knowing her cheeks were flushed, her eyes overbright—and not from the chill of the cold night air, either.

'Molly…?'

She froze at the sound of Gideon's voice, her shoulders tense as she slowly turned to face him, her expression wary. 'Yes?' she prompted reluctantly.

He was scowling darkly, drawing in a harsh breath before answering. 'Nothing.' He shook his head impatiently. 'Let's go and look for this silly dog.'

But ten minutes of shouting and looking proved completely unsuccessful. Merlin was nowhere in sight. Sam was looking worried rather than impatient when the three of them once again joined up outside the house.

'He's probably gone off chasing rabbits again,' Molly reassured lightly. 'You know how he loves to do that.'

'Maybe,' Sam answered slowly. 'I just—' He broke off as a whining and scrabbling noise suddenly became apparent to them all. 'What the—?' He strode determinedly round the side of the house, with Molly and Gideon following him just in time to see him open the door to the garden shed, and a relieved Merlin rushing out into the darkness to jump up at him ecstatically.

'Panic over,' Gideon drawled ruefully as they strolled over to join Sam and the happily barking dog.

'Shh, Merlin, you'll wake Peter up,' Sam murmured, still stroking the dog as he looked around distractedly.

'Everything okay?' Gideon prompted concernedly.

'Hmm.' Sam nodded, straightening. 'I'm just wondering how Merlin got shut in the shed in the first place, that's all.' He shrugged. 'Probably I just left it open earlier and it blew shut behind him,' he decided.

'He's safe now. That's the important thing,' Molly said encouragingly as she linked her arm with his. 'Let's all go in out of the cold, hmm?' She smiled reassuringly.

But her inner thoughts were less assured. Those strange telephone calls today—definitely not from any mistress of Sam's! The car headlights she had seen at the end of the driveway earlier—and now Merlin somehow getting himself shut in the garden shed.

It was that 'somehow' that bothered her.

Sam might have forgotten to shut the shed earlier. And Merlin might have wandered inside. And the wind might have blown the door shut behind him.

It just seemed to Molly that there were an awful lot of 'mights' in the scenario…

CHAPTER TEN

'WAITING up so that you can tell Father Christmas personally that you've been nice rather than naughty?' an all-too-familiar voice drawled mockingly as Molly sat alone in the kitchen two hours later, drinking a mug of coffee.

She had drawn in a sharp breath at the first sound of Gideon's voice, and released that breath in a heavy sigh as she registered the deliberate insult in his words. 'My mother always told me that if you can't say anything nice, don't say anything at all!' Molly snapped impatiently, leaning back in her chair to look at Gideon where he stood in the doorway.

Sam had settled Merlin down in the kitchen before going up to bed when they had all come in a couple of hours ago, and Molly and Gideon had followed him up the stairs to their own bedrooms. But, having undressed and gotten into bed, Molly had found herself unable to sleep. Finally she had given up the effort half an hour ago, in favour of pulling on a pair of denims and an old rugby top of Sam's to come downstairs and make herself a pot of coffee.

From the look of Gideon he had also gone to bed. He was no longer wearing his dinner suit, but a pair of faded blue denims and a dark blue tee shirt, his hair slightly tousled.

In fact, he looked altogether too approachably attractive for Molly's peace of mind.

He moved farther into the dimly lit room, the light

over the Aga their only illumination. 'Having now met Caroline, I appreciate what a graciously beautiful woman she is, and I stand corrected,' he drawled, pouring himself a mug of coffee from the pot and pulling out the chair opposite Molly's to sit down at the table.

Molly eyed him defensively. 'Hard to believe such a "graciously beautiful" woman could be my mother, isn't it?' she snapped disgustedly.

Gideon gave a humourless smile. 'I didn't say that.'

'You didn't have to,' Molly scorned. 'You—'

'Molly, I didn't come down here to argue with you,' he cut in quietly.

She eyed him warily for several long seconds, and Gideon steadily returned that gaze. 'Then why did you come down?' she finally prompted slowly.

He shrugged. 'For the same reason as you, I expect; because I couldn't sleep.'

Her mouth twisted derisively. 'Worried in case Father Christmas doesn't think you've been nice this year, either?'

He smiled as she neatly returned his jibe. 'There is that, I suppose,' he allowed. 'But, actually, no.' He sobered, frowning. 'Molly, what do you think is going on?'

She gave him a startled look. Was it so obvious that she was in a complete turmoil concerning her recently realised feelings for this man? If it was, then she—

'I'm talking about those telephone calls,' Gideon continued evenly.

Molly glared at him. 'I've already told you—they are not, as you suggested earlier, from any mistress of Sam's!'

He nodded. 'I'm beginning to agree with you.'

'Big of you!' she snapped scathingly.

Gideon gave a sigh. 'Molly, whatever the argument might be between the two of us, let's just forget it for a moment and concentrate on this other matter, hmm?'

Whatever the argument might be between the two of them...

It wasn't exactly an argument any more, was it? Gideon either insulted her or kissed her. And as for her own feelings...

'What other matter?' she prompted impatiently, wishing she had never come down here for a mug of coffee. The last thing that was going to help her get to sleep was another of these heated conversations with Gideon!

'The telephone calls—don't jump in again, Molly,' he said wearily. 'Just hear me out, hmm?' he suggested firmly. 'You have to admit those telephone calls are odd, to say the least.'

'Yes,' she allowed abruptly.

'Then Merlin disappeared and we found him shut in the garden shed,' Gideon murmured frowningly.

'Somehow,' Molly confirmed.

'Exactly.' Gideon nodded. 'What is it?' He eyed Molly searchingly as she chewed on her bottom lip. 'What else has happened?' he guessed shrewdly.

Was her face really that easy to read? If it was, in view of the way she had discovered she felt towards this man, she had better start guarding her expression a bit more!

She shrugged. 'It could just be nothing...'

Gideon sat forward tensely. 'What could?'

She grimaced, not sure that the two of them weren't just becoming paranoid. 'There was a car in the driveway earlier. When you were all at church. But whoever it was they didn't stay there—just turned around and drove away again,' she added quickly as Gideon's frown turned to a scowl. 'It could have been Diana Chisholm, I suppose,' she said suddenly, brightening slightly. 'Maybe she got her house-call over quite quickly and thought she could join us in going to church, after all, and then she saw how late it was and changed her mind?' She trailed off weakly as she realised she sounded as if she was grasping at straws.

'Maybe,' Gideon acknowledged slowly, not seeming to think she was grasping at straws at all. 'It might be worth calling her tomorrow and checking that out.'

Molly frowned when she saw how grim Gideon still looked. 'Gideon, what do *you* think is going on?'

'I have no idea,' he answered her honestly.

But the fact that he did think something was going on only reawakened Molly's earlier feelings of unease—just when she had been prepared to dismiss her fears as being late-night jitters and tiredness.

There was no denying that it hadn't only been thoughts of Gideon that had been keeping her from sleeping earlier.

Only thoughts of Gideon...

It was like saying it was only an iceberg—when you knew very well that ninety per cent of it was below the surface of the water, and—like Gideon—extremely dangerous to the unsuspecting.

But she had also been wondering if there was any connection between those telephone calls, the car she had seen earlier, and Merlin's disappearance. Why she had been wondering that, she had no idea, but if Gideon's thoughts and concerns were anything to go by she wasn't the only one with a vivid imagination.

'It's probably nothing, you know,' she told him ruefully.

'Probably,' he agreed unconvincingly.

Molly gave him a sharp look. 'I don't think you should mention any of this to Crys and Sam,' she warned softly.

He gave her a piercing look. 'I'm not completely stupid.'

She had never for a moment thought he was in the least stupid—many other things, but stupid certainly wasn't amongst them.

She gave a deep sigh, standing up to place her empty mug in the dishwasher. 'I think I'm ready to go back to bed.'

Gideon raised a dark blond brow. 'Is that an invitation?' he drawled mockingly.

It hadn't taken him long to return to being that derisive stranger.

Molly eyed him tauntingly. 'What do you think?'

He grimaced, smiling slightly. 'I think I would be pushing my luck to expect you to say anything but no. But you can't blame a man for trying!'

This man she could blame. Because once in this man's arms it would be easy to forget that he didn't like her, so good to forget that. But the repercussions certainly wouldn't be worth it.

'I suppose not,' she answered dryly, knowing she should leave, but slightly reluctant to do so. These few minutes' conversation, during the quiet early hours of the morning, had been something of a truce. Tomorrow, she didn't doubt, they would be back to their normal armed warfare.

Gideon eyed the rugby top she wore. 'Sam's?' he guessed dryly.

The top reached almost down to her knees, and the sleeves were pushed back so that the cuffs shouldn't hang off the ends of her hands. But it was comfortable, and at three-thirty in the morning that was what she wanted to be.

'I certainly hope so—otherwise I've lost an awful lot of weight!' she teased lightly.

'You're perfect just as you are,' Gideon said huskily.

Molly's breath caught in her throat, her eyes wide as she stared at him. Had Gideon, of all people, just given her a compliment?

No, he couldn't have done.

Could he...?

Gideon gave a slight smile as he saw the disbelief on her face that she was just too surprised to hide. 'I've given you rather a hard time over the last few days, haven't I?' he murmured huskily.

Molly eyed him warily. 'No harder than I've given you,' she answered guardedly, remembering his anger earlier this evening when she had mentioned his feelings towards Crys.

Feelings, she realised with a sudden jolt, that he had been angry about her mentioning but had never actually denied...

Gideon stood up abruptly. 'Don't start letting your imagination run away with you again,' he advised her harshly.

Molly's chin rose defensively. 'Isn't that what we've both been doing these last few minutes?' she challenged. 'There is probably no connection at all between those telephone calls, the car I saw and Merlin getting lost,' she said impatiently. 'Emotions just seem to run a little high at Christmas time.' She gave a derisive shake of her head.

'Is that what it is?' Gideon murmured softly, moving silently across the kitchen to stand only inches away from her. 'Is that the reason that at any given moment

I either want to smack your bottom or kiss you? And I'm never quite sure which it's going to be until the moment happens.' He shook his head. 'Does that mean that in two days' time this madness is going to stop?' he added hopefully.

Molly stared up at him, too much aware of the silence of the sleeping house and its inhabitants not to know how dangerous this particular situation was. Especially as she knew herself to be in love with this man.

But how did Gideon feel about her? Like smacking her or kissing her, he had claimed, with little to choose between the emotions.

'I expect it does.' She nodded abruptly.

'Pity,' Gideon bit out, holding her gaze locked with his.

Molly moistened dry lips, swallowing hard. Exactly what had he meant by that? He couldn't actually be *enjoying* this roller coaster of feelings every time the two of them were together?

'You're very kissable, you know, Molly,' he added huskily, his gaze sliding to the movement of her tongue across her lips.

He eyes widened in alarm at how quickly the atmosphere had changed between them. From antagonism to intimacy in a matter of seconds. And it was wrong. All wrong.

She eyed him with deliberate mockery. 'So I've been told,' she taunted.

His head came up, his mouth tight as his narrowed gaze clashed with hers. Clashed and held, in the mental battle of wills taking place between them.

To Molly's chagrin she was the first to look away, unable to sustain the challenge she had initiated between them because Gideon was standing close enough for her to be able to feel the heat of his body, to faintly smell the aftershave she knew he favoured.

'You did that on purpose,' he rasped suddenly, reaching out to grasp the tops of her arms.

Well, of course she had done it on purpose—how else could she have broken the intimacy that had been deepening between them by the second? Although she only seemed to have made the situation worse—Gideon was actually touching her now. And every time he did that her legs went weak at the knees.

'Why, Molly?' He shook her slightly. 'What are you running away from?'

'You, of course,' she gasped, staring up at him incredulously. 'It isn't very comfortable for me being on the receiving end of your wanting to either smack my bottom or kiss me.'

Gideon became very still, his eyes dark as he looked at her. 'At the moment I want to kiss you,' he murmured throatily.

'I know,' she groaned.

She had known that for the last few minutes—would be a fool not to know that. But where would that get them? Nowhere, she knew. Which was why it would be better for everyone if it didn't happen.

Except she wanted him to kiss her, too—ached to have him kiss her, to finish what they had started earlier!

'Molly...!' Gideon had time to murmur her name gruffly before his mouth once again claimed hers.

He was right. This was madness. But it was a madness Molly was no more able to stop than Gideon apparently was, and her lips parted to the pressure of his, her body curving against his hard contours even as her hands moved up over his shoulders, her fingers becoming entwined in the blond thickness of his hair.

These emotions had just been put on hold, she realised dazedly. Sam's interruption earlier had been only a respite from a desire neither of them seemed able to resist.

Gideon raised his head slightly to look at her. 'Why is it we're always in the kitchen when I kiss you?' he murmured self-derisively, his lips lightly grazing her temple.

'Because it's the warmest room in the house?' she suggested huskily, aware of this man with every fibre of her body.

Gideon looked at her with dark, fathomless eyes. 'I'm very warm. Aren't you?'

Warm? She was on fire!

'Quite warm,' she answered softly, suddenly shy. The time, the stillness of the house, was making it seem as if they were the only two people on the planet.

'Let's go into the sitting-room,' Gideon suggested gruffly, and he took her hand in his and turned to leave the kitchen.

Molly hesitated. The fire still glowed in the sitting-room. There was a sofa—a very comfortable one—in the sitting-room. And this was Gideon, a man who had expressed nothing but contempt for her.

She shook her head. 'Gideon, I don't think—'

'No—don't think,' he encouraged throatily, turning back to cup one side of her face with the warmth of his hand. 'Whenever the two of us start to think, collectively or singly, that's when things go wrong between us.' He bent his head to kiss her lingeringly on the lips. 'Don't think, Molly,' he urged persuasively.

She couldn't. Not when he kissed her with such aching passion. And she followed as he once again turned to leave the room.

She had been right about the sofa; it was comfortable. She sank back against the cushions as Gideon began to kiss her once again.

'You did look very beautiful tonight in that red dress,' he told her huskily as his lips travelled the length of her neck to the hollows of her throat. 'But all I wanted to do all evening was strip it from you!' he added achingly, before his lips returned to hers, fierce passion making any more talk between them impossible.

Molly's heart had leapt in her chest at Gideon's admission concerning her red dress, and her lips opened to his now as he deepened the kiss to intimacy.

His back was warm beneath his tee shirt, the muscles rippling beneath her fingertips as she touched him there, gasping slightly as his hands began to caress beneath her own top.

Only intending to come downstairs for a quick mug of coffee, she had merely pulled the rugby top and denims on over her nakedness, and Gideon groaned his approval as his searching hand encountered her bare breast.

It was Molly's turn to groan as Gideon cupped and caressed her nakedness, her nipple already pert and inviting as a thumbtip moved across it in a light caress.

And all the time his lips continued to possess hers, and Molly was aware only of him, of the touch of his mouth and hands on her lips and body.

Her hands clutched convulsively in the hair at his nape as he moved his lips to her naked breast, and she seemed to stop breathing altogether as he drew the sensitive tip into the moist warmth of his mouth, his tongue a rasping caress.

Molly was aware of every muscle and sinew of him as he lay half across her on the length of the sofa, his long legs entangled with her own, the hardness of his thighs telling of his own desire—if she had needed any telling.

'I want you, Molly,' he groaned as his mouth returned to hers and his hands now caressed the fiery tips of her breasts. 'God, how much I want you.'

She wanted him, too—too much to be able to say no to anything he asked of her.

His face was slightly flushed, his eyes glittering darkly as he raised his head to look at her, one of his hands moving to cup beneath her chin, his thumb running lightly over lips swollen from the hungry kisses they had just shared. 'Say you want me, too, Molly,' he encouraged huskily.

She didn't have to say it—knew it had to be obvious when her whole body was on fire. Even the blood in her veins seemed to flow more heatedly, making her aware of every pulsing inch of her body, from the soles of her feet to the top of her head.

'Say it, Molly!' he urged again. 'Tell me—' He broke off abruptly. 'What's that?' He frowned his confusion.

Molly frowned too as she became aware of a loud scrabbling noise somewhere in the house.

'A sleigh with eight reindeer on the roof, do you think?' Gideon suggested incredulously.

Molly gave a shaky smile. 'Somehow I doubt that very much,' she answered ruefully, very much aware of their closeness. Gideon's bared chest was against her own, covered in that downy blond hair, as she had imagined it was.

'So do I.' Gideon gave a dazed shake of his head as he raised himself slightly. 'What the—?' He gasped as the sound of loud barking suddenly broke the silence around them.

'It's Merlin,' Molly said concernedly, struggling to sit up.

'I realise that, but—hell, if we don't stop him he's going to wake the whole house up in a minute!' Gideon rasped, standing up to stride forcefully from the room with the obvious intention of silencing the dog.

Molly took a little longer to regain her equilibrium, still trembling with desire as she sat up to watch Gideon leave, her cheeks fiery red as she hastily pulled the rugby shirt down over her nakedness.

'Saved by the dog' didn't sound quite the same as the original quote, but it was no less the truth, for all that. If Merlin hadn't begun barking like this, shattering the intimacy between them, then she knew she would have told Gideon just how much she wanted him.

Too much!

CHAPTER ELEVEN

NOT that Gideon seemed to be doing too good a job of silencing Merlin. The sound of the dog's barking was interspersed with low growls, too, now, and the cacophony became louder as Molly hurried down the hallway to the kitchen.

Merlin was scrabbling at the back door when Molly entered the room, and Gideon was doing everything he could to calm him—from talking to him soothingly to raising his voice sharply, even going down on his haunches and trying to hold the dog and silence him that way.

This was something Merlin took great exception to, growling even deeper in his throat, baring his teeth in displeasure.

'He wants to go outside,' Molly advised him worriedly.

Gideon turned to scowl at her. 'I know what he wants, Molly,' he bit out frustratedly. 'I'm just not sure it's a good idea to let him out,' he added slowly.

She looked down at him frowningly. 'Why not?'

'Because... Just because.' He amended whatever he had originally been going to say, straightening to look down frustratedly as Merlin still scrabbled frantically at the door. 'I know this is a large house, but nevertheless I have no doubt that he's woken everyone in it by now—'

'He has indeed,' Sam muttered grimly as he came into the room. 'Silence, Merlin!' he instructed sharply.

Amazingly, the huge dog went quiet—although he still stood staring at the back door, panting heavily.

Sam, a white bathrobe pulled on over his nakedness, ran a hand through his already tousled hair. 'This is turning into one hell of a Christmas.' He shook his head dazedly.

'Isn't it?' Gideon agreed dryly.

Molly didn't look at him—couldn't look at him—but nevertheless she knew that last remark had been directed at her as much as at Sam.

It was turning into one hell of a Christmas for her, too. So much so that Molly had no idea where it was all going to end. But end it must. With or without this situation resolved between Gideon and herself.

'What's wrong with him?' Sam frowned as Merlin dropped to the floor, his nose pressed against the door as he once again began to rumble low in this throat.

Gideon straightened. 'Something outside disturbed him. A cat, possibly a fox.' He shrugged.

'I see,' Sam said slowly, seeming to look at the two of them for the first time and frowning thoughtfully as he took in their dressed appearance. 'And the two of you rushed down here to try to quieten him before he woke us all up?'

'Yes—'

'No,' Molly cut across Gideon's deliberate evasion, feeling the warmth in her cheeks as he looked at her frowningly and at Sam speculatively. 'We were already down here. Having a cup of coffee.' She indicated the still-warming percolator, shooting Gideon a look that said the-truth-is-usually-the-best-policy as she did so.

Sam knew damn well that the coffee percolator had been turned off when he went up to bed three hours ago; she had seen him check it.

'Merlin just seemed to go wild,' she added ruefully.

'Hmm. Well.' Sam gave a weary sigh. 'He seems to have calmed down again now,' he noted with some relief. Merlin was still lying beside the door, but no longer looking agitated. 'Back to bed, I guess.' He grimaced. 'Maybe we can all get another couple of hours' sleep before the next disturbance occurs,' he added ruefully.

Molly didn't need another disturbance to know she wasn't going to get any sleep tonight—thoughts of Gideon, of the intimacy they had shared, were enough to keep her awake for a week.

'How's Peter?' she prompted as the three of them went up the stairs.

Sam grinned. 'It seems a little trite to say "sleeping like a baby"—but that's exactly what he's doing. He's fine,' he assured her warmly. 'Although—' he sobered '—if Merlin carries on like that again I may just have to make him comfortable outside rather than in the house.' He didn't look at all happy at the idea.

'I'm sure it was just a one-off thing.' Gideon was the one to reassure him. 'Well, good night again, Molly.' He turned to her pointedly as they reached the top of the first staircase.

Her eyes widened at this obvious ploy to get rid of her. Gideon's guest bedroom was on the same floor as her own—surely it was more natural for the two of them both to say good night to Sam and go up together?

Not if you were regretting the intimacy that had occurred fifteen minutes ago. Then you would avoid being alone together again at all costs.

'Good night,' she said abruptly, not looking at either man before she hurried over to the second staircase and ran up to her bedroom, closing the door firmly behind her and leaning weakly back against it.

How could anyone be as changeable as Gideon obviously was? One minute telling her that she was beautiful, and how much he wanted her, the next coldly wishing her good night?

He could if he didn't want anyone else to know that the two of them had almost made love together. If he regretted it had ever happened.

Well, she regretted it, too.

But not as much as she regretted the fact that she was in love with him...

'I love Christmas, don't you?' Crys said happily the next morning as they gathered in the sitting-room to open presents beneath the tree.

'Gathered' as the result of Sam going along the hallways knocking on all the bedroom doors to wake everyone up with the cry, 'Time to get up, Father Christmas has been.'

And it was rather lovely. Sam had lit a fresh fire in the hearth before waking everyone else, the lights glowed on the tree, and even a little gentle seasonal snow was falling as they looked out of the huge bay windows.

'Love it,' Molly agreed with forced warmth.

One glance at Gideon had been enough—his expression was less than encouraging. Just normal Gideon, really. It was the warm and sensual man of last night who had been the exception.

'For you.' Sam handed her a gaily wrapped parcel, standing in as Father Christmas as he distributed the presents from beneath the tree.

One glance at the label showed that the lumpy-looking parcel was from David. Molly glanced across at him before opening it.

'Don't blame me,' he warned her laughingly as he strolled over to join them. 'I asked Crys, and she told me you collect them!'

In that case, Molly knew exactly what it was, and laughed as she opened the present and saw a cuddly pig holding a red rose in its trotter.

'Now I feel guilty that I only got you a book.' She grinned up at David.

'But what a book.' He grinned back. 'You probably won't get any sense out of me for the rest of Christmas. Okay, okay.' He laughed when Molly gave him a teasing look. 'You don't get much sense out of me anyway,' he accepted.

'Now, would I have said that?' she teased.

'Undoubtedly,' David said dryly.

Why was it so much easier to laugh and joke with David like this than it was with Gideon, the man she was in love with?

Probably because she *was* in love with him, she acknowledged ruefully.

And no longer had any idea what he felt for her.

Although, if the way he was scowling across the room at her now was anything to go by, after last night he held her in more contempt than ever.

'Another one for you.' Sam gave her a second package before resuming his present-giving duties.

Molly's hand began to tremble as she read 'To Molly, From Gideon' on the label. No frills or fancies about that. No 'love', either. Probably even 'best wishes' would have been asking for too much. And she would have preferred some cheerful robins on the wrapping paper rather than cold silver bells.

All of which meant she was totally unprepared for the beautiful cashmere scarf she found inside the package, so soft to the touch it felt like silk. But, more importantly, it was of the deepest pink—a colour Gideon had already assured her didn't suit her red hair.

'In contrast to the suit you were wearing on Sunday, this is the shade of pink that *does* go with your colouring.'

Molly looked up sharply as Gideon spoke, her hand closing convulsively on the scarf. She had been unaware until that moment that Gideon had crossed the room to stand beside her.

She swallowed hard. 'It's beautiful,' she told him sincerely. 'Thank you.'

He gave the ghost of a smile. 'Did it hurt to say that?'

She shrugged. 'Only a little.'

His smile widened. 'That's something, I suppose.'

It *was* something—considering she was slightly overwhelmed by his gift. 'Impersonal' was the way he had described the buying of her gift to him, and yet this scarf, obviously chosen to go with her particular colouring, couldn't be put in that category.

Crys stood up to announce briskly, 'Time for breakfast, I think.'

'I'll come and help,' Molly offered instantly, grateful for an excuse to stand up and break the air of intimacy that had been developing between herself and Gideon.

'We'll all help,' he said firmly. 'Just because both of you can, doesn't mean that you two women *should* do all the cooking around here.'

Which was probably about as close to a compliment for her cooking last night's meal as she was going to get from Gideon, Molly accepted ruefully.

'Oh, don't worry,' Crys paused to say laughingly. 'You aren't going to just sit here with nothing to do; you three men can amuse Peter for half an hour or so.'

And leave us two women alone to have a gossip in privacy, Molly guessed easily as she followed Crys to the kitchen. No doubt Sam had told Crys that Molly and Gideon had been downstairs together during the night, and her friend wanted to know all the details.

Something Molly had no intention of confiding in anyone—not even her best friend.

'So, come on—spill the beans,' Crys encouraged predictably as soon as the two women were safely ensconced in the kitchen.

Molly sighed, knowing that pretending not to know what her friend was talking about would be a waste of time; Crys could be dogged when she set her mind to it. 'I couldn't sleep and came downstairs for some coffee. Gideon had the same idea about half an hour later.' She shrugged dismissively.

Crys straightened from getting the eggs out of the fridge to eye Molly reprovingly. 'And that's it?' she said sceptically.

'More or less.' Molly nodded, determinedly turning her attention to laying the table.

How much more, Crys really didn't need to know.

Crys obviously wasn't of the same opinion. 'Well?' she prompted pointedly.

'Well, nothing,' Molly dismissed lightly. 'We both had a mug of coffee, and then Merlin started barking.' And in between that she had completely lost her heart, amongst other things.

'I don't understand the two of you.' Crys gave her an exasperated look. 'Gideon is gorgeous. You're beautiful—'

'Thank you,' Molly accepted teasingly.

'The two of you might at least have a flirtation—if

only to satisfy my romantic inclinations!' Crys complained frustratedly.

Molly couldn't help but laugh at her friend's disgruntled expression. 'Nice try, Crys.' She shook her head indulgently. 'But I've already told you—you're wasting your time where Gideon and I are concerned.'

'Obviously.' Crys frowned. 'But as two of my dearest friends, I do think you might have indulged me just a little.'

'Sorry,' Molly said unconcernedly.

'Oh, scramble these eggs,' Crys muttered frustratedly, before concentrating on preparing the other ingredients for breakfast.

Molly only wished she could distract her heart as easily as she seemed to have distracted Crys. But her heart wasn't as easily deceived. She knew without a doubt that she was in love with Gideon.

She flattered herself that she did quite a good job of hiding it as the day progressed. Not that it was too difficult to do, when Gideon seemed just as determined to avoid her company, too.

In fact, by the time they had all collapsed in the evening, after yet another sumptuous meal, Molly could honestly say that they hadn't exchanged more than a few words all day—and even those had only been of the polite category, such as 'Could you pass the salt, please?'

At least this respite from Gideon's company gave her a chance to rebuild her defences—defences that had been badly damaged during their closeness the night before. And she felt restored enough that she felt no qualms about joining Gideon and Sam for Merlin's evening stroll. In fact, after a day spent eating, chatting, and watching the occasional programme on television—a special Christmas *Bailey* being one of them—she welcomed the opportunity for some fresh air.

Although, from the scowl on Gideon's face as she went outside, it seemed he would rather she hadn't joined them.

Well, too bad. Sam was her brother, and this was her Christmas, too.

The three of them walked in the grounds in silence for some time, the moon's reflection on the light scattering of snow on the ground making it a clear night.

'I'm glad you decided to join us, Molly.' Sam suddenly spoke heavily 'Gideon has told me exactly what's been happening the last few days, and I think you should know—'

'I disagree, Sam,' Gideon cut in harshly. 'In fact, I don't think it's a good idea for you to talk about this,' he added determinedly.

Sam turned to frown at the other man. 'Why not?'

'Because I don't.' Gideon's expression was harshly forbidding, his face appearing all hard angles in the moonlight.

Molly's own face, she knew, was pale; she had felt the colour drain from her cheeks at Sam's opening comment. How could Gideon have told her brother what had happened between the two of them during the night? How *could* he?

'I disagree, Gideon,' Sam told the other man ruefully. 'I know you think you're being protective, but Molly is far from being a child—'

'Obviously,' she snapped, utterly humiliated at the thought of Gideon discussing her in those terms—with her stepbrother, of all people. In fact, if he had been in the least a gentleman he wouldn't have discussed last night with *anyone*.

'Molly—'

'Oh, forget it, Sam.' She interrupted his placating words impatiently. 'Gideon has spoken,' she snapped angrily, feeling the heated colour return to her cheeks as she turned to glare at Gideon in the semi-darkness. 'Too much, by the sound of it,' she accused furiously.

'Molly—'

'Stay out of this, Sam,' she told him coldly, her gaze still locked on Gideon. 'You are without doubt the most arrogant, self-opinionated, horrible man it has ever been my misfortune to meet,' she bit out accusingly.

'Molly, please let me explain—' Sam tried.

'Leave it, Sam,' Gideon rasped. His expression had become even grimmer at Molly's tirade of accusations, and his face was starkly etched against the moonlight. 'I'm sure Molly feels she is perfectly entitled to express her opinion of me.'

'Yes, but—'

'Too right I am!' she snapped, her hands clenched at her sides now. 'And arrogant doesn't even begin to cover what you are!'

He smiled without humour. 'Self-opinionated and horrible were two other descriptions, I believe,' he drawled hardly.

'Oh, I could go on,' she assured him scornfully. 'But, don't worry, I'm not about to,' she added scathingly as she saw how dismayed Sam was looking. 'I'm going back to the house now,' she told them both abruptly, before turning on her heel and marching furiously away.

The tears were falling hotly down her cheeks before

she had gone half a dozen steps, and she brushed them away impatiently as she began to run rather than walk.

How could he?

How could he?

CHAPTER TWELVE

'BUT you can't leave now,' Crys protested in dismay when Molly joined her in the kitchen before lunch the next day and told her of her intention of doing just that. 'It's still only Boxing Day,' she added incredulously.

Molly was well aware of what day it was. She was also aware, after yet another night of not sleeping, that she simply couldn't stay here a moment longer. If only so that she might go back to the flat she was renting in London and get some much-needed sleep.

Although that was far from the real reason for the decision she had come to during the wakeful night hours...

She would never forgive Gideon for confiding in Sam in the way that he had. Her humiliation had been complete the evening before, when Sam and Gideon had returned to the house and Gideon had ignored her. She'd sat talking to David. At least, she had been trying to talk to David—inside she'd been too disturbed to be able to think straight—before he'd made his excuses and disappeared upstairs to bed.

Molly had waited only minutes before doing the same thing, glad of the privacy of her bedroom to lick her wounds in private.

'I know what day it is, Crys,' Molly assured her friend lightly. 'But the traffic will be easier today for a long drive, and I still have lots of boxes to unpack.' She grimaced at the thought of the disorder she had left behind in her new flat in London.

Crys looked unconvinced by these arguments. 'But it's still Christmas.' She frowned.

'I've been here four days already, Crys,' she reasoned cajolingly. 'And it isn't as if you don't have other guests who will be staying on for several more days.' Her voice hardened at the thought that Gideon was one of those guests.

The real reason for her abrupt departure.

'I know that, but— Sam, talk some sense into Molly.' She turned to plead with her husband as he strolled in from walking Merlin. 'She says she's leaving today,' Crys told him frustratedly.

Molly could feel the blush in her cheeks as Sam paused in discarding his jacket to look at her with obvious surprise. But surely he more than anyone should realise that she simply couldn't stay on here another moment longer?

'Really?' her stepbrother murmured slowly.

'Really,' Crys echoed impatiently. 'Talk to her, Sam,' she encouraged forcefully.

Molly wasn't happy at breaking up everyone's Christmas like this, and was aware of how hard Crys had worked towards it, but at the same time she knew that the increasing tension between herself and Gideon was going to ruin it all anyway if something wasn't done to stop it. The only option appeared to be to remove one of the protagonists. And, as she doubted Gideon intended going anywhere, that only left her to be the one to make the move...

'Molly?' Sam prompted quietly.

'Sam, you know why I want to leave,' she told him exasperatedly.

'No,' he said slowly. 'I don't think I do. Crys, darling—' he turned to her smilingly '—would you mind if I just took Molly into my study with me for a while?'

'If you can persuade her into staying on you can keep her in there all day,' Crys assured him. 'In fact, if you can't persuade her, lock her in there until she agrees to stay.'

Sam chuckled ruefully, and even Molly had to smile at her friend's obvious frustration with her decision to leave today.

But there was nothing Sam could say to her that was going to make her change her mind...

'Is someone leaving?' Gideon questioned sharply as he walked into the kitchen.

Molly stiffened at the first sound of his voice, her expression guarded as she turned to look at him. 'I am,' she told him with determination.

Blue eyes looked at her calmly for several long seconds. 'Rather ungrateful of you, isn't it?' he finally murmured coolly. 'After all Sam and Crys have tried to do for us.'

She could feel the heat in her cheeks at this unmistakable reprimand. But he must know why she couldn't stay on here any longer.

'Don't give that another thought, Gideon,' Crys assured him. 'It's been a pleasure having you all here. It's just...' She grimaced. 'Sam is going to try to talk her into changing her mind,' she added confidently.

Molly wished they would all just let her leave and stop making such a fuss about it. After all, Sam at least knew exactly why she wanted to leave.

'Let me talk to her,' Gideon soothed.

That really was going too far.

'I don't think so, thanks,' she bit out disgustedly. He was the last person she wanted to talk to—the last person who could possibly persuade her into staying on here another day.

'Sam—' Gideon completely ignored her protest as he turned to the other man. '—I heard Peter stirring as I came down just now. And as Crys is busy preparing lunch... Come on, Molly.' He took a firm hold of her arm and practically marched her out of the room.

Molly tried to free herself. 'What do you think you're doing?'

'What do you think *you're* doing?' Gideon came back grimly, maintaining that grip of her arm. 'Stop fighting me, Molly; you'll only end up hurting yourself,' he advised coldly.

'As opposed to you hurting me?' she accused heatedly, not giving up on trying to pry his fingers from her arm. Not succeeding, either. But that didn't mean she wasn't going to keep trying.

Gideon came to an abrupt halt, turning her to face him in the hallway. 'Me?' he repeated harshly. 'What the hell have I done to hurt you?' he demanded impatiently.

Kissed her until her head spun. Made love to her. Made her fall in love with him.

She was breathing hard in her agitation. 'I have absolutely nothing to say to you—'

'Too bad—because I have a few things I want to say to you!' he ground out, pulling her into the sitting-room and finally releasing her as he closed the door firmly behind them.

The room where they had almost made love. The sofa where they had been so close. Too close.

Molly turned her back on the sofa, on those disturbing memories, glaring up at Gideon. 'Say away!' she challenged, her chin held defensively high.

Gideon looked down at her exasperatedly for several seconds, and then he gave an impatient shake of his head. 'You are, without doubt, the most stubborn person—'

'It takes one to know one.' Molly scorned.

'Doesn't it just?' he accepted ruefully, moving away to thrust his hands into his pockets. 'Molly, I don't think it's a good idea for you to leave here just now—'

'Surprise, surprise—I don't care what you think!' she told him incredulously.

His mouth twisted humourlessly. 'Do you think I don't already know that?'

Her eyes widened. 'Then why—?'

'Molly, there's something...' He paused, sighing exasperatedly at the situation. 'I really would rather not explain at this juncture.' He shook his head.

'Because there's nothing to explain,' Molly assured him scornfully. 'I already know you made a mistake kissing me the other night.'

'Is that what you think this is all about?' His eyes were narrowed to glittering blue slits, a nerve pulsing in his tightly clenched jaw.

'What else?' she said derisively. 'But you really don't have to worry about the other night, Gideon. I can assure you that I, for one, would much rather forget that it had ever happened at all!' She was breathing hard in her agitation.

'Do you think I don't know that?' Gideon drew in a sharp breath. 'You've made that all too damned obvious by the way you've been avoiding my company ever since,' he ground out accusingly.

'What did you want me to do?' Molly scorned. 'Fall all over you like some lovesick idiot?'

Again he gave that humourless smile. 'That would be asking too much.'

'Too right it would!' Her vehemence was all the deeper because that was exactly what she would rather have done.

It was what she wanted to do now...

Looking at him, being with him, brought home to her how much she loved this man, how much she wanted to throw herself into his arms and have him tell her that it was all right, that he was in love with her, too.

But she had stopped believing in fairy tales a long time ago, and was well aware that Gideon didn't love her. Oh, he might find her desirable—after the other night he really couldn't deny that—but it was against his own wishes to feel that way, was something he fought against all the time. And most of the time he succeeded...

'Okay.' He gave a heavy sigh. 'I accept that you want as little to do with me as possible. But do you have to leave to achieve that? I thought we had been managing to avoid each other quite well the last twenty-four hours?'

Oh, they had. She had. And so, from his comment just now, had Gideon. She just wasn't sure how much longer she could keep up this bravado, pretend not to give a damn.

But would she love Gideon any less for being alone in London? The answer to that was a definite no.

'I don't want to stay on here.' But even as she said it she knew her voice lacked the conviction it had had a few minutes ago.

'That isn't true, and you know it.' Gideon sighed. 'You don't want to stay here with me as a guest, too.

So the question is, do you want me to be the one to leave?'

Her eyes widened. 'Are you seriously offering?'

His mouth thinned. 'Yes, I'm seriously offering.'

Molly stared at him. Would he really do that? More to the point, could she ask him to do that?

Three days ago, when she had first learnt that he and David were to be guests here, too, over Christmas, she had considered Gideon to be an interloper, an intrusion on what should have been a family Christmas. But over those last three days she had come to realise that he wasn't an interloper at all, that he was as much a part of Crys and Sam's family as she was.

She moistened dry lips. 'I—' She broke off as she heard the doorbell ring. 'Are we expecting anyone today?' She frowned.

'I have no idea,' Gideon answered grimly. 'Wait here while I go and see,' he instructed abruptly, before striding from the room.

Wait here while I go and see, Molly's thoughts echoed resentfully; like hell she would.

Gideon had reached the door by the time she came out of the sitting-room, turning to give her a reproving glare as he heard her in the hallway behind him.

'It's okay, I'll get it.' He spoke to someone over Molly's shoulder.

Molly turned in time to see Crys shrug before returning to the kitchen.

Gideon was still glaring at her when she turned back. 'I thought I told you— Oh, never mind,' he snapped impatiently as Molly stood her ground, and reached out to wrench the front door open. 'Diana!' he greeted, his voice containing none of the ice of a few seconds before, when he had spoken to Molly.

'I hope I haven't arrived too early,' Diana apologised ruefully. 'Hi, Molly,' she said with a smile as she glanced around Gideon. 'Crys didn't actually specify a time when she invited me to come and spend the day with you all.'

'I'm sure you aren't too early.' Gideon opened the door wider for the doctor to enter. 'Especially as you seem to have arrived bearing gifts,' he added lightly, as the bag that Diana carried chinked tellingly.

'I couldn't possibly have accepted Crys's invitation without contributing in some way,' Diana Chisholm assured them, and laughed huskily. 'Besides, one of my partners has offered to be on call today—he has two aged aunts and his mother-in-law staying with him over the holidays,' she added pointedly. 'Which means I have an unexpected day off,' she said happily.

'That's good,' Molly told her sincerely, having a genuine liking for the pretty doctor. 'And I'm sure that if you do happen to have too much wine then Crys and Sam will be only too happy for you to stay here tonight,' she added.

'Oh, I doubt that I shall do that, but thanks,' Diana answered lightly. 'I noticed on my drive over here that there seem to be an awful lot of police cars in the area— no doubt on the lookout for drunk drivers going home from the pub.' She grimaced.

'Actually, you've arrived just in time to add your weight to the argument for Molly not to return to London today,' Gideon told the other woman lightly, and the gleam of challenge in his eyes was for Molly alone as he glanced across at her.

It was a glance Molly deliberately didn't meet as she turned to smile at Diana.

'Oh, no, you can't possibly,' Diana told Molly con-

cernedly. 'I moved here from London three years ago.'
She shook her head. 'It has to be the loneliest place on
earth at Christmas-time if you aren't with family.'

Any place was lonely if you weren't with people you
loved—the man you loved. Molly already knew that.
But being here with Gideon, when her love wasn't returned, was painful, too.

'Do stay, Molly,' Diana encouraged warmly. 'I did
so want to have a chat with you. I'm an avid fan of the
Bailey series, you know.'

Molly smiled. 'In that case it's David you should be
talking to, not me.'

Diana looked nonplussed. 'Oh, but he mentioned that
you're going to be in the new series with him?'

'Did he, indeed?' Molly laughed exasperatedly. 'David!'
She turned to open the library door—she had seen
David disappear in there an hour or so earlier. He was
still there, sitting in the window, gazing out at the snow-
covered landscape, a book lying untouched in his lap.
'And they say women gossip!' she teased as she preceded Diana and Gideon into the room.

David looked slightly surprised to see Diana, putting
the book down on the table to slowly stand up. 'What
did I do now?' He gave a quizzical smile, that smile
not quite reaching the sadness of his eyes.

'Never mind,' Molly dismissed lightly, moving to
link her arm with his, instinctively sensing that he had
spent enough time alone with obviously unhappy
thoughts. 'As there's no sun today, I have no idea
whether or not it's over the yard-arm yet—but let's all
go and join Crys and Sam in the kitchen and open up
a bottle of wine while we help prepare lunch.'

'Sounds like a good idea to me.' David nodded.
'Lead on, MacDuff,' he invited lightly.

Somewhere between opening the red wine Diana had brought with her, pouring it into glasses, and helping Crys prepare the vegetables for lunch, Molly's decision to leave was forgotten by all of them.

Deliberately so by the others, Molly was sure. But with Diana's arrival it seemed churlish to pursue her plans to leave. Besides, Crys had prepared her delicious trout dish for lunch—a culinary experience that no one should miss.

'It was a pity you didn't get back the other evening to join us in going to church.' Gideon spoke lightly to Diana as the six of them sat around the dining-table, eating their main course.

Diana, sitting to his left, grimaced slightly. 'I don't know what it is, but babies always decide they want to be born on Christmas Day. This one also decided it couldn't wait for the ambulance to arrive and take its mother to hospital, and I ended up delivering it myself, just after midnight. A healthy little boy, I'm glad to say, and mother and baby nicely tucked up in bed shortly after one o'clock. A home birth has to be the most wonderful experience,' she added softly.

Molly gave Gideon a sharp glance, sure that he had deliberately mentioned Christmas Eve in an effort to see whether or not it had been Diana's car in the driveway that night. From what the doctor had just told them, it obviously hadn't.

But if that had been Gideon's intention Molly could see he certainly wasn't going to share that knowledge with her—unless she was very much mistaken, once again he was deliberately avoiding meeting her gaze.

In fact, he had been noticeably aloof towards her during the whole meal as she'd sat across the table from him, while at the same time warmly considerate to Diana Chisholm.

Encouraged by Crys, she had to acknowledge. Her friend, having taken Molly's uninterest in Gideon literally, now appeared to be deliberately encouraging a friendship between Gideon and Diana.

Jealousy wasn't an emotion that Molly had known for a long time, and never as she felt it now—aware of every word spoken between Gideon and Diana, every laugh they shared.

'What are you up to now?' she demanded of Crys as she followed her friend into the kitchen to help carry in the desserts.

'Sorry?' Crys looked at her blankly.

Deliberately so, Molly was sure, when she saw the mischievous twinkle in her friend's laughing grey eyes. 'Don't play the innocent with me.' She grimaced wryly. 'Gideon and Diana?' she said pointedly as Crys continued to look at her blandly.

'Oh, that.' Crys nodded slowly.

'Yes—that!' Molly snapped tersely.

'Aren't you being a little dog in the manger, Molly?' Crys came back knowingly.

Molly could feel the blush in her cheeks at her friend's correct assessment of the situation. 'Don't be ridiculous, Crys,' she bit out shortly.

Crys gave a husky laugh. 'Is that what I'm being?' She raised blond brows as she moved briskly about the kitchen, preparing the whisky cream to go with oranges that had been marinading in liquor overnight.

Molly sighed heavily. 'You know that you are. Gideon is— Crys, you simply can't be this blind—you must know it's you Gideon loves!' she burst out forcefully.

Crys came to an abrupt halt, giving Molly a stunned stare. 'Now who's being ridiculous?' she finally said incredulously. 'Of course Gideon isn't in love with me.' She shook her head. 'He's James's brother,' she added dismissively.

'So?' Molly returned exasperatedly. She couldn't believe her friend was unaware of how Gideon felt about her.

'So he's James's brother!' Crys repeated impatiently, her smile rueful. 'Really, Molly, I don't know how you came to such a conclusion, but I can assure you—'

'Gideon himself,' Molly cut in frustratedly.

'What?' Crys gasped incredulously.

'From watching Gideon whenever he's with you,' Molly said tersely. 'He adores you, Crys—'

'I hope that he does,' Crys cut in. 'Because I adore him, too. After James died, and then my parents six months later, Gideon was the only family I had left. But that's all it is, Molly,' she added frowningly. 'All it's ever been.'

She shook her head with certainty. 'Not on Gideon's side.'

'Yes, on Gideon's side,' Crys insisted evenly. 'Molly, is this the reason you've been staying clear of Gideon? Because if it is—'

'I've been "staying clear of Gideon", as you put it, because he doesn't like me,' she came back impatiently.

'Rubbish!' Crys came back, just as firmly. 'If you want my opinion, Molly, then you haven't given him a chance to like or dislike—'

'I don't,' she cut in firmly.

'Okay.' Crys shrugged. 'In that case, carry the oranges and cream through for me while I bring the *crème brûlées*.' She gave an exasperated shake of her head. 'I really don't know what you were thinking of, Molly,' she added reprovingly as she picked up the tray. 'Gideon is the big brother I never had.'

But just because that was the way Crys felt about the relationship, it still didn't mean that Gideon felt the same way…

'Move, Molly,' Crys ordered determinedly. 'And if I'm wrong, and you do want Gideon, then I advise you to start showing it a little more,' she advised. 'Otherwise Diana may just pip you to the post,' she added wryly.

If she wanted Gideon…

She wanted Gideon more than she had ever wanted anything or anyone in her life before. But—

There was always a 'but' in her dealings with Gideon.

And Molly still thought Crys was wrong in her dismissal of Gideon's feelings towards her…

CHAPTER THIRTEEN

'YOU never did answer my question earlier.'

Molly tensed at the sound of Gideon's voice, turning slowly to find that he had joined her where she sat on the hearthrug in the sitting-room, playing with baby Peter's toes while the other adults all sat in chairs—or lay on the sofa in Crys and Sam's case—dozing after the filling lunch they had all eaten. Until this moment she had thought Gideon asleep in a chair, too.

'You like babies, don't you?' Gideon murmured huskily before she had a chance to answer his initial statement, gently touching Peter's hand as he sat on the rug beside them.

She frowned, keeping her voice low so that they shouldn't disturb the others with their conversation. 'Doesn't everyone?'

He shrugged. 'I haven't always found that to be the case, no,' he answered ruefully. 'For instance, my own mother wasn't particularly maternal.' He grimaced.

Molly's eyes widened. 'But she had you and James.'

He nodded. 'I was the necessary "heir". James's arrival, ten years later, as the "spare", was an accident she never let anyone forget. Including James himself,' he added grimly. 'She walked out on all of us, taking most of my father's money with her, I might add— when James was only four. I was fourteen.'

Molly blinked, surprised by this confidence coming from a man she knew to be completely sufficient unto himself. But maybe this was an insight into the reason he was like that...?

Gideon gave a humourless smile as he glanced up and saw the expression on her face. 'Not exactly what you expected, was it?'

What *had* she expected? From his obvious wealth and self-confidence now, yes, she had assumed that Gideon had always led a charmed life—as had James seemed to. But these revelations seemed to point towards a completely different sort of childhood from the one she had imagined for them.

But why should Gideon assume she had expected anything? That she had even given his past life a second thought...?

'My father did the best he could, of course. He sent me to university, engaged nannies and then found a boarding-school for James,' Gideon continued softly. 'But unfortunately he died from a heart attack when I was twenty and James only ten.'

Not the background she had imagined at all for this often seemingly arrogant man!

She frowned slightly. 'Why are you telling me these things, Gideon?' she asked slowly, voicing her puzzlement.

He gave a husky laugh. 'Truthfully? I have no idea!' he admitted self-derisively. 'Perhaps it was watching your gentleness with Peter just now. Or to explain why a family Christmas like this is special to me.' He gave a rueful shake of his head. 'Or, more probably, I just drank too much wine with lunch!'

Molly stared at him for several seconds—at the way his hair fell endearingly over his forehead, the softness in his eyes; even his mouth was not set in that forbidding line as he gazed down at Peter.

'Which question were you referring to a few minutes ago?' she prompted huskily.

Gideon glanced up at her. 'About my being the one to leave here. Because if you want me to go—'

'I don't,' she hastily assured him; it would be cruelly insensitive of her to even suggest he leave this place where he obviously felt so much at home, when he had no other family to go to.

That could have been the reason he had told her those things about his childhood, of course—although somehow she very much doubted that Gideon was a man who would ever play upon another person's feelings in that way; he was simply too emotionally aloof to ever welcome an emotion in others that might be interpreted as pity.

He seemed to guess some of her thoughts, his mouth twisting scornfully. 'Don't feel sorry for me, Molly,' he rasped harshly. 'I can assure you I'm actually doing very nicely, thank you!'

Yes, he was. He was obviously financially secure, and had a career that made him much in demand. It was only in the area of having a family of his own that Gideon seemed lacking, but Molly felt sure that had to be from personal preference; she didn't doubt for a moment that there were dozens of women who were attracted to his blond, arrogant good looks, who would willingly have married him and shared their life with him.

Herself, to name but one...

She straightened, knowing she must never let him guess that. 'And I can assure you I don't feel in the least sorry for you, Gideon,' she told him briskly, keeping her face averted as she bent down to pick Peter up, at once feeling more relaxed as she held his scented softness against her. 'He's adorable, isn't he?' she murmured indulgently as the baby nuzzled into her neck and promptly fell asleep.

Gideon gave a brief smile. 'He's certainly found a comfortable place to sleep!'

Molly gave him a searching glance, frowning slightly. Had there been a slight edge of wistfulness in Gideon's tone, or had she just imagined it?

You just imagined it, she told herself firmly, knowing from the way he had virtually ignored her during lunch that there was absolutely no reason why Gideon should ever want to fall asleep on her shoulder.

If it was her shoulder he had been referring to…

Her gaze narrowed on him questioningly, and was instantly answered by Gideon's mocking grin.

No, it wasn't her shoulder he'd been referring to.

'Let me take him from you and put him in his cradle,' Gideon offered, reaching out to take the baby, his fingers brushing lightly against Molly's breast as he did so.

Molly's skin seemed to burn where those fingers had lightly touched.

Had that touch been accidental or deliberate? she wondered as she watched Gideon cross the room and carefully place the baby in the cradle before covering him with a blanket. She still had found no answer to that question when Gideon returned to stand beside her.

'Shall we leave them to sleep and take Merlin for a walk?' he suggested huskily, even as he held out a hand as an offer to help pull her to her feet.

Molly looked at that long, artistic hand, clearly remembering its touch upon her skin, its caresses seeking, finding her complete response. It would be dangerous to her own peace of mind to go outside alone with him. But not to go would be just as unacceptable to her heart!

'That sounds like a good idea,' she agreed abruptly, ignoring his hand to get agilely to her feet unaided.

Gideon gave a rueful smile in acknowledgement of her obvious rejection, his arm falling back to his side. He thrust his hand into his denims pocket. 'Wrap up warm,' he advised briskly as they walked down the hallway to the kitchen. 'There's more snow forecast for later this afternoon.'

Molly felt slightly self-conscious as she wrapped the deep pink cashmere scarf he had given her for Christmas around the bottom half of her face and neck before pulling on her thick sheepskin jacket. It was such a beautiful scarf, and so soft to the touch, that it would be churlish not to wear it just because Gideon had given it to her.

'Here—let me,' he offered as the scarf became slightly dislodged by her coat collar. His fingers were warm against her cheeks as he deftly pulled the scarf back into place. 'It really does look wonderful against the rich auburn of your hair,' he stepped back to remark admiringly. 'But, then, I knew that it would.' He nodded his satisfaction.

Molly looked up at him from beneath her lashes, slightly breathless at the compliment. 'Thank you,' she accepted self-consciously.

Gideon chuckled at her obvious wariness. 'You're welcome. Come on—let's go.' He threw open the door, a blast of icy cold air instantly hitting them.

It really was cold outside, and Molly was grateful to be able to burrow down in her scarf, her hands thrust into the deep pockets of her coat. The scarf about her lower face also served to hide the blush to her cheeks caused by Gideon's unexpected compliment.

'You didn't think I would remember you, did you?' Gideon remarked quietly after they had walked in silence for several minutes. Merlin was happily running on ahead, obviously fascinated by the cold white stuff that covered the ground.

Molly gave Gideon a sharp glance. 'Sorry?'

'From James and Crys's apartment over three years ago,' he answered evenly.

So they were back to that, were they? So much for hoping they might be learning a new tolerance between them.

She turned away, hunched down in her jacket. 'I don't recall ever giving it a second thought,' she answered dismissively.

She didn't remember giving it a *second* thought because she had followed that by dozens of others once she'd known Gideon was to be at Peter's christening.

She gave an impatient sigh. 'Gideon, did you invite me to share this walk with you just so that you could pick another argument with me?'

His face lit up in a smile, eyes laughingly blue. 'Strangely enough, no!'

Molly gave an irritated shake of her head. 'Then you have a very funny way of showing it!'

'Funny, strange—not funny, ha-ha?' he drawled derisively.

'Oh, definitely funny, strange!' she answered impatiently, stopping abruptly as they reached the gate that would take them out into the country lane. 'Gideon, how many times do I have to tell you that I did not—however briefly—ever have an affair with James?'

He met her gaze unblinkingly, his expression unreadable. 'I don't believe you ever have told me that...'

Molly's frown deepened. 'But—of course I have!' she dismissed before walking on, stiff with indignation, only to find herself swung back to face Gideon as he took a firm hold of her arm. 'Let me go, Gideon,' she instructed coldly.

To her surprise he instantly did exactly that, holding up his hands before stepping away from her. 'No, you never did, Molly,' he assured her softly.

She blinked, thinking back over the conversations they had had together over the last four days—most of them unpleasant. And that unpleasantness had merged into one long battle of wills between the two of them. When they hadn't been in each other's arms, of course.

No, she couldn't remember specifically telling him that she hadn't had an affair with James. But even so...

'Well, I did not have an affair with your brother! Or, more to the point, Crys's husband,' she added, indignation starting to rise in her voice. 'Crys is my best friend,' she added firmly. 'She always has been. Always will be. And I would never, ever do anything that might hurt her. I think having an affair with her husband might just have done that, don't you?' she scorned.

'Undoubtedly,' Gideon acknowledged quietly.

'Well, she won't be hurt, because I didn't.' Molly was warming to her subject now, wanting to get all of this off her chest while she had the chance to do so. 'Yes, I was at Crys and James's apartment that night when Crys was away, but not because I was having an affair with James. And if you knew anything about me at all—'

'I believe you.'

'—you would believe me when I tell you that's—'

'I believe you.'

'—the truth… I beg your pardon?' She looked at Gideon warily as his words finally penetrated her indignation.

Gideon drew in a deep breath, looking down at her intently. 'I said, I believe you, Molly,' he repeated softly.

She blinked, wondering if this wasn't another ploy on his part, if he wouldn't later somehow twist her words to suit his less-than-flattering opinion of her.

'Oh,' she said noncommittally.

Gideon gave a heavy sigh. 'Now it's you who doesn't believe *me*.'

'Can you blame me?' Her eyes flashed darkly. 'You've done nothing but accuse me of one indiscretion or another since we met again on Sunday. To accept that you now believe my version of what happened over three years ago is a little hard to take.'

He grimaced. 'I'm sure it must be,' he acknowledged. 'Although, if you think back carefully over the early part of this conversation, you might recall that you didn't actually give me your version of what happened. I told you—I believe you, anyway,' he pointed out huskily.

Molly, after days of this man's taunts and put-downs, was beginning to feel slightly as if her legs were being taken out from under her. Where was Gideon's antagonism now? Why was he being so nice to her?

'Would it help if I were to apologise for all the less-than-flattering remarks I've made to you over the last few days?' Gideon asked grimly.

'It might,' she allowed warily.

It was a wariness Gideon seemed all too aware of, and he sighed heavily. 'Molly, I think the two of us need to talk, and I'm not sure here is the best place.'

'Everything all right here, sir?'

Molly turned sharply at the sound of that voice, her eyes widening as she saw a policeman standing on the other side of the gate. She had been so taken up with this unexpected exchange with Gideon that she hadn't even noticed the police car parked beside the road, let alone this man's approach.

Gideon gave the policeman a reassuring smile. 'Everything is fine, officer.' He nodded. 'Miss Barton and I are just taking the dog for an after-lunch stroll.'

The other man nodded, eyeing the watchful Merlin with a certain amount of caution. 'You'll be two of the guests staying at Falcon House, sir, with Mr and Mrs Wyngard?'

'Yes, we are.' Gideon moved slightly in order to take a proprietorial hold of Molly's arm. 'Is there any news?'

The policeman nodded. 'I'm just on my way to see Mr Wyngard now.'

'With good news, I hope?' Gideon prompted guardedly, his fingers tightening slightly on Molly's arm.

The policeman looked grim. 'Depends on how you look at it, sir,' the policeman answered noncommittally. 'Well, I'll just pop along and see Mr Wyngard now, and leave the two of you to continue your walk,' he added briskly. 'Nice day for it,' he added, before strolling off to get into the squad car, giving them a wave as he drove off towards Falcon House.

Molly frowned as she watched him drive away, totally lost as to what the conversation between the two men had been about. She had no idea what news, good or bad, the policeman could possibly have to give to Sam.

But obviously, from their brief conversation, Gideon knew.

CHAPTER FOURTEEN

'OKAY.' Molly turned determinedly towards Gideon. 'Exactly what is going on? And please don't insult my intelligence by answering "nothing",' she added forcefully.

Gideon gave the ghost of a smile. 'I wasn't about to do that,' he drawled. 'But I think it might be better if we return to the house and I leave it to Sam to explain,' he added grimly.

'But—'

'It really isn't up to me, Molly,' Gideon cut in firmly. 'But maybe once he's explained you'll excuse some of my behaviour over the last couple of days,' he added frowningly.

'I wouldn't count on it!' Molly told him hardly, even as she turned and began to walk back to the house.

'That's what I'm afraid of.' Gideon caught up with her after only a couple of strides, Merlin trailing along obediently behind him.

Molly gave a disbelieving snort. 'You aren't afraid of anything!'

'Oh, but you're wrong there, Molly,' he answered softly, causing her to give him a sharp look. 'I'm very much afraid you aren't going to forgive me once Sam has made his explanations,' he told her grimly.

She gave an exasperated shake of her head. 'I'm sure any lack of forgiveness on my part isn't going to keep you awake at night!'

His expression became even grimmer. 'You'd be surprised!'

'Yes—I would,' she dismissed scornfully.

Gideon drew in a controlling breath. 'I've really messed things up between us, haven't I?'

'There's never been any "us" to mess up,' Molly assured him.

His hands were painful on her arms as he pulled her to a stop before they entered the house. He turned her to face him, his expression harshly remote. 'Will you at least agree to talk to me in private after the policeman has said his bit and gone?'

'What would be the point?' She sighed.

'Will you?' He shook her slightly.

'If that's what you want—yes!' she agreed, impatient to be inside.

'It is what I want.' He nodded grimly.

'Fine,' Molly dismissed. 'Now can we go inside?'

He gave an impatient snort before releasing her, following behind as she hurried into the house.

No one was asleep when Molly entered the sitting-room a few seconds later. Crys and Sam were sitting on the edge of the sofa now, and David and Diana were all attention, too, as they sat forward in their chairs. The policeman held all their attention as he stood in front of the fireplace, nodding acknowledgement of Molly and Gideon's arrival in the room even as he continued with what he had been saying.

'Unfortunately Miss Gibson was involved in an accident about two miles from here just over an hour ago,' he informed them briskly. 'She's dead, I'm afraid,' he added evenly.

Miss Gibson? Rachel Gibson? Sam's ex-fiancée of twelve years ago? The woman who had told all those lies about Sam to the newspapers after he'd broken their engagement because he had realised she was emotionally unstable? The woman who had made all of their lives such a misery twelve years ago—so much so for Sam that he had moved to the wilds of Yorkshire in order to escape her vitriol?

'Oh, no...' Crys had gasped at the policeman's news. 'I hated what she was doing to us, but... How awful!' She turned her face into Sam's chest.

Sam's arm closed protectively about his wife. 'How did it happen?' he asked the policeman quietly, his face ashen.

'Her car went off the mountain road and down into a deep ravine,' the other man informed him. 'She was already dead when the rescue services arrived,' he added apologetically. 'I'm sorry to bring you such bad news over Christmas, sir,' he added regretfully. 'Although, in view of the charges against her, if we had caught up with her...!' He trailed off pointedly.

'Yes,' Sam acknowledged heavily.

'What charges?' Molly turned to Gideon with wide, bewildered eyes. 'Is that *Rachel* Gibson they're talking about?' she demanded disbelievingly.

'It is,' Gideon answered hardly. 'Come on,' he encouraged, his arm about her shoulders as he guided her out of the room. 'You don't need to hear any more of that,' he told her briskly, and he took her into the library, sitting her down in one of the armchairs before moving to pour her some whisky from the decanter on the table. 'Please drink some of it,' he said, as he came down on his haunches beside her to give her the glass.

Molly didn't need any prompting, totally numb from the shocking news she had just heard.

But though her emotions felt numb, her brain seemed

able to coolly and calmly dissect the events of the last few days, to pick out all the incidents that at the time hadn't seemed to make any sense.

She looked at Gideon with clouded brown eyes. 'She's been stalking Sam, hasn't she?' she guessed heavily. 'She was the one making those telephone calls on Christmas Eve. And that night,' she continued determinedly, 'the noises outside that so disturbed Merlin... Even his getting shut in the shed in that way,' she recalled dazedly. 'It was all her, wasn't it?'

'We believe so,' Gideon said grimly. 'Although we'll never really know now, I'm afraid,' he added heavily.

Molly gave a shiver at the reason why they would never know.

Twelve years ago Rachel had been a blight on all their lives, her lies encouraging the press to hound Sam, and the whole family, until their parents had been forced to move out of their home. Molly had had to begin anew in another school, and Sam had isolated himself in the wilds of Yorkshire.

But, even so, Molly knew that none of them would have wished the other woman dead...

'It was her,' Molly said with certainty. 'But how did she...? The newspaper article about Peter's christening!' she realised with a groan.

'Sam seems to think so,' Gideon confirmed gently.

'But—it—I—it's been twelve years!' she gasped. 'Twelve years, for goodness' sake!'

'Yes,' Gideon acknowledged heavily. 'But something happened over the weekend—something that seems to have sent her completely over the edge.' He frowned grimly. 'The police have been looking for her ever since.'

Those charges the policeman had mentioned...

'What?' Molly breathed intently. 'What happened over the weekend?'

'Molly, she's dead.'

'What happened?' she demanded through gritted teeth.

Gideon drew in a deeply controlling breath. 'She killed someone. The man she was living with,' he continued firmly at Molly's shocked gasp. 'She discovered him with another woman and—she killed him.' He frowned darkly.

Molly swallowed hard. 'How?'

'Molly, you don't need to know—'

'Tell me,' she demanded harshly.

'She stabbed him,' he said flatly. 'The woman he was with managed to escape, but unfortunately the man had died from his wounds before the police got there.'

Molly felt sick, waves of nausea washing over her as she realised that it could have been Sam—that if he hadn't broken their engagement twelve years ago Rachel could have...

'Bend down and put your head between your knees,' Gideon encouraged gently, taking the glass from her hand as she did exactly that.

It took several minutes for the waves of nausea to stop, the light-headedness to dissipate. But they were minutes when her brain once again seemed capable of functioning without any help from her.

She straightened. 'You knew about all of this,' she said accusingly. 'All this time you've known—'

'I've known for precisely one day,' Gideon corrected her firmly. 'Since I mentioned my misgivings to Sam after you went to bed that night and he came clean on the subject. One of those telephone calls he had to return on Monday morning was to the police,' he explained, as Molly would once again have spoken accusingly. 'Rachel Gibson had been reported as being seen in the area, and, following investigations, they discovered that she and Sam had once been engaged...' He shrugged. 'The police wanted to inform Sam of the—incident, only as a matter of courtesy, because of their past connection. I don't believe they really thought she would come after him here.'

'Then they were wrong, weren't they?' Molly rasped. 'Finally knowing where Sam was, seeing that photograph, seeing his happiness with Crys and Peter. My God, did Crys know about all this, too?' She frowned as the thought suddenly occurred to her. She'd have a deeper respect for Crys if she *had* known; to all intents and purposes, apart from that scare with Peter, Crys had seemed caught up in the gaiety of Christmas.

Gideon smiled without humour. 'Sam doesn't have any secrets from Crys.'

'Unlike you with regard to me,' Molly snapped, picking up the whisky glass and downing the contents. 'I suppose now you're going to accuse me of being a lush again?' she challenged, two fiery spots of angry colour in her cheeks.

It wasn't logical, and she knew that it wasn't, but nonetheless she couldn't help her feelings of anger towards Gideon for treating her as if she were a child who couldn't handle the truth. She felt the same anger towards Sam, too. But Gideon was the one here in front of her, and as such he was the one who would bear the brunt of her anger.

'Molly—'

'Don't touch me!' she told him fiercely, brushing past him to stand up.

Gideon eyed her warily and slowly stood up. 'Molly, there was no point in worrying you, too—'

'Don't tell me whether or not I should worry!' she snapped furiously, her eyes glittering brightly. 'I'll worry if I want to—not when someone else decided that I should!' she continued illogically. 'God, you're an arrogant—'

'I advise you to stop right there,' he warned coldly.

'—pig,' she concluded challengingly. 'A chauvinist pig to boot,' she continued wildly. '*You* were the one who stopped Sam from telling me the truth.' She realised what had happened now, what it was Sam had wanted to talk to her about. But he had been stopped from doing so by Gideon's warnings of caution. 'I can hear it all now. "Don't tell the little woman",' she mimicked. '"It will only worry her".'

'It wasn't like that—'

'Yes, it was,' she snapped hardly. 'It was exactly like that! Well, do you know something, Gideon Webber? You can go to hell,' she continued, without giving him an opportunity to answer.

She turned sharply on her heel and ran from the room, taking the stairs two at a time until she reached the sanctuary of her bedroom, where she threw herself down on the bed, her anger quickly turning to tears.

She cried for poor, sick Rachel, and the obsession for Sam that had never completely left her. She cried for the mess that was Gideon and her, for all the misunderstandings between them. But most of all she cried because in spite of everything she knew she still loved him.

'Hey,' Crys chided gently as she moved to sit beside Molly on the bed a few minutes later. Molly had been crying so deeply she hadn't heard her friend enter the room. 'Molly,' she said firmly, 'it's over now. Come on.' She pulled Molly into her arms, hugging her tightly as the tears finally began to stop. 'Who are you crying for, Molly? Poor Rachel? Or Gideon?' she added astutely.

Molly moved back to look at her friend. 'Is it so obvious that I'm in love with him?'

Crys gave her an encouraging smile. 'Only to me. Gideon doesn't have a clue, I can assure you,' she added ruefully. 'In fact, from what he said to me just now, he seems utterly convinced that you hate him.' She looked questioningly at Molly.

She swallowed hard, wiping the tears from her cheeks. 'It's him who hates me,' she contradicted. 'And all because—because... Crys, there's something I should have told you long ago,' she said huskily. 'Something about James. And...and me.'

Crys frowned. 'Yes?'

Molly closed her eyes briefly, taking a deep breath before she began talking, knowing it all had to come out now, and that Crys should have been told long ago. 'Do you remember my disastrous love affair with Derek? Of course you do.' She answered her own question with obvious self-derision. 'You tried to warn me at the time about the dangers of falling in love with a man so recently separated from his wife—that very often they patched up their differences and were reconciled. I didn't listen, as you know.' She sighed heavily. 'And I ended up getting very hurt when Derek did exactly that.'

Crys looked confused. 'You don't still love him, do you?'

'No, of course not,' Molly dismissed instantly. 'I'm not sure I ever did,' she added huskily. The way she now felt about Gideon made that other love pale into insignificance. 'Maybe I was just flattered.' She sighed again. 'He was an internationally known actor, very good-looking, and it was *me* he wanted to be with! At least I thought it was at the time…' She shook her head. 'I was devastated when he returned to his wife.'

'I know that.' Crys nodded, still looking puzzled.

'Yes,' Molly said firmly. 'But what you don't know—what I've never told you—is that the night Derek went back to his wife I got very drunk—'

'You were entitled,' Crys replied. 'He wasn't exactly gentle about it, if I remember—just arrived at a party with her one night. A party where he was supposed to be meeting you,' she recalled disapprovingly.

Molly winced at the memory. 'The night I got dr—'

'Alcoholically challenged,' Crys corrected decisively. 'You drank a little more than you would usually, that's all. James assured me that you certainly were not drunk.'

Molly blinked, her mouth feeling very dry. 'James did…?'

'Of course,' her friend dismissed. 'I was glad that you went to him. Sorry I wasn't there to help, of course, but James assured me he had done a good job of taking care of you.'

'He did,' Molly confirmed numbly. 'But—I—you *knew* about that night?'

'Well, of course I did,' Crys assured her lightly.

She frowned dazedly. 'But I… All this time…' she shook her head '…and you've never said.'

Crys gave a rueful smile. 'What could I have said? Derek was a very selfish man, and he hurt you very badly; there was no point in my bringing up the subject again when you obviously didn't want to talk about him.'

'But the night I stayed at your apartment—'

'What of it?' Crys asked. 'Look, Molly, you're my best friend and I trust you implicitly, just as I trusted James, so what was there for me to say about that night? Without reminding you of Derek's duplicity, that is,' she added grimly.

Molly shook her head dazedly. 'I can't believe you've known all this time that I stayed at your apartment with James when you were away...'

Crys smiled. 'I've known and never for a moment thought there was anything wrong with it. Why should I have done?' she said unconcernedly.

'Well, Gideon certainly thought there was something wrong with it!' Molly snapped disgustedly.

'Gideon did?' Crys looked more puzzled than ever, and then her brow cleared in understanding. 'Oh, you mean because he called in to see James that morning and saw you there? Molly, Gideon didn't think that you and James were having an affair, did he?' She gasped as the idea suddenly occurred to her. 'No! He can't have done. Can he?' She frowned dazedly. 'He did, didn't he?' she realized incredulously. And then she began to laugh.

'Crys, it really isn't funny,' Molly told her disgruntledly. She was relieved that Crys had known the truth all along, but utterly bemused by her friend's reaction to knowing what conclusion Gideon had come to concerning Molly's presence in Crys and James's apartment that morning.

'No, it really isn't,' Crys agreed, sobering slightly. 'You and Gideon are incredible, do you know that?' She stood up. 'You think he's in love with me—which he most definitely is not,' she added firmly as Molly would have spoken. 'And Gideon thinks you had an affair with James—which you most definitely did not. You know, for two very intelligent people, you've both been incredibly stupid.'

'Thanks!' Molly grimaced, not sure she agreed with Crys's summing up of the situation at all.

'You're welcome,' Crys assured her dryly. 'Not completely stupid, of course,' she continued conversationally. 'Somewhere amongst all this confusion the two of you have managed to fall in love with each other anyway, so I suppose I can forgive you.'

'Gideon isn't in love with me,' she cut in dismissively.

'Oh, yes—he is,' Crys said with certainty. 'Who do you think sent me up here because you were so upset? Who do you think is even now pacing up and down my kitchen wearing out the flagstones as he waits for me to go back downstairs and reassure him that you're okay?'

Molly swallowed hard, suddenly still, a slight hope beginning to burn somewhere deep inside her. 'Gideon…?' she said hopefully.

'The one and only.' Crys nodded, pulling her to her feet. 'Come downstairs with me—'

'I can't!' Molly resisted, jerkily shaking her head. 'I really can't, Crys,' she added, as her friend gave her a look of reproof. 'What if you're wrong?'

'I'm not,' Crys assured her.

'But if you are?'

'I'm not,' her friend repeated firmly. 'Although maybe the kitchen isn't quite the place for…' She paused, obviously thinking. 'Okay.' She nodded as she came to a decision. 'You stay here and I'll send Gideon up—'

'He won't come,' Molly told her with certainty.

'We'll see,' Crys murmured speculatively. 'Just don't stay up here together all afternoon—otherwise, knowing Sam, he's likely to come looking for the two of you and demand that Gideon make an honest woman of you!' She grinned.

Molly frowned. 'I wish you would stop making a joke out of all this, Crys.'

'Can I be chief bridesmaid?' Crys asked conversationally. 'I've never been a bridesmaid, you know, and—'

'Oh, go away!' Molly told her irritably.

'I'm going,' her friend assured her. 'But no attempting to climb down the drainpipe after I've gone,' she warned on her way out of the room. 'You won't look a very elegant bride with your leg in plaster!' She grinned again as she made her parting shot.

Molly gave an exasperated shake of her head once she was alone, thinking that Crys was turning into as much of a tease as Sam.

Although that didn't change the fact that even now Crys was probably down in the kitchen talking to Gideon.

Was Crys right? Would Gideon come up here to see her once he had spoken to Crys?

She would have the answer to that question in the next few minutes.

CHAPTER FIFTEEN

'CRYS said that you're feeling a little better...?'

Molly's heart leapt as she turned to see Gideon standing hesitantly in the bedroom doorway, his face guarded, the expression in his deep blue eyes wary.

She swallowed hard before speaking. 'Er—yes, I'm feeling better.' She nodded. 'I—I'm sorry I shouted at you. Before.'

Wonderful, Molly, she inwardly chided herself; she sounded like a tongue-tied idiot.

But that was probably because she *felt* like a tongue-tied idiot!

Just because Gideon was here, as Crys had said he would be, that did not mean anything more than that he wanted to apologize for upsetting her concerning not telling her earlier about Rachel Gibson.

'Perfectly understandable in the circumstances,' he allowed abruptly. 'It was arrogant of me to ask Sam not to tell you.'

Arrogant, yes—but it could also have another interpretation... 'Why did you do it, Gideon?' she prompted.

He drew in a harsh breath. 'I—do you think I could come in?' He grimaced. 'It's a little—public, standing out here in the hallway.'

Considering that besides themselves only David had a bedroom on this floor of the house, and he was probably still in conversation with the others downstairs, she wouldn't exactly have called it 'public'. But if Gideon wanted to come into her bedroom...

'Please do,' she invited, standing awkwardly in front of the window as he entered the room and closed the door quietly behind him, her hands twisting tightly together as she eyed him warily.

Gideon gave a strained smile obviously as uncomfortable as she was.

'I—' Molly hesitated, shaking her head, not really sure where to begin. Or what she was actually beginning!

Gideon drew in a harsh breath. 'Will it help the—the situation if I tell you that I'm not in love with Crys?' he bit out abruptly. 'That I never have been.'

Molly felt a sinking sensation in her stomach. Okay, so he wasn't in love with Crys, but that didn't mean he was in love with her.

She bit her lip painfully to stop it trembling. 'I was never in love with James, either,' she told him huskily. 'And I certainly didn't have an affair with him,' she added firmly.

'I know that.'

She nodded. 'Crys will have told you—'

'No,' Gideon cut in determinedly. 'Crys didn't tell me anything.'

Her eyes widened. 'But—'

'She didn't have to,' he continued evenly. 'Molly, I know that I owe you an apology for—for the things I've said to you over the last few days.' He gave a self-disgusted shake of his head, thrusting his hands into his pockets. 'I saw you in James's apartment that morning and I—'

'Drew your own conclusions?' she finished heavily.

Gideon shook his head. 'No, that isn't what happened at all.' He gave another strained smile. 'I looked at you that morning, your hair all tousled, your face sleepy, your long legs bare beneath that ridiculous shirt, and I—' He drew in a harsh breath. 'You were the most beautiful woman I had ever seen!' he told her gruffly.

Molly's eyes widened incredulously. 'I looked awful! My hair was a mess, my face all puffy, and James's shirt was the only thing I could find to pull on when I needed to go to the bathroom. You can't possibly have… Did you really think me beautiful?' She looked at him dazedly.

'Really.' Gideon nodded self-derisively. 'But it appeared you belonged to my brother,' he added hardly.

'But I didn't,' Molly told him exasperatedly. 'I never did. How many times do I have to tell you that?'

'You don't,' he assured her heavily. 'You see, it made no difference; I fell in love with you anyway that morning—'

'You couldn't have done!' Molly gasped disbelievingly.

'Oh, yes, I could.' Gideon nodded. 'And I spent the next few months telling myself what a fool I was—that just being attracted to you was dangerous, that falling in love with you was an act of madness, that it would be better for everyone if I just forgot I had ever seen you. I almost succeeded in believing that, too.' His mouth twisted ruefully. 'Until I saw you again the morning of the christening…'

'You were so horrible to me,' Molly reminded him breathlessly, that faint glow of hope she had known when talking to Crys now starting to explode inside her.

Had Gideon really just told her that he had fallen in love with her more than three years ago?

'I know,' he accepted flatly. 'Deliberately so. I simply couldn't believe that I still felt the same way about you, that those years might just as well not have been.

Your relationship with James, what the knowledge of it might do to Crys—' He gave a self-disgusted shake of his head. 'In spite of all that I was still in love with you.'

Molly gave a pained frown. 'But you said just now that you believed me when I said I didn't have an affair with James...?'

'No.' He sighed. 'What I actually said was that I *know* you didn't have an affair with him. And I know that because over the last few days I've come to know you, Molly. You're not only the most beautiful woman I've ever seen, you are also the kindest, most compassionate woman I've ever known. Your loyalty to Crys and Sam is unmistakable, your love for them, too. Your compassion for David is only to be admired. And as for your gentle caring for Peter... Molly, you would never have allowed yourself to have an affair with James even if you had been in love with him!'

'No,' she acknowledged. 'But I wasn't in love with him. I did think myself in love with someone else, though,' she hurried on, as Gideon would have spoken. 'A man separated from his wife. The night before you saw me at the apartment he had gone back to her,' she confided evenly. 'Not my finest hour.' She grimaced.

'But don't you see, Molly? It doesn't matter,' Gideon said forcefully. 'Unless you're still in love with him, of course,' he added uncertainly.

Uncertain? Gideon? It certainly wasn't a feeling that Molly would normally have equated with him!

But hadn't he just told her that he had fallen in love with her at first sight? That he'd only had to see her again over three years later to know that he still loved her?

She moistened dry lips. 'No, I'm not still in love with

him, Gideon,' she told him quietly. 'How could I be when I'm in love with you?' she added almost shyly.

His eyed widened, emotion blazing in those dark blue depths. He took a step towards her, then stopped, hesitating.

Molly was the one to take the two last steps that took her into his arms; in fact she almost threw herself into them, her arms about his waist as she held him tightly to her. 'I love you, Gideon,' she told him forcefully. 'I love you so much.'

His hands moved up to cup either side of her face. 'Will you marry me?' he asked emotionally. 'Will you? I swear I'll love you until the day I die!' He looked down at her intently. 'Molly, I only wanted to protect you by not telling you about Rachel Gibson. I've never thought of you as less than you are, and I never will,' he promised. 'I just want to protect and love you for the rest of our lives!'

'Yes,' Molly accepted chokingly, wanting to laugh and cry at the same time. 'Oh, yes, Gideon, I'll marry you!'

As he moved to kiss her with infinite gentleness, with all of the love he felt for her in that loving caress, Molly knew that she had at last found the man she truly loved, and who truly loved her.

'You look adorable,' Gideon assured her lovingly. 'Although I'm not sure it was a good idea for me to suggest you put on one of David's shirts.' He frowned darkly. 'It just makes me want to throw you on the bed and make love to you!'

Molly laughed huskily. 'Not here, darling.' She looked around pointedly at the crowded studio, at the director and technicians all on the *Bailey* set, and David already in the bed, waiting for her to supposedly appear out of an adjoining bathroom.

'Later, then,' he promised gruffly.

'Later,' Molly echoed throatily.

The two of them had been married for three months now. Crys had got her wish to be chief bridesmaid, with Sam acting as Gideon's best man.

It had been three months of pure happiness as far as Molly and Gideon were concerned. The two of them were working together a lot of the time, too, as Gideon had turned out to be the new designer of all the sets for the *Bailey* series. Neatly answering Molly's question of how an actor, David, and an interior designer, Gideon, could possibly have met before they had all spent Christmas together.

But it was because of Gideon's involvement with the new *Bailey* series that he had been able to have some input into the nude scene that had been mentioned over Christmas. Knowing of Molly's aversion to it—and having certain objections of his own concerning his wife appearing nude on public television—he had come up with the suggestion of Molly undressing off-set and coming back wearing David's shirt.

The fact that he had made the suggestion at all, so reminiscent of the first time they had met, told Molly how unimportant all that had been. If she had needed any reassuring. Which, after three ecstatic months as Gideon's wife, she most certainly didn't.

'Actually—' she leaned into Gideon '—I think it's as well that I do this scene now. Another couple of months and I won't be able to.'

Gideon looked down at her concernedly. 'Why not? Molly, what's wrong?' His arms moved about her protectively.

'Absolutely nothing.' She laughed reassuringly. 'But it's going to be interesting seeing Sam cope with introducing a pregnant girlfriend for Bailey,' she added teasingly, gazing lovingly into her husband's face as the importance of what she had just said slowly dawned on him.

'Molly...?' he finally gasped, his arms tightening about her as he stared down at her disbelievingly.

Molly snuggled into the warmth of his chest. 'In about seven months' time Peter is going to have a little cousin,' she confirmed huskily. Her happiness was overwhelming at the knowledge that she carried their child.

'I—you—how...?' Gideon was obviously having trouble speaking at all, but his eyes glowed brightly with love as he looked down at her.

'You know very well *how*,' Molly teased him huskily. 'And, yes, it was you and I.' She nodded happily. 'Isn't it wonderful?'

'Wonderful,' he confirmed, slightly dazedly. 'Oh, Molly, I do love you,' he told her intensely.

'And I love you,' she assured him seriously. 'All my life,' she promised.

'All my life,' Gideon echoed forcefully, before his mouth claimed hers in a kiss of infinite sweetness.

'I hate to interrupt,' David called out dryly several minutes later, 'but I'm in danger of genuinely falling asleep if you don't soon make your entrance, Molly.'

Gideon raised his head to grin down at her ruefully. 'I think your presence is required, my love.'

'I think David is just a little full of himself after his weekend away; apparently he drove up to Yorkshire at the weekend and took Diana Chisholm out to dinner,' she told her husband speculatively.

'That's good news.' Gideon smiled.

'Isn't it?' She grinned up at him. 'Maybe we're going to have another wedding in the ''family'' soon.'

Gideon's smile turned to an indulgent chuckle. 'You're getting as bad as Crys with your matchmaking.'

Molly reached up to gently touch his cheek. 'Maybe because, like Crys, I want everyone else to be as happy as we are,' she told him seriously.

Gideon shook his head. 'They couldn't possibly be,' he said with certainty.

No, she didn't think they could. She had never known such happiness, such contentment, as she had found being Gideon's wife.

'Molly!' David called out complainingly.

'I have to go.' She grimaced ruefully.

Gideon nodded. 'We'll celebrate our good news later.'

'We could go to Crystal's,' she agreed happily; Crys's restaurant was one of the most exclusive in London, but Gerry, the manager, always managed to find a table for 'family'.

Gideon's smile became intimate. 'I wasn't thinking of going out.'

'Even better,' Molly agreed instantly, feeling a glow deep inside her at the promise in Gideon's gaze.

'Molly, if you don't get in here in the next ten seconds I'm going to come and get you.' David warned.

'Later,' Molly told Gideon as she hurriedly turned to leave.

'Always,' he called after her.

What a wonderful, lovely word!

CHRISTMAS EVE MARRIAGE

by

Jessica Hart

Jessica Hart was born in West Africa, and has suffered from itchy feet ever since, travelling and working around the world in a wide variety of interesting but very lowly jobs, all of which have provided inspiration on which to draw when it comes to the settings and plots of her stories. Now she lives a rather more settled existence in York, where she has been able to pursue her interest in history, although she still yearns sometimes for wider horizons. If you'd like to know more about Jessica, visit her website, www.jessicahart.co.uk.

Don't miss Jessica Hart's exciting new novel, *Promoted: to Wife and Mother*, out in March 2008 from Mills & Boon® Romance.

CHAPTER ONE

NOTHING.

Thea closed the fridge with a sigh and began investigating the kitchen cupboards, but they were equally empty of anything remotely resembling breakfast.

What a great start to the holiday! A nightmare journey, an unfriendly neighbour, less than four hours' sleep, and now nothing to eat.

'Have a fortnight in Crete, she said,' Thea muttered her sister's words as she bent to peer. 'You need a break. It'll be beautiful. Nothing to do but read, relax…starve to death…'

'What are you doing?'

Clara's voice made Thea straighten and push her tangled hair away from her face. Her niece was at the bottom of the stairs, looking sleepy and tousled and very sweet in a baggy pink T-shirt. There was no doubt that it was a look that was easier to pull off after four hours' sleep at nine, when you had peachy skin and a nice, firm little body, than at thirty-four, when peachy skin and a firm body had never figured largely among your assets in the first place.

'Trying to find some breakfast,' she said, yawning.

'Oh, good. I'm hungry.'

'Me too,' said Thea glumly.

Nothing new there, then. Easy to tell that she and Clara were related. You'd think they'd be too tired to be hungry. It had been nearly half past five before they got to bed that morning, and it was only just after nine now. Any normal stomach would be daunted by a nightmare trip, arriving in

5

a strange country and utter exhaustion, but Martindale stomachs were tougher than that! A massive asteroid could be hurtling towards earth and her stomach would still be going, Mmm, nine o'clock, no wonder I'm a bit peckish… Bacon and eggs would be nice, or perhaps a little croissant before the end of the world… Oh, and make that a double cappuccino while you're at it.

She hadn't even lost weight over Harry. It wasn't fair. All her friends lost their appetites the moment they hit an emotional crisis, but the misery diet never worked for Thea. She just went in for comfort eating on a massive scale.

Not that there was much chance of eating now, worse luck.

'I can't find anything to eat,' she told Clara. 'I think we may have to go shopping before breakfast.'

Clara's face fell. 'But there aren't any shops here. We'll have to drive all the way back to that town we passed last night, and it'll take ages. It's *miles* away.'

'I know.' Thea grimaced at the memory of their hair-raising journey through the hills in the small hours. 'I'm not sure I can face those hairpin bends again, let alone on an empty stomach,' she said with a sigh.

'What shall we do?'

'Well, first I think we should ring your mother and ask her why she booked a villa in the middle of nowhere, instead of a nice beach apartment near shops and restaurants!'

Clara grinned. 'She did say it was isolated.'

'It's that all right.'

Thea eyed the view through the kitchen window without enthusiasm. Rocky hillsides, olive groves and the spectacular peaks of the White Mountains in the distance were all very well, but right then she would have sacrificed picturesque for the odd blot on the landscape, an ugly supermarket, say, or a nice plastic restaurant—preferably one that delivered coffee by the gallon and an assortment of calorie-laden breakfasts.

She nibbled her thumb as she tried to think, but her brain really needed caffeine before it would function properly.

'We're just going to have to ask the people in the other villas if they can let us have some bread or something until we can get to the shops,' she decided eventually.

'We don't have to ask that grumpy man we met last night, do we?'

Clara looked a little apprehensive, as well she might, thought Thea, remembering their disastrous arrival.

'I think there are three villas, aren't there? We'll try the other one first,' she said, trying to sound positive. 'Maybe they'll be friendlier.'

They couldn't be less friendly, anyway, she thought glumly. So much for her relaxing holiday. She hadn't planned to kick it off begging for a bit of bread and water. Why did these things happen to her?

Oh, well. Better get on with it.

They got dressed, which in Thea's case meant shorts and a T-shirt, while Clara simply pulled a T-shirt over her swimming costume, and then headed off in search of breakfast.

In spite of their hunger, they hesitated on the terrace and took in their surroundings. It was the first time they had seen the villas. Three stone-built houses were set around a communal pool that glinted bright and blue in the dazzling Greek sunlight.

'Cool,' breathed Clara. 'Can I swim after breakfast?'

It was very quiet. The air was already warm and filled with the drifting scent of herbs, and Thea sniffed appreciatively. 'Lovely...thyme and oregano...let's get some lamb to cook tonight.'

'Let's get breakfast first,' said the more practical Clara.

Their villa sat between the two others, looking directly

out over the pool to the mountains beyond. On the right was the villa they had stumbled into by mistake the night before.

'Let's try this way first,' said Thea, pointing left.

All was very quiet as they climbed the steps leading up to the terrace. 'Hello?' Thea called, but there was no reply. 'Hello?'

'I don't think there's anyone here,' Clara whispered, affected by the silence.

'It doesn't look like it.'

Reluctantly, as one, they turned to look at the villa opposite. They had a much better view across the pool than from their own terrace, and they could clearly see the man sitting at a table under a vine-laden pergola. A little girl was slumped in a chair beside him, scuffing her shoes sulkily.

'There he is.' This time it was Thea whispering.

'He still looks cross,' said Clara.

It was too far to read his expression, in fact, but Thea knew what her niece meant. There was something off-putting about the body language on the opposite terrace.

She bit her lip doubtfully. She had already experienced the rough side of his tongue, and she didn't fancy it again. OK, the mistake was theirs, but there had been no need for him to be quite that fierce, had there?

If she had any self-respect, she would go and find the car keys and brave the hairpin bends before she would ask him for so much as a glass of water.

It was a battle between pride and her stomach, and her stomach won. No surprises there then.

'He's probably got a nice wife inside,' she suggested to Clara. 'She might feel guilty about the way he shouted at us. We weren't making *that* much noise.'

'It was five in the morning,' said Clara gloomily. 'And you did crash into his car.'

'It was just a little bump.'

Clara's mouth turned down at the corners. 'Maybe we should go to that town after all,' she said, but Thea had stiffened.

'Look.' She nudged her niece as she spotted a cup and a cafetière on the table. 'He's got coffee!'

She felt quite giddy at the thought. She would do anything for a cup of coffee right then. 'Let's just go and see,' she encouraged Clara. 'He's not going to be rude in front of his little girl, is he?'

Clara was clearly unconvinced, but she could see that her aunt was determined. 'OK, but you do the talking,' she warned.

Buoyed up at the prospect of coffee, Thea bore her niece around the pool and back past their own villa. It was only at the bottom of the steps that her nerve began to fail. Close to, the man's face was very grim as he looked out at the view. He was evidently lost in his thoughts, and it didn't look as if they were particularly happy ones.

He hadn't seen them yet, and Thea faltered. 'Maybe this isn't such a good idea after all,' she muttered.

'Go on,' whispered Clara, giving her a push. 'We're here now, and I'm starving!'

Thea opened her mouth to argue, but just then the little girl spotted them and sat up curiously. She tugged at her father's sleeve, and he turned his head and saw them lurking at the bottom of the steps. The intimidating brows rose in surprise and Thea gulped. It was too late to turn and run now.

Squaring her shoulders, she trod up the steps with an assumption of confidence, Clara following reluctantly in her wake.

'Morning!' She produced a bright smile, the kind of smile she might give someone she had never met before. Someone who had never shouted at her furiously.

He looked a little taken aback by her smile as he got to his feet. 'Good morning.'

His voice was cool but civil. That was something, thought Thea, looking on the bright side. At least he hadn't leapt to his feet and roared at them the way he had only a matter of hours ago. It wasn't the warmest welcome she had ever received, but Thea had to admit that she probably didn't deserve one of those.

'Hello.' She smiled a little nervously at the little girl and received a blank stare in return. Oh. That grimness must run in the family.

She turned back to the man. 'We…er…thought we should come over and apologise for last night…well, this morning.'

Distracted by the smell of coffee, her gaze wandered in spite of herself over to the cafetière, and she had to force herself to look back at him. 'I'm very sorry for waking you up and…er…and for crashing into your car.'

To her surprise, the sternness in his face lightened somewhat. 'I think I'm the one who should apologise,' he said. 'I'm afraid I was very rude to you. I'd had a difficult day,' he went on, his own gaze straying involuntarily towards his daughter, 'and an even worse evening, so I was in a filthy temper long before you arrived. It wasn't fair to take it out on you.'

An apology from him was the last thing Thea had expected, and she was completely thrown. 'I don't blame you for being annoyed,' she said, stammering slightly. 'It was very late and we were making a lot of noise, I know.

'It was just that we'd had such a nightmare journey,' she tried to explain. 'The plane was delayed, of course, and then there was some problem with the baggage handling at the airport, which meant that we had to wait ages for our cases. By the time we'd found the car hire place, I was so tired I was like some kind of zombie—and that was before we had to find our way here in the dark.'

'It's not an easy drive at the best of times,' he said, which was nice of him, Thea thought. Especially when she doubted very much that he would have found it difficult at any time of day. He had an air of calm competence about him that could be intimidating or incredibly reassuring, depending on how much you really needed someone competent with you.

'I'd no idea it would be so far, or that the roads would be that scary,' she told him. 'It's not as if I'm a good driver to begin with—I'm more used to taking cabs—and I really thought we'd never get here. We'd been creeping along for miles in the dark, terrified we were going to go over the edge...don't you think somebody would have thought of putting up safety barriers at some point?...and it was such a relief to get here at last that I probably stopped concentrating.

'We came round that corner there,' she went on, pointing. 'And the next thing I knew there was this big bang. I didn't see your car until it was too late. I wasn't going that fast,' she added guiltily and risked a glance at him. Fortunately he was looking more amused than anything. Phew. A big change from last night!

'It was just a little bump really, but I suppose it was the last straw. We were both so tired by then that we started to laugh. It was that or cry.'

'So that's what all the giggling was about,' he said dryly. 'I wondered what was so funny.'

'I think it was hysteria rather than amusement, but once we'd started laughing we couldn't stop. You know what it's like when you start snorting, and then you set each other off...' Thea trailed off as she realised that he was just looking at her.

No, of course he didn't. Obviously not.

'Well…anyway…we didn't realise how much noise we were making, obviously,' she hurried on. 'And then when we found ourselves in the wrong villa, it just seemed even funnier.'

Or had, until he had come roaring down the stairs and demanded to know what the hell they thought they were doing. He had been furious. As well he might be, Thea thought contritely. If she'd been woken up in the early hours of the morning by the sound of someone crashing into her car, and if they had then started fooling around, laughing loudly and breaking into her house, she probably wouldn't have been that amused either.

'I'm really sorry,' she said, wondering why it suddenly seemed so important to convince him that she wasn't as silly as she had been last night. Or not often, anyway.

'Forget it,' he said. 'It wasn't your fault that I'd completely mislaid my sense of humour last night. I think we should pretend that we've never clapped eyes on each other before and start again, don't you?'

'That's very nice of you.' Thea smiled gratefully at him. 'I'm Thea Martindale, and this is my niece, Clara.'

'Rhys Kingsford.'

Nice hands, Thea thought involuntarily as they shook hands. Warm, firm, capable. No clamminess or knobbly knuckles or suggestive little squeezes. Yes, full marks on the hand front.

And the rest of him was bearing up well to closer scrutiny as well. A bit severe-looking maybe, with those dark brows and stern features, but he was certainly more attractive than she had realised last night. Not handsome like Harry, of course—no one was as good-looking as Harry—but still… yes, definitely attractive.

Certainly attractive enough for Thea to wish that she had

taken the time to brush her hair properly and put on something more flattering before she came out.

Rhys was gesturing towards the little girl who was still sitting at the table, refusing to show the slightest interest in what was going on. 'My daughter, Sophie.'

'Hi, Sophie,' said Thea, and Clara smiled in a friendly fashion.

His mouth thinned somewhat as she merely hunched a shoulder. 'Say hello, Sophie,' he said, a note of warning in his voice.

''lo,' she muttered.

A muscle beat in his jaw, but he turned back to Thea and smiled with an obvious attempt to master his frustration. 'Well...how about some coffee? There's plenty in the pot and it's still hot.'

Thea had been afraid he would never ask. The relationship between Rhys and his daughter was obviously strained but she was slavering too much over the smell of coffee to make a polite excuse and leave them to sort out their differences.

'That would be lovely,' she said firmly before the invitation could be withdrawn. 'Actually, we came over to ask if you could possibly spare us some bread or something for breakfast,' she went on in response to a nudge from Clara. 'We haven't got anything in the villa, and it's a long drive to the shops.'

'Of course,' said Rhys. 'Sophie, why don't you go and see what you can find for breakfast—and bring a cup for Thea.'

Sophie's brows drew together mutinously, and for a moment she looked uncannily like her father had earlier that morning. 'I don't know where the cups are.'

'Try looking in the cupboard,' he told her, keeping his temper with an effort. 'There's some bread and jam on the table. You could bring that out, and whatever Clara would like to drink.'

'I'll help you,' offered Clara quickly as Sophie opened her mouth to protest.

Sophie looked deeply suspicious, but after a glance at her implacable father she deigned to drag herself off her chair and scuffed her way inside, accompanied by an unfazed Clara.

There was a slightly awkward pause. 'Sorry about that,' said Rhys, running an exasperated hand through his hair and gesturing for Thea to sit down. 'She's going through a difficult phase at the moment.'

'How old is she?' Thea hoped she would hurry back with that cup. That coffee smell was driving her wild.

'Nearly eight.'

'Clara's nine. They should get on like a house on fire.'

He sighed. 'I'm not sure Sophie gets on with anybody at the moment.'

'Well, Clara gets on with everybody,' said Thea cheerfully. 'I bet you anything that they're friends in no time.'

Rhys looked as if he wanted to believe her, but couldn't quite let himself. 'Clara seems a very nice little girl,' he said.

'She is,' said Thea with an affectionate smile. 'It's a bit disheartening sometimes to find that your nine-year-old niece is more sensible than you are, but apart from that she's a star! She's great company too. It's easy to forget that she's only nine sometimes.'

'Is it just the two of you on holiday?'

'Yes. Clara was supposed to be coming with my sister but Nell slipped off some steps at the beach three weeks ago and managed to break a foot and a wrist, which means she's been effectively immobilised ever since. There was no question of her being able to drive or walk, so she'd have been completely stuck up here, even if she'd been able to get here in the first place.'

'Unfortunate,' said Rhys. 'Was she insured?'

Thea nodded. 'Oh, yes, Nell's always very sensible about things like that. I'm sure she would have been able to claim the cost of cancelling the holiday, but Clara would have been so disappointed. She's been looking forward to this for ages. Her father never takes her on holiday.'

She scowled, thinking about her sister's ex-husband. 'He's got a new family now, and his new wife doesn't like Clara very much. I think she's probably jealous of her.'

'Clara's parents are divorced?' Rhys looked surprised. 'She seems so...happy.'

'She's fine,' said Thea. 'She was very small when Simon left, so she's always taken the fact that her parents live separately for granted. She sees Simon regularly, and Nell's been very careful not to expose her to any bitterness.'

'Maybe she and Clara will have something in common after all.'

Ah. Thea had been wondering about Sophie's mother. 'You're divorced as well?'

He nodded, his face set. 'Sophie hasn't adjusted as well as Clara, though. She wasn't even two when Lynda left, so she's not used to us living together either.

'I was working in North Africa at the time,' he went on. 'My work took me to the desert a lot and Lynda said it wasn't a suitable place to bring up a child. I suppose it was difficult for her, but...'

His mouth twisted slightly at the memory and he made a visible effort to shrug it aside. 'Anyway, she came home and we divorced. Nobody else was involved, and it was as free of bitterness as a divorce can be. We're still on good terms.'

'That must make it easier for Sophie, doesn't it?'

'The trouble is that I've seen so little of her.' Rhys drank his coffee morosely. 'My job kept me in Morocco for another five years. Whenever I had leave and could get back to the UK, I saw Sophie, of course, but it wasn't that often, and I guess I am pretty much a stranger to her.'

'That must be hard,' said Thea carefully.

His mouth turned down as he nodded. 'The last time I came home, I realised that I didn't know my daughter at all, and I didn't want it to be like that. I want to be a proper father to her, not just someone who turns up with presents every now and then. So I got myself a job in London, where I could live nearby, and I'm trying to see her more regularly now, but…'

'But what?' she prompted. 'It sounds to me as if you did exactly the right thing.'

'I'm just afraid I may have left it too late,' said Rhys reluctantly. 'I know I only came back a few weeks ago, but it's as if Sophie is determined not to be won over.'

'It might take a little time,' said Thea, hearing the hurt in his voice. 'It's probably confusing for her too, to suddenly have a full-time father.'

'I suppose so.' He sighed and raked a hand through his hair in a weary gesture. 'I was hoping that coming away on holiday together would be a good chance for us to get to know each other properly and get used to each other, but it hasn't been a great success so far. I imagined us going for long walks together and talking, but Sophie doesn't like walking and half the time she won't talk to me either. She says she's bored.'

'Aren't there any other children here?'

'Yes, there are two boys staying in the other villa.' Rhys nodded across the pool. 'Unfortunately, they're very well behaved. Sophie says they're boring, too.'

'I'm sure Clara will sort them all out,' said Thea comfortably as Sophie came back out on to the terrace, looking marginally less sullen.

She thrust a cup at Thea. 'Here.'

'Thanks.' Thea took it with a smile. Clara would have known that her aunt was desperate for coffee, she thought gratefully, but Rhys was frowning at his daughter's gracelessness.

'What about a saucer?' he asked, but Sophie was already on her way back to the kitchen.

'Honestly, this is fine,' said Thea quickly before he followed her. It was all she could do to contain herself as Rhys poured coffee into her cup.

'That smells wonderful.' She sighed, breathing in deeply. 'Mmm....' She took a sip and closed her eyes blissfully. 'God, that tastes good!'

Lowering the cup, she smiled at Rhys, a wide, warm smile that lit up her face and left him looking oddly startled for a moment. 'I've been fantasising about this all morning!'

He raised a brow. 'Nice to meet a woman whose fantasies are so easily satisfied!' he said dryly.

His eyes were an unusual greenish-grey colour, their paleness striking in his brown face. Thea was surprised that she hadn't noticed them before, and, distracted, it took her a moment to register what he had said.

A faint flush stained her cheeks when she did, and she made herself look away. 'Some of them, anyway.'

There was a pause while Thea drank her coffee and gazed studiously at the view, wishing she could think of something to say.

The sudden silence was interrupted, much to her relief, by Sophie and Clara, bearing breakfast. Bread and jam were laid carefully on the table, along with some ripe peaches, a pot of Greek yoghurt and some honey.

'This looks wonderful, Sophie,' said Thea, although she

was fairly sure that her practical niece had taken a leading role in procuring the lavish spread. Sophie had that pale, thin look of a child with no interest in food. 'Thank you so much.'

Sophie hunched a shoulder in acknowledgment and resumed her slumped posture on the chair, but Thea noticed that, beneath her fringe, her eyes were alert as she watched them tucking into breakfast with relish.

Rhys watched them too, with quiet amusement. 'It's a pleasure to see girls with such healthy appetites,' he said as Thea poured honey over a bowlful of yoghurt, handing it to Clara before preparing one of her own.

'We're very hungry,' she said a little defensively. 'We haven't eaten since the meal on the plane, have we, Clara?'

Clara shook her head, her mouth full. 'This is so good,' she said when she could. 'Can we have yoghurt and honey for breakfast every day?'

'Sure,' said Thea. 'We'll get some when we replace everything we've eaten now.'

'Don't worry about it,' said Rhys, resigned. 'I bought most of it for Sophie, anyway. I thought it would be good to have a real Greek breakfast, but she won't touch it, will you?' he added to his daughter.

Sophie's lower lip stuck out. 'Mum doesn't eat dairy products, so why should I have to?'

'No dairy products?' Thea stared at her, appalled. 'No cheese? No milk? No butter?'

'Or red meat or potatoes or bread or salt...' Rhys said, sounding tired.

That was Thea's entire diet out of the window then. 'Chocolate? Biscuits?' She didn't even think it was worth mentioning alcohol.

His smile twisted. 'You're kidding, aren't you? Lynda's

permanently on some faddy diet or another. She's obsessive about every mouthful.'

No wonder Sophie had looked so surprised when she saw them guzzling breakfast. Imagine having that kind of self-control.

'She must have a lovely figure,' said Thea, wishing she hadn't had quite such a large bowl of yoghurt.

Sophie nodded. 'She does.'

'I think she's too thin,' said Rhys.

Thea tried to imagine anyone saying that about her. *The thing about Thea is she's just too thin.* No, it just didn't sound right. Totally unconvincing, in fact. A bit like saying, *The thing about George Clooney is he's just too ugly.*

On the other hand, it sounded as if Rhys might actually prefer his women to have a few more curves than a stick insect. That was good.

Whoops, where had *that* thought come from? Thea caught herself up guiltily. She wasn't the slightest bit interested in how he liked his women.

'I wish I had that kind of self-discipline,' she said with a sigh. 'I'm always trying to diet, but I'm lucky if I make it to lunch without devouring a packet of Hob Nobs to make up for just a grapefruit for breakfast.'

'You don't need to diet,' Clara leapt in loyally. 'Mum says you're silly to worry about your weight. She says you've got a sexy figure and men much prefer that to thin girls.'

'Clara!' Mortified, Thea tried to kick her under the table.

'Well, she does,' insisted Clara, and then made things a million times worse by turning to Rhys. 'It's true, isn't it?'

'*Clara...*'

Unperturbed by the directness of the question, Rhys had turned and was studying Thea. 'I think your mother's right,' he said, straight-faced, and Clara sat back, satisfied.

'See?' she said to Thea, who was blushing furiously.

'If you've finished your breakfast, maybe you'd like to go and have a swim?' she suggested through her teeth.

'Cool!' Clara leapt to her feet. 'Come on, Sophie.'

Sophie looked warily at her father. 'Can I go?'

'Of course,' he said, and she slid off her chair and ran after Clara.

Thea buried her burning face in her coffee cup, but when she risked a glance at him saw that the disconcerting eyes were green and light with amusement.

'Is she always that direct?'

'If I didn't love her so much, I could kill her sometimes!' Thea gave in and laughed. 'She can be disastrously honest, and if she likes you she'll stop at nothing to get you what you want—or what she thinks you need!'

She shook her head ruefully. 'Clara's like her mother that way. They're both so determined, it's often easiest just to give in and do as they say!'

A smile twitched at the corner of Rhys's mouth. 'What if they don't like you? Does it work the other way?'

'Unfortunately, yes.' Thea's own smile faded as she remembered how much Nell and Clara had disliked Harry. She had never been able to understand that. Harry was so good-looking and charming. How could anyone *not* like him?

'I'd keep on her good side if I were you,' she said to Rhys, and the intriguing dent at the corner of his mouth deepened in amusement.

'I'll remember that. Now, how about some fresh coffee?' He picked up the cafetière and waved it tantalisingly.

'Well…' She didn't want to seem too greedy.

'Go on, fulfil those fantasies! You know you want it,' he tempted her, and smiled at her, a swift and totally unexpected smile that illuminated his face and left Thea with the peculiar sensation of having missed a step as her breath stumbled.

She swallowed. 'That would be lovely.'

The coffee smelt just as good as before when he came back, but this time Thea was less easily distracted by it. She found herself studying him under her lashes instead as he sat back in his chair, hands curled around his cup, watching the girls in the pool.

He wasn't *that* attractive, not really. He was compactly-built and obviously fit, and he had that air of toughness and confidence she associated with men who spent most of their life outdoors. He had mentioned working in the desert, and Thea could imagine him in a wild setting like that, unfazed by the heat and the emptiness of the elements as he narrowed his eyes at the far horizon.

Of course, it might just be the tan that made her think that.

Her gaze dropped to his hands, and the memory of how his palm had felt touching hers was enough to send a tiny shiver down her spine. Yes, nice hands, nice eyes.

Nice mouth, too, now she came to think of it. Cool and firm looking, with just a hint of sensuousness about the bottom lip. It was a shame it seemed normally set in such a stern line, but the effect when he smiled was literally breathtaking.

Hmm.

Thea was uneasily aware that her hormones, long fixated on Harry, were definitely stirring and taking an interest. Odd. She frowned slightly. Rhys wasn't her type at all. He couldn't have been more different from Harry.

She shifted in her chair, trying to shake the feeling off. Maybe it was the sleepless night catching up on her, she thought hopefully, although she was definitely feeling better after that breakfast.

'Listen!' Rhys sat forward suddenly, startling Thea out of her thoughts.

'What?'

'Sophie's laughing.'

CHAPTER TWO

THERE was such an odd note in his voice that Thea looked to where the two little girls were running around the pool and dive-bombing with much shrieking and giggling.

'They'll be inseparable now,' she said. 'I'm afraid you won't see nearly so much of her.'

'I don't mind as long as she's happy.'

Something about his expression made Thea's heart twist. Underneath that tough exterior, he was clearly vulnerable about his daughter. He struck her as the kind of man who would dismiss emotions as 'touchy feely', but it was easy to see that he loved Sophie desperately and was bothered more than he cared to admit by his inability to bond with her.

And Sophie obviously wasn't making it easy for him. Remembering that sullen expression and the stubborn set to that little chin, Thea couldn't help feeling that he had a long way to go. She felt sorry for him.

Which was much better than feeling disturbed by him.

Draining her coffee, she pushed back her chair. 'Thank you so much for breakfast,' she said gratefully. 'I feel as if I can face that awful drive now that I've got some caffeine inside me. I was dreading getting back in the car again.'

'If it's any help, I'm going down myself in a bit,' he said casually, getting to his feet at the same time. 'We need to stock up as well, so I could give you a lift if you really don't like the idea of driving.'

She really *didn't*, but Thea hesitated. 'That would be wonderful,' she said, trying not to sound too eager. 'I feel as if I'd be exploiting you, though. So far you've provided breakfast and coffee, and all I've done is wake you up in the middle of the night and crash into your car. It's rather a one-sided relationship, isn't it?' she joked a little uneasily.

For answer, Rhys cocked his ear in the direction of the pool where the girls could be heard giggling together. 'That's the first time Sophie has laughed in a week,' he said simply. 'She actually sounds as if she's enjoying herself. A pot of yoghurt, a cup of coffee and a lift into town when I was going anyway doesn't seem much compared to that.'

'Well, if you're sure…' Thea let herself be persuaded. Pride had never been her strong point anyway, and there was no point in both of them driving down that road again, was there?

'That's settled then,' said Rhys briskly. 'If I can persuade the girls out of the pool, will you be ready to leave in half an hour?'

'Half an hour's fine,' she said, calculating that would give her plenty of time to change. She wasn't sitting next to Rhys in these shorts, that was for sure.

Oh, to have lovely long, slender thighs that you could flaunt without worrying about how they would look splayed out over the passenger seat. The only alternative was to sit with her feet braced to keep the weight off her thighs, and that drive was stressful enough as it was. The last thing she needed was the added anxiety of keeping cellulite under control.

Not that there was any reason to suppose that Rhys would even notice what her thighs were doing.

Or for her to care whether he did or not.

It was just habit, Thea told herself, frantically dragging clothes out of her case. She had been in no state to unpack when they arrived in the early hours, and now everything was disastrously crumpled. She was used to constantly fretting about her appearance with Harry, who was super-critical and forever remembering how beautifully groomed Isabelle was.

The thought of Harry and Isabelle made her wince, but it wasn't that awful lacerating pain it had once been. The realisation made Thea pause. Perhaps Nell had been right when she said a change of scenery was what Thea needed.

'There's no point in moping around while you wait for Harry to make up his mind,' her sister had said. 'Go somewhere different. Think about something different.'

Like the smile in Rhys's eyes and the feel of his hand touching hers.

Thea went back to pulling clothes out of her case, but more slowly. Yes, maybe Nell had a point. Coming out to Crete in Nell's place had forced her out of her rut. It had been so long since she had been anywhere new, met anyone new, thought about anything other than Harry that her reactions were all over the place.

That would explain her peculiar physical reaction to Rhys, wouldn't it? She wasn't *attracted* to him. No, she was simply adjusting to the unfamiliar, and obviously lack of sleep—not to mention acute caffeine deprivation—hadn't helped her behave normally.

Still, that was no reason not to look her best. She would feel more herself when she was properly dressed. But in what?

'Dress or skirt and top?' Thea held the alternative outfits up for Clara's inspection when her niece appeared, still dripping from the pool.

Clara considered. 'The dress is pretty, but it's all creased.'

'Linen's supposed to look a bit creased,' said Thea, relieved to have had the decision made for her. Clara had her mother's taste and even as a very little girl her opinion had been worth having.

Tossing aside the skirt and top, she rummaged around in her case for a pair of strappy sandals. 'It's part of its charm.'

'Are we going out?'

'Didn't Rhys tell you? He's giving us a lift to the supermarket in that town we passed.'

Clara eyed her aunt suspiciously. 'Why are you getting dressed up to go shopping?'

'I'm only putting on a dress!' Thea protested.

'And you've got lipstick on.'

Trust Clara to notice that. 'I often wear lipstick. It doesn't mean anything.'

'Rhys is nice, isn't he?'

It was Thea's turn to look suspicious at the airy change of subject. 'He seems nice, yes.'

'Do you think he's good-looking?'

'He's OK,' said Thea. Nothing like Harry, of course, but yes, definitely OK.

She didn't want Clara matchmaking, though. Her niece didn't like Harry and was tireless in suggesting alternative boyfriends—encouraged by her mother, Thea thought darkly. If Clara got it into her head that Rhys would do for her aunt, she would be shameless in promoting their relationship, and Thea could foresee huge potential for embarrassment.

'Sophie says he's really cross the whole time,' Clara was continuing artlessly, 'but he didn't seem cross to me. He's got lovely smiley eyes.'

Thea didn't feel like admitting that she had noticed his eyes herself. 'Really?' she said discouragingly instead.

'Maybe he could be your boyfriend?' Clara suggested, evidently deciding to go for the direct approach after all. 'Sophie says he hasn't got a girlfriend.'

Thea filed that little piece of information away to consider when her niece's gimlet eyes weren't fixed upon her.

'I'm not looking for a boyfriend,' she said firmly. 'You know I'm still in love with Harry. You don't get over somebody just like that.'

Clara set her chin stubbornly. 'Rhys would be much better for you than Harry,' she said, sounding so like her mother that Thea was quite taken aback.

'Well, I'm sorry to disappoint you, but I'm afraid he's not really my type,' she said, wishing that Clara would go so that she could check her make-up.

Just because Rhys wasn't her type didn't mean she should let standards slip.

'I think you should give him a try. I'm sure he'd be nicer to you than Harry.'

'Clara, we're going shopping not embarking on a new relationship, all right? And if you *dare* say anything like that to Rhys or Sophie, I'll…I'll be very cross,' she finished in a threatening voice that had absolutely no effect on her niece, who grinned and skipped out of the room to change out of her wet swimming costume.

Without making any promises at all, Thea noticed.

Rhys had hired a sturdy 4x4 which dwarfed the tinny little model Thea had driven up the road in the small hours. She eyed its gleaming exterior nervously. It looked like an expensive car to repair.

'Did I do any damage last night?'

'Barely a scratch, in spite of all that noise,' said Rhys, giving the bonnet an affectionate slap, much as he might pat a horse. 'She's solid as anything. It might be worth checking your own bumpers, though.'

'I'll do that when we get back,' said Thea vaguely, with no intention of doing anything of the kind. She would worry about any damage when she returned the car. For now, she would be quite happy if she didn't have to go anywhere near it for the next two weeks.

Thea enjoyed the drive much more than she had expected to. It was wonderful not having to worry about the lack of safety barriers or the precipitous drops, or being responsible for getting the car round each of the tortuous bends. She could sit back, relax and enjoy the view.

Or she would have been able to if only she could stop her eyes drifting over to Rhys. He was an incredibly calm and reassuring driver. Unlike her, he didn't get his gears muddled up. He didn't shout at the car or swear or panic about which side of the road he was supposed to be driving on. He just sat there, hands sure and steady on the steering wheel, and Thea felt utterly safe in a way she never had with Harry, who drove a flash model and couldn't bear to have another car on the road in front of him.

Rhys was the kind of person you wanted to be sitting next to on a plane when both pilots went down with some mysterious disease and all the passengers were left to panic. Thea had seen a late-night movie like that once. Everyone flapped around and in the end the heroine had to get the plane down, but if Rhys had been there things would have been different. He would have taken over the controls and calmly landed the plane.

Of course, it wouldn't have made for such an exciting movie.

On the other hand, if the director added in fizzing sexual tension between Rhys and the heroine, who probably bore an uncanny resemblance to Thea herself, it might work. The two of them could end up shut in a room together—quarantine, Thea decided, blithely disposing of all the other passengers—and someone would have made a mistake so there was just a double bed and neither of them would have any pyjamas with them, naturally, and Rhys would say, Well, no point in wasting it, is there? At which point *she*…

Good grief, what was she *thinking* about? Thea jerked

herself back from the brink of fantasy just in time. For a moment there she had felt quite...hot.

This getting-out-of-a-rut business was doing very odd things to those hormones of hers. From having their interest piqued earlier over breakfast, they were now standing up, putting on their lipstick and patting their hair into place, ready for action.

Down, girls, Thea told them sternly. Concentrate on the view instead.

Fortunately, Clara was chatting away with her usual disarming friendliness in the back seat. Thea herself felt too shaky to carry on a conversation. It was all she could do to stare unseeingly out of the window and will her hormones to relapse into lethargy once more.

'Don't worry, we'll be there soon.' Rhys's voice made her start.

'What?'

He smiled. 'You're looking a bit nervous. The worst of the road is over now.'

'Oh. Right. Yes.' Thea cleared her throat. 'I suppose I was a bit nervous.'

That was true enough, but it wasn't about the lack of safety barriers.

Once at the supermarket, they split up. Sophie trailed listlessly behind her father, responding to his suggestions about what she would like to eat with her usual hunched shoulder.

'Whatever,' was all she would say, while Clara and Thea puzzled over the Greek alphabet.

'We'll just have to go by the pictures,' said Thea, tossing what she hoped was a tin of tuna into the trolley. It was either that or pilchards.

'I think Rhys really likes you,' whispered Clara in a stage whisper. 'I saw the way he was smiling at you in the car.'

'Shh!' Thea glared at her, pointing frantically to indicate that Rhys and Sophie might be in the next aisle.

'We should invite them to dinner,' Clara pursued in the same stage whisper, ignoring her.

Thea closed her eyes briefly. 'Clara, I really don't think—'

'To thank them for breakfast and giving us a lift,' Clara added innocently. 'I'm sure Mum would say we should.'

She would, too. 'We're on holiday. We don't want to spend a lot of time cooking,' said Thea, conscious that she was fighting a losing battle.

'I'll help you. We just need to make something simple. Sophie says her dad's always going on about how he likes home cooking, but he can only do about three things himself. He'd probably really like it if you cooked something for him.'

In the end, Thea gave in to shut Clara up. She knew quite well that her niece had visions of whisking Sophie away so that she and Rhys would be left sharing a romantic dinner for two on the terrace in the dark, with just the stars for company.

Put like that, it didn't sound too bad, did it? Thea's hormones rustled with something dangerously like excitement at the thought. They were completely out of order today.

Besides, Clara was right. A meal in return for all Rhys's help was the least she could offer. She would make the invitation very casual. If he didn't want to come, she would have done her duty and she could tell Clara that Rhys wasn't really interested.

But when she mentioned it, as casually as she could, Rhys didn't even put up a token show of reluctance. 'That sounds great,' he said. 'We'd like that, wouldn't we, Sophie?'

'Better than eating with stupid Damian and Hugo,' she muttered.

Thea raised her brows at Rhys, who was looking uncomfortable at his daughter's lack of manners. 'Damian and Hugo?'

'The two boys in the other villa,' he explained. 'The Paines are here for three weeks as well. They've been very hospitable all week, a little too hospitable as far as Sophie's concerned. They're always asking us over for meals.'

'You don't like them either,' said Sophie sullenly.

'That's not true,' he protested, although not very convincingly, Thea thought.

They were sitting at a taverna in the village square, under the shade of an enormous plane tree. The shopping had been safely stashed in the car, and Thea was starving again. When Rhys had suggested lunch she had agreed with alacrity and had ordered *souvlaki* and chips with an enormous Greek salad, reasoning that it was too late to start pretending that a lettuce leaf was all she usually had for lunch, with perhaps a low fat yoghurt if she was indulging herself.

'Well, Clara and I are very honoured that you'd rather eat with us than Hugo and Damian, Sophie,' she said lightly, and Sophie hung her head.

'Yes, I would. Thanks,' she mumbled from behind her hair.

'It'll be great,' said Clara. 'Can Sophie and I go shopping?'

'Shopping?' Thea stared at her niece. 'Where?'

'They had some postcards at the supermarket.'

Thea strongly suspected that Clara was concocting an excuse to leave her alone with Rhys, but she could hardly accuse her of that now. She contented herself with a meaningful look.

'All right, but don't be too long, and stay together.'

'OK. Come on, Sophie.'

She bore Sophie off on a wave of enthusiasm that poor

Sophie was powerless to resist, and Thea and Rhys were left alone.

There was a slightly awkward silence. For some reason Thea's nerve endings were on alert, only amber so far, perhaps, but with those treacherous hormones egging them on Thea couldn't discount the alarming possibility that they would suddenly switch to red alert and start shrieking like an intruder alarm at a high security facility.

Desperately, she gazed around the village square but, stare as hard as she might at the whitewashed walls and the dusty geraniums straggling out of painted oil barrels and the gnarled old men sitting morosely in the shade, her attention was fixated on Rhys.

He was sitting next to her at the small square table, resting his forearms tantalisingly close to hers on the checked plastic tablecloth. Thea was acutely aware of the soft, dark hairs by his broad wrist, of the unpretentious watch, and the square, capable hands, and her fingers tingled with speculation about how it would feel to lay her own over them.

The very idea made the breath dry in her throat. Something was very wrong, she thought, confused. Her body appeared to have forgotten that she was pining for Harry. It was *Harry* whose warm skin she wanted to touch.

Only yesterday, Harry had dominated her thoughts, and now when she made the effort to conjure up his handsome face all she could see was Rhys, turning his head to smile at her, the sunlight in his eyes.

Thea felt as if the earth beneath her feet had suddenly started to crumble. She was just tired, she told herself desperately. How could she be thinking clearly after less than four hours' sleep? She would be fine after a siesta.

The waiter brought a little jug of retsina, and Thea tried not to stare at Rhys's hand as he poured, but her own was unsteady as she picked up her drink and their eyes met as they chinked glasses. She must get a grip.

Looking quickly away, she reached out for a fat green olive. 'Is it true what Sophie said?'

'What about?'

'That you don't like our neighbours? What are they called again…the Paines?'

'Oh, that.' Rhys looked a little uncomfortable. He swirled the liquid in his glass as he picked his words with care. 'They're very…kind,' he said at last.

'But?'

He grimaced. 'They're just a bit much, I suppose. Especially Kate. She's one of those women who believe everybody ought to be part of a couple, and seems to take the fact that I haven't married again as a personal affront. I'm not sure where she thinks I would have found a suitable wife in the Sahara!' he added dryly.

'Oh, God,' groaned Thea. 'Don't tell me I've come all the way to Crete to end up next to the kind of people who think being single is just a deliberately selfish attempt to throw out the seating plans for their dinner parties?'

The creases around Rhys's eyes deepened in amusement. 'Oh, you've met them, then?'

Glumly, Thea helped herself to another olive. 'They're part of an extended sub-species, *copulus smugus*, otherwise known as smug married couples.' She sighed. 'Oh, well, I suppose forewarned is forearmed,' she went on as she discarded the stone. 'I'll be ready for pitying looks and questions about why I haven't married and advice about not leaving it too long to have babies, because time's ticking away, isn't it?'

'I can't believe you'd get those kind of comments very often,' said Rhys, and she stared at him.

'Why not?'

He looked a bit taken aback by her vehemence. 'Well...I don't know. I'd just assumed that someone like you would always be with somebody.'

Someone like you. What did *that* mean?

'No, I seem to be a serial singleton.' Thea picked up her retsina and drank morosely.

The truth was that even when she had been with Harry she had never really felt part of a couple. She had kept waiting for someone to point a finger and say, Who do you think you're kidding? You're just playing at having a man.

Rhys was studying her vivid face over the rim of his own glass, noting the cloud of soft brown hair, the smoke-grey eyes, the generous curve of her mouth and the lush body. 'You surprise me,' he said.

Thea hadn't been expecting that. Startled, her eyes veered towards his and then skidded away. That smiling green gaze of his was unnerving enough at the best of times.

He was only being polite, anyway. What else could he say? Lose a couple of stone and do something about your hair, and you might be in with a chance?

She sipped her retsina, willing the faint colour across her cheekbones to fade. 'At least you're divorced,' she said. 'I've always assumed that would be better. And you've got a child, too. You don't need to prove you're normal!'

'Don't you believe it!' said Rhys with a twisted smile. 'Kate is on a mission now to fix me up with another wife. Every time we go over for a meal she tells me about another "awfully nice" friend of hers she thinks I would like.'

'Can't you just not go?'

'It's difficult. The Paines are friends of Lynda's—that's how we ended up here. I haven't been back in London that long, and the summer holidays seemed like a good opportunity to take Sophie away and spend a proper chunk of time together. It suited Lynda, too. She had some conference or something to go to, so we agreed that I would have Sophie for three weeks.'

'It's a very isolated place to spend three weeks,' commented Thea. 'I think I'd have taken her to somewhere more lively.'

Rhys nodded ruefully. 'That's what I should have done, but I didn't even think about going to a resort. I thought a beach would get really boring. You can't just lie in the sun for three weeks.'

Couldn't you? Thea looked at him. He was obviously one of those hearty ten-mile walk before breakfast types who always liked to be doing things. The art of lying on a sunbed and flicking through magazines with nothing more strenuous to do than contemplate what to eat and drink next would be quite lost on him. Shame, really.

'If I'd been a more hands-on father I'd have known what Sophie would like.' Rhys was frowning down at his glass. 'As it was, Lynda told me that the villa here was available because the friends who were originally coming out with the Paines had dropped out.

'It seemed like a good idea at the time,' he went on, lifting his eyes to Thea once more, obviously trying to justify the decision to himself. 'I thought that if the Paines were friends of Lynda's, Sophie would know the children and be able to play with them, but as it turned out they've got absolutely nothing in common.

'Meanwhile, Kate and Nick are desperate to look after us. Lynda obviously confides in Kate—she seems to know an unnerving amount about my marriage and divorce—and because they're friends, short of being outright rude, I can't get out of it.'

'It sounds a bit of a nightmare,' said Thea sympathetically.

'It is,' said Rhys, reaching for the jug of retsina and topping up her glass. 'Kate's impervious to hints that I'm quite capable of looking after myself. She went on and on about all these single friends of hers she wants to introduce me to when we get home, and I could foresee endless dinner parties if I didn't put a stop to it. Eventually I just told her I had met someone special already and that I was committed to her.'

Thea was conscious of a sinking feeling in the pit of her stomach that she didn't want to analyse. 'Oh,' she said. 'Have you?'

He gave a short, mirthless laugh. 'When would I have been able to meet anyone, let alone anyone special? I've been working in the middle of the desert for most of the past five years, and in the few weeks I've been back every minute of my time has been taken up with settling into a new job, buying and moving into a house and trying to coax two words out of my daughter.'

'You lied,' said Thea admiringly, trying to ignore the sudden lightening of her spirits at the news that Rhys did not, in fact, have a girlfriend.

'I had to,' he said, assuming a mock martyred expression, and she laughed as she picked up her drink once more.

'Well, thanks for the tip. I might invent an adoring fiancé back home myself before Kate gets me in her clutches!'

'Unless you'd like to be my girlfriend?' said Rhys.

Thea paused with the glass halfway to her lips. 'Sorry?'

'Well, if we're both going to pretend, we might as well back each other up,' he pointed out. 'If my supposed girlfriend was here in person, that would really shut Kate up.'

'But she'd know that I wasn't your girlfriend,' objected Thea, not entirely sure whether he was joking or not.

'How? I've never told her a name or anything about my girlfriend other than the fact that she exists, and Kate doesn't know who was booked into the villa. She told me herself that she was wondering who would turn up and hoping that it would be a ''nice family''. They didn't see you arrive last night, and they were off on some day trip before you got up, so she still doesn't know how disappointed she's going to be.'

His face seemed straight, but that was definitely an ironic gleam in those disconcertingly light eyes, and Thea was pretty sure she had seen the corner of his mouth twitch. So he *was* joking.

Phew.

She thought.

Sipping her retsina, she decided that she might as well enter into the spirit of the thing. It was just a joke, after all.

'Wouldn't you have told her I was coming?'

'Maybe you decided to surprise me?'

Thea laughed. 'What, by barging into the middle of the holiday you'd planned to spend alone with your daughter? I think that's a bit tactless, don't you? Frankly, I can't believe I'd be that insensitive!'

He was good at keeping a straight face but there was a definite twitch to his mouth now. 'Perhaps we'd originally planned to spend it together but you couldn't make it?' he suggested.

'But if I know you're going to be pleased to see me, why book a separate villa?' Thea was beginning to enjoy herself. 'I mean, we *do* sleep together, don't we?' she joked.

Rhys looked across the table at her, his gaze dropping from the wide, quirky mouth to the generous cleavage revealed by her sundress. 'Definitely,' he said and, when he looked back into her eyes, Thea was mortified to find herself blushing.

'That's good,' she said, although not quite as casually as she would have liked. 'I wouldn't want Kate to think that I was no fun.'

'No danger of that,' said Rhys, taking in the wide grey eyes and the mobile mouth that tilted up at the corners and seemed permanently on the point of breaking into a smile.

OK, this was getting silly. Look away from his eyes now, Thea told herself. *Now*, she added urgently and at last managed to jerk her gaze away. This was just a joke, she reminded herself as she tried to get her breathing under control. That was it, inflate the lungs, breathe out…and again…

'Ah, so you just want me for my body?' She tossed her head and the cloudy brown hair tumbled around her face. 'I thought you loved me!'

'I do,' said Rhys. 'Madly. You're the woman I've been waiting my whole life for.'

Thea hated the way he could say things like that and look so *normal*, as if the idea—absurd though it was—wasn't causing little flutters in the pit of his stomach or interfering with the smooth functioning of his lungs at all.

'Then why aren't we sharing a villa, if you love me so much?' she asked almost tartly.

Rhys thought for a moment. 'You've got Clara with you because of your sister's accident and you need more space?'

Thea wrinkled her nose. 'She and Sophie could always share a room,' she pointed out. 'It's not as if the villas are pokey. There's plenty of room for four in ours, and—oh, I've got it!' She held up a hand dramatically, and Rhys lifted an amused eyebrow.

'Go on, then.'

'You've kept me a secret from Sophie so far,' she said slowly, thinking her way through it as she spoke. 'You're not sure how she'll react when she finds out that you've got a girlfriend.'

He nodded encouragingly. 'OK.'

'And I'm a bit fed up with this. If you love me as much as you say you do, why won't you introduce me to Sophie?

She's the most important part of your life, and I want to be part of it too. You keep saying that you don't want to rush things, and you think it's too soon.'

'I'm still a relatively new feature in her life,' said Rhys. 'I probably *would* think it was too soon to introduce another new person into it.'

'Well, there you are. But what you *don't* realise,' Thea went on in the same portentous tone, 'is that I'm sick of the way you're refusing to commit, and now I'm putting on the pressure. I've decided to force the issue by coming out with Clara but, because I'm not quite sure how you're going to react, I've booked a separate villa for us.'

Rhys considered. 'Aren't you afraid I'll be angry?'

'That's a risk I'm prepared to take,' she said solemnly. 'You might be cross, but you can't ignore me. By booking my own villa, I'll be forcing you to introduce me to Sophie, just as a friend initially, but at least then you won't be able to pretend that I don't exist.'

She was getting so into the story by now that she was almost starting to feel resentful at the way Rhys kept shutting her out of his life. 'And with my own villa I won't be crowding you, so you can't be *too* angry. In fact, I've probably planned to be quite independent with Clara once I've made my point.'

Pleased with her own inventiveness, Thea sat back in her chair. 'What do you think?'

Rhys was looking at her with open admiration. 'I think it would convince Kate, and if it would convince her it would convince anybody!'

They both laughed, releasing the tension that had underlain the game, until Thea realised that Rhys had stopped laughing and was looking thoughtful instead, and the chuckle dried in her throat.

'You're not serious?'

CHAPTER THREE

RHYS looked at her for a long moment, and then seemed to shake himself back to reality.

'No, of course not,' he said heartily. 'I couldn't possibly ask you to do something like that.' He leant forward and picked up the jug to refill their glasses. 'Have some more retsina.'

She had probably had enough, thought Thea, watching the golden liquid pouring into her glass. The retsina was probably the reason why she had been sitting there joking about anything quite so silly.

Because it *was* silly, and they hadn't been serious, and she ought to be running a mile from a strange man who would even suggest such a thing. She didn't know anything about Rhys Kingsford, other than what he had chosen to tell her this morning.

But it didn't feel that way. It felt as if she had known him for a very long time. It felt almost as if he had always been part of her life.

They sipped their retsina in silence for a while, both thinking about what a ridiculous idea it was to go to such lengths just to avoid being patronised by a woman who meant nothing to either of them.

But still thinking about it, anyway.

'It would be very embarrassing if Kate and Nick found out that we were pretending, wouldn't it?' said Thea eventually as if carrying on the unspoken conversation between them.

'Probably,' Rhys agreed. 'On the other hand, would it be

as bad as spending the next two weeks finding excuses not to go over to dinner?'

'Or explaining why I'm a sad person without a boy-friend,' said Thea.

There was another silence.

It was Thea who broke it again. 'Do you really think we could convince them?'

'I don't see why not,' he said, considering the matter all over again.

'We'd have to pretend that we were in love,' she said, as if the idea had only just occurred to her.

'Yes,' he agreed.

They glanced at each other and then away.

'But that shouldn't really be a problem, should it?' she reassured herself. 'I mean, they won't expect us to be all over each other, will they? Even if we were a real couple, we wouldn't be sticking our tongues down each other's throats in company.'

'Quite,' said Rhys in a dry voice. He hesitated. 'I might have to put an arm round you occasionally or something, though. Would you mind that?'

Thea managed a careless shrug. 'I ought to be able to manage that,' she said as lightly as she could, but it wasn't easy when his lean, solid body tugged at the corner of her eye and the mere thought of being held against it was enough to give her a severe attack of the flutters.

The truth was, she wouldn't mind at all.

'So what are we saying?' said Rhys at last.

Thea took a deep breath. 'I will if you will,' she said.

'Are you sure?'

'Why not?' She sat up straighter. 'It's just a bit of fun. It's not as if you really do have a girlfriend who would be hurt if she found out... Is it?' she added, hoping that she didn't sound too anxious to have this little point confirmed.

'No,' he said with a wry smile. 'I'm keeping all my attention for Sophie at the moment. What about you? No boyfriend likely to turn up and start acting jealously?'

'No.' Thea shook her head a little sadly. She would have loved to have been able to imagine Harry turning up out of the blue and glowering jealously at Rhys, but jealousy had never been Harry's thing, at least as far as she had been concerned. 'I don't think he'll be doing that.'

Rhys hesitated. 'But there is a boyfriend?'

'I'm not sure.'

'You don't know?' he asked in surprise.

'No. I suspect not, but…no, I'm just not sure.' Thea ran a finger around the rim of her glass, her face sad as she remembered.

'I met Harry a year ago, and fell for him like a ton of bricks. He was a dream come true—incredibly attractive, charming, glamorous…and honest. He told me all about his split with his ex-girlfriend and how close he still felt to her. Isabelle is the complete opposite of me.'

'You met her?'

She shook her head. 'No, but Harry spent most of his time talking about her. She's very pretty and petite, apparently, and she works in the City like him. She's got some high-powered job that means she's constantly under pressure and it doesn't help that she's completely neurotic anyway. That's not what Harry says, of course,' Thea added with a twisted smile. 'He says she's "highly strung."'

'I can see that you might be a relief after someone like that,' said Rhys carefully.

'That's what Harry used to say, but I always felt he secretly thought I was a bit dull after Isabelle's histrionics. According to Harry, it was an amicable split, and they both agreed that they would be free to see other people, but as far as Isabelle was concerned she still had first call on his time. At the first hint of a crisis she'd ring him up and he would drop everything to rush round and sort it out for her.'

Rhys's eyes rested on her averted face. 'That must have been difficult for you.'

'It wasn't easy.' Thea managed a shrug. 'Nell—Clara's mother—thinks Harry is weak and selfish, but I told her she didn't understand. Harry's a kind person. He feels that Isabelle needs him and that he wants to be a good friend to her.'

'What about being a good friend to you?'

She glanced at him. 'Funny, that's what Nell used to say, too!' Heaving her shoulders, she let them slump back. 'Oh, I don't know...I suppose I was prepared to put up with anything as long as Harry came back to me. And he did. He'd tell me that Isabelle was just needy, and that I was the one he loved and, of course, I let myself believe it.'

'So how come you're here now, not sure whether you've got a boyfriend or not?' asked Rhys after a moment.

'We'd booked a holiday together.' It still hurt Thea to think about how much she'd looked forward to that holiday. 'I'd found a perfect little cottage in Provence and it was going to be just the two of us, away from Isabelle, but about a month before we were due to go Harry started to back-pedal, saying he wasn't sure it was good timing and maybe we should think about postponing it.

'It turned out that Isabelle had to have some operation on her foot. It wasn't anything major, and she was just an out-patient at the hospital, but she decided that she needed Harry to feed her cat, water her plants, make her little cups of herbal tea, and generally dance attendance on her.'

Thea blew out her cheeks and pushed the hair away from her face. 'Sorry, that sounds bitchy. I'm sure she didn't choose to have the operation just then, and for all I know it was very uncomfortable for her. It was just the last straw for me.'

'So you told Harry he had to choose between you?'

'More or less.' She hated remembering that awful day, and how heartsick she had been. It had felt as if she were deliberately destroying her only chance at love and that she would never be happy again.

'We had a long talk, Harry and I, and I told him how I felt. Harry said that he felt guilty about being constantly torn between the two of us, and that sometimes he felt smothered, so I suggested that he take some time to think about what he really wanted.'

One of the worst things had been seeing the unmistakable relief that had leapt to Harry's eyes, as if he had been trapped, longing for her to open the door for him.

'Harry agreed that he needed some space, so that's what he's doing, deciding which of us he wants.'

'And in the meantime you're left hanging on, hoping that you might still have a boyfriend, but not sure if you do or not?' Rhys's voice was unusually hard, and Thea glanced at him. What was it to him, anyway?

'The last time I heard from him, he still couldn't make up his mind,' she admitted. 'At least that means I can still hope. I didn't get my holiday in Provence, but then Nell had her accident and asked if I would come out with Clara in her place, so…here I am!'

Rhys was frowning down into his glass again, a muscle beating in his jaw as if he was angry about something, but when he looked up after a few moments, he smiled. 'I'm sorry if it wasn't the holiday you wanted, Thea,' he said, 'but I for one am very glad you're here.'

'I think it's Clara you should be grateful for,' she said, conscious of a dangerous little glow flickering into life inside her.

He shook his head. 'You too,' he said firmly, and the glow spread a little further.

Thea looked around her, at the rickety tables dappled with sunlight through the plane leaves, at the pots of bright flowers and the massively gnarled tree trunk dwarfing them all. The air was warm and full of the tantalising smell of grilling lamb while beyond the shade the light glared and a car tooted in a failed attempt to disrupt the peaceful atmosphere.

'I'm glad I'm here too,' she said. 'It's been good to get away.'

'I'm glad you told me about Harry, as well,' Rhys went on. 'I think it makes things easier in a way.'

'What do you mean?'

'Well…it means that there's no danger of either of us taking the pretence too seriously, doesn't it?' he said, not quite awkwardly, but as if he wasn't entirely sure how she would react.

'Oh. No. Quite.'

And that would explain why that glow was still seeping along her veins and she still had that weird fluttery feeling under her skin at the thought of touching him, wouldn't it, Thea?

'No danger at all,' she said firmly.

Rhys smiled and held out his hand. 'Let's shake on it then.'

Oh, dear, touching him just *wasn't* a good idea at the moment. Why hadn't he suggested drinking to it instead? Chinking glasses would have been fine. Even shaking hands seemed fraught with complications given the confused state her hormones were in right then.

But she couldn't see any way to refuse without looking a complete idiot. Thea eyed his hand as if measuring a jump over an abyss, which was almost what it felt like. All she had to do was lift her own hand, touch palms, curl her fingers around his—*briefly*, remember—and let go. How difficult could that be?

Thea took a deep breath, put her hand in his and yanked it back before he could do anything alarming like squeeze it or hold it for too long or anything at all to prolong the warmth that was tingling up her arm as it was.

Rhys looked a little surprised but picked up his glass. 'Here's to pretence,' he said, toasting her.

Why couldn't he have done that before?

'I'm not sure we've really thought this through,' she injected a note of caution as she resisted the urge to rub her arm where it jangled still from his touch. 'We're going to have to explain to Clara, and Sophie knows quite well that I'm not your girlfriend, even one you've been keeping secret up to now. What will she think?'

'It's impossible to tell with Sophie,' he said wryly. 'I can only try. If she doesn't want to play along, we'll have to leave it. One thing, she won't tell Kate,' he added. 'She can't bear her, and is always embarrassingly rude to her. It's partly Kate's fault,' he said in defence of his daughter. 'She will keep criticizing Sophie's behaviour in front of her and comparing it to her boys'.'

'I would have thought that would just make her worse.'

'It does,' said Rhys with feeling, and then his face lightened. 'Ah, here's our lunch.'

The waiter was bearing down on them, plates stacked up his arm, and Thea's mouth watered at the appetising smell. Clara, attuned to food like her aunt, had already noticed the arrival of the meal and was galloping back across the square, followed by Sophie.

'I'm starving!' she said, flopping down into her chair.

Thea caught Rhys's eye and knew that he was thinking about the huge breakfast they had consumed not so long ago. 'Martindale girls have healthy appetites,' she said.

'So I see,' he said with a smile, and his gaze travelled on to his daughter who was picking up her knife and fork with an enthusiasm Thea guessed was unusual. Her thin little face was flushed, and her eyes were brighter as she tucked into grilled chicken.

Wisely, Rhys refrained from commenting on her improved appetite, but waited until they had finished eating before outlining their plan so casually that Thea could only gape at him with admiration. He made it sound a perfectly reasonable idea that two complete strangers should go to such elaborate lengths just to avoid a tedious neighbour.

Clara certainly didn't have any problems with it. 'Cool,' she said, and her bright eyes sparkled, and her enthusiasm won over Sophie, who was clearly uncertain how to react at first.

'The thing is, you two are in on the secret. You won't have to say or do anything, but we'd need to know that you weren't going to give us away,' said Rhys carefully. 'How would you feel about that?'

'I think it would be fun,' said Clara buoyantly, but then she would. Thea could practically see her calculating opportunities to throw her aunt together with Rhys.

'What about you, Sophie?' he asked. 'Would you mind?'

She shook her head. 'No,' she said. It sounded grudging after Clara's effervescence, but it was a big step for Sophie.

'I think you should be engaged, not just girlfriend-boyfriend,' Clara was saying, oblivious to the way Rhys was looking at his daughter.

Thea frowned her down. 'There's no need to go that far, Clara.'

'But if you're just a girlfriend, this Kate person won't think Rhys is really serious,' Clara protested.

'You know, I think Clara might have a point,' said Rhys, eyeing her niece with respect. 'I wouldn't put it past Kate to keep thinking up potential girlfriends for me in case you turn out not to be suitable after all. What difference does it make, after all? We'll still be pretending.'

'True.' Thea looked from her niece's bright face to Rhys and back again. Really, that girl was going to go far. She was only nine, and already she had manipulation down to a fine art. But she could hardly tell Rhys that she didn't want to pretend to be his fiancée because it might give Clara ideas, could she?

'Oh, well, in for a penny, in for a pound.' She sighed, resigned, and Clara sat back with a smug smile.

'What about a ring, things like that?' To Thea's consternation, Rhys was actually looking to Clara for advice. Didn't he realise that she was only nine, for heaven's sake?

'That won't be necessary,' she intervened quickly before Clara could pronounce. 'We'll just say that you were so thrilled to see me at five o'clock this morning that the scales fell from your eyes. You want to spend the rest of your life with me, and you don't want to waste any more time, so you asked me to marry you there and then.'

'What, at five in the morning?' said Rhys incredulously.

It didn't sound that convincing put like that, Thea had to admit. Would she really want to be proposed to in the early hours after a drive like that without her make-up on? No.

'OK, we got engaged this morning, when you'd had a chance to realise that we really do belong together.'

There was one of those sizzling pauses you couldn't plan in a million years, when Thea's words seemed to echo round the village square, booming back at her. *We belong together.*

Rhys broke it first. 'This is our engagement lunch, then?' he said, and Clara seized her lemonade, playing it for laughs. 'Congratulations!' she said, lifting her glass.

What a little drama queen she was! Thea shook her head

at her, but she and Rhys laughed and chinked their glasses against hers and, after a moment, Sophie lifted her glass too.

'Congratulations!' she said, and when she smiled Thea felt as if she'd conquered Everest.

Another silence threatened, and this time it was Thea who rushed to fill it. 'You know, you could be difficult if you wanted to, Sophie,' she suggested. 'You could pretend to make a big fuss and say you hate me, then that would be a reason for you to go off on your own with your dad.'

'But then I wouldn't be able to play with Clara,' Sophie objected.

'Oh, I don't know. You could be nice to Clara because you feel sorry for her stuck with me all the time. And whenever I come by you could glower and look sulky.' Thea demonstrated by putting on a moody face, and Sophie was surprised into a reluctant giggle.

'I think she'd be pleased if you were her dad's girlfriend,' said Clara loyally. 'Thea's my favourite aunt.'

She turned to Sophie, but Thea could tell that her words were aimed elsewhere. 'It's always fun when she comes round. I wish my dad had married someone like her,' she added, one eye on Rhys. 'My stepmother's really boring. I'm not allowed to make a mess when I'm there, and she never lets me try on any of her make-up or clothes. I could never curl up on a sofa and have a chat with her the way I can with Thea. She makes yummy meals, too, not all low-fat and healthy like my stepmother does.'

Such blatant promotion made Thea cringe. She didn't dare look at Rhys to see how he was taking Clara's transformation into professional matchmaker. Any more of this and she would be negotiating a dowry.

'Yes, well, none of this matters, Clara,' she said hastily. 'We're just pretending here, remember? Sophie doesn't really want me to be her dad's girlfriend.'

'I wouldn't mind,' said Sophie shyly, and Clara shot Thea a triumphant look.

Oh, God, here came another of those awkward pauses. Thea still hadn't risked a glance at Rhys, but she was very conscious of Clara's bright eyes whisking interestedly between them and she rushed into speech before her niece could do anything else to embarrass her.

'We should decide how we met. Kate's bound to ask. What about at a party?'

Rhys looked unconvinced. 'I'm not really a party animal,' he said. 'I'm sure Lynda will have told Kate that. It was one of the things she always used to complain about me.'

'You could have decided to change your life since you've come back to the UK,' Thea pointed out. 'You could say you'd had a personality transformation.'

He made a face. 'I don't think I could carry off being the life and soul of the party, particularly as I've spent the last week trying to convince Kate and Nick how unsociable I am. How about if we met on a blind date? I could have seen your ad in a newspaper and thought you sounded interesting.'

Thea bridled. 'I'm not telling Kate that I've been advertising! She'll think I'm desperate.'

'She's going to think that anyway if you're pursuing me out to Crete.'

'Look, who is it who invented the girlfriend in the first place?' she said crossly. 'I don't mind appearing pushy, but I'm not going to be sad!'

Rhys held his hands up in mock surrender, and she subsided slightly. 'Could we have met through work? That's where most people get together, after all.'

'I don't know. What do you do?'

'Oh, a bit of this and a bit of that, as they say. I'm still waiting to stumble into a career,' said Thea with a sigh.

It must be nice to be able to answer the dreaded What do you do? question with confidence. I'm a doctor. I'm a solicitor. I'm a gardener. I'm in sewage disposal. Anything as long as you sounded like you knew what you were doing with your life.

'I keep changing jobs,' she went on. 'It drives my mother wild! I'm a PA in a public relations company at the moment.' She brightened. 'Maybe we could have been raising the profile of your organisation, or changing the focus of your sales? Or—I know!—the key element of what you do needs re-branding, so of course you needed to talk to my boss but as soon as you laid eyes on me, you knew I was the one and naturally you couldn't concentrate on business after *that* and—' She stopped, seeing Rhys's face. 'What?'

'I was just trying to imagine how you could re-brand rocks.'

'*Rocks?*' echoed Thea, completely thrown. She had been getting quite carried away there, imagining just how it would have been when he walked into her office and their eyes had met…a bit like the way they had met earlier, in fact.

'I'm a geologist,' Rhys explained. 'I'm interested in rocks that are millions of years old. Geology is the most important thing there is.'

Thea, Clara and Sophie exchanged a look. 'More important than shoes?' asked Thea innocently.

'Or shopping?' added Clara, never one to be left out.

Rhys rose beautifully to the bait. '*Shopping? Shoes?*' he echoed incredulously. 'You can't even begin to compare them! Everything you do, everything you see, everywhere you walk, is shaped by geology,' he argued, roused to passion, Thea was interested to note, by a few rocks. 'How can you understand the world around you if you don't under-

stand how it's made? They ought to teach geology in primary schools. If I had my way—'

He stopped as he saw Thea and Clara giggling as they
mimed falling asleep with boredom, closing their eyes and
letting their elbows slip off the edge of the table, and he
grinned reluctantly.

'OK, so not everybody finds rocks as interesting as I do,'
he conceded.

Sophie was watching them with huge eyes. It had obviously never occurred to her that it was possible to tease her
formidable father, but when she saw that he was laughing
too, she giggled.

Thea judged that it was time to bring them back to the
business in hand. 'Well, if geologists are too grand to deal
with PR, we'd better fall back on that tried and trusty matchmaking activity, the dinner party. We can say a friend of
mine works with a friend of yours or something, and we
both ended up at the same dinner.'

Rhys shrugged. 'Sounds reasonable enough to me—and
not something Kate can disprove either. She's an intimidating woman, but I'd have thought even she would draw the
line at demanding names and addresses.'

'OK, a dinner party it was, then. And naturally, when you
talked about rocks and showed me how important they were
in my life, I was completely dazzled!'

Rhys acknowledged her mockery with another grin. 'Ah,
so it was love at first sight for you, too, was it?'

Thea looked at the old men playing backgammon at the
next table and wondered what had happened to the air in
her lungs. 'I think it probably was,' she said.

The alarm dragged Thea out of a deep sleep, and for a while
she lay utterly still, groggily wondering where she was and

why there was bright sunshine outside when her body was telling her it was the middle of the night.

She felt totally disorientated. Vivid images kept coming to her in puzzling flashes, none of which seemed to connect in any way. Clutching the steering wheel as she drove endlessly through the dark—she remembered *that*—but then she had a very clear image of Clara positively smirking as well. Surely not?

Then there was a checked tablecloth and a man's arm and Rhys...*Rhys*!

Thea jerked upright. It was all coming back to her now. Yes, she had had coffee with him, and then they had driven down the mountain together. That had all been fine.

But that ridiculous plan they had concocted... What had she been *thinking* of? The retsina must have gone to her head.

'Oh, *God*!' Thea dragged her hands through her hair. What had she got herself into?

The worst thing was remembering how reasonable it had all seemed at the time. They had talked about it as they drove home with their shopping, the girls giggling in the back seat. They had actually *laughed* about it!

Thea blenched, thinking about it now. Nell would have a fit if she knew that Thea had thrown herself and Nell's precious daughter's lot in with a perfectly strange man for the entire holiday!

She would have to get up and explain that she hadn't been thinking clearly, and that they couldn't possibly go through with it. Rhys had seemed the sensible type. He had probably been having second thoughts himself, Thea reasoned, and as for the girls, well, they could just pretend that it had all been a joke.

How did she get herself into these things? Thea wondered

in despair, as she struggled to disentangle herself from her sheet. She had only been in Crete a matter of hours!

It was very hot still, even in the shady bedroom, and the thought of getting dressed properly was just too much to contemplate on top of all the other disastrous situations she seemed to have got herself involved in. Digging out her favourite sarong, she wrapped it around her. Its soft cotton was cool and comforting against her bare skin.

Tiredness had hit her like a freight train on the way back. One moment she had been gaily chatting away in the front seat—extraordinary how she had seemed to have so much to say to Rhys, considering that she didn't know him from Adam…maybe that had been down to the retsina too—and the next her head had been lolling on to her chest.

It had been all she could do to unpack the shopping and shove most of the contents of the bags into the fridge before collapsing into bed. Clara had opted to keep going in the pool, and now Thea wished that she had done the same. She felt lousy, dopey, disorientated, faintly sick and shivery. It was a bit like having a monumental hangover, but without the headache.

She padded downstairs. Perhaps a swim would freshen her up too. She would just check to see that the dreaded Paines weren't back. She didn't want to face Kate for the first time in a swimsuit. That really would put her at a disadvantage. Opening the front door, she stepped cautiously out on to the terrace.

'Thea!'

Thea nearly leapt out of her skin. Clutching her sarong, she swung round to find herself staring at Rhys and an elegantly-groomed blonde who Thea had no difficulty at all in identifying as Kate Paine.

So, instead of meeting her in a swimsuit, their first encounter had Thea tousled and half-naked in a piece of material so old and worn it was practically see-through. Her eyes were piggy with sleep still, and her hair was its usual tangled mess. Instinctively, Thea lifted a finger and wiped it under her eyes.

It came away black. She had been too tired to take her make-up off when she fell into bed, which meant that she had mascara circles under her eyes and looked like a panda.

Excellent.

Rhys and Kate had evidently met on the terrace and seemed as startled to see Thea as she had been to see them. Why? Thea wondered crossly. It was *her* terrace.

For a moment the three of them just looked at each other, and Thea was just wondering if she could, in fact, simply turn and walk back inside and close the door, when Rhys pulled himself together.

'There you are, darling!' he said, advancing on Thea with a warm smile. He put an arm round her before she could follow her instincts and bolt back inside. 'I was just coming over to see if you were awake yet! How do you feel?'

'A bit odd, to tell you the truth,' said Thea huskily, finding her voice at last.

Ooh, look, she had suddenly turned into the Queen of Understatement. Now that *was* odd. Odd was much too ordinary a word to use for the way it felt to have Rhys's arm around her.

He held her firmly, his arm strong and solid and warm through the fine material of her sarong, and Thea was agonizingly conscious of her nakedness against him. The merest whisper of cotton separated her skin from his, and the thought was peculiarly exciting. It was all very well reminding herself that she hardly knew this man, but the sad truth was that his arm felt...well, *good*. Right, even.

Disturbingly so, in fact.

'I've just been telling Kate how you surprised me last

night,' Rhys said with a warning squeeze which Thea could have done without. Her sarong was in a precarious enough position as it was, not to mention her nerves.

It wasn't even as if she needed reminding of the situation when she was pressed up against his body like this. It felt satisfyingly unyielding. He might not have Harry's glamorous looks, but he was all bone and muscle.

'Remember I mentioned the family staying in the third villa?' he was saying to Thea, as if they hadn't spent their entire lunch working out how they could avoid them as much as possible. 'This is Kate Paine. She's here with her husband, Nick, and their two boys.'

Everything about Kate said cool and crisp. She had icy blue eyes and her hair was both stylish and practical. She radiated the kind of confidence that left Thea feeling the way she had at primary school when faced with a particularly brisk teacher. It was impossible to imagine her ever getting dirty or flustered.

Thea eyed her pristine white shirt and immaculately ironed stone-coloured trousers with disbelief. It would be bad enough to think that Kate had unpacked them looking like that, but Thea was prepared to bet on the much scarier thought that here was someone who not only took an iron on holiday, but used it!

'Hugo and Damian,' Kate was explaining graciously, but her eyes were coolly assessing as they rested on Thea in a return inspection. She didn't look over-impressed.

Thea couldn't blame her. She knew what she looked like when she woke up, and it wasn't a pretty sight.

'Hello,' she said, managing a sickly smile.

'Kate, this is Thea.' Rhys sounded positively adoring, and now he was smiling down into her face as if he thought that she was beautiful instead of ridiculously smeared with mascara.

Who would have thought a geologist could act like that?

'Kate's kindly invited us for drinks on their terrace tonight,' he went on with another of those alarming squeezes.

'Oh, well, that's very kind of you,' Thea began, but Kate interrupted her before she could formulate a decent excuse.

'Just a drink to welcome you,' she insisted. 'Rhys has explained that this is a special day for you, but we *would* like to help you celebrate your engagement as well.'

'Well...'

'I'm sure you'll want a chance to freshen up,' Kate said kindly, although the eyes that inspected Thea from head to toe were unmistakably critical. Clearly the slatternly look held no appeal for her. 'We'll expect you at six, shall we?'

CHAPTER FOUR

'Why didn't you make some excuse?' muttered Thea as Kate clicked off on her perfectly polished shoes. 'I thought the whole point of the pretence was to avoid them, not spend our time having drinks with them.'

Rhys waited until Kate was out of sight before dropping his arm. Having willed him to do just that, Thea found that she missed its warm support and perversely wished that he would put it back.

'We had to go some time,' he said as she concentrated fiercely on her sarong instead, tying it in such a tight knot that she was in danger of cutting off her circulation altogether.

'We might as well get it over and done with,' he went on. 'I'd rather have waited until tomorrow, but when I saw her heading over here I thought I'd better come and cut her off. I managed to stop her before she got to your door, and told her about our touching little romance. Agreeing to drinks was the best way I could think of to get rid of her. I didn't think you'd want to meet her unprepared.'

'No, really, I'm delighted I could meet her like this instead,' said Thea with more than a touch of sarcasm. She gestured down at her sarong, but carefully. She didn't trust the slippery material. 'With me looking so smart and all!'

Rhys smiled, one of those swift, disturbing smiles of his. 'I didn't know you were going to open the door just then,' he pointed out. 'Anyway, you look great.'

'It's all right,' said Thea, flushing slightly. 'You don't need to act when the Paines aren't here.'

'No, I mean it,' he said.

Uh-oh, here came one of those tingly moments again. Thea didn't want to look at him, but it was as if her eyes had a will of their own, dragging her head round until she was gazing straight at him.

'Really,' he said with a smile.

Oh, please don't do that, Thea wanted to say. She was having enough trouble coping with the peculiar behaviour of her hormones as it was.

She moistened her lips. 'I keep forgetting you've been out in the desert with no women for the last few years,' she said, and he laughed, which just made things worse.

Sighing inwardly, Thea made an effort to pull herself together. Really, it would be much easier if he would just go back to being grumpy and disagreeable, the way he had been when they had first encountered each... Was it only that morning? She felt as if she had known him a lifetime.

'So.' From somewhere she produced a bright smile. 'We're committed now. Kate seemed to believe that we've known each other longer than a few hours.'

'So far, anyway,' Rhys agreed. 'We've still got to get through the inevitable interrogation over drinks, but if we brush through that, we should be fine. I hope they'll leave us to do our own thing after that. Kate wanted us to go over for supper, but I compromised on drinks, the subtext being, I hope, that a quick gin and tonic was all we could manage without ripping our clothes off each other. I thought drinks would be enough to cope with!'

'Quite enough,' said Thea, trying not to imagine the clothes ripping scenario too clearly.

Glancing at her watch, she saw that it was already almost six. 'I was on my way to check on Clara and have a swim, but I think I'd better have a shower now. Have you seen Clara at all?'

'I have. I've been keeping an eye on them all, and it took her about five minutes to subvert the Paine children from good little boys to shouting, splashing and dive-bombing with the best of them,' said Rhys with a grin. 'They're all having a great time, although Kate didn't look too happy with the transformation in her sons.'

'Oh, dear. Do you think I should go and have a word with Clara?'

'No. The other three have been staring at each other all week, and it's taken Clara less than a day to get them all playing together. They'll enjoy the rest of the holiday now. I'd say Clara was more than a match for Kate, anyway!'

Thea laughed. 'You're probably right. I'll go down and see what's going on when I've had my shower.'

'I'll see you at the pool, then, and we can go over to the Paines' together.'

With a wave, Rhys set off down the steps, leaving Thea to wonder why she should feel vaguely resentful, and then to be horrified when she realised that it was because he had gone without kissing her goodbye.

God, she *must* pull herself together! They were pretending, remember? Rhys didn't really want to marry her and he didn't have to kiss her at all, and she shouldn't want him to. She was supposed to be broken-hearted about Harry, anyway.

Turning to go inside, she reassured herself that she was just confused after a long day. She would be fine tomorrow, and in the meantime maybe a shower would help.

Preferably a cold one.

Thea was aghast when she caught sight of herself in the bathroom mirror. With her hair all over the place, a white pasty face, bleary eyes and horrible black mascara smears, she looked as if she had stumbled off the set of a horror movie. *The Afternoon Nap of the Undead* perhaps. No wonder Kate had looked unimpressed!

Clearly drastic measures were called for. Thea jumped into the shower, washed her hair and slathered on the curl control cream. This was no time for restraint on the lotions and potions front.

By the time she had dried her hair it didn't look *too* bad. Still no sleek, shining curtain, but at least it looked more like a fluffy cloud and less like a haystack. It had been worth bringing that hair-dryer after all. Nell had said that she wouldn't need one, and it was nice to know that her big sister could be wrong sometimes.

Glad that there was no Clara this time to ask awkward questions, Thea made up her eyes carefully and pulled on a cherry-red dress. It was one of her favourites, quite old now, but still the most flattering for her curvaceous figure, emphasising her cleavage and drawing attention well away from her hips and thighs. Lovely soft material too, that floated around her bare legs. Wearing it always made her feel sexy.

The only trouble was that it creased badly. Thea tried smoothing down the skirt again, but it didn't make much difference. Still, it would have to do. With any luck it would get dark soon anyway, and she was damned if she was going to ask Kate if she could borrow her iron!

Six o'clock... Thea squinted at her watch. 'OK,' she muttered, scrabbling through her make-up bag for a lipstick. 'Lipstick...lipstick...lipstick...ah, there you are! Now... shoes...earrings...*earrings!*...God, what did I do with my earrings?'

She looked wildly around the room. If only it wasn't in such a mess where she had pulled everything out of the case earlier. She'd never be able to find anything now.

Thea was frantically tipping various cosmetic bags out on

to the bed in search of her jewellery when she suddenly realised that she was hyperventilating, as breathless and excited as if she were going out on a heavy date.

'Calm down,' she told herself and took some deep breaths. It was just drinks with tiresome neighbours.

And supper with Rhys, that sly inner voice whispered.

Yes, well, that too, but really she was dressing to convince Kate that she didn't always look like an extra from *Buffy the Vampire Slayer,* Thea tried to convince herself. All this effort was simply in aid of the pretence.

Sure, said the voice.

It was a bit much when your own inner voices went sarcastic on you, Thea reflected glumly, spotting her earrings at last. They were supposed to restrict themselves to the occasional note of caution, not outright mockery and discomfiture.

Maybe it *did* look as if she had made too much effort for casual drinks, though? Thea's confidence, ever shaky, faltered as she squinted at herself in the bathroom mirror while her nerve got ready to run off and hide in the bushes with its tail between its legs.

Thea bit her lip. There was no time to change now. She was late already. Whistling her nerve to heel once more, she straightened her shoulders. It wasn't as if she was togged up in sequins and a tiara. She was only wearing a dress, for heaven's sake.

'Get a grip,' she said sternly to her reflection.

Judging by the squeals, splashes and giggles emanating from the pool, Clara hadn't spent the afternoon missing the care and sound counsel of an adult, although Thea was relieved to know that Rhys had been keeping an eye on the girls while she had been crashed out in bed.

By rights Clara should have been exhausted too, but no,

there she was, in the thick of it and, by the looks of things, all four of the children were thoroughly over-excited.

Obviously Thea wasn't the only one who thought so. As she came down on to the poolside, she saw Kate, as immaculate as ever but looking exceedingly tight-lipped as she watched a little boy leap off the side of the pool and land with a terrific splash.

'Hugo! Damian!' she was shouting. 'How many times have I told you not to jump in like that? Get out right now!'

'Oh, *Mu-um*…'

Poor kids. Imagine not being allowed to dive-bomb in a private pool on holiday, thought Thea. The Paine household was obviously run as a very tight ship, with instant obedience the norm to judge by their mother's astonishment at being answered back.

'It's after six, boys,' Kate said, careful to sound reasonable, because clearly Kate was the perfect mother who never lost her temper. 'You know perfectly well that you always have a bath now, and then you're ready for the evening.'

'But we're playing this brilliant game,' one of the boys objected.

'Everyone is getting out now, anyway.' Kate's eye fell on Thea. 'Ah, good, there you are,' she said briskly, as if Thea was an errant pupil who had turned up late without a proper excuse. 'You want Clara out now, don't you, Thea?'

Behind Kate's back, Thea could see Clara shaking her head emphatically. 'I don't see why, if she's enjoying herself.'

'But she must be tired!'

'She's on holiday,' said Thea with a touch of defiance, trying to ignore the jubilant thumbs-up signs Clara was making from the pool. 'She can sleep in the morning if she wants.'

Kate sucked in her breath. 'Are you sure that's wise? I

gather Clara is your niece, and it's obviously tempting to be indulgent when it's not your own child,' she added patronisingly, 'but parents know that children really need routines.'

'At home, maybe, but I would have thought that the whole point of a holiday is to give the child a break from routine,' said Thea, ultra-reasonable.

Balked, Kate swung back to the pool. 'Well, the other three are certainly getting out now,' she said crossly. 'I'm sure your father will think *you've* had enough, Sophie.'

'Enough what?'

At the sound of Rhys's voice behind them, Thea's heart leapt into her throat and lodged there, quivering, as she swung round. He had put on a clean shirt and shorts, and he looked crisp and clean and self-assured, but there was nothing special about him. He didn't have Harry's romantically floppy hair or dazzling blue eyes or chiselled features. He was just ordinary, really.

So why did it feel as if every cell in her body had jerked to attention at the sight of him? Why, after knowing him only a matter of hours, did he seem so familiar, and yet so joltingly immediate at the same time?

And why did the way his cheeks creased as he smiled— yes, like that—dry the breath in her throat?

'You look wonderful,' he said, ignoring Kate completely, and slipped an arm around her waist. Before Thea—and possibly he—had quite realised what was happening, he had dropped a warm, casual kiss on her mouth.

Caught unawares, Thea's heart, already in turmoil, seemed to stop altogether. The paving round the pool dropped away beneath her feet, and for a moment she swung dizzily in space, her only anchor the searing, dangerously exciting touch of his lips.

It was just a moment, though. The next Rhys was lifting

his head, and as their eyes met fleetingly, Thea thought he looked as shaken as she felt. It was almost as if he had acted without thinking, and now wasn't sure what had happened.

Kate was tapping her foot impatiently. 'I was suggesting that all the children get out of the pool now and get ready for bed,' she told Rhys, apparently unaware that his arm was all that was keeping Thea upright. 'They're all getting over-excited, and the boys have been in there quite long enough. When they've had their baths, I think they should sit quietly and read so they can all calm down before they go to bed.'

Rhys looked at the children in the pool. 'They don't look to me like they're in much of a mood for reading,' he said.

'That's because they're playing this silly game,' said Kate, exasperated.

'Games are supposed to be silly, aren't they? Isn't that the point of them?'

'The point *is*,' Kate said icily, 'that Sophie isn't usually in the pool this late, is she?'

'Oh, *Dad*,' begged Sophie, who had been hanging around near the edge waiting to hear her fate. 'Don't say I have to go to bed yet! We're playing this totally cool game, and Thea says Clara doesn't have to get out.'

'Hugo and Damian are getting out,' Kate intervened, provoking another chorus of moans from her sons, 'so Clara will get pretty lonely in there on her own.'

Rhys let go of Thea and went over to squat by the edge of the pool so that he could talk to Sophie. 'You can stay in with Clara while we have drink,' he told her, 'but when I call you, I want you both out straight away.'

'Thanks, Dad!' Sophie could hardly believe her luck.

'That goes for you too, Clara.'

'OK.' Clara beamed, and celebrated by doing a handstand

on the bottom of the pool. 'Thanks Rhys, thanks Thea!' she called when she surfaced.

'Rhys.' Kate lowered her voice as he straightened and came back towards her and Thea, whose legs were doing the most amazing impersonation of cotton wool and who was still rooted to the spot where he had left her, afraid to move in case she simply collapsed.

'Are you sure it's wise to give in to her like that?' Kate went on in concern. 'I know Lynda believes in setting very strict boundaries, otherwise Sophie can be, as you know, quite…well, *difficult*…'

'I know all about Lynda's boundaries, thank you, Kate,' said Rhys in a cool voice. 'Lynda's not here, I am responsible for my daughter, and for once she seems to be having a good time. I'm not going to spoil that by insisting on needless confrontation. Now, did someone say something about a drink?' he finished, closing the discussion firmly.

Wow, assertive or what? Thea watched, incredibly impressed, as Kate gave ground. She obviously longed to make an issue of it, but there was something in Rhys's face that evidently made her decide not to push the matter.

'Yes, of course,' she said, forcing a tight smile. 'Nick's waiting for us now.'

Kate's husband was waiting for them at the top of the steps. He was a big, florid man, exuding *bonhomie*. 'Come up, come up,' he urged them, and wrung Thea's hand. 'I'm Nick, Nick Paine. Paine by name, pain by nature!' He laughed heartily.

You said it, thought Thea. What was it about people who laughed at their own jokes that made them so intensely irritating? She had hardly stepped on to the terrace and already her teeth were on edge. No wonder Rhys had been so keen to find a way to avoid them. Thank God she had listened to him, instead of insisting on finding out what the Paines were like for herself. It would have been too late then.

'Thea Martindale,' she replied with a polite smile, extracting her hand with some difficulty from Nick's clammy clasp, an extra incentive, if one was needed, to make her pretend engagement to Rhys as convincing as possible.

'But not for much longer, I gather?' Nick ogled her cleavage. 'That Rhys is a dark horse! He never breathed a word about you, and now Kate tells me that you're getting married!'

'That's right.' Thea stepped back before Nick actually fell down her cleavage and took Rhys's hand, which was warm and strong and dry and infinitely comforting. A contrast to Nick's, in fact. 'We're so happy.'

'We must toast your health.'

Thea sensed that Kate was not overly pleased by this unexpected development. She might be in favour of Rhys getting married again, but only to someone of her choice, and definitely not anyone related to subversive influences around the pool!

Still, to do her justice, she wasn't going to say it outright, however much she might want to.

'Nick, get the wine.' Kate didn't quite snap her fingers, but she might as well have done the way Nick leapt to obey.

Thea sat down next to Rhys on a bench and wondered whether Lynda was like her friend. She couldn't imagine Rhys responding well to a barked order.

'Well, here we here!' Kate waited until Nick had poured out four glasses, and lifted her glass. 'Congratulations!' she said, but smiled in a way that made Thea a little nervous. 'You must tell us everything!'

Ah, the interrogation. 'Have you known each other long?'

'Not long, no,' said Rhys, and Thea quickly trotted out the dinner party story to explain how they had met.

Kate frowned slightly. 'I thought Lynda said that you'd been abroad so long you didn't know anyone in London?' she said. 'She was quite worried about you when you came back.'

'I know these friends who had the dinner party,' said Rhys coolly, 'and of course I know Thea now.'

He rested his hand on the back of the bench and his thumb caressed the nape of Thea's neck, sending delicious shivers down her spine. She would never be able to concentrate if he kept on doing that.

'I'm surprised you're engaged already,' said Kate, disapproving. 'You can hardly know each other.'

'I knew the moment I saw Thea that she was the woman I wanted to spend the rest of my life with,' said Rhys, sounding so convincing that Thea lost track of her breathing for a moment.

And then he lowered his arm from her neck to take her hand instead, lifting it to his mouth and kissing it. 'You don't need time to fall in love, do you, Thea?'

She shook her head dumbly, her fingers curling hopelessly around his. 'No,' she said, but her voice came out as barely more than a croak.

'Have you told Lynda yet?' asked Kate, which Thea thought was a bit tactless of her. On the other hand, if it was her friend, she would probably want to know too.

'No,' said Rhys evenly, 'but I will, of course, when we get home. We only got engaged today,' he explained. 'It was a spur of the moment thing, but it feels absolutely right.'

'I see.' Kate looked between them, an oddly calculating look, and it occurred to Thea that she might not be as convinced by their story as they had hoped.

'We're getting married at Christmas,' she put in, feeling that a few corroborating details were required.

'Christmas is only four months away!'

'I know, but I've always wanted a Christmas wedding,' said Thea disingenuously. 'We'll have plenty of time to organise things. We don't want anything too elaborate, do we, darling?'

She took the opportunity to snuggle closer to Rhys and gaze winsomely up at him. 'Just family and close friends, and of course Sophie and Clara as bridesmaids. It'll be lovely,' she finished with a misty look. She was tempted to heave a sigh as well, but didn't want to overdo it.

'Sure you know what you're doing, Rhys?' On his way round with the bottle to top up their glasses, Nick gave him a nudge that nearly made Rhys spill his wine. 'I'd make the most of my freedom, if I were you! You haven't been back from the desert long, and there are lots of nice girls out there.'

'I don't want a nice girl,' said Rhys. 'I want this one.'

Laying a warm palm against her far cheek, he turned her head until she was facing him, and very gently he touched his mouth to hers. It was a brief, sweet touch, over much too soon.

Rhys drew back and for a moment they just looked at each other, before leaning towards each other once more, their lips moving as if they had a will of their own, catching and clinging with a kind of desperation. Nick and Kate were forgotten as they kissed, and that strange glow that had been simmering inside Thea since she had seen Rhys smile for the first time ignited with a whoosh, spilling fire along her veins.

The feeling was so intense that when Rhys broke the kiss once more, it was all she could do not to grab him back to her and make him kiss her again. But he was sitting back, saying something to Nick and apparently carrying on the conversation as if nothing had happened at all.

How did he *do* that? It was taking everything Thea had not to slide off the bench into a puddle on the terrace. She was quivering inside and out, and her pulse was booming so loudly in her ears that she could hardly hear a thing. It was only when she realised that the other three were looking at her curiously that she realised that she was being asked a question.

'Sorry?' she said huskily.

'I was just asking what you do.' Kate's perfectly shaped brows rose slightly, as if in faint surprise that Rhys should have chosen someone apparently incapable of following a simple conversation.

'Oh...I...er...I'm a secretary.' Thank God Kate hadn't asked her anything more difficult.

'A *secretary*?' Kate echoed as if she had said something extraordinary.

'Yes. Well, a PA, really. In a PR firm.'

'Oh.' Kate was clearly deeply unimpressed. She glanced at Rhys. 'Thea is obviously very different from Lynda!'

'She is indeed.' Rhys put his arm around Thea once more and met Kate's eyes squarely. 'Very different.'

Kate didn't seem to think that the point had been adequately made. 'Lynda was a lawyer when I first met her,' she told Thea. 'She's gone on to start up her own business. She's a marvel, isn't she, Rhys?'

'She certainly seems to have become very successful,' he said, non-committal.

'And you're just a secretary.' Kate sighed, turning back to Thea. 'It *does* seem a waste,' she lamented. 'I mean, you seem quite intelligent, Thea. Haven't you ever thought about a proper career?'

'What sort of thing did you have in mind?' asked Thea, who was finding it hard to concentrate on what Kate was saying. She was burningly conscious of the strong arm around her and longing to turn her face into Rhys's shoulder, to burrow into him.

'Oh, you know,' said Kate. 'A solicitor, for instance.'

'I can't quite see myself as a lawyer,' Thea confessed. 'I'm not very ambitious, I'm afraid. To be honest, I'd be just as happy having children and looking after a home. We're planning a big family, aren't we?' she added to Rhys.

'At least four children,' he agreed solemnly.

Kate pursed her lips. 'What about Sophie?'

'Sophie will be part of the family,' said Thea, meeting Kate's disapproving eyes, her own very clear and direct. 'Of course she will.'

Thea and Clara had breakfast on their own terrace the next morning. They had their own coffee, their own yoghurt and honey, their own peaches, but somehow none of it tasted quite as good as it had the day before.

It wasn't the same without Rhys and Sophie. They had agreed the night before that they shouldn't feel obliged to spend all their time together and that was good, naturally, but it was as if the light was less bright this morning, her appetite less sharp, the sounds and scents drifting in the air less intense.

Clara felt it too. 'Can I go and see if Sophie wants to play?' she asked as soon as she had finished her peach.

'OK. I'll be down in a minute,' said Thea and then, as Clara skipped off, she added, 'Oh, if you see Rhys, tell him I'm going to spend the day by the pool, so I'll keep an eye on Sophie if he wants to go out.'

There, that sounded perfectly natural, as if she didn't really care whether she saw him or not. As if she hadn't spent hours lying in bed last night remembering those kisses and reliving the way they had sat talking on the terrace after supper, listening to the cicadas rasping frantically in the dark.

They hadn't got round to cooking a proper meal. Rhys had barbecued some lamb and Thea made a salad, and afterwards the girls disappeared. Sitting side by side, feet up on the low terrace wall, Thea hadn't been touching Rhys, but she'd been agonisingly aware of him, of his lean, solid strength, of the line of his jaw, of the gleam of his eyes when he'd turned his head to look at her.

He was nothing special, she kept telling herself. There was no reason for her pulse to kick whenever he smiled. She was just on the rebound from Harry.

Yes, that was it. Harry's departure to think about things had left an emptiness in her life and now she was subconsciously casting around for someone to fill it. Rhys simply happened to be the first man who had swum into her orbit.

Of course, there had been Neil at work, who had asked her out several times so, strictly speaking, Rhys wasn't quite the first…or the second, now she came to think of it. She'd forgotten about Andy from the flat downstairs, who was always offering to sort out her CD player for her. Both would have been ideal rebound material, now Thea came to think of it. She hadn't felt like this about either of them.

Thea had picked a piece of mint from the pot on the terrace and rubbed it between her fingers, enjoying the smell even as she tried to justify her unaccountable attraction for Rhys to herself.

So she wasn't desperate… Well, that was a good thing, wasn't it? Maybe it was more a question of timing? She was alone and on holiday and the normal conventions didn't apply. It was the classic scenario for a holiday romance, in fact. You fancied yourself attracted to someone quite different but you weren't committed to anything, because you both knew that at the end of two weeks you'd say goodbye, so you could relax and have your confidence boosted by having a good time with no strings attached.

It made sense, Thea had thought, lifting the mint to her nose and feeling better. Of course, with Clara and Sophie around, there was no question of embarking on a fling with Rhys, but at least now she could explain her own peculiar reactions to herself.

So now she could relax and stop feeling guilty and confused about the way Rhys made her feel, right?

Thea had studied Rhys under her lashes. He was pointing at the velvet blue sky, and telling her about the stars in the desert, his face animated, and she had felt something shift deep inside her as she'd watched him.

Yeah, right.

Now Thea gazed down at the pool, glinting in the bright morning sunshine. Clara and Sophie were already there, sitting on the edge and dangling their feet in the turquoise water, their heads bent together as if they hadn't spent most of the night before talking.

She would see Rhys again today. He might come to the pool and, even if he didn't, she owed him dinner. Thea smiled and stretched luxuriously. The day stretched lazily ahead of her, with absolutely nothing to do but try and convince him that she wasn't quite such an idiot as Kate had made her appear. She might not be a dynamic businesswoman, but she too could be cool, calm and in control.

Today was the perfect opportunity to christen her new swimsuit. Sadly, bikinis and her figure didn't go together, but she had found a one-piece that was really quite flattering if she held her tummy in and lay very still.

When Rhys found her, she was draped decoratively over one of the sun loungers by the pool, one leg oh-so-casually bent to avoid splayed thigh syndrome, and apparently absorbed in the book Nell had lent her. According to the cover, it had been short-listed for several literary prizes, and Nell had raved about it.

'You *must* read it, Thea,' she had insisted, and Thea had judged it easier to pack it rather than protest that she would be much happier with a rollicking blockbuster. Now she was pleased that she had. The book lent her a certain *gravitas*, she felt, and she had secreted a couple of glossy magazines under the lounger for later when no one was looking.

'Good morning, Thea.'

Thea lifted her sunglasses and squinted up at Rhys. 'Oh…hi.'

Her voice was a bit squeaky, but otherwise she didn't think it sounded too bad for someone whose heart had just done an elaborate series of somersaults. The way it did when you were cool and calm and in control.

He sat down on the edge of the lounger beside her. 'You look very comfortable.'

'I am. I'm planning a lazy day to recover from all yesterday's excitements.'

Rhys twisted his head round to read the title of her book. 'Are you enjoying that?'

'It's marvellous,' said Thea, who hadn't a clue what was going on, and had been stuck on the same page for at least half an hour. She didn't understand why books like this had to be such hard work, but she was glad now that she hadn't succumbed to the lure of *Marie Claire*. It wouldn't do Rhys any harm to see that even secretaries could engage in literary discussion before lunch.

'Have you read it?' she asked him, mentally crossing her fingers, and hoping devoutly that he hadn't. If he wanted an in-depth analysis of the plot, she'd be sunk. Fortunately, he was a scientist. Chances were that he didn't go in for any arty-farty stuff like this.

But Rhys was nodding. Really, why couldn't he conform to his stereotype? Thea wondered crossly.

'I thought it was rubbish,' he said. 'You're obviously more intellectual than I am. I didn't understand a word of it.'

Phew! Thea beamed at him in relief. 'Well, I've only just started it,' she said, settling her glasses back on her nose. 'I might persevere with it for a while. I haven't got anything else to do all day, so if you wanted to go off and do anything on your own, here's your chance.'

Translation: here's your chance to say that you'd rather stay here with me.

'Are you sure? Clara did mention that you were happy to keep an eye on Sophie, and there is a walk that I've wanted to do for some time. It's too long for Sophie, though, so this might be an opportunity.'

So much for the seductive effect of her swimsuit, Thea thought glumly. He couldn't wait to get away. Perhaps she had intimidated him by seeming too intellectual. That would be a first, anyway!

'I feel a bit guilty, though,' Rhys was confiding. 'I should really be spending time with Sophie, not leaping at the chance to go off on my own.'

He sounded so unsure of himself that Thea put the book aside and sat up to reassure him. 'You have been spending time with her,' she pointed out. 'What you should be doing is letting her have a good time, and she is. Look at her now.'

Rhys followed her gaze to where Sophie and Clara were hanging off a lilo and chatting animatedly as they drifted around the pool.

'She's transformed,' he agreed. 'Normally she converses in monosyllables, but she was positively chatty at breakfast this morning. I don't know how to thank you,' he added, and the expression in his eyes made Thea's throat tighten.

'It's nothing to do with me,' she told him. 'Thank Clara.'

He looked back at the pool. 'I will,' he said.

CHAPTER FIVE

THERE was a tiny silence, and then Rhys got to his feet. 'Will you be all right having Sophie for the day?' he asked, looking down at Thea, who put on a martyred air.

'It'll be a terrible struggle lying here in the sun all day—' she sighed '—but I expect I'll cope somehow.'

Rhys laughed and got up from the lounger. Walking over to the pool, he hunkered down to have a word with Sophie. Behind her glasses, Thea admired his back view. Not many British men could carry off shorts that well, but Rhys had just the right lean, brown, I-spend-my-life-squinting-at-far-horizons look about him.

Clara was splashing over to talk to Rhys, hauling herself up to fold her arms on the edge of the pool and dangle there while she carried on an animated conversation with him, punctuated by giggles from both girls.

'What was all that about?' Thea asked as Rhys straightened and headed back to her with an odd expression on his face.

He didn't answer directly, nodding down at her lounger instead. 'May I?'

'Sure.' A little surprised, Thea shifted her legs over so that he could sit down, and put down her book again.

It felt very intimate to have him so close. He was sitting facing her, so that her arm was very close to his bare knees and her legs were almost touching his thigh.

Her heart had started that slow, painful thumping that interfered with her breathing again, and she was very glad of the sunglasses that hid most of her expression, which otherwise would be a dead giveaway. Without them she might as well have *kiss me, kiss me!* emblazoned on her forehead.

That was it, Thea, cool, calm and in control!

She swallowed hard. 'If Clara was putting in a plea for an ice-cream run later, we've got a whole tub in the freezer.'

'No,' said Rhys slowly, 'it was a little bit more delicate than that.'

'What?' God, it was hard to concentrate when her entire body was jangling with the awareness of how close his hand was and how easily he could smooth it along her thigh.

'She was pointing out that Kate was making a poor job of pretending not to watch us from her terrace.'

Thea lowered her sunglasses and glanced surreptitiously over the rim to the Paines' terrace, where Kate was indeed sitting at the table where she had a perfect view of what was going on at the pool.

'You can hardly go over and tell her to stop looking,' she pointed out. 'It's her terrace. She can sit where she wants, surely.'

'That's not quite what Clara had in mind.' There was a thread of amusement in Rhys's voice that made Thea look at him suspiciously.

'Oh? What exactly *does* Clara have in mind?'

'She thinks it would be a very good idea if I kissed you goodbye.'

'Oh...' The breath leaked out of Thea's lungs and she couldn't get it back, especially when Rhys smiled quizzically.

'She seems to be taking the whole pretence very seriously!'

That was because Clara was determined to turn pretence into reality, thought Thea, but she had better not tell Rhys that.

'I know.' Her answering smile was decidedly nervous. 'I think it's something to do with having a vivid imagination. I wonder where she gets her ideas from sometimes. Television, I suppose. Nell's always complaining that she watches too many soaps.'

Oh, great, now she was babbling. Rhys was talking about kissing her, and all she could do was witter on about television. Thea took a deep breath and made herself shut up.

'So what do you think?' asked Rhys after a tiny pause, presumably to check that she wasn't going to start drivelling on about something else.

'Um…about a goodbye kiss?'

'Yes.'

'Well, I…I suppose it wouldn't do any harm. I wasn't sure Kate was entirely convinced last night.'

'That's what I thought.'

Another silence, longer this time. Long enough for Thea to wonder if he could actually hear her pulse booming.

'We'd better make it look good, then,' said Rhys.

'Might as well.'

Thea was mortified to hear her voice disappear into a squeak. 'Let's give it a go,' she tried again. That was better—casual, relaxed, no big deal. This wasn't about getting involved, it was about feeling good and keeping it light.

The trouble was that it didn't feel light. It felt dangerous and disturbing as Rhys leant forward, very slowly. She could change her mind if she wanted to, but now his hand was on her thigh, warm and firm, and her heart was slamming against her ribs, making it hard to breathe and even harder to think.

Deep inside her, anticipation churned, quivering out to the ends of her fingers and the tips of her toes, but all at once he was hesitating. Don't say he had changed *his* mind?

It was too much for Thea. As if of their own accord, her

hands lifted to his arms, sliding upwards to wind around his neck and pull him towards her, or maybe she didn't need to pull him, maybe Rhys was closing the distance between them anyway. But, however it happened, they were kissing at last and the release from all that anticipation was so intense that Thea gasped in spite of herself.

His lips were so tantalising, the hand smoothing over her thigh so warm and so sure, it was enough to make a girl forget what she was doing. Thea certainly forgot to think, forgot anything but the sheer pleasure of kissing and being kissed, of being able to touch him at last, run her hands over his back and savour the feel of his hard, strong body.

Fortunately, Rhys had himself under better control, or who knew where it would have ended? He pulled back slightly to look down into her face with an expression Thea couldn't quite identify.

'Very good, Thea,' he said.

'Just getting into my part,' she said a little unsteadily, and Rhys smiled.

'You're a natural.' Reaching out, he stroked a finger down her cheek in a gesture so tender it dried the breath in Thea's throat, and then got to his feet. 'I'd better go. See you later, girls,' he called as he headed off to his villa.

'Bye!' they yelled, as if nothing unusual had happened at all and it was perfectly normal for him to kiss Thea and then get up and walk off.

Thea was just grateful that she was already lying down and didn't have to try and walk anywhere. She was quite sure that her legs wouldn't have held her if she had been upright. It was bad enough trying to behave normally as it was, with this shaky feeling and that odd jittery sensation under her skin.

So much for calm, cool and in control.

Across the pool, she saw Clara wave and make a cheeky

thumbs-up sign. Really, that girl was too clever for her own good, thought Thea, shaking her head back at her. She would have a word with Nell about her when she got home.

Picking up her book with hands that trembled slightly, she tried to read, but the words were dancing in front of her eyes. How could she be expected to concentrate on impenetrable prose when her lips were still tingling from that kiss, when her thigh was burning where he had touched her?

Her whole body was pulsating. This was ridiculous, Thea scolded herself. It was only a kiss. She was completely overreacting, as usual. Hadn't she decided last night that she was just suffering the symptoms of a holiday romance, and that there wouldn't be a problem if she could keep things light-hearted?

Thea laid her fingers against her skin where his hand had been, and squirmed at the memory. For a light-hearted romance, it sure felt very intense. That kiss had been wonderful—warm and exciting and, if she was honest with herself, much, much too short.

And just a pretence. Don't forget that bit, Thea.

To hell with this stupid book! She had been staring at the same page for what felt like days. Tossing it aside, Thea leant under her lounger and pulled out one of her magazines instead. She was never going to stop thinking about Rhys and that kiss when she didn't understand half the words on the page. What she needed now was a distraction. The new look on the catwalk, the latest mascara, a little celebrity gossip and she would soon regain her equilibrium.

As it turned out, this was an excellent idea, and Thea was absorbed in the marital difficulties of two of Hollywood's biggest stars when a shadow fell over her. Kate was standing there, perfect eyebrows oh-so-slightly lifted as she checked out Thea's reading matter.

Oops, how not to impress Kate! Kate was clearly much

too clever to waste her time with magazines, let alone gossip. Quickly, Thea flicked over the page. She could at least pretend to be stuck into one of the more serious articles about women's issues, but found herself instead staring at a headline trumpeting 'Sex that makes *you* look slim and *him* feel huge!'

Perhaps she should show Kate the article and they could have a girlish giggle together about it? Or perhaps not, Thea decided, glancing at the immaculate Kate with her air of efficient sophistication. Kate just wasn't the type for a giggle.

With an inward sigh, Thea closed the magazine altogether, but made a mental note to go back to it. She was always up for a laugh, and she would try anything that promised to make her look slimmer without the hassle of dieting or going to the gym.

'Do you mind if I join you?' asked Kate, dropping her bag on to the next lounger without waiting for Thea's answer.

Well, what could she say? 'Of course not.'

Kate was wearing a sarong, just as Thea had the day before, but where Thea's had kept slipping and falling apart, Kate's was elegantly and securely tied. Now she was unwrapping it to reveal a perfectly tanned and toned body in the kind of bikini Thea could only ever dream of wearing.

The kind of bikini that might have been specifically designed to make Thea feel fat and blowsy. Give her some whiskers and a couple of tusks, and she'd be a dead ringer for those great, blubbery walruses you saw floundering around the beach in their rolls of fat on nature programmes, she thought glumly. It was amazing to think that she had been quite pleased with her appearance earlier.

She eyed Kate with resentment. Look at her, not even having to hold her stomach in as she sat and oiled herself complacently, perfectly aware of the contrast her trim, taut figure made with Thea's voluptuous curves.

If only her mother hadn't brought her up to be so polite, Thea could have moved to the other side of the pool, or preferably taken that tube of suntan lotion and squeezed it all over Kate's shiny blonde hair. As it was, she was stuck feeling fat and inadequate and making polite conversation.

'Where are Damian and Hugo today? I was expecting to see them in the pool with the girls.'

'Nick's taken them to the archaeological museum in Heraklion.'

'Gosh, won't they be bored?'

'Certainly not,' said Kate crisply. 'They're both very interested in history. Hugo's a member of the local archaeological society. He's got his own trowel.'

Thea laughed until she realised that Kate was not being humorous. Should have known better, she thought with an inward sigh.

'It's so important that children learn something about the culture of the country they're staying in,' Kate was saying. 'I'm sure you agree.'

'Oh, yes, absolutely,' said Thea, who couldn't be bothered to argue. She amused herself instead imagining Clara's reaction if she suggested that she might like to forgo a day in the pool to go to a museum.

Kate settled herself on the lounger. 'Is Rhys not joining you today?' she asked delicately, as if she hadn't been watching him say goodbye to Thea from her observation post on her terrace.

'He's gone for a hike,' said Thea, conscious of a warm little thrill down her spine at the mere memory of how he had said goodbye.

'I think it's marvellous of you not to mind him going off on his own on your first day here.'

Thea looked at her sharply. It was hard to tell whether Kate took her seriously or not. In the end, she managed a careless shrug.

'I'm feeling lazy, and you know Rhys. He's not one for sitting around.' At least, she didn't know whether he was or not, but he hadn't struck her as a man who would be very interested in sunbathing, and it was a fairly safe bet that Kate wouldn't know either.

To her surprise, Kate took this very seriously. 'Yes, I gathered from Lynda that Rhys has problems relaxing.'

'I didn't say that,' said Thea, unaccountably annoyed. 'Just that he didn't like sunbathing.'

'Nick and I think it's marvellous Rhys has met someone at last,' Kate confided earnestly. 'I know Lynda was quite worried about him for a while. She was afraid he was never going to get over her leaving. She's often said to me that she knows how much damage she did to him, and she feels very guilty about that.' Kate leant towards Thea. 'Apparently he was absolutely devastated when she left. He absolutely adored her.'

'Really?' said Thea discouragingly.

She didn't want to hear about Rhys from Kate, and she certainly didn't want to hear about how much he loved Lynda, and frankly she thought it was monumentally tactless for Kate to assume that she would. As far as she knew they really were engaged, after all.

Picking up her magazine, she opened it once more in the hope that Kate would take the hint, but the woman clearly had the hide of a rhinoceros.

'No, Lynda says that he never really seemed to accept that she had left for good,' Kate went on in the same concerned tone. 'She really wanted him to be able to move on, but of course the first thing he did when he got back to

London was to buy a house just around the corner from Lynda.'

'It's possible that he wanted to be near his daughter, not Lynda,' Thea was provoked into saying, and Kate nodded as if she had made an interesting point. Wrong, but interesting.

'That's what Lynda hoped, but I think she was secretly afraid that he was trying to be part of her life again. It wouldn't be surprising if he did. Lynda is a beautiful woman and very talented. It's an old-fashioned word,' she went on, oblivious to Thea's unreceptive attitude, 'but I always think that Lynda is really *accomplished*.'

'Really?' said Thea coldly again.

The chill in her voice was lost on Kate, who was still burbling on about Rhys's ex-wife. 'Did you know that she set up her own business selling alternative therapies? They're absolutely marvellous and we all swear by them!'

Kate's cold blue eyes swept over Thea. 'I'm sure she'd have something that could help you lose weight,' she added as an aside and then swept on while Thea was still open-mouthed at her rudeness and spluttering for a retort.

'She only started it up two or three years ago, but the turnover last year was phenomenal, apparently.' Kate shook her head admiringly. 'She really is a fantastic person—very astute, extremely successful, amazingly insightful... I can't think of anything she isn't good at, in fact. Really, she could make a success of anything she put her mind to.'

Pity she didn't try making her marriage work in that case, thought Thea, fed up with hearing about how marvellous Lynda was. If she was that clever, why were Rhys and Sophie out here on their own?

'Well, perhaps hearing about our engagement will put Lynda's mind at rest about Rhys,' she said acidly, but sarcasm was evidently wasted on Kate too.

'Oh, yes, I'm sure it will,' she agreed. 'She'll be delighted.'

Flexing her toes, she smiled patronisingly at Thea. 'Here's me chatting on, and you want to get back to your magazine. I should have brought something down to read myself.'

'Here, you can borrow this if you want.' Thea fished Nell's book out from under her lounger and offered it to Kate.

Kate's face changed as she saw it. 'Oh, you've got *that*? I hear it's marvellous.' It was obvious that she hadn't expected Thea to be able to read books without pictures in them. 'Lynda's read it twice and told me I should read it. She said it was one of the best books she'd ever read.'

'I think it's rubbish.' Thea smiled sweetly as she quoted Rhys. 'You're welcome to it.'

Defiantly, Thea went back to her celebrity scandal, too cross with Kate by then to care what she thought of her. The other woman had no business gossiping about Rhys's affairs anyway, and that Lynda seemed to take an unhealthy interest in her ex-husband's affairs.

Thea wished Kate hadn't told her anything. Especially, she wished she didn't know how heartbroken Rhys had been when Lynda left. He must have loved her a lot—but then, he seemed to Thea the kind of man who wouldn't get married unless he did love deeply.

Thea turned a page morosely. She couldn't get into the article any more. She had been enjoying it, too, she thought, shooting Kate a resentful glance. It was all her fault.

Be honest, Thea told herself. You don't like the idea of Rhys being in love with anyone else at all.

It shouldn't matter to her one way or another. It wasn't as if there was anything between them. Their relationship was entirely imaginary, and if Rhys was as obsessed with his ex-wife as Kate had implied, it would be better if it stayed that way. Thea had had enough of playing second fiddle to the ex with Harry, and if there was one thing she had learnt, it was that you couldn't compete with emotional history.

Time to stop flirting with the idea of a holiday romance, she decided a little sadly. That would be the sensible thing to do.

It was late afternoon before Rhys returned. Thea was doing her nails in the shade by the pool, and when she saw him she quickly whipped the emery board and polish into her bag. She might have decided not to get too involved, but she didn't want him thinking that she was hopelessly superficial either, even if she was.

She would just have to stick with the natural look for the next two weeks. Lynda was probably far too busy being successful and talented and insightful to do her nails, unless of course she had someone to do them for her. Thea's eyes narrowed at the thought. She sounded like the kind of person who had a weekly manicure. Thea was beginning to dislike her intensely on principle.

Rhys lifted a hand as he saw her, and Thea's heart did a silly little lift of its own in return. Stop it, she told herself firmly, and forced herself to stop smiling quite so widely.

He was on his way round the pool to join her when Sophie called out to him. 'Dad! Dad! Look at this!'

Even from the other side of the pool, Thea could see the blaze of expression in Rhys's face as his daughter demanded his attention, and he stopped to watch her perform a handstand, legs flailing wildly above water for a moment before she surfaced, gasping and spluttering and looking extremely pleased with herself.

'Did you see?'

'I certainly did. I'm impressed! When did you learn to do that?'

'Today. Clara taught me.'

'Have you had a good time, then?'

'Yes.'

Sophie's burst of volubility was evidently over. She went back to practising handstands, and Rhys carried on round the pool to Thea, trying—unsuccessfully—to disguise how moved he was by the brief, tentative connection he was making with his daughter at last.

He was looking hot and dusty after walking all day, but his smile as he sat down beside Thea illuminated his whole face, and she wouldn't have been able to prevent herself smiling back at him even if she had wanted to.

'How was your walk?'

'Hot,' said Rhys, swinging his legs up on to the lounger and leaning back with the contented sigh of someone who had put in a hard day's physical exertion and is entitled to put his feet up. 'Good, though.'

'Lots of interesting rocks, then?'

It was easier to tease him than to think about how much she wanted to be able to go over and sit next to him, the way he had sat next to her that morning, and press her lips to the pulse in his neck below his ear. To kiss her way up his throat and along his jaw to his mouth, to kiss him hello the way they had kissed goodbye earlier.

'Fascinating,' said Rhys. 'I found some great samples of igneous rock. I brought them back to show Sophie and Clara, in fact. I'm sure they'd be interested to know about Crete's ancient volcanic landscape, so I've prepared a short talk. I thought perhaps after supper?'

It took a little while for his words to filter through, and there was a short delay before Thea found herself jolted out of her fantasy of kissing him. He had planned *what*?

'Er, are you sure that's a good idea?'

'Why not?' Rhys met her startled gaze blandly until he gave in and grinned at her expression. 'Don't worry, I'm joking! I wouldn't do that to them, even if they didn't have the attention spans of gnats.'

Lying back, he put his hands behind his head. 'Have they been in that pool all day? They must be completely water-logged!'

'Pretty much,' said Thea, cross with herself for falling for his teasing, but glad in a way that he had made her laugh. It had released some of the tension of meeting for the first time since that kiss. 'I made them get out for a couple of hours in the middle of the day, and we had lunch in the shade, but they're real water babies, both of them.'

'I didn't realise Sophie liked swimming so much.' Rhys sounded a little sad, as if it was something he should have known about his daughter. 'She didn't spend so much time in the pool last week.'

'I don't think it's swimming so much as splashing around and chatting,' said Thea reassuringly. 'She just needed a friend to do that with, and if there's one thing Clara can do, it's chat!

'Tell me about your walk, anyway,' she went on, trying to keep the conversation on safe ground. 'What was there to see apart from those extremely interesting rocks you mentioned?'

'I went up into the White Mountains and followed a gorge down again. It's wild country, but beautiful.' He glanced at her. 'You should come with me some time. I'm sure you would like it.'

Thea, whose plans hadn't included venturing any further than the poolside, thought about spending the day on a wild hillside, alone with the heat and the light and the drifting scent of wild herbs.

And Rhys.

Something turned over inside her at the thought. 'Maybe I will.'

Her eyes met his then slid away, and there was a pause. 'Well…I'm glad you had a good time.'

'Yes, I did,' said Rhys slowly, 'but, funnily enough, not as much as I expected to.'

'Oh?'

He looked at her, and even in the shade his eyes seemed very light and clear in his brown face. 'It sounds strange, but I missed you.'

'Oh,' she said again, but this time her throat was so tight that she could barely manage a croak. So much for dispersing the tension. The memory of how they had kissed was back with a vengeance, resonating in the air, drumming along Thea's veins, so vivid that Thea couldn't believe that Rhys couldn't feel it too.

But he was looking at the pool, frowning slightly as his gaze rested on Sophie and Clara. 'And the girls,' he was saying. 'It's odd. Most of my work is very solitary, so I'm used to spending a lot of time on my own, and it's never been a problem before, but today I found myself thinking about you all, wondering what you were doing…wishing I was with you.'

He looked back to meet Thea's eyes. 'In the end I took the quicker route back.'

Thea swallowed and reminded herself fiercely about not getting too involved. 'I missed you too,' she said as lightly as she could. 'I had to deal with Kate on my own!'

'Oh, dear.' Rhys grimaced sympathetically. 'Did it go all right?'

'I didn't have to talk much, which was something. She was very keen to tell me how pleased Lynda will be to hear about our engagement. Apparently she has been very worried by you being on your own.'

He made a sound somewhere between a snort and a sniff. 'Kate's quite an authority on my relationship with Lynda, isn't she?' he said sardonically. 'She spent most of the first week telling me how worried Lynda was about my failings as a father.

'I don't spend enough time with Sophie, it turns out, and when I do see her I give her the wrong things to eat, read her the wrong stories, buy her the wrong presents, and let her watch the wrong programmes on television. Basically, I'm the wrong father,' he went on, unable to keep the bitterness from his voice. 'Kate thinks I'm compounding the error of being an absent father by trying too hard, which is probably true.'

'Maybe,' said Thea, 'but it's not up to Kate to tell you what kind of father you should and shouldn't be.'

'Oh, she wasn't saying anything I haven't heard plenty of times from Lynda.' He sighed. 'I missed a whole chunk of Sophie's childhood. I don't know her the way Lynda does.'

'No, but then I gather it wasn't you who left and took Sophie away so you couldn't see her regularly,' Thea pointed out calmly.

'No,' he admitted, 'but I still feel guilty about the missing years. Lynda was right about one thing. I should have been prepared to give up my job in North Africa. Effectively, I put my career ahead of my daughter.'

Having a wife laying down ultimatums about choosing between them couldn't have helped either, thought Thea.

'Could you have got a job in the UK?'

'Not then—or not doing the same thing, anyway.' He lifted his shoulders. 'The fact is that I enjoy my job, and I was involved in what seemed to me an important project. I didn't feel that I could just give up on it—but that doesn't justify the fact that I didn't,' he added quickly.

'It's a good reason for Lynda coming to a compromise, though,' said Thea, and he rubbed his face wearily, his smile a little twisted.

'Lynda doesn't do compromise. She's a very strong-minded woman, and once she decides what's going to happen, that's what happens. She didn't want to live in North Africa any longer, so she left. It was an obvious decision from her point of view.'

He sounded frustrated rather than heartbroken by Lynda's behaviour, Thea couldn't help noticing. Maybe he hadn't been quite as devastated as Kate had made out. On the other hand, it *was* five years ago. He might have got over it, no matter what Lynda wanted to think.

'Lynda wanted a divorce so she could start afresh,' said Rhys, 'and, although I thought about moving back to London the next year so I could share in looking after Sophie, I found myself in the absurd situation where the only way I could pay Lynda the maintenance she wanted while she was setting up her business was to continue working overseas.

'It was only this year that Lynda's business took off and I found a position at a comparable salary so that I can live in London and support Sophie, but now I'm afraid it may be too late. I've missed so much time with her.'

'I don't think you should worry too much,' said Thea comfortingly. 'You haven't been back long and Sophie will come round in time. You saw what she was like just now.'

He wouldn't look at her. 'She's just enjoying herself because Clara is there.'

'Partly, but she was also looking for you. She's been waiting for you to come back so that she could show you that she had learnt how to do handstands. It's the little things that are important,' she told him. 'You can't expect her to turn into a daddy's girl overnight.'

'No, I suppose not.' Rhys sighed in spite of himself.

'Kate was right about one thing, at least,' said Thea gently. 'You *don't* need to try so hard with Sophie. You're her father and she loves you because of that. She just doesn't know how to show it at the moment. All you need to do is be yourself, and let her know that you love her, however sulky and badly behaved she is.'

His face relaxed into a smile. 'You sound very wise for someone who doesn't actually have any children.'

'Oh, I'm an experienced armchair parent,' she told him with a sigh. 'I'm an armchair divorcee too, come to that. You wouldn't believe the crises I've been through with my sister and friends. I've seen it all before!'

'Well, I wish you'd been here at the beginning of the holiday,' said Rhys. 'You might have saved me a difficult week.'

'It's never too late for advice from Auntie Thea,' she said smugly. 'And if I *had* been here last week, we'd have all arrived together and we would have been in Kate and Nick's clutches before we had a chance to concoct some elaborate pretence to get out of seeing them, so you could say it's all worked out for the best!'

He looked at her, sitting comfortably on her lounger, her face glowing from a day in the sun and her hair tumbling in its habitual disorder to her shoulders. She had taken her sunglasses off in the shade, and her grey eyes were warm, the humorous mouth tilted in a smile.

'I'm beginning to think it has,' he said.

CHAPTER SIX

RHYS turned his gaze back to the White Mountains where he had been walking, leaving Thea to wonder just what he had meant by *that*.

'You're good with children.' He returned to the earlier part of the conversation after a while. 'Would you like children of your own?'

'Oh, yes.' Thea sighed a little. 'I'd really like that big family I told Kate and Nick we were going to have, but it takes two, doesn't it? There's not much chance of it at the moment, and I'm not getting any younger either.'

She brooded silently on the matter for a few moments. 'Sometimes I can't help thinking that it would all have been so much easier if my parents had just arranged a marriage for me!'

'Who would they have chosen for you?' asked Rhys, amused.

Absently, she picked a leaf off the geranium beside her and twirled it under her nose as she considered.

'My mother would have picked a man with a nice steady job,' she decided eventually, 'and my father wouldn't have cared as long as he played cricket, so I'd have ended up with a braying, bat-toting accountant in white flannels. I'd probably have been very happy,' she added glumly.

Rhys lifted disbelieving brows and Thea sighed again.

'Or not,' she conceded. 'Of course I don't just want children. I want to spend my life with someone I love and who loves me, someone who makes me laugh and likes me the way I am. Someone who'll stand by me in good times and in bad and won't mind if my hair's a mess or if I put on a couple of extra pounds. Is that too much to ask?'

'It's too much to expect without a lot of hard work,' said Rhys slowly. 'It's not too much to dream about and to aim for, no.'

'I'm always being told I'm a hopeless romantic,' said Thea, shredding the leaf between her fingers. 'Maybe I am. I decided a long time ago that I didn't want to compromise. I always thought that if you wanted everything to be perfect, you should hang out for the right man…but then you find what you think is the right man and it turns out not to be so perfect after all,' she finished, and let the last pieces of leaf drift sadly to the ground.

'I'm sure it will work out for you, Thea.' Rhys sat up and put his feet down so that he could face her. 'I can't imagine Harry won't realise how special you are. If I were in his shoes, I would be on the first plane out here I could find. He might even be on his way now.'

'He doesn't know I'm in Crete,' she said, not meeting his eyes, not wanting to see the kindness and the sincerity and the complete lack of jealousy there.

'Your sister knows, doesn't she?'

She nodded reluctantly. 'Nell doesn't like Harry, though.'

'If Harry could convince her that all he wanted to do was to make you happy, I bet she'd tell him the address anyway,' said Rhys stoutly. 'And if he had any sense he'd be out here now, on his knees and begging you to forgive him and take him back. I know I would.'

Thea smiled a little sadly. She couldn't imagine Harry on his knees to anyone—with the exception of Isabelle, of course.

'The thing is, Rhys, Harry's not like you.'

His face changed. 'No, I know. I'm sorry,' he said heavily. 'I didn't mean to sound as if I was criticising Harry.

He's the one you love, and sometimes there's no accounting for why we love the people who hurt us the most.'

Thea wondered if he was thinking about Lynda, who had hurt him so badly. He looked so solid, so sharply defined in the light. She couldn't imagine how anyone could leave him.

'No, there isn't,' she agreed.

'It doesn't stop you loving them, though, does it?'

She stared down at her hands, all at once desperate to remember how much she loved Harry, but all she could see was Rhys, his light eyes and his strong jaw and his cool, cool mouth.

'No,' she said, feeling suddenly uncertain, as if the ground was sliding away beneath her.

'Don't look like that, Thea.' Rhys put out an involuntary hand and took hold of hers. 'Don't give up hope. Maybe not knowing where you are will make Harry realise how much he misses you.'

That was what Thea had hoped when she left England, but now it was hard to imagine Harry even noticing that she was gone, hard to think about anything when Rhys's fingers were warm and strong and infinitely reassuring around hers.

'Maybe.'

'Look, why don't we do something all together tomorrow?' Rhys released her hand and sat back, and she tried not to mind too much.

'Sure.' It was definitely time to lighten the atmosphere, and she produced a bright smile. 'We could go to the archaeological museum like Hugo and Damian!'

He quirked an eyebrow at her. 'Are you going to try asking the girls if they'd like to do that, or will I have to do it?'

'I think I'll save my breath,' she admitted. 'Where were you thinking of?'

'Knossos. It's a bit of a drive from here, but then so is everything, and you can't come to Crete and not see one of the oldest and most important archaeological sites in the world.'

That was what Nell had said, too. Thea remembered her reply. 'Clara and I won't be visiting any boring old ruins, Nell. We'll be at the pool, or in the shops, and that's the limit of our cultural activities this holiday!'

Somehow the idea was a lot more appealing now that Rhys had suggested it. It would be good for the girls, Thea justified her change of mind to herself. They couldn't spend their whole time swimming and, if they weren't careful, Clara would end up monopolising Sophie and Rhys would hardly get to see his daughter at all. At least if they all went, he would get to spend some time with her.

And if it meant that Thea spent more time with him, well, that was just incidental.

'That sounds great,' she said. 'Always providing we can get the girls out of the pool!'

Rhys put the idea to them over supper. 'Thea's keen to go,' he finished, and Thea shot a warning look at Clara, who knew perfectly well that the words Thea and keen rarely coincided in the context of visiting ruins.

But Clara had evidently not forgotten her plans to distract Thea from Harry and throw her together with Rhys instead. When Rhys asked if she would like to go, she was enthusiastic and carried poor Sophie along in her wake, offering the ultimate accolade.

'Cool.'

In the event, Thea found Knossos much more interesting than she had expected. She couldn't make much sense of the labyrinth of stone steps and passageways, or the higgledy-piggledy collection of palace rooms and tiny storerooms, but there was no doubt that the place had an atmosphere. Just thinking about how old it was made her feel dizzy.

Although that might also have had something to do with the fact that Rhys was beside her, very real and very solid and somehow very immediate amongst the old, old stones.

He steered them away from the crowds of tourists to the quiet parts of the ruined palace in the shade of the pine trees, and he told the girls the story of Theseus and the Minotaur, complete with the kind of blood-curdling detail that had even the streetwise Clara saucer-eyed.

'You mean all that happened *here*?' she asked, and Sophie moved closer to her father.

'The monster's not here any more, is it?'

'No,' he said, putting an arm round her, and she let him draw her into the security of his body as he looked around him. 'They're all long gone.'

'Tell us another story,' she said.

It was very hot, even in the shade. Thea was acutely aware of her surroundings. The air was full of the scent of pine needles, and the cicadas sawed in a deafening chorus. She let Rhys's voice roll over her, feeling the warm, ancient stones beneath her palms, and it was as if all the confusion and the uncertainty and the anguish she had felt since Harry had left was draining slowly but steadily out of her until she was quite empty, and then she was filling up again with a feeling she didn't recognise, but which left her strangely restored.

Her gaze rested on Rhys. After Harry's passion and volatility, he was so restrained, so self-contained, so at ease with himself and where he was and what he was doing. What did it take to rouse a man like him to passion—apart from igneous rocks, of course?

Thea closed her eyes and let herself imagine what it would be like if there was no pretence. No Paines, no Lynda lurking in the background, no Clara watching everything with interest, not even Sophie. If there were just the two of them, and a wide white bed, like the ones in the villas.

Would he pull her down on to the crisp sheets? Would his hands be slow and tantalising, or hard and demanding? Would he smile against her skin, and oh! how would it feel to be able to touch him properly, to wrap her arms around him and let her lips drift over that taut brown body?

The image was so vivid, the desire clenching at the base of her spine so intense, that Thea took a sharp intake of breath and opened her eyes wide to find Rhys and the two girls staring at her in concern.

'Thea?' said Rhys cautiously. 'Are you OK?'

Dizzy and disorientated, struggling against the vertiginous tug of her fantasy, Thea blinked and swallowed hard. 'Yes…yes, I was just…'

Thinking about you kissing me. About kissing you back. About making love.

'…just…um…'

Her voice trailed off, her mind so full of imagining what it would have been like that she couldn't think of a single thing that she might legitimately have been thinking about. In the end, she gave up and she stared dumbly back at him and wondered what it was about someone so ordinary-looking that had her aching with desire like this.

Even Harry, the love of her life, had never made her feel *this*, this raw, physical longing. With Harry, it had almost been enough to be with him, and let the dazzle of his presence envelop her. She had never quite believed that she wasn't dreaming when she was with him.

She had never experienced this piercing desire before, this feeling that if she couldn't reach out and touch Rhys, if she couldn't press her lips to his throat, if he didn't pull her into his arms and lay her down in the dust and the pine needles right there and then she would simply shatter into a million pieces.

The feeling was so intense that Thea was shaken, almost scared. Her mouth was dry and she felt giddy, almost ill. She closed her eyes again in the desperate hope that when she opened them again everything would be back to normal.

'You don't look well,' said Rhys. 'It is quite hot. Perhaps we'd better just sit here in the shade for a while.'

That was it, the heat! She really *was* ill, thought Thea with relief, and she drew a deep breath.

'Do you feel faint? Put your head between your knees.'

It was easier to pretend than to explain, and anyway, she did feel dizzy. Thea dropped her head obediently and Rhys put a comforting hand on her back. She could feel the imprint of his palm burning through the thin material of her dress.

'Better?' he asked after a while.

Thea nodded and straightened slowly. 'I'm fine,' she said, although not with any degree of certainty. 'I don't know what came over me.'

'It's easy to underestimate the heat.'

After studying her with narrowed eyes, Rhys took his hand away at last. Thea wasn't sure whether to be relieved or disappointed. Not that it made much difference, in any case. She could still feel her back tingling where his palm had pressed into her. If she took her dress off, she was sure they would find a perfect imprint of his hand on her skin. They could probably take his fingerprints off it.

'Where are the girls?'

'They've found some kittens,' said Rhys in a resigned tone, and nodded over to a corner of the ruins where Clara and Sophie were crouched down and cooing 'oh...so cute' in a kind of harmony. 'The cats will be wild and probably covered in fleas, but try telling those two that!'

'Oh, well, the fleas won't stand much of a chance. Clara and Sophie spend so much time in the pool any flea will drown in no time.'

'Unless they pass them on to Hugo and Damian first. Then we'll be unpopular!'

Thea laughed and felt better. 'I'm sure no flea would dare to jump on to a Paine. Kate just wouldn't have it. The flea would be sent packing and told that kind of behaviour just wasn't acceptable!'

'You know, you're a very restful person to be with,' said Rhys unexpectedly.

'Me?' She was taken aback. 'Am I?'

'Most of the women I know—like Kate, or Lynda come to that—would be ordering the girls to leave the kittens alone. They'd be worrying about them picking up some nasty disease, and insisting that they did a complete tour of the site with the guide instead, and then organising lunch and fretting about what time we'd need to leave...'

He smiled at Thea. 'I can't tell you how much easier it is to come here with someone like you. You don't worry about any of those things, or if you do, you keep it to yourself. You seem happy just to sit and absorb the atmosphere.'

'I think that just means I'm lazy,' said Thea with a rueful smile. 'That's what Harry used to say, anyway.'

He had used to say that a lot, she realised now she came to think about it. And he had hated the way she dressed. He was always trying to make her smarter, to get her to have her eyebrows shaped, and her hair highlighted. To look more like Isabelle, in fact. Why hadn't she realised that before?

'Restful sounds better than lazy, doesn't it?' said Rhys. 'Restful, relaxing, easygoing...calm...'

Calm? Calm was the last thing Thea felt when she was near him.

'Placid, boring, dull,' she offered instead.

Rhys shook his head at her as he got up. 'Thea Martindale, your self-confidence needs a lot of work!' He held out a hand to help her to her feet. 'I think you'd better stick with me until we can do something about that negative image you have of yourself.'

Thea looked at his hand for a moment before she took it and felt the by now familiar thrill run up her arm and settle with a shiver of pleasure deep inside her. And the equally familiar pang as he let her go.

'I think I better had,' she said.

Afterwards, looking back, Thea was amazed at how little time it took them to fall into a routine. The days drifted timelessly by. Whenever she thought about them later, each one seemed to be drenched in sunlight and permeated with the smell of thyme and dust, with cicadas whirring and clicking in the background.

If it had been up to them, Sophie and Clara would have spent every minute in the pool, but they usually let themselves be persuaded to go out, on condition that they could swim when they got back. It took several days of badgering for Rhys to get them to consider a walk and, after much grumbling and groaning, they agreed.

'Just to shut you up,' warned Thea, but actually, once she was out there, she loved it.

They walked along the bottom of the gorge, overhung by trees which provided cool shade splashed by patches of bright sunlight. The river bed was dry, and the girls clambered over boulders and dabbled their fingers in the occasional pool of water that remained, and forgot to moan about the fact that the batteries had run out in Clara's portable CD player.

Another day, Rhys took them up into the mountains and

they had a picnic on a rocky hillside, observed incuriously by a flock of goats. Careless of the dust, Thea lay back in the fragrant scrub and looked up at Rhys's profile, outlined against the deep blue sky.

In the crystalline light, she could see the lines around his eyes and the first few grey hairs at his temple. She could see the texture of his skin, the crease in his cheek and the hint of stubble along his strong jaw, and when he turned his head to smile down at her, his eyes were warm and light.

'Are you comfortable down there?' he asked.

'Very comfortable,' said Thea, fighting the same vertiginous feeling that had swept over her at Knossos. At least this time she was lying down. If she closed her eyes, she would swear that she could feel the earth turning slowly beneath her.

It got harder and harder to remember Harry and how desperately unhappy she had been when he left and she had put her life on hold while he took the time to sort out how he really felt.

Much, much harder, too, to remember everything that she had decided about not getting involved with Rhys. Occasionally, Thea would remind herself that time was passing, even if it didn't feel like it. The holiday would come to an end, and when these two weeks were over there would be no reason to pretend any more. No long, lazy days, no starlit nights on the terrace, just the two of them, while inside the girls gossiped and giggled.

No Rhys.

They talked easily, like old friends. Rhys talked about Sophie and about his determination to be a good father. He told Thea about his job and what it was like to stand on a dune in the middle of the Sahara and turn three hundred and sixty degrees and see nothing but sand and sky. He tried to explain his fascination for rocks, and she tried to explain her fascination for shoes. They laughed a lot, and they talked about everything really.

Everything except what would happen when the holiday ended.

Thea always shied away from thinking about that, and she would put it firmly out of her mind. How could she think about leaving when the sun was shining and Rhys was waiting for her on the terrace? She was afraid of thinking beyond the here and now, and of spoiling what they had.

Not that they 'had' anything. They might pretend to be lovers when they saw Kate or Nick at the pool, but they were just friends. There was no question of them being anything else with Sophie and Clara there in any case, and no indication that Rhys was even thinking about it. Thea told herself that it was just as well, and that friendship was enough.

Only it wasn't, not really.

Rhys preferred to be out in the wild hills, but he was outnumbered by the girls and Thea, who liked the beach best, so he gave in with good grace and drove them down to the coast whenever they asked. They had a favourite beach, on a curving bay where the waves rolled gently in and sighed against the sand, and the sea was a deep turquoise colour and the water so clear that you could see the tiny fish that nibbled your toes if you dawdled too long in the shallows.

Clara and Sophie would run past them, shrieking, and throw themselves into the deep water, diving into the waves like seals. Thea would rather have liked to do the same, but didn't think it would look very dignified.

They were there again towards the end of the second week, although Thea was in denial about the fact that they had only a couple of days left and refusing to even think about it. She stood on the edge of the water with Rhys,

watching the girls dash in past the fish, and remembered the
sharp little bite she had got last time instead.

'Come on, let's go in too,' said Rhys and set off, only to
stop when he realised that Thea was still safely on dry sand.
'Aren't you coming?' he asked, apparently unbothered by
the fact that the fish might be swarming towards him like
mini piranhas even then.

'Yes,' said Thea, but she hesitated. She wished she hadn't
started thinking about swarming fish and their potential for
a feeding frenzy.

'Don't tell me you're scared of a few little fish, too!'

'Certainly not.' She put up her chin, and then dropped it
as she met his amused gaze. 'Well, not much, anyway. They
can give you a very nasty nip, you know.'

Rhys laughed and splashed back through the shallows.
Before Thea had realised what he had in mind, he had
scooped her up and was heading back into the sea.

Instinctively linking her arms around his neck, she was
torn between laughter and embarrassment and the excruci-
ating awareness of his body against hers. His arm was under
her knees, hers around his powerful shoulders and the meeting of bare skin was like an electric shock.

He carried her out to where the sand shelved away and
paused. Thea thought that he was going to drop her in, and
braced herself for the splash, tightening her arms around his
neck.

'Don't,' she begged, half breathless, half laughing.

'Don't what?' he said, laughing down into her face.

'Don't throw me in. Please,' she added, clutching him
with a mock imploring look. 'I'll do anything!'

'Anything?'

'Yes! I promise!'

Rhys's smile faded. 'I'll remember that,' he said, and

Thea's own laughter evaporated along with the last of her breath as she found her eyes locked with his.

Very slowly, without taking his eyes from her face, he took his arm out from under her knees so that she slid down his body until her feet touched the bottom. They stood very close, her arms still wound around his neck, his hands strong and warm against her back, as the sea rocked gently around them, lapping Thea's waist.

She stood stock-still, afraid to move in case he let her go. *Kiss me*, she willed him as his eyes darkened. *Kiss me now.* She knew that he wanted to, she could see it in his face, but of course he couldn't kiss her, not here, not now, with the girls swimming over to join them.

But later, on the dark terrace, when the girls were asleep…he might kiss her then.

Please, please, please let him kiss her then.

As Sophie and Clara splashed up, Rhys let her go at last and turned to the girls, listening to them clamour for him to pick them up and throw them into the waves. Rather shakily, Thea swam further out to sea, well out of splash range, and floated on her back for a while as she tried to calm her thunderous pulse and the insistent booming of her body.

The waves rose and fell gently beneath her as they rolled into the shore, and Thea faced up to the truth at last. Being friends was not enough. She wanted him, ached for him, *needed* him. The sea was cool, like silk against her body, but she felt as if it should be steaming and sizzling around her, as she thought about running her hands over his shoulders, down his back, all over him, about feeling his skin against her, his mouth on her…

Desperately, Thea rolled over and trod water. She wished she could be like Sophie and Clara, who could clamber over him like puppies. She could hear their squeals of delight as

Rhys swung them round and round before launching them into the deep water.

He was standing sturdily, his body braced to keep them safe. There was nothing obvious about him—ever—but he was toughly-built, strong yet contained and, to Thea right then, irresistible.

She could see the water droplets gleaming on his back and the wonderful sleek line of his shoulders. The sunlight on the water threw a rocking pattern of reflections over his skin, and his muscles rippled as he lifted Clara high in the air and tossed her into a wave. Sophie was already jumping beside him, wanting her turn again.

Lucky girls, thought Thea wistfully. They could keep the being thrown into the water bit, although that was obviously the highlight for them. All she wanted was to be held against him, to slide her arms around him and taste the salt on his skin.

All right, stop it now, Thea, she told herself sternly. She was getting carried away. This was just lust, a purely physical thing. Maybe she was seeing him in his swimming shorts too often? It was hard to avoid noticing that lean, strong body when you were on the beach. If she only ever saw him in a suit and tie, she probably wouldn't be getting into this state.

But things were no better when they were dressed once more and she was sitting next to him in the car. In long trousers and a short-sleeved shirt, Rhys could hardly be accused of flaunting his body, and she still wanted to crawl over him, to press herself against him and feel his hands unlock her.

This was awful. Thea linked her fingers desperately together in her lap to stop them reaching out for him. If only Rhys would give some indication that he was feeling the same tug of attraction, she would feel better. At least then she might look forward to being alone with him later.

But, apart from that one moment when he had let her slide down his body and held her in the sea while he looked in her eyes, Rhys was behaving with intimidating normality.

He put the key in the ignition but didn't switch it on, glancing at his watch instead and turning in his seat so that he could look at her and at the girls in the back seat at the same time.

'It's half past four,' he said. 'We don't need to go back just yet. Why don't we go on to Agios Nikolaos and have a look around there? It's a nice old port. Maybe we could have some supper too? We're having drinks with the Paines tomorrow night, so this is our last chance for a farewell bash.'

'Will there be shops?' asked Clara, leaning forward so that she could cross her arms on the back of his seat and focusing on essentials.

'Lots, I should think.'

'Good. I need to buy a present for Mum.'

Sophie had brightened as well. 'I've got some money left, too. We could go shopping.'

'Thea?'

Thea was still flinching from his casual reference to a farewell supper. Could they really only have one more day?

She forced a smile. 'Shopping sounds good to me.'

'And there was me thinking you'd be more interested in the restaurants,' said Rhys, putting the car into gear. 'Let me buy you a slap-up meal, anyway!'

Well, here was a turn up for the books. She, Thea Martindale, wasn't hungry! She must have it bad if she had lost her appetite, Thea tried to joke herself out of it, but she couldn't get rid of that sick little feeling that came with knowing that very soon she was going to have to say goodbye.

Agios Nikolaos was a bustling port, with ferries, cruise ships and gaily painted fishing boats jostling in the harbour, restaurants ranged along the waterfront and, to the girls' delight, plenty of shops. It was early evening when they got there, and the town was bathed in a golden light as they wandered around.

Clara must have been into almost every shop before she was satisfied with a present for Nell, while Sophie gave the choice of a fridge magnet the same kind of attention Thea would a mortgage. More, probably.

Since she was there, Thea took the opportunity to buy a few presents, too, and told herself that shopping made her feel better. If she could only find a decent shoe shop, she would be almost herself again.

Rhys bore it all with commendable patience and finally managed to drag them away from the shops. They found a restaurant overlooking the small inner harbour where it was quieter, and the girls sat down long enough to compare their purchases over a Coke before they were itching to be off again.

'I suppose it's too much to expect you to sit still and converse nicely until the food arrives?' said Thea, resigned.

'Oh, please say we can, Thea!' Clara wheedled, hugging her from behind. 'We won't go far.'

'We might as well let them go,' said Rhys. 'They'll just fidget otherwise.'

'Thanks, Dad. Come on, Clara,' said Sophie quickly, and the two of them ran off to explore before Thea could raise any further objections.

That left Thea alone with Rhys and unable to think of a single thing to say. Paralysed by a new kind of shyness, she concentrated on pulling a piece of bread apart and on trying to keep her eyes from crawling all over him.

She was excruciatingly aware of him, of the strong brown forearm resting easily on the tablecloth, of the fingers that curled around his glass. Of the broad wrist and the firm jaw and his mouth, especially his mouth. Her entire body was tense with the need to reach across the table and touch him, to remind herself that he was here and real, to store up the memory of how he felt before he was gone.

Her tongue felt as if it was stuck to the roof of her mouth as the silence stretched unbearably, but Rhys was unperturbed by it. He had pushed his chair back slightly so that he could watch the hustle and bustle around the harbour, and he looked utterly relaxed.

Utterly unconcerned by the fact that they would be going their separate ways very soon.

'I'd forgotten we'd agreed to have drinks with the Paines tomorrow.' Her voice sounded horribly stilted, but at least she had broken the awful silence. 'I didn't realise that would be our last night.'

'Neither did I when Kate suggested it,' Rhys admitted, 'but she seemed so keen on meeting up that it was hard to say no. After all, we've got out of seeing them very successfully over the last couple of weeks.'

'I suppose it won't kill us to go and be pleasant for an hour or two,' Thea agreed. 'I just hope Clara behaves herself. Kate's not at all charmed by her. It's obvious she thinks that Clara is a subversive influence around the pool.'

'Yes, I've noticed Hugo and Damian have been a lot less well-behaved since your niece took charge of activities!'

Thea couldn't help laughing, but that was a mistake. Their eyes met as he smiled, and the conversation promptly dried up once more.

Damn, and she had been doing so well sounding normal there for a while!

'Dad!' Fortunately Sophie was back, hanging off Rhys's chair. 'Dad, have you got two euros? We need two coins.'

'What on earth for?'

'We want to have a go on the Mouth of Truth.' Sophie gestured across to where Clara was waiting impatiently beside a stone mask set into the wall. 'It's a hand analyser,' she explained. 'It reads your palm and you get a computer printout that tells you your fortune, and you can choose if it's in Greek or English.'

'Oh, well, that'll be worth the money then,' said Rhys with a sigh. 'You do realise, don't you, Sophie, that this printout will just be a random sample of total nonsense?'

'Yes, yes…' His daughter nodded, shifting from foot to foot, evidently not listening to a word. 'But can we have a go?'

Rolling his eyes, Rhys dug in his pocket for two coins while Thea suppressed a smile, glad to have been distracted from that terrible tension. It was such a pleasure to see how Sophie had blossomed over the two weeks, she reflected. She had filled out, and now had a lovely golden glow to her, and her relationship with her father was transformed beyond recognition.

The girls were soon back, bearing sheets of computer printout. Sophie thrust hers at Rhys. 'Can you read mine for me, Dad?'

Rhys sighed and fished the glasses he wore for reading and driving out of his shirt pocket. He settled them on his nose, looking over the rims at the girls with mock exasperation, and that was when it hit Thea.

There was an extraordinary moment of utter stillness, as if the world had simply stopped. The wooden boats rocking in the harbour, the boys on their skateboards, the waiter weaving his way through the tables, even Clara and Sophie waiting eagerly to hear what the printout said...all froze and faded in Thea's consciousness, until there was just Rhys.

Just Rhys and the sudden certainty that she was completely, hopelessly and utterly in love with him.

CHAPTER SEVEN

So IT was Rhys. How about that?

Rhys. With one peculiarly detached part of her mind, Thea was astounded. It had been odd enough when she had thought that wanting this ordinary-looking man with his slightly greying hair and his reading glasses and his passion for rocks was a purely physical thing.

And now she had to face the fact that it was so much more than that.

She had never felt this before—this sense of recognition, of utter certainty that he was the one, the man she could love for the rest of her life. There he was, peering over his glasses, the only man who could make her happy, and, odd or not, no one else would do.

It was an amazing feeling. Thea felt her heart swell and lift with the simple relief of being able to look at him, to think *I love you* and be absolutely sure. She shook her head slightly with a kind of dazed and joyful disbelief. All he had done was to put his glasses on, and this had happened!

Thea looked slowly around, expecting everything to be different and was unable to understand why it wasn't. The world hadn't stopped at all. The boys were still showing off on their skateboards, the boats still rocked gently on their moorings, the waiter had deposited a bottle on the next table and disappeared back into the kitchen. Clara and Sophie were listening avidly to Rhys.

Not one of them realised that her life had changed completely in a single instant and would never be the same again.

'"You sometimes feel dissatisfied by everything,"' Rhys finished reading Sophie's printout, '"but you will have a long and happy life." So that's all right then.' He put down the piece of paper. 'What does yours say, Clara?'

Clara smoothed the paper out on the table in front of her while Rhys took off his glasses and glanced across at Thea with a smile that turned her bones to water.

'Let's see if the Mouth of Truth can get to grips with Clara!'

'"You could be seriously disappointed by rash ventures,"' Clara read out loud. '"You are full of vitality and physical pleasures."' Her face changed as she read the next line. '"Beware of trying to be too clever,"' she read with an outraged expression, only to grin reluctantly when she saw the others laughing. 'Stupid thing.'

'I'm beginning to think there might be something in this hand analyser after all!' said Rhys.

'You have a go, Dad!'

'Yes, go on, Rhys,' urged Clara. 'You too, Thea!'

In the end it was easier to give in. Resigned, Rhys found another couple of coins, and they inserted their hands in the hole in the wall, feeling decidedly foolish.

'I'll read yours if you like, Thea,' Clara offered when they were back at the table.

Her eyes scanned the page. 'OK...the Mouth of Truth says that you are a very kind and loving person—that's true, isn't it?' She looked up triumphantly. 'You see, it *does* work!'

'Sure,' said Thea, rolling her eyes. 'What else does it say?'

'Um...you have good health but you often look for love in the wrong place. Well, that means Harry, of course!'

'Who's Harry?' asked Sophie, puzzled.

'Thea's boyfriend. He's awful.' Clara made a face. 'He

looks all right and he says all the right things, but you just *know* he doesn't mean them.'

She hadn't noticed Thea's expression, but Rhys had. 'Read mine, Clara,' he said quickly.

'Oh...OK.' Diverted, Clara took his printout and prepared to read. 'The Mouth of Truth says that you are a per... per...a *perfectionist*,' she said carefully after a whispered consultation with Thea. 'With a sometimes obsessive attention to detail. Does that sound right?'

'It's not too far off the mark,' he admitted grudgingly.

'Oh, and listen to this!' Clara looked up excitedly to make sure she had all their attention before she read the next prediction. 'One of those rare, brilliant marriages which often happens to the really fortunate seems to lie in store.'

'That shows how much the Mouth of Truth knows then, doesn't it?' said Rhys. 'Funny that it didn't know I'm divorced if it's so clever!'

'It could mean a second marriage,' said Clara and Sophie nodded.

'Maybe it means when you marry Thea, Dad.'

There was a tiny pause.

'Thea and I aren't getting married, Sophie,' said Rhys carefully after a moment. 'We were just pretending when we told the Paines that we were engaged.'

'Oh, yes. I keep forgetting.'

Rhys didn't so much as glance at Thea.

'It's easy to do,' he reassured his daughter. 'Sometimes I do it myself!'

'Can Sophie sleep over?' Clara begged when they got back to the villa later that evening.

'I don't know, Clara,' said Thea doubtfully. 'It's quite late already.'

'But it's our last chance! Rhys says we won't be able to

do it tomorrow night because we're leaving so early the next morning and we have to pack.'

It was her last chance to talk to Rhys, too, thought Thea. Once the girls were in bed she would be alone with him, and she could tell him about that incredible moment of revelation on the harbourside that evening, when he had put on his glasses and she had fallen in love.

Quite how she was going to do that, Thea wasn't sure yet, but she would think of something. After all, she had seen the expression in his eyes when he carried her out into the sea, and he had told Sophie that he forgot they were only pretending to be engaged sometimes, hadn't he?

Of course that *might* have been a joke, just to make Sophie feel better. Thea's confidence, ever fragile, faltered and began to trickle away. There hadn't been so much as a flicker of a meaningful glance since then, had there? No accidental brush of the fingers, no murmured aside that he must talk to her soon, and now it sounded as if he was planning an orderly departure with no fuss and no emotions.

Having persuaded her aunt to agree, Clara danced off to convey the good news to Sophie, and a few minutes later the two girls reappeared, accompanied by Rhys, who was carrying Sophie's bedding.

'Just on the off-chance they'll stop talking long enough to go to sleep,' he said.

Thea kissed the girls goodnight and left Rhys to give them a stern five minute warning. 'I don't suppose they'll take much notice,' he said in a resigned voice as he came downstairs.

'You can get heavy-handed with the discipline when you get home,' said Thea. Having longed for the time when they would be alone together, she felt incredibly nervous now that it had come. 'They're still on holiday.' She swallowed. 'So are we. I think we should all make the most of it.'

There, could there be a better cue than that? *Let me make the most of it by taking you in my arms and kissing you until you tell me you love me and want to spend the rest of your life with me.* That was all Rhys had to say now.

He didn't, of course.

'I expect you're right,' he said instead, sounding tired and not in the least romantic. He rubbed his face wearily.

'It's been a long day,' said Thea. 'Come and have a drink and relax.'

Rhys followed her out on to the terrace and took the glass she handed him. 'Thanks,' he said as he sat down. 'This is just what I need.'

Thea had hoped that it would be easier in the dark, sitting where they always sat, but there was an edginess to the atmosphere that had never been there before. She longed to tell him how much she loved him, but she didn't know how. It wasn't the kind of thing you could just blurt out in the middle of the conversation, was it? *Oh, by the way, I'm in love with you.*

So she sat and twisted her fingers in her lap and tried to get back that wonderful sense of certainty she had had in Agios Nikolaos.

'You're very quiet tonight,' said Rhys after a while. 'What are you thinking about?'

About loving you. About wanting you. About needing you. About how I'm going to manage without you.

She didn't say any of those things, of course. She looked down into the glass she was turning slowly between her fingers. 'Oh…about tomorrow being our last night. I can't believe it's over.'

There, another opening for him. *It doesn't have to be over.* How easy would it be for him to say that?

'No, the last two weeks have gone quickly, haven't they?'

He looked up from his drink with a ghost of a smile. 'I've had a good time.'

Oh, dear, it was all beginning to sound very final. Thea swallowed.

'Me, too.'

She was just going to have to say something herself. If only she didn't feel so ridiculously shy. It was so *silly*, too. They were friends. She had never had any problem talking to him when she hadn't known that she was in love with him.

The silence began to twang.

OK, Thea told herself. Take it easy. Begin by saying that there's something you want to say to him, and take it from there.

Shoulders back. One deep breath. Two.

She had just opened her mouth when Rhys put down his glass with a click and stood up.

'I should go.' He sounded terse and so unlike himself that Thea, already thrown off by being interrupted just when she had plucked up the courage to tell him how she felt, could only gape at him.

'What's the matter?'

He couldn't go yet. Not now, just when she was ready to tell him the truth.

'Nothing...well, *something*, I suppose.' For the first time he seemed unsure of himself. 'But it's nothing to do with you,' he assured her. 'That is, it *is* about you, but—'

Rhys broke off and swore, raking his hands through his hair in frustration.

Thea had never seen him like this before, and it helped her to pull herself together.

'Rhys, sit down,' she said.

He stared at her for a moment and then sat abruptly.

Thea shifted round in her chair so that she was facing
him. 'Now, tell me.'

'I was thinking about what you said,' said Rhys after a
long, long pause.

'Something *I* said? What about?'

'About making the most of what was left of the holiday.'

He looked squarely into her eyes, and it was as if all the
air had been sucked out of Thea's lungs.

'And I thought about how much I wanted to kiss you
today,' he went on, his voice very deep and very low. 'I
know it's just a holiday thing, and you're still confused and
hurt about Harry, but today in the sea, when I was holding
you, I wanted to forget all that and kiss you anyway.'

'Why didn't you?' asked Thea, her mouth so dry that the
words came out as barely more than a husky whisper.

Rhys sighed and leant forward to rest his arms on his
knees, looking away from her. 'Because it would have been
a mistake.'

'Would it?'

'We're going home tomorrow, Thea. You know what
these things are like.'

'What things?' she asked unsteadily, but she knew what
he was going to say already.

'Being on holiday. You get thrown together, the way we
have been, and everything is much more intense than it is
at home, but it's not real. This is a time out of time. Right
now, with the stars and the smell of the garden and the warm
breeze, this seems like the only reality there is, but when
we get back to London and our separate lives we'll realise
that that's what real life is, and all this will be like a dream.'

She hadn't wanted him to say it, but he was right, wasn't
he?

'I know,' she said.

Rhys's head came up at the sadness in her voice. 'I'm

sorry, Thea, I shouldn't have said anything. I didn't want to spoil things, especially now. You've been so wonderful.'

He dropped his head back into his hands. 'It's not as if I don't know how you feel about Harry. You probably can't wait to get back to London to see him. I've been there myself. I know what it's like to keep on loving someone and needing them, even when they've hurt you.'

Was that a way of telling her that Kate was right, and that he'd never got over Lynda?

Thea opened her mouth to put him right about Harry, but she had hesitated too long while she thought about what he had said, and Rhys was carrying on.

'It's not even as if I want to get distracted by a relationship with anyone. I came back to be a better father to Sophie, and that's what I need to concentrate on when I get home. I haven't got time to think about anybody else right now. Sophie hasn't had enough of my attention as it is over the last few years.'

Right, so now she knew. Thea stared out at the velvety sky embedded with stars and felt her heart constrict.

No more doubt, no more confusion. Rhys had told it like it was. He had no room in his life for her once they got home. He might want her now, but not for ever. Not even next week.

Thank God she hadn't blurted out that she loved him. It was all she could think.

And really, *did* she love him? Or was it, like he said, just a holiday thing? She had wondered herself for long enough, after all.

She had thought she was in love with Harry, too, and look how different the two men were. Rhys had none of Harry's dash and glamour. There was no reason to fall in love with him other than the fact that he *wasn't* Harry, and maybe that was all it was. She had turned to him because he was there and because he was different, just as Harry had turned to her after his relationship with Isabelle fell apart.

It would be easy to accept that.

But Thea couldn't. Deep down, she knew that moment in Agios Nikolaos was the only reality that meant anything. She did love Rhys, she was certain of it in the very core of her being, and for someone normally so wavering and unconfident and easily swayed it was a comfort to have for once such an unshakeable belief in her own feelings. It *was* real. She just had to accept one thing.

Rhys didn't love her back.

Thea drew a deep breath. She couldn't change his mind, not now. But there might be a chance to see him again when they got home. He might miss her.

Perhaps it was a mistake to think too much about the future. He was here, next to her in the dark, and he had said that he wanted to kiss her. And she wanted to kiss him too. Why deny that for the sake of a bit of pride?

She didn't need to tell him how she really felt. She didn't need to think about the future, how life would be without him. For now, all she needed was to kiss him and hold him and feel his arms around her. Like Scarlett O'Hara, she would worry about the rest tomorrow.

'There's no need to be sorry,' she said slowly. 'I know what you mean about this being a time out of time. You're right, it's not about real, or for ever, but the truth is that I wanted you to kiss me today too.'

He jerked round at that and his eyes fixed on her face.

'What are you saying?'

'This is our last night. Let's not waste it. You want to kiss me, and I want to kiss you. We both understand that it doesn't mean anything, that it's not about for ever.'

'Then what is it?' asked Rhys slowly, without taking his eyes from her face.

'A celebration of the last two weeks?' she suggested, getting up and going over to his chair. 'Clearing the air? A moment that's just for now, just between the two of us.'

He took her by the hand and drew her gently down into his lap. Taking a lock of her hair, he rubbed it between his fingers. 'Are you sure, Thea?'

Instead of answering, she shifted so that she could lean down and touch her lips to the pulse under his ear, the way she had fantasised about doing all day, all week.

'I'm sure.' She sighed into his throat. Now that she was here, close to him, with his arms around her, she couldn't stop kissing him. 'I'm sure,' she murmured again, nibbling little kisses along his jaw. 'This is just for us, just for now.'

And then he was turning his head and their lips met at last and the love and the longing shattered inside Thea. She melted into him with a tiny sigh of release. At last, at last, they were kissing, kissing properly, kissing not because Kate was watching, but because they both wanted to.

She couldn't get close enough to him, couldn't feel enough of him. Her lips and her fingers drifted over his face, his hair, his skin, those lovely sleek muscles in his shoulders, and all the while Rhys's hands were moving hungrily over her, exploring her, sliding under her skirt, smoothing over her thigh, until Thea thought she would dissolve with pleasure.

She clung to him, loving him, loving the feel of him, and their kisses grew deeper and more desperate. It was the first time that they had kissed like this, and the last time. However much Thea tried to shut the thought out, she couldn't.

This was the last time she would kiss Rhys. She couldn't bear it to end, couldn't bear time to have moved on to a time when it was over and all she had was the memory instead of this surge of sensation, this feeling of coming home, this sense that her life had been all about getting to this place and this time and this man.

But it did end, of course. Rhys's hand was tugging down the zip of her dress, his mouth burning along her clavicle when he forced himself to pause.

'The girls…'

Girls? What girls? Thea pressed closer and he drew a ragged breath.

'We need to stop while I still can.'

No, thought Thea. We need to *not* stop. We need to go up to the big white bed upstairs. We need to kiss each other all over. We need to never let each other go. But stop? No.

Girls… Rhys's voice reached her through a haze of desire, and a dullness crept over her as reality filtered back at last. Sophie and Clara were upstairs, probably still talking. Of course they had to stop. There would be no making love. It would be all letting go from now on.

Slowly she straightened. 'Of course, you're right,' she said, and from somewhere found a wavering smile for him. 'It was nice while it lasted, though!'

Something changed in his face. 'It was very nice,' he said softly.

She mustn't look at him. If she looked into his eyes she would blurt out the truth. Thea closed her eyes briefly to gather the strength to disentangle herself from him. Getting off his lap, she went over to the wall where the honeysuckle was entwined with jasmine and the heady scent enveloped her as she brushed against the flowers.

'And we've cleared the air,' she said, forcing brightness into her voice and keeping her back firmly turned to him. 'That's good.'

'I hope so.'

Thea heard the scrape of the chair as Rhys got to his feet and came to stand behind her. He put his hands on her shoulders and she squeezed her eyes shut against the temptation to lean back against him.

'You're a very special woman, Thea,' he said. 'I hope Harry's waiting for you at the airport.'

She didn't want Harry. She wanted Rhys, but how could she tell him that now? *It doesn't mean anything,* she had promised. *It's not about for ever. It's about here and now.* She couldn't change the rules now.

'It's our last day tomorrow,' he said, dropping his hands and stepping back. 'Let's make the most of that, too.'

They tried to make it a good day, but it just didn't work. Having chatted most of the night, Clara and Sophie were fractious and sulky about having to go home.

'I don't want to go,' grumbled Sophie.

'Your mum will be waiting to see you.' Thea tried to make her look on the bright side but it was hard when her own heart was like a leaden weight inside her. 'It'll be lovely to see her again, won't it?'

'Yes, but then I have to go back to school on Tuesday,' said Sophie glumly.

Well, she couldn't do anything about the start of term. Thea abandoned her efforts to be cheerful. Frankly, it was all she could do to keep the tears that clogged her own throat at bay.

If she had had the heart for it, she would have laughed at the idea of clearing the air with that kiss. Had they really believed that a kiss would somehow dissolve the tension between them?

Instead, it had had the opposite effect, so that now they could hardly talk to each other without the air thronging with memories of how it had felt to be able to kiss and to touch. Rhys made no reference to what they had shared, and neither did Thea, but she couldn't stop thinking about how right it had felt, about the sweetness and the gathering excitement. And with the good memories, like a bitter counterpoint, came the aching realisation that they wouldn't happen again. It was over.

None of them felt like going out. The children played in the pool and moaned about having to go back to school. Rhys was abstracted, and spent a lot of time checking the car.

Thea drifted drearily around the villa, picking up discarded towels and swimming costumes and books she had never got round to reading. Clara had spread her belongings all over the house. Thea found a Game Boy in the bathroom, a T-shirt on the floor in the living area, hair bands in the kitchen.

Nell would have made Clara pick them up herself, but Thea was glad of something to do other than ache for Rhys. It was her fault. She shouldn't have pushed that kiss. It hadn't made it better between them. It was much, much worse to know how close she had come and what she was going to miss.

It was almost a relief when it was time to have the promised drinks with the Paines. Instructed to be on their best behaviour, Sophie and Clara trailed over behind Rhys and Thea. 'We could be in the pool instead of having stupid drinks,' they grumbled.

'You can have a last swim later, but for now you can sit and be polite, or you won't be swimming again at all.' Rhys sounded sharp for him, and the girls exchanged glances.

As it turned out, Kate had no intention of the children taking part in the conversation anyway. She sent them inside to play cards with Hugo and Damian. 'I don't want you getting dirty,' she warned the boys.

Nick was despatched to find glasses, and she turned to Rhys and Thea. 'Now, we can sit and enjoy our last evening in peace! Hasn't it been a marvellous holiday?'

Thea thought about the sunlit days, about the smell of thyme and the sound of the cicadas. About sitting at local tavernas, and laughing with the girls, and the gleam of Rhys's smile in the darkness.

'It's been perfect,' she said, and glanced at him, sitting beside her with a set face. He didn't look as if he had had a perfect holiday. 'None of us want to go home,' she told Kate to distract her from the fact that Rhys clearly wasn't in a mood to make polite conversation.

'I always look forward to getting back,' said Kate briskly as Nick reappeared and to Thea's relief began handing out drinks. 'I like to have three weeks to recharge my batteries, but I'm itching to get to work now. There's always so much to sort out in the office. I sometimes wonder if it's worth going away at all.'

Right, what did three weeks with your children count for when it came to keeping your in-tray under control?

Thea's mind began to wander as Kate rabbited on about her job and how the entire legal system ground to a halt when she wasn't there to organise everybody. Rhys was staring morosely down into his glass, and she remembered how he had smiled the night before as he'd pulled her down into his lap, and her body clenched with longing.

'I see you haven't got a ring yet.' Thea was caught unawares when Kate switched the subject without warning and fixed an eagle eye on her naked hand. 'I'd have thought you would take the opportunity to get one while you're here. I mean, it's not that long until the wedding, is it?'

Thea moistened her lips. 'No, but there's no hurry. We thought we'd wait until we got home.'

'What have you got in mind? Diamonds, I suppose?' Kate

looked complacently at the massive cluster of diamonds on her own finger.

'Diamonds would be too cold for Thea.' Rhys's voice was curt as he took an unexpected part in the conversation. He took Thea's hand and studied it as if picturing a ring on her finger. 'She needs a different stone—a sapphire, perhaps?'

'I love sapphires,' stammered Thea, agonizingly aware of his touch.

'Oh.' Kate looked down her nose. 'Well, if that's what you like...Nick, go and see what those children are doing,' she snapped suddenly. 'They're making a lot of noise in there. I don't want Hugo and Damian running around.'

Poor Nick rose obediently, and she turned back to Rhys and Thea. 'I must confess I always think sapphires a little bit...' she searched for an alternative to common, which she was clearly longing to say '...ordinary,' she decided eventually. 'Diamonds are classic, so simple and elegant.'

'Well, I'm an ordinary person,' said Thea, trying to make a joke of it, but Rhys's brows drew together and he looked more forbidding than she had ever seen him.

'You're not ordinary,' he snapped. 'And nor are sapphires. They're beautiful and warm. Like Thea,' he finished, looking challengingly at Kate.

'The one advantage of going home is that we won't be exposed to that woman any longer,' said Rhys under his breath when they finally managed to leave. 'For the first two minutes you think she's not as bad as you remembered, and after five minutes you're ready to scream at how insufferable she can be. I don't know how Nick puts up with her.'

'I think he's worse,' said Thea. 'He spent half an hour showing me how his mobile phone works!'

They had gathered up Sophie and Clara, Clara in very

bad odour with Kate again for inciting the boys into playing hide-and-seek, first in the house and then in the garden, as a result of which all four of them were extremely grubby. Now they were sitting by the pool in the dark while the girls had their promised last swim, much to the envy of Hugo and Damian.

'You'll have a hard time shaking her off,' said Thea, desperate to keep the conversation going. She wasn't sure how to deal with Rhys in this new, grim mood. 'Did you hear her suggesting that we go over to their house for dinner one night so that we could compare photos?'

'I did. I also heard you say that would be lovely!'

'I had to say something,' she protested. 'I could hardly tell her we wouldn't be seeing each other, let alone them, could I?'

He glanced at her and then away. 'No,' he agreed in a flat voice.

'Kate's the kind of person who follows up invitations like that, too,' Thea warned. 'She'll track you down via Lynda and keep on and on at you until you agree to go, so you'd better be ready to explain why I'm not around.'

Rhys stared at the pool, which was unfamiliar in the darkness. 'I'll just say we've split up.'

'She'll ask you why. The Kates of this world always do.'

'I'll tell her that you snore,' he said with the first glimmer of humour he had shown all evening, and Thea was so relieved to see it that she even managed a laugh.

'You dare!'

'No, I'll tell her the truth,' said Rhys after a moment and she stared at him.

'What?'

'Oh, not about the pretending,' he said. 'I'll just explain that when I met you, you were on the rebound from a previous affair, but when you got home your old boyfriend was waiting for you and you realised that you'd made a mistake. I hope it'll be true, too—the bit about Harry waiting for you, anyway. You deserve the best.'

Why was he so keen on her getting back together with Harry, anyway? Thea wondered crossly. She was sick of hearing how much he hoped Harry would come up trumps. And she would decide who was best for her, thank you very much!

What was it with men, always telling you how you deserved someone better than them, as if you couldn't work out for yourself who you wanted? Nell said it was a way of avoiding responsibility.

'What "you deserve someone better than me" actually means is "I can't be bothered to make the effort for you",' she had told Thea.

So by pushing her towards Harry, Rhys could pretend that her falling in love was nothing to do with him, Thea thought, welcoming the way her resentment was growing. It was easier to feel angry than to bear the aching emptiness of imagining life without him.

He liked her, he'd wanted her last night, and he'd been in a bad mood all day at the thought of saying goodbye, but none of that was enough to make him stop and think that maybe he could change his mind, that he could be a good father and still have a relationship. That all he needed to do was tell her that he loved her and they could both be happy.

But it was easier to believe that Harry was responsible for making her happy, wasn't it? Rhys could reassure himself that it was nothing to do with him. He had kissed her and held her and listened to her and made her laugh and smiled at her, but hey, it wasn't his fault that she had fallen in love with him, was it?

And it wasn't really, Thea realised sadly. She had fallen in love with him all by herself.

'It'll be a relief not to have to pretend any more, anyway,' Rhys said after a while.

For him, maybe. She was going to have to carry on, pretending that last night's kiss didn't mean anything to her, pretending that she didn't love him, pretending that she was bright and cheerful and that her heart wasn't breaking even as she smiled.

'Yes. Still, it's been two weeks to remember. It's not every holiday you get to be engaged!'

Or fall in love.

'I'm sorry you won't be getting that sapphire ring.' At least now Rhys was making the effort to play along, to make these last few hours bearable.

Thea managed a brilliant smile. 'Ah well, better luck next time! You never know, maybe Harry will come through after all.'

Although Harry would opt for diamonds if he did. He would never think about buying her sapphires because they were warm and beautiful and reminded him of her.

Another silence fell.

'The girls are going to miss each other,' she said at last.

'They can meet up in London. They don't live that far away from each other, so I'm sure we can organise something.'

We presumably meant him and Lynda, though, or possibly him and Nell, Thea thought with a tinge of jealousy. Rhys would probably meet her sister, who had always been so much prettier, so much nicer, so much more sensible. Nell was exactly the kind of woman Rhys would fall for if he ever let himself.

Oh, she could probably arrange to be around sometimes, but what would be the point? Rhys had made it very clear that he didn't want a relationship, and Thea was sick of falling in love with men who didn't love her back.

That was one pattern she was going to break, she vowed. She was just going to have to bandage up her heart and get on with her life, and maybe one day she would meet a man who was prepared to love her wholeheartedly, the way she needed to be loved.

As long as she didn't spend her life wishing that man could be Rhys.

CHAPTER EIGHT

THEA stood in the baggage claim hall and watched the luggage juddering slowly around the carousel. It had been a long, dreary journey, starting in the small hours, and she was gritty-eyed with exhaustion and the sheer strain of keeping tears at bay for so long.

No sign of their cases yet, and they seemed to have been standing there for hours. Maybe they were lost. Thea couldn't decide whether that would be a good thing or not. It would delay the moment of saying goodbye for a few minutes longer, but she was dreading losing control so much that part of her longed to get it over with.

Rhys was stepping forward and lifting a suitcase off the carousel, and the next moment Clara was at her elbow, pointing. 'There's my case! And that's Sophie's, look.'

Let mine be lost, prayed Thea in panic, suddenly faced with the fact that as soon as her case appeared there would be no reason to stand here next to Rhys any longer. She would have to walk out into the arrivals hall and into her old life, and he would be gone.

But here it came, wedged between a set of golf clubs and a battered rucksack. For a moment, Thea was tempted to pretend that she hadn't seen it, but Clara was already pointing it out to Rhys, who lifted it easily off the carousel and put in on their trolley.

'Ah, there you are!' Kate came bustling up. 'We're all ready to go, so we'll say goodbye. It's been super to meet you.'

She thrust her cheek forward for an air kiss, and Thea

131

dutifully obliged. 'I presume I can reach you at Rhys's number? I'll give you a call,' she went on without waiting for Thea's reply, 'and we'll fix up supper. Now, must dash. Hugo, Damian! Come along!'

She breezed off, utterly sure of herself and everybody else, and Thea and Rhys were left alone, isolated in the middle of the crowded hall.

'How are you getting home?' asked Rhys stiltedly. 'I left the car here, so we could give you and Clara a lift if you wanted.'

Thea could have wept. 'Nell's going to meet us. She's not up to driving, but I'm sure my father will have brought her in the car.'

Why did she have to have a close and loving family? Right then, Thea would willingly have disposed of them all if she could only have a little longer with Rhys.

'I see,' he said. 'Good. Well, I'm glad you won't be struggling with those cases on the tube.'

'No, we'll be fine.'

How had it come to this? It wasn't that long since she had been lost in his arms, and now they were reduced to small talk.

'So,' said Rhys after a moment. 'It looks like this is it.'

The breath leaked out of Thea's body. 'Yes.'

With every fibre of her being she longed for him to suggest meeting up some time, ask for her number, anything to give her hope that he was thinking about seeing her again, but he was giving Clara a goodbye hug and making her giggle, so it looked as if that was that.

Thea kissed Sophie. 'I'll miss you,' she told her.

'When will I see you again?' asked Sophie, clinging to her.

'I'm…not sure, Sophie. Some time, I hope.'

'Soon?'

'I hope so.' What else could she say?

Sophie let her go reluctantly and turned to hug Clara, and the moment Thea had been dreading had come.

She made herself smile at Rhys. The smile came out a bit wavery, but it was the best she could do, and at least she wasn't throwing herself on his chest, wailing and screaming and begging him not to let her go, which was what she felt like doing. She hoped he was grateful.

'Well…' she said and kept the smile fixed in place with an enormous effort.

'Thea—' said Rhys, and then stopped.

Her heart was hammering painfully. 'Yes?' she prompted when he didn't go on, but he had clearly changed his mind about whatever it was he had been going to say.

'Just…thanks for everything.'

'I should be thanking you,' she managed.

'What for?'

'For looking after us and driving us around,' she said. 'We'd never have left the pool if it hadn't been for you.'

And she would never have had that wonderful moment of knowing that she had found him and that he was all that she would ever want.

Reaching up, she kissed him, just on the cheek, but her lips touched the corner of his mouth. She felt his hands close hard around her for a moment, holding her still, and then he released her, letting her step back.

'Goodbye.' Her voice cracked slightly and she drew a steadying breath as she took hold of the baggage trolley. She couldn't let go now. 'Come on,' she said to Clara. 'Let's see if we can find Mum.'

She made herself walk away from Rhys without looking back. It was one of the hardest things she had ever done. Hardly aware of where she was going, she pushed the trolley through Customs, and suddenly they were out into the

Arrivals Hall, disorientated for a moment by finding themselves faced with an enormous crowd of people waiting to greet friends and family.

They hesitated, scanning the faces. 'There she is!' cried Clara as she spotted the familiar figure at last, and she rushed over to her mother, almost knocking her off her crutches. 'Mum! Mum, we had such a cool time!'

Thea followed more slowly and was greeted by a warm hug from her father who, as expected, had driven the car for the still-incapacitated Nell. 'Hello, love. You don't look too happy for someone who's just had two weeks in Crete.'

'I'm fine.' She hugged her father back, feeling awful because over his shoulder she was trying to catch a last glimpse of Rhys. It was no good, anyway. He had already gone.

'I'm just tired,' she told him as he let her go. 'We had a very early start.'

'Well, I've got some news that might make you feel better,' said Nell, kissing her sister.

Right then, the only thing that could make Thea feel better was to see Rhys pushing his way through the crowds towards her, but she managed a smile for Nell.

'Oh?'

'Harry rang.'

Harry. How odd. He had been the beat of her heart for over a year, and when she had left for Crete she would have given everything she possessed to know that he would contact her sister.

And now…now she couldn't remember why it had mattered so much.

'Really?' she said, wanting to sound thrilled for Nell's sake, but obviously not being convincing enough. Nell looked puzzled, as well she might, having put up with months of Thea obsessing about Harry.

'Poor Thea, you *are* tired, aren't you?'

'What did Harry say?'

'That he had been trying to phone you but couldn't get a reply, and that he was worried about you. I did point out that he had had two months to ring you and he hadn't, so it was a bit much to start worrying about you now. In the end, I told him that you were fine and on holiday, so if he wanted to talk to you he was just going to have to wait. I didn't think it would do him any harm after all the waiting around he's made *you* do.'

'Quite,' agreed Thea with a twisted smile. Harry must have been worried if he had rung Nell. The two of them had never got on, and he wouldn't have appreciated getting the sharp end of a devoted sister's tongue.

'You know I've never had much time for Harry,' said Nell, 'but he did sound suitably apologetic, and so desperate to get hold of you that I guess that he's got something to say that you'll want to hear. I told him that you would be back today, so he'll probably ring you later.

'I hope that's OK,' she finished, looking understandably anxious at Thea's lack of enthusiasm. By rights, Thea should have been dancing around the airport shouting and singing with relief.

'Of course.' Thea smiled widely until her jaw ached to show just how happy she was. 'Thanks, Nell. I just hope he doesn't ring until I've had a chance to catch up on my sleep.'

If only sleep was all she needed. Thea went to bed that night hoping that she would wake up and realise that she had just been confused, and that away from the bright light and hot hillsides of Crete Rhys would seem as distant and unreal as Harry had done when she was there.

Only it didn't work like that. In a last burst of summer, just in time for the start of school, London was hot and sunny, but for once the glorious weather wasn't enough to lift Thea's spirits.

She woke the next morning with a leaden sense of despair. Post-holiday blues, she told herself firmly. It was Monday and she had to go back to work, sunshine or no sunshine. No wonder she was depressed.

But that didn't account for the rawness of her heart or the aching sense that a vital part of her was missing. Thea talked and smiled, and agreed with everyone at work that, yes, the weather in Crete had been great and that she had had a wonderful holiday, but inside she felt completely numb.

She tried telling herself that she would get over Rhys the same way she had got over Harry, but it was different this time. When Harry had decided to leave she had felt miserable and hurt and disappointed at the way things had worked out, but there had always been that glimmer of hope too to console her.

She hadn't felt desolate without Harry, the way she was desolate without Rhys. She hadn't had this terrible sense that life without him was empty and meaningless, the way it was empty and meaningless now, and the thought of the future, stretching inutterably bleak and lonely before her, hadn't been unendurable, the way it was unendurable now.

By the end of the week Thea was exhausted by the simple effort of getting from day to day, and she was beginning to feel desperate. She couldn't go on like this. Surely she would start to feel better soon.

Dutifully, she took her photos in to be developed, but when she went to pick them up she realised that she couldn't bear to look at them, so she sent them to Clara instead.

'They're wonderful,' Nell said when she rang up to thank her. 'It looks so beautiful, and it was great to see Sophie and Rhys after hearing so much about them from Clara.'

Rhys. Just the sound of his name was enough to make Thea flinch with longing.

'Why don't you come over for supper?' Nell went on. 'There's so much to talk about!'

The two sisters had always been close and it didn't take Nell long to realise that there was more amiss with Thea than the shock of going back to work when she saw her.

'Is it that bloody Harry again?' she demanded fiercely. 'Didn't he ring after all that?'

'Yes, he rang,' said Thea, remembering how odd it had been to hear Harry's voice again.

'What did he have to say for himself?'

Thea let out a long breath. 'He wanted to try again. He said that he loved me.' Once, less than a month ago, his call would have been a dream come true, but when Harry had rung she had found herself doodling as she listened to him.

'He said that he had had plenty of time to think over the summer and that he realised that he had had trouble cutting himself off from Isabelle when their relationship ended.'

'Well, that's one way of describing being kept dangling on the end of a string, I suppose,' said Nell sarcastically.

'According to Harry, Isabelle has found someone new to lean on, so everything would be different for us now.'

Nell sniffed, profoundly unimpressed. 'I suppose you realise that as soon as her new guy takes off she'll be snapping her fingers for Harry again?'

'Yes, I know,' said Thea with a tired smile, and Nell put down her glass and looked at her sharply.

'So what did you say?'

'I said that I thought it was too late and that I wasn't going to settle for being second best any more.'

What she hadn't told him, but what she had thought, was that meeting Rhys had made her realise that she wanted to be loved and needed for herself, that she wanted to be essential to the man she loved, not just a diversion or a fall-back position.

Nell sat back, looking relieved. 'Good for you!'

'Aren't you going to say "I told you so"?' asked Thea wryly.

'That's the last thing you want to hear when things go wrong,' said Nell, 'and I should know! People said it to me often enough when Simon left,' she added with a touch of bitterness.

'But I can't pretend I don't think you made the right decision telling Harry where to get off,' she went on. 'I couldn't see that he was ever going to make you happy.'

'No, I know that now.'

Nell looked concerned at the flatness in Thea's voice. 'Are you OK? Not regretting it?'

'No.' Thea shook her head. 'I'm fine. I'm just…tired, I suppose.'

'You can't still be tired! You've been back a week—' Nell broke off, her face clearing. 'It's Rhys, isn't it?'

'I don't know what you mean,' said Thea feebly, but her face must have given the game away.

'Come on, Thea.' Her sister shook her head at her own obtuseness. 'I should have clicked before, but I thought you were still wrapped up in Harry. Clara's done nothing but talk about Sophie and Rhys all week. She told me all about your engagement.'

'It wasn't an engagement,' Thea protested. 'We were pretending, as Clara knows perfectly well.'

'Pretending to be in love is a dangerous game,' said Nell. 'It's got a nasty habit of turning into the real thing without you noticing!'

'Why didn't you warn me about that before I went to Crete?' said Thea miserably.

'Well, I thought you'd be too busy looking after my

daughter to get involved in mock engagements with strange men,' teased Nell, but Thea couldn't even muster a smile. 'Look, what's the problem, anyway? He looks really nice in the photos and Clara likes him a lot. She thinks he's perfect for you.'

'I think he's perfect for me too. It just doesn't work the other way round. I'm not perfect for Rhys.' To her horror, Thea heard her voice crack on his name, and she put a hand up to cover her trembling mouth.

There was nothing she could do about the hot tears scalding her eyes, though, and Nell pushed back her chair quickly and came round to give her sister a comforting hug.

'Hey! Come on, it can't be that bad!'

'It is,' wept Thea, losing her battle against tears. 'What's wrong with me, Nell?'

'Nothing's wrong with you!'

'Then why do I keep falling in love with men who can't love me back?'

'How do you know Rhys doesn't love you?' asked Nell, handing over a box of tissues.

Thea took one and blew her nose noisily. 'He doesn't want to get involved. He told me he didn't have the time or energy for a proper relationship.'

'Hmm.' Nell looked sceptical. 'Spending two weeks with you and doing everything together doesn't strike me as the right way to go about not getting involved!'

'It was just a holiday thing, and anyway nothing happened, not really. We were just friends, and now... Oh, God, I miss him so much, Nell!' Thea dissolved into fresh tears and her sister patted her back absently, her expression slightly puzzled.

'Give him a ring if you miss him.'

'I can't!'

'Why not? You just said you were friends. Friends are allowed to ring each other.'

'It's not like that,' said Thea indistinctly through another tissue. 'Rhys made it clear that his priority is to spend time with Sophie. He would feel guilty getting emotionally involved with anyone else when the whole point of him coming home was to be with his daughter and try and make up for the time he's lost. He thinks he needs to concentrate on her for the time being, and I can't argue against that, can I?'

Nell wasn't looking convinced. 'It's all very well in theory, but I can't see that devoting his entire life to his daughter is particularly healthy in practice. And once you've got used to having someone to be with, even if you are just pretending, you're going to miss them when they're not there any more. Anyway, from what Clara told me, I wouldn't be at all surprised if he got in touch with you.'

'He doesn't have my number.' Thea scrubbed at her face with a tissue. 'He didn't even ask for it.'

'He looked pretty competent to me,' Nell pointed out. 'I don't think finding out your number would be much of a challenge for him.'

'If he'd missed me, he would have called by now,' said Thea with one of those ragged sighs that came after crying. There was no use in getting her hopes up. 'He won't ring.'

That was Friday evening, and on Saturday Thea let herself into her flat and dumped a load of carrier bags on the kitchen floor. She had spent most of the morning fighting her way around the supermarket and had suddenly understood why everybody else hated it so much.

Thea had always secretly enjoyed pushing her trolley up and down the aisles, tossing in whatever happened to catch her eye, but today she had been completely lacking in inspiration. Even the cheese counter had failed to cheer her up.

Typical! All those years longing for her appetite to desert her, and now she was too miserable to enjoy the fact that for once in her life comfort eating had lost its appeal.

Her fridge had never looked so spartan. Thea finished unpacking the last of the bags and decided to go wild and celebrate with a glass of mineral water. Perhaps this was the start of a new, healthier her, and she would look back in years to come at this miserable weekend as a turning point in her life? She might screw up her face in an effort to remember why she had been so unhappy and why Rhys had mattered so much.

There, now she was beginning to think more positively, Thea congratulated herself. She was letting herself imagine a time when none of this would matter. That had to be a step in the right direction. She was well on the way to recovery.

The light on her answer machine was flashing, and she pushed the play button idly as she found a glass and unscrewed the top of the water.

'Thea, it's Rhys. I got your number via Sophie and—'

Thea jerked involuntarily at the sound of his voice, spilling water everywhere, and she leapt for the machine to save the message and play it again.

'...I got your number via Sophie and Clara, and eventually your sister, who sounds very nice. I wanted to ask you a favour, and wondered if you could give me a ring when you get in?'

He had left his number and signed off with a simple, 'Hope to talk to you soon.'

Thea listened to the message three times, her hand shaking so much that she couldn't write down his number properly. The figures staggered over the page as if some drunken spider was in charge of her pen, and all the time her heart sang, It was him, it was him! He called me!

Her knees felt quite weak by the time she had finished, and she had to sit down, staring down at the piece of paper clutched in her hand.

So much for being well on the way to recovery! The sound of his voice was all it had taken to put her right back at square one.

Unable to help herself, Thea reached out and played the message once more. It wasn't exactly lover-like and he hadn't said anything about missing her, it was true. But he had thought about her, he had called her! Thea's spirits, their downward spiral abruptly halted, were now zooming skywards once more.

What was this favour he wanted to ask? Once more her finger pressed the play button, convinced that she might have missed something vital the first ten times she had listened to it. But no, it was infuriatingly uninformative. He had a favour to ask, and he wanted her to ring him.

If she wanted to find out what it was, the obvious thing would be to ring him, wouldn't it?

She rang Nell instead.

'Didn't I say he'd ring?' her sister greeted her. 'He sounds absolutely lovely, I must say. We had quite a chat.'

'Nell, if you said anything about me...'

'Of course I didn't,' Nell soothed her. 'I just said that I'd heard a lot about him from Clara. I did say that I was sure you'd be pleased to hear from him, though. Now, why are you ringing me and not him?'

'I'm just so nervous,' confessed Thea. 'I'm terrified I'll say something stupid and make a mess of it.'

'What's there to make a mess of? He asked you to ring him. Call him back, listen to what he wants and if this mysterious favour is a reasonable one—and it probably is, as

Rhys sounds a reasonable man—all you have to do is to say OK. And then you'll get to see him again, which is what you want. If he wants you to do something unreasonable, you just have to say no. You might not get to see him in that case, but if he's being that unreasonable you probably won't want to, will you?'

Right. Funny how easy it was to think clearly when it wasn't your heart that was hammering in your throat, or your stomach churning with nerves. Thea stared at the phone when Nell had rung off and concentrated on breathing calmly. Several times she reached out to pick it up once more, only to snatch her hand back at the last minute as her nerve failed her.

OK. More deep breaths. In, out. In, out. Pick up phone. Dial number.

Thea listened to Rhys's phone ring. Once, twice, three times. He was out. Was she going to have to go through this all over again, or could she cope with leaving a message? Oh, God…

'Rhys Kingsford.'

Her hands were so slippery by this stage that she almost dropped the phone when he answered.

'It's me,' she said stupidly. Not that he would recognize who 'me' was with her voice wavering up and down like a demented duck. 'Thea.'

'Thea!'

She could almost hear him smile, and he sounded so warm and so strong and so familiar that the terrible jitters began to subside somewhat.

'It's good to hear from you,' he was saying. 'Thank you so much for ringing back. How are you?'

'Oh…fine, fine,' she lied. 'How about you?'

They exchanged rather stilted chit-chat for a bit. Thea asked about Sophie, and going back to work, and whether he'd had his photos developed, while what she really wanted to ask was whether he'd missed her, if he remembered kissing her, if he thought he could ever bring himself to love her.

'You mentioned a favour,' she said at last, desperate in case she ended up blurting one of them out anyway.

'Yes,' said Rhys slowly. 'I feel a bit awkward about it, to tell you the truth. I'd rather explain face to face, if possible. Look, I don't suppose you're free any time this weekend?

Not the time to start playing hard to get, thought Thea.

'When were you thinking of?'

'Any chance of this evening?'

It was nice of him to sound dubious. Any self-respecting girl would be out partying of a Saturday evening, but Thea had long abandoned her pride as a lost cause.

'Fine by me,' she said.

They agreed to meet at a wine bar Thea knew, about halfway between them. 'See you there at seven, then,' said Rhys as he rang off.

That only left Thea six hours to dither around and let the jitters build up all over again.

It was no use pretending that he had sounded remotely lover-like. He hadn't said anything about missing her, so whatever Rhys had in mind it clearly *wasn't* a proposal of marriage or a suggestion that he might whisk her back to his house and ravish her.

Shame.

Still, she would see him; that was what mattered. Thea's senses sang at the prospect. She kept picking things up and putting them down again, forgetting what she had meant to do with them, unable to settle to anything.

Then there was deciding what to wear. That took *ages*. Naturally, she didn't want to look as if she was trying too hard, but on the other hand, what if the whisking and ravishing scenario materialised after all? She needed to make a bit of effort.

Reluctantly, Thea laid aside a flirty little skirt and opted for black trousers instead. At least they were well cut, and one advantage of the last miserable week was the fact that they fitted quite comfortably now. She would wear them with a pale pink cardigan that she had picked up for a song in the sales. It hit just the right note between classy and sexy, and had that irresistible softness that practically screamed *touch me*.

She saw Rhys as soon as she walked in the door that evening. He was sitting at a table, looking brown and self-contained, and somehow more definite than everybody else in the bar. Thea's jangling nerves stilled abruptly at the sight of him, and she filled instead with that wonderful sense of certainty she had felt in Agios Nikolaos. He was the man she loved and he was waiting there for her. For now that was all that she wanted.

Rhys got to his feet as he spotted her, and his expression made her feel ten feet tall. She smiled.

'Hello.'

'Thea, you look…wonderful!'

They faced each other, suddenly uncertain of the most appropriate way to greet each other and, after a moment, Thea leant forward and kissed him on the cheek.

'It's good to see you again, Rhys.'

A masterly understatement, if ever she made one. Her eyes devoured him, hardly able to believe that he was there and solid. She longed to be able to burrow into him, to sink on to his lap and kiss the way they had kissed in Crete, but Rhys was already heading to the bar to get her a drink, and she had to sit down instead and get her hands firmly under control.

She was very glad when he brought back a glass of wine. It gave her something to hold on to, and stopped her hands from wandering towards him of their own accord.

'I've been thinking about you a lot,' said Rhys, sitting next to her, tantalisingly close, but not close enough to touch.

Thea's heart lurched. Maybe she had it all wrong? Maybe he was thinking along ravishing lines after all?

'Oh?' she said unsteadily.

'I wondered if you'd heard from Harry since you got back.'

'Oh,' she said again, in a very different voice. 'Yes, yes, I did actually, but…' She trailed off. How could she explain to Rhys about Harry? He would never believe that she could have changed her mind so quickly and so completely.

He was waiting for her to finish, a look of concern on his face. 'It didn't work out,' was all she said in the end.

'I'm sorry.' He sounded as if he meant it.

'Honestly, I'm fine about it,' said Thea, summoning a bright smile to prove her point. 'Nell keeps telling me that it's all for the best, and I think she's right.'

She wondered about reassuring Rhys that she was heart whole and fancy-free, but decided that it was too much of a heavy hint. Surely he would have got the point that Harry was out of the picture, in any case, which left it wide open for any move he might want to make.

'Tell me about you, anyway,' she said when Rhys gave no sign of following up the opening she had offered. 'What's this favour you mentioned? Don't tell me you haven't been able to fob Kate off on the dinner party front?'

Rhys gave a twisted smile. 'This time it's not really Kate that's the problem,' he said. 'It's Sophie.'

'Sophie?' Thea echoed incredulously. 'What's wrong with her?'

'There's nothing wrong, she's fine,' he said hastily. 'She's just...well, prolonging our engagement, I guess you could say.'

'Prolonging...?' She stared at him. 'What do you mean?'

Rhys took his glass of beer and moved it around the table, as if making a pattern with the wet ring it left.

'It's all my fault, really,' he said. 'As expected, Kate told Lynda all about you but, instead of asking me about it, Lynda questioned Sophie. I should have realised she'd do that,' he added with a sigh.

'What did Sophie say?'

'She said it was all true, and that she really liked you. She certainly gave Lynda to understand that we were very serious. She told her that I was going to buy you a ring and that we were planning to get married at Christmas. They must have picked up more of our conversations than we realised.'

Thea grimaced slightly. 'How did Lynda react?'

'She was straight on the phone to me, demanding to know what was going on. I'd planned to tell her that there wasn't anything serious between us, and that if she asked I'd just say we'd decided to call it a day, but... Well, the truth is that I didn't want her to be able to accuse Sophie of not being completely honest. I should never have put her in that position to begin with.'

'So you played along?'

He nodded. 'At first I thought it would just be for another couple of weeks and then we'd go back to the original plan.'

Thea looked at him. 'It sounds like there's a "but" coming?'

'There is,' said Rhys. 'Now Lynda wants to meet you.'

CHAPTER NINE

SHE'S been quite insistent about it,' Rhys went on ruefully, 'and I'm running out of excuses. That's when I wondered if you would consider coming along and having a drink with Lynda, and pretending that you really are engaged to me for one more night.'

'So that's the favour?'

'That's the favour,' he said. 'I don't like to ask you, especially when you must still be upset about Harry, but it really would just be for one evening. It doesn't need to be a whole evening either. Just an hour or so would do.'

An hour or so. Was that all she was going to have with him? Thea's heart contracted. He seemed very keen to keep it short. But then, she didn't want to spend an entire evening with his ex-wife either, did she?

'Perhaps we could have dinner afterwards,' Rhys went on, and her spirits did an abrupt U-turn in mid nosedive. She could practically hear the squeal of slamming brakes and then the revving as they roared upwards once more.

OK, so it wasn't a passionate declaration of love, but at least they would be alone together. That had to be a step in the right direction.

'That would be lovely,' she said.

His face lit up. 'You mean you'll do it?'

'Of course,' said Thea. 'It's a bit late for me to object to pretending on principle, don't you think? Anyway, I'd like to see Sophie again. It'll be like old times. I've missed them,' she added lightly, wanting to say, I've missed you, but not quite daring, not yet.

Rhys looked at her, as if remembering how she had been in Crete, bare feet resting on the terrace wall, tousled hair tumbling to her shoulders, her skin luminous in the starlight.

'So have I,' he said.

The meeting with Lynda was eventually arranged for that Wednesday. Rhys and Thea agreed to meet at South Kensington station and catch the tube out to Wimbledon together after work.

This allowed Thea to spend Monday and Tuesday agonizing over the eternal question of what to wear. Kate would have told Lynda how hopelessly scruffy she had been in Crete, so she was determined to make an effort to look smart for once. It was going to be intimidating enough meeting the beautiful, successful, talented Lynda as it was without feeling her usual mess as well.

How come she had never possessed one of those outfits that were supposed to go effortlessly from day to evening? Thea chewed her thumb as she contemplated her wardrobe, depressed by the utter lack of anything remotely stylish that she could wear to the office, to have a drink with Lynda and then move on to dinner with Rhys. It was a pity he had already seen that pink cardigan.

In the end, she threw money at the problem and bought a little grey suit in her lunch hour on Tuesday. She had never owned anything classic before, and she was quite pleased with the effect, although she nearly lost her nerve when presented with the total. Still, it would have been silly not to take the ivory silk top that went so perfectly with it at the same time, and the shoes made sense too. Didn't they say you should always buy a complete outfit?

Thea scribbled her name and decided to worry about paying for it later. What was the point of having a credit card if you couldn't use it in an emergency like this?

Anyway, it was worth it, she thought, admiring herself in

the mirror on Wednesday morning. She should have tried the classy look before. It was just a shame she didn't have that lovely glossy blonde hair you could sweep up into a chignon. A mop of brown curls didn't have quite the same effect.

The downside was putting up with everyone in the office gawping at her as if she had never worn a skirt before. She got a bit sick of people telling her how smart she looked and then asking what was up, and her boss claimed to have hardly recognized her, which was a bit much given that she was sitting at her usual desk and he could only see her top half anyway.

She realised what he meant, though, when she saw Rhys that evening. She hardly recognized him, either. It was raining and she was sheltering inside the entrance, shaking out her umbrella, when she saw him running across the road. He was wearing a dark grey suit and tie, which surprisingly suited his austere features, but made him look very different from the lean, brown, outdoors man she remembered from Crete.

Conscious of a quite ridiculous feeling of shyness, Thea waved as he reached the ticket barriers and looked around for her.

'I'm here,' she said. 'You ran right past me!'

'I didn't recognize you,' said Rhys, just as her boss had. He looked her up and down, taking in the suit and the elegant new shoes, and mentally comparing her to the woman he had known in Crete, with her bright, creased sundresses and casual tops. 'I've never seen you in a suit before. You look…quite different.'

'Do you know, I was going to say *exactly* the same thing to you,' Thea confided, and felt that moment of shyness evaporate as he managed to grin and grimace at the same time.

'I hate wearing a tie,' he said, running a finger around his collar. 'I never needed one out in the desert. I forgot that coming back to London would mean putting on a suit every day.'

Thea eyed the constant stream of people heading purposefully into the station, determined to get home out of the rain as soon as they could. 'I don't suppose you did a lot of commuting in the Sahara either.'

'No.' Rhys sighed a little. 'I can't say that I enjoy it, but then who does?'

And it meant that he could see Sophie. If it hadn't been for her, he would be out under the vast desert sky, in the heat and the space and the light. He belonged out there, not here in a suit and tie, with crowds pushing past them to get through the ticket barriers, puddles on the floor and the dank smell of wet coats.

For the first time Thea realised what he had given up to do the right thing by his daughter. She wished she could find a way to tell him that she admired him without sounding patronising, but in the end all she could think of to do was to lay a hand on his arm.

'Sophie's worth it, though, isn't she?'

Rhys looked down into Thea's warm grey gaze. 'Yes, she is,' he said, covering her hand with his own and tightening his clasp.

The suit might be different, but those light greeny-grey eyes were still the same, and they had the same transfixing effect on Thea, who felt herself melting inside, just the way she had in Crete. For a moment the two of them might have been back there, isolated in a private bubble from the rush hour crowds jostling around them.

It was Rhys who was jolted back to reality by a bump from a passing commuter. 'Oh, I nearly forgot,' he said as he slipped his hand inside his jacket and pulled out a little box. 'I bought you a ring to wear this evening.'

'That's not necessary, surely?' she said awkwardly.

He shrugged. 'I thought I might as well get something. It's the kind of detail that Lynda notices. Here, see what you think.'

Thea had little choice but to take the box from him. Opening it slowly, she saw the simple ring inside and her throat tightened.

'Sapphires,' she said, managing an unsteady smile.

'Did you think I'd forget?'

She glanced at him, knowing that they were both remembering that conversation on Kate's terrace. 'It seems a long time ago, doesn't it?' she said a little sadly.

There was a tiny pause.

'What do you think of it?' asked Rhys, nodding at the ring.

What did it matter what she thought of it? Thea wondered. It was only for this evening. She looked down at the box where the sapphires gleamed against a plain gold band.

'It's beautiful,' she said, and meant it.

'Try it on,' he said, taking the ring out of the box and sliding it on to her finger. 'I hope it fits. I had to guess at the size.'

It was a little loose, but not too bad. Thea bit her lip. It was impossible not to think of what it would feel like if this were for real, if he had bought her the ring because he loved her and needed her and wanted to spend the rest of his life with her, and not just to provide an extra detail to convince his ex-wife.

'Rhys, I—' She stopped at the sudden realisation that they were being watched.

'Aah!' A plump woman nudged her companion as she

spotted the ring on Thea's finger, and they both stopped to stare openly.

Within a matter of seconds, it seemed, Thea and Rhys had attracted a curious crowd. Some were watching in the hope of a sentimental scene, some were evidently up for any diversion from the usual routine, while others were simply staring because everybody else was staring.

'Say yes, darlin',' shouted a wag from the crowd and there was a ripple of laughter.

It was such an absurd situation to find themselves in at a tube station in the middle of a wet rush hour that Thea couldn't help laughing.

Rhys's lips were twitching too. 'I think you'd better say yes,' he murmured, 'or we might never get out of here!'

'Oh, all right, then,' said Thea loud enough for everyone to hear, and there was such a cheer that she began to think there might be something to be said for public proposals after all.

'Go on, give her a kiss!' someone else suggested and others took it up. 'Yes, give her a kiss!'

Thea's eyes met Rhys's. 'You started it,' she said, *sotto voce*.

A smile hovered around his mouth. 'And it would be a shame to disappoint them, wouldn't it?' he said as he reached out and gathered her into his arms.

A barrage of whistles and clapping broke out, but Thea hardly heard it. She melted into his kiss, flooded with a dazzling sense of coming home. It was so wonderful to be close to him again, to be able to kiss him back and feel his arms around her. Her own arms slid of their own volition beneath his jacket and tightened around his back, holding him close so that she would never have to bear to let him go.

But she had to, of course. 'Come on, move it along here.'

A bad-tempered official managed to push his way through the crowd at last and tapped Rhys on the shoulder. 'Find somewhere else to get engaged, mate,' he said to a chorus of boos. 'You're blocking the entrance here.'

'Sorry.' Rhys let Thea go and acknowledged the cheery crowd that was reluctantly dispersing with a lifted hand and a wry smile. 'I think we'd better go,' he said to Thea.

Somehow she found her travel pass, got through the barrier and down the steps to the platform. She felt utterly boneless—it was a surprise to find that she could stand up at all on her own, let alone walk—and so woozy that she was practically reeling along the platform. She was very glad Rhys was there beside her, the one fixed point in a swirling, spinning world.

'Well, at least we provided them with some entertainment,' he said dryly as they found a space to wait for the train.

'It was quite funny, really,' Thea managed.

He glanced at her and then away. 'Very funny,' he agreed, but not as if he found it very humorous.

They had to wait for ages for the Wimbledon train and, when it did arrive, it was packed. Thea didn't mind. She got to stand pressed up against Rhys.

'Do you want to hold on to me?' he asked as the doors squeezed shut and everybody held their breath.

Well, *there* was a question. Thea wondered what he would say if she told him that she did, she wanted to hold on to him for ever.

Except she knew what he would say, didn't she? He might be very nice about it, but essentially he would say what he had said in Crete, that for now the only person he wanted to hold on to was his daughter.

So she just nodded and took the opportunity to lean against him while she could. He was holding on to the overhead rail with one hand, his body braced against the lurching of the train, which meant that she could put an arm around his waist and balance against him.

It was a disappointment when a whole lot of passengers got off at Earl's Court. They found seats side by side. Thea stared up at an advertisement for cheap flights on the internet and tried not to think about reaching out for his hand, climbing into his lap, making him kiss her again...

The doors hissed open once more. They were only at Fulham Broadway. Thea sighed and fiddled with the unfamiliar ring on her finger. They couldn't sit in silence all the way to Wimbledon.

She cleared her throat. 'I presume we stick to the same story as before? About how we met and what I was doing pursuing you out to Crete?'

'I think that would be best, don't you?' said Rhys, who seemed annoyingly relaxed and not at all like someone who was longing to get her on her own so that he could kiss her properly in private.

'Is there anything I should know before I meet Lynda?'

'She can seem a little intimidating sometimes,' he said after thinking about it for a few moments, 'but that's just her manner. Don't let her put you off.'

If Rhys thought Lynda could be intimidating, Thea didn't give much for her own chances of not being put off by his ex. He had to be the least easily intimidated person she had ever met.

'I gathered from Kate that she's a very successful businesswoman.'

'She is. She's a clever woman, with a huge amount of drive and determination, and she's ambitious too. I remember when I asked her to marry me, I was amazed when she agreed. I never thought she'd settle for less than a millionaire.'

Oh, so he had been besotted enough to want Lynda, even thinking something like that about her. Thea's lips tightened at the thought of Rhys loving Lynda enough to risk rejection. How thrilled he must have been, how dazzled by her, when she agreed.

'You obviously didn't make the mistake of asking her in the middle of a tube station,' she said almost tartly, and Rhys was startled into a grin.

'No, I didn't do that.'

'How did you propose?' Thea asked in spite of herself.

'The usual clichés. A restaurant, candlelight, roses...I was very young,' he added, as if excusing himself.

'Oh, those old chestnuts,' said Thea enviously. She wouldn't have said no either if Rhys had laid on the clichés for her. 'I'm not sure I wouldn't prefer a wet tube station, myself,' she lied.

The corner of Rhys's mouth lifted as he looked at her, sitting bright-eyed in her suit, the raindrops still spangling the mass of brown hair. 'I'll remember that,' he said.

It was still raining when they eventually emerged from the underground station at Wimbledon, so they shared Thea's umbrella, walking close to keep as dry as possible. Thea normally hated the rain, but she would have been happy to have walked like that for hours with Rhys. All too soon, though, he was indicating a house ahead.

'Here we are.'

They stood in the shelter of the porch and Thea shook the worst of the rain from her umbrella.

'Nervous?' asked Rhys as they rang the doorbell.

'Should I be?'

'You'll be fine,' he reassured her.

The door opened, and Thea realised that (a) he hadn't answered her question directly, and (b) exactly why he had used that reassuring tone of voice.

She had been expecting someone crisp and conventional like Kate, but Lynda wasn't like that at all. Instead she was dark and dramatic, almost exotic-looking, with huge brown eyes and a cascade of beautiful dark hair down her back. Very slender—infuriatingly so, in fact—she wore black jeans that clung to her perfectly yoga-honed body and a sexy, sleeveless vest that Thea wouldn't have been able to carry off in a million years.

Just to make Thea feel even more lumpy and bourgeois, she was barefoot, presumably to show off her toe-ring. The message, clearly, was that Lynda was too intense and spiritual to waste her time with superficial things like shoes.

Thea was torn between intense irritation and wanting to sink through the floor. She had seen Lynda's eyes flick dismissively over the suit she had been so proud of. It had felt so smart and sexy that morning; now it seemed merely cheap and conservative and utterly, utterly boring. She would have been better off in her crumpled sundress.

Why hadn't Rhys warned her? Thea raged internally. It was a bit late to hint at the need to be nervous when she was actually at the door!

He was kissing Lynda's cheek, all very friendly and amicable. No bitter divorce for the likes of Lynda, obviously. 'I've brought Thea to meet you, as promised,' he said.

'Hello.'

Thea's smile felt stiff as she held out her hand. No doubt shaking hands was as bourgeois and outdated as wearing a suit to work. Lynda probably expected her to exchange some spiritually sound greeting, chink their crystals together, perhaps, or press their hands to heart and forehead.

Lynda didn't exactly shun her hand, but she clasped it warmly between both of hers as if to indicate that a simple shake would be too repressed and buttoned up for her.

'It's marvellous to meet you at last, Thea,' she said, her voice deep and breathy. 'Come in.'

She ushered them into an incredibly cool, uncluttered room that had Feng Shui all over it. Comparing it to her own unbelievably chaotic sitting room, with its mismatched curtains and junk shop furniture, Thea suppressed a sigh. Funny, just when you thought you could feel as inadequate as it was possible to feel, you could manage to feel it just that little bit more.

The sound of feet charging down the stairs made her turn, and the next second Sophie burst into the room. 'Thea!'

'Sophie!' Thea was so glad to see her and to find her exactly the same that tears pricked at her eyes as she hugged the little girl. 'I've missed you! So has Clara.'

'Oh, yes, I've heard a lot about Clara.' Lynda's laugh held a slight edge, and Thea guessed that she had been talking to Kate. 'She sounds quite a character!'

'Yes, she is,' Thea agreed.

'Come and see my room,' said Sophie, tugging at her hand.

'Sophie,' Lynda interrupted reproachfully. 'Aren't you going to say hello to your father?'

'Sorry, Dad.' She ran over to give him a hug. 'I was just excited to see Thea again.'

He grinned down at her and tweaked her nose. 'I know how you feel, Sophie!'

'Come on, then, Thea.'

Sophie headed for the door and Thea hesitated. She could see that Lynda was looking a little tight-lipped, but when she glanced at Rhys he nodded encouragingly.

She admired Sophie's room, which looked remarkably like Clara's, right down to the photo board. In pride of place, she was interested to see, was a picture of the four of them by the pool in Crete.

Thea remembered the day Nick had taken it for them. Rhys had been at one end and Thea at the other, with Sophie and Clara in between them. They were all laughing, squinting a little into the sun, and they looked so happy and relaxed that Thea's heart contracted.

'We had a good time in Crete, didn't we?' she said to Sophie, who heaved a sigh.

'I asked Dad if we could go again with you next year.'

'What did he say?'

'He said, ''We'll see'',' said Sophie, and Thea couldn't help laughing at her disgusted expression.

'I'm afraid that's the kind of thing parents say!' She looked at her watch. 'I'd better go down and talk to your mum,' she said. 'That's why I came, really.'

'OK.'

Sophie jumped off the bed and took her back down to where whatever words Lynda and Rhys might have had about their daughter had obviously been resolved. As Thea came down the stairs she could see them through the open doorway. They were sitting together on the sofa, talking. Lynda was leaning earnestly towards Rhys, her dark eyes fixed on his face, and Thea's eyes narrowed suspiciously. Lynda's body language said that she still had a more than proprietorial interest in him.

Fixing on a bright smile, she let Sophie lead the way into the room.

'There you are!' Lynda uncoiled herself from the sofa and got to her feet. 'Come and have that drink, Thea. Rhys, you know where everything is, don't you?'

'Of course,' he said and smiled at Thea as he stood up. 'What would you like, darling?'

For a terrible moment, Thea thought that he was speaking to Lynda. Then she remembered the ring on her finger and the part she was supposed to be playing.

'My usual, please,' she said innocently. Let him make of that what he would!

'Can I have a lemonade?' asked Sophie.

'You know I won't have lemonade in the house,' said Lynda in a sharp voice. 'Rhys, you don't give her lemonade, do you?'

'Occasionally,' he said from the kitchen.

'I wish you wouldn't. Those drinks are full of additives.'

'Oh, Mum...'

'That's enough, Sophie. You're not having anything. Anyway, you haven't done your violin practice yet. Dad will come up and listen to you while I'm talking to Thea.'

'I want to stay with Thea,' grumbled Sophie and Lynda's fine brows drew together.

'Answering back seems to be a little habit you've picked up on holiday, Sophie,' she said, which Thea was sure was a dig at Clara. It sounded exactly like something Kate would say, anyway. 'I don't like it. Now, off you go.'

Sophie scuffed off crossly and could be heard stomping upstairs as Rhys came back in with a glass of white wine for Thea and some murky-looking juice for Lynda, who had sunk gracefully into the lotus position on the floor.

'Organic cranberry and ginger,' she said, following Thea's appalled gaze, and took a sip. 'Delicious.'

'I'm sure,' said Thea politely, glad that Rhys had given her wine. She had a feeling she was going to need it, even if it wasn't the gin and tonic she had been craving. No doubt they had too many additives to be allowed in Lynda's house too.

'Darling, I told Sophie you'd go and listen to her violin practice,' said Lynda as Rhys made to sit down next to Thea.

Darling, eh? Thea's eyes narrowed slightly. It would be interesting to know whether Lynda called everyone darling, or if it had been a deliberate slip in response to the fact that he had called Thea darling so obviously.

'You can take your drink with you,' Lynda was overriding Rhys's attempts to object. 'You're always saying you want to be more involved with what Sophie's doing,' she added reproachfully. 'Or is that just for effect?'

In the end, Rhys had little choice but to follow his daughter. He could hardly insist on staying when Lynda was so insistent and, anyway, Thea could see that the merest suggestion that he might not be prepared to pull his weight with Sophie had stung.

'Now,' said Lynda, turning back to Thea, 'we can have a good chat without him cramping our style.'

'Right,' said Thea a little nervously.

'I hope you won't think I'm nosy, but naturally I want to know as much as I can about anyone proposing to spend what will inevitably be a lot of time with my daughter.'

Well, that seemed fair enough. 'I can understand that.'

'And, then again, I'm still very fond of Rhys,' Lynda went on. 'If he really *has* found someone he can be happy with, no one would be more delighted than me, I promise you.'

She sighed and ran a hand through the dark rippling hair. 'I've felt so responsible for the fact that he's had such difficulty forming relationships since our divorce. I know I damaged him, and I want so much for him to recover, but…'

Ah. Thea had had a feeling that a but was coming.

Lynda lowered sweeping lashes. 'I don't quite know how to say this,' she said, her voice positively throbbing with sincerity, 'but I want to be sure that Rhys has found the right woman for him. He's such a special person.'

'I know he is,' said Thea evenly. 'That's why I'm in love with him.'

'Ah, then you *do* understand that!'

As opposed to not understanding everything else? Thea wondered with rising irritation. Perhaps it was time to go on the offensive.

'Are you trying to say that you don't think I am the right woman for him?'

Lynda held up her hands. 'Please, Thea, don't get defensive. I'm only trying to ensure that you and Rhys don't make a terrible mistake. It may be that you are meant for each other but, if not, it's surely better to find out now. Nobody knows better than I do what agony divorce can be.'

Thea thought about her sister, who probably knew just as much about the pain of divorce as Lynda, who had waltzed off of her own accord.

'What exactly makes you think that we might be making a mistake?' she asked coldly.

'It's just one or two things Kate said that made me wonder,' said Lynda, still oozing warmth and sincerity.

Thea eyed her with acute dislike. 'Really?' she said. 'What kind of things?'

'We-ell, she mentioned that you were a secretary, for a start.'

'Yes, I work for a PR firm. Is that a problem?'

'Oh, not a *problem* as such. It's just that Rhys has always been a bit of an intellectual. I remember I used to feel quite intimidated by him sometimes.' She gave a little trill of laughter as if to show that she knew how incredible this seemed. 'He's got a marvellous mind,' she added earnestly. 'He's someone who really needs an intellectual equal.'

Right, so that ruled Thea out, obviously.

She wondered about telling Lynda about her degree, but decided not to bother. It wouldn't make any difference.

Lynda could talk all she liked about wanting Rhys to be happy, but to Thea it was pretty clear that she had no intention of letting him out of her sphere of influence. She didn't want to be married to him herself, but she didn't want anyone else to have him either. In Lynda's world, Rhys belonged firmly on the end of her string, to be jerked whenever she chose.

Just like Harry and Isabelle.

It turned out that she wasn't cosmopolitan enough for Rhys either. A few holidays on the Continent and a trip to New York didn't make her a suitable companion for a man as well-travelled as Rhys, it seemed.

'I feel he really needs someone who has spent some time in developing countries and is used to expatriate life,' said Lynda.

'He's not an expatriate now,' Thea couldn't help pointing out. 'He's living in Wimbledon!'

Lynda frowned a little at her obtuseness. 'I don't think that's quite the point, Thea.'

From upstairs, Thea could hear the scraping of Sophie's violin. She wished the two of them would come down and rescue her.

'What exactly *is* the point?'

'The point is that to be really happy Rhys needs someone with a similar background and experiences to his. You can't just start from scratch. I always think the history each person brings to a relationship is almost as important as the present. Don't you agree?'

Thea thought about Harry again. 'As a matter of fact, I do, yes.'

'I mean, holiday romances are all very well, but when it comes down to it, it's being able to share the important experiences of life that makes the strongest bond. Things like marriage and having children. You just can't understand what that's like until you've been there. You, for instance, have never been married, have you, Thea?'

'No.'

'And you haven't got any children?'

'No.' Thea felt as if she were failing spectacularly at an important interview. 'But I really like children,' she offered, hating herself for sounding as if she was seeking approval. 'I spend a lot of time with my niece.'

'Ye-es.' Lynda's lack of enthusiasm was perfectly judged. 'I've heard a lot about Clara. She's obviously given a lot more freedom than Sophie is used to.'

The subtext being that Thea was clearly irresponsible and an unfit person to be in charge of children. Thea bit back an angry retort.

'I'm just trying to say that you don't always have to have had a baby to know about children.'

'No, but it's not the same, is it? You can have no idea of what it's like to hold your newborn baby in your arms, or to see them take their first steps. Rhys does. That's something you can't share with him.'

'It's not your fault,' Lynda went on so patronisingly that it was all Thea could do not to grind her teeth. 'The fact is that, as far as the important things in life are concerned, you and he don't share much common ground, and I'm not sure that bodes well for a long-term relationship, let alone marriage. Sharing the same kind of experiences, the same kind of life, the same way of thinking...these things are fundamental to any strong relationship.'

Thea took a defiant slurp of her wine, but her heart was sinking.

The very worst thing was that Lynda was right.

'I think you should ask yourself what you and Rhys really have in common,' said Lynda in that hateful gentle voice that made Thea want to stand up and scream.

This was Sophie's mother, though, so she couldn't do that. She looked at the sapphires gleaming on her finger instead and thought about Rhys, about those long sunny days and the starlit nights and the way his smile warmed her. She thought about how safe she felt when she was with him and the deep thrill that ran through her whenever he touched her and the terrible emptiness when he had gone.

Lifting her eyes, she looked directly at Lynda. 'We love each other,' she said.

Lynda sighed regretfully. 'Sometimes love isn't enough. I'll be honest with you, Thea,' she said. 'I was rather afraid that Rhys would do something like this.'

'Like what?'

'Get involved with someone on the rebound from our divorce.'

Thea gaped at her. 'You've been divorced five years! It's a bit late for a rebound, isn't it?'

'Not if you think that Rhys has been in something of a limbo since then. He's only been back in the country a few weeks. You must be about the first woman he has had the chance to meet.'

'Oh, I didn't realise there weren't any women in Morocco.'

'Sarcasm is a very negative reaction, Thea,' said Lynda reproachfully. 'Remember, I'm only trying to help. I care too much about Rhys to want him to get involved in something that might only hurt both of you.'

If she was waiting for Thea to thank her for her concern, she had a long wait ahead of her. Thea set her chin stubbornly.

'Rhys came back to get to know Sophie properly before it's too late,' Lynda went on, evidently abandoning hope of any gratitude on Thea's part. 'He's got a lot of years to make up for, and I think it's best if he does that before he gets involved with anyone else.'

It was all sounding very familiar. Had the whole concentrate-on-Sophie idea come from Lynda in the first place? It was a perfect way for her to maintain her influence without actually going to the bother of marrying Rhys again. The first sign that another woman might become part of his life, and all Lynda had to do was press the guilt button. Oh, yes, Thea could see it all.

She wasn't about to give Lynda the satisfaction of admitting that she was beaten, though. She smiled sweetly at the other woman.

'*I* think it's best that Rhys decides for himself,' she said. 'I can understand why you're concerned about Sophie, but all I can tell you is that I love her, and I love Rhys. I love him very much, and I want to spend the rest of my life with him. It might not—'

Thea broke off as Lynda's great dark eyes widened suddenly, and she looked over her shoulder to see Rhys standing in the doorway.

'How long have you been there?' asked Lynda sharply.

Rhys smiled. 'Long enough.' He came into the room to stand behind the sofa where Thea was sitting and rested his hand at the nape of her neck, and she closed her eyes in involuntary pleasure at the warmth of his touch. 'I love you, too,' he said softly.

CHAPTER TEN

THEA was quiet as they walked back towards the station. It had stopped raining by then but the sky was still dull and grey.

Like her spirits.

In spite of her fragile appearance, Lynda was a strong woman. It was clear that she wanted to keep Rhys close to home, and she wasn't about to let Thea interfere. Thea didn't think that she was jealous. For all her talk about caring, she hadn't got the impression that Lynda was still in love with Rhys, or wanted him back.

No, it just suited her to have him around. Thea could see how flattering it would be for Lynda to believe that he was inconsolable. To be able to imply, as she obviously had to Kate, that he had never really got over her.

The role of lost love was perfect for Lynda, and she wouldn't give it up easily. It wouldn't be quite so convincing if Rhys was demonstrably happy with somebody else though, was it? No wonder she was keen to suggest—with the best possible motives, of *course*—that he wasn't ready for any relationship.

The question was, did Thea love Rhys enough to take Lynda on?

It was easy to see what would happen. Lynda would be all sweetness and light, but whenever Thea had a special dinner planned there would be an urgent request for Rhys to have Sophie for the night. If they were going somewhere special, she would have forgotten to tell him about a PTA meeting, or a violin lesson that Lynda couldn't make, so could Rhys just drop everything and take Sophie instead?

And how could Thea complain if Rhys was being a good father? There was no way she could insist that he put her before his daughter. Of course he would have to go.

His guilt about Sophie gave Lynda a huge advantage, and Thea knew that she would play it for all it was worth. It wasn't even personal. Lynda would be the same with any woman who ventured into Rhys's life.

And Thea couldn't be sure that Rhys cared enough to do anything about it. She wasn't going to be silly and suspect that he was still in love with Lynda. That was just Lynda's propaganda. Rhys had said nothing to suggest that was the case.

On the other hand, he had said nothing to suggest that he was in love with her either. He was doing exactly what he said he wanted to do, and that was to make his daughter his priority.

That left Thea with a stark choice. She could stand up to Lynda and fight for Rhys. Or she could walk away and leave him until he worked out what he wanted himself.

She loved him. The truth of that rang deep inside Thea. It wasn't something she could analyse or explain, but in the very core of her being she felt that he was the only man she would ever love, the only man she would ever need. The thought of going through life without him was unendurable.

Thea had seen enough to know that a love like that was a very special thing, a gift, and not to be treated lightly. It was worth more than a 'maybe it will, maybe it won't work' approach. Shouldn't she do everything she could to give it a chance to flower and see if Rhys might come to feel the same?

But she was afraid. Afraid that too many last minute summonses from Lynda would sour any relationship that they managed to build. Thea could see herself growing snippy and resentful every time Rhys had to drop everything the moment Lynda decided to make him feel guilty about Sophie, and he would end up torn and exhausted by conflicting demands.

Just like Harry.

No, Thea had had enough of triangular relationships. They didn't work, she knew that to her own cost already.

Rhys would need to decide whether he wanted to make a new life for himself, and if he wanted her to be part of it, but she had to let him make that decision on his own. She had to stand aside now, or she would only get hurt, just like Lynda had said.

'You're very quiet,' said Rhys after a while.

'I'm sorry. I was just thinking.'

Thinking about how hopeful she had felt when she had dressed that morning. The thought of dinner with Rhys had held out so much promise, the chance of a new and wonderful life, loving and being loved the way she had always dreamed of being loved.

'You look sad,' he said. 'Were you thinking about Harry?'

Thea concentrated on fastening her umbrella. 'In a way, yes.'

'I thought you said you were OK about the way it had worked out?'

'I know, and I am really,' she said, picking her words with care. 'It's just that sometimes it's harder to put it all behind you than at others.'

Rhys hesitated. 'Do you want to talk about it?'

'I don't think I do now,' said Thea slowly, knowing that once she started to talk the truth would come out, and Rhys didn't need that. 'But thanks.'

'OK.' He nodded, accepting that immediately in a way

Harry would never have done. Harry would have pushed and pushed, and she would have found herself in tears and it would have ended with them both feeling guilty. 'Tell me how you got on with Lynda instead.'

'Ah, Lynda.' Thea put her head on one side, wondering how to put it. 'Let's just say that she's not sure our engagement is a good idea.'

'*What?*' To her surprise, Rhys sounded outraged. 'Lynda told me that she was thrilled for me!'

And he had obviously believed her. That was men for you.

'That was before she met me,' said Thea delicately. 'I gather she doesn't think I'm quite right for you.'

Rhys scowled. 'Why the hell not?' Anyone would think that he had forgotten all about the pretence, she thought with a pang.

'Well, we don't have that much in common when you come to think about it—as Lynda obviously has.' She glanced up at him. 'I thought you'd overheard that bit?'

'No,' he said. 'I only heard you say that you loved me.'

'Oh, that,' said Thea after a tiny pause. 'Did I sound convincing?'

'Very.'

Keep it light, she told herself fiercely. 'You didn't do so badly yourself. That hand on my neck was a master stroke, I thought.'

Rhys looked down at her, just as she risked another glance at him, and their eyes met for a brief moment before both looked away. For a while, there was silence, broken only by the sound of their footsteps on the pavement.

Rhys's mouth was set in an alarmingly grim line. 'What's it got to do with Lynda, anyway?' he demanded.

'It doesn't really matter, does it?' said Thea, determinedly avoiding meeting his gaze once more. 'In fact, I was think-ing that it might be a good reason to end our engagement.'

'What would be?'

She had never heard Rhys sound so short before. Something had put him in a really bad mood, and she wasn't sure whether it made it easier for her or more difficult.

'The fact that we've got nothing in common.'

'Oh, that,' he said, echoing her words with a touch of sarcasm.

'You can say that we realised that she was right, and it would have been a mistake for us to marry.'

Lynda would like that, Thea thought wryly. It went against the grain to give her the satisfaction of thinking that they had taken her advice. On the other hand, they had suc-cessfully fooled her into believing that theirs was a genuine relationship, or she would never have gone to so much trou-ble to dissuade Thea from pursuing it. It was good to know that Lynda wasn't *that* perceptive, whatever Kate might claim for her famous insight.

They had reached the turning to the station. 'There's a nice little restaurant just down here,' said Rhys, nodding straight ahead. 'I was thinking we might go there.'

Thea took a deep breath. 'Actually, I think I'll pass on dinner if you don't mind.'

'Don't you want anything to eat?'

'I'm not really that hungry.' It was true, too, although Rhys might have trouble believing it after the way she had tucked into her food in Crete.

Rhys looked puzzled, as well he might. 'What about an-other night, then? How would Friday do for you?'

'I...don't think so,' said Thea with difficulty. 'Things are a bit complicated at the moment.'

'I see.'

An awkward silence fell. Biting her lip, Thea tugged the ring off her finger.

'I almost forgot. Here, you'd better have this back.'

Rhys made no move to take it from her. 'Why don't you keep it?' he said abruptly. 'Have it as a thank you.'

'What for?'

'For tonight. For Sophie.' He hesitated. 'For Crete.'

Thea swallowed. 'Rhys, I can't. It's much too expensive.' She tried a smile, but it wasn't a very successful one. 'I couldn't wear it anyway. It's an engagement ring.'

'No, you're right. Of course.' Rhys took the ring from her and put it in his jacket pocket.

'I'll...um...get the tube back from here, then,' she said after a painful moment.

'I'll see you home.'

'Don't be silly, it's still early. I'll be fine.'

Rhys insisted on walking her to the station, but she managed to dissuade him from taking her all the way home.

'Thank you for this evening,' he said formally as she attempted to fish out her travel pass.

Thea summoned another smile, not much more successful than the last one. 'It was nice to see Sophie again.'

Ah, there was her pass at last. She tried not to think about the last time she had been through the ticket barrier, and the way he had kissed her in front of everybody.

'Well... I'd better go,' she said.

'Goodbye, Thea.'

Rhys's face was set as he watched her put her ticket through the machine. On the other side, Thea hesitated, looking back at him, longing to push her way back through the barrier and tell him that she had changed her mind, that she would like to go out to dinner, and then for him to see her all the way home.

But every time it got more difficult to say goodbye. Better to make a clean break now than prolong the agony.

'Bye, then,' she said and lifted a hand before she made herself turn away and walk down to where a train was just pulling into the platform.

'But *why*?' asked Nell plaintively. 'You didn't even give him a chance to choose you over Lynda!'

'It's not a choice between me and Lynda. It's a choice between me and Sophie, and he has to choose Sophie.'

Thea sipped miserably at the tea Nell had made her when she had dissolved into tears on her doorstep.

'I'm sick of falling for men with all this emotional baggage,' she complained. 'Next time I fall in love, it's going to be with someone who doesn't have a past to screw him up!'

'You'd better start looking for a toy boy, then,' said Nell practically. 'Stick to men under twenty and you should be OK.'

'But I don't want a toy boy. I want a real man.'

Rhys, in fact.

Nell sighed. 'If you want a man of your own age, you're going to have to accept that he's going to come with an emotional history, Thea. Most normal men are going to have had at least one serious relationship by the time they hit their mid-thirties and, if they're available, the chances are that it's going to have ended in tears—just like yours did.

'Let's face it, we've all got emotional baggage. I certainly have, and you have too. If you hadn't been messed around by Harry, you wouldn't be scared of making a go of it with Rhys now.'

'I'm not scared,' Thea protested. 'I'm just trying to be realistic about the problems. I couldn't bear it if it all turned nasty and I turned into some horrible, bitter cow.'

'Well, then, you'll have to make sure that you don't let it turn nasty,' said Nell. 'Of course it would be difficult sometimes, but show me a relationship that isn't. If a relationship is worth having, it's worth working for.'

She paused, and then went on more gently, 'You know, not everyone is lucky enough to find someone they can love the way you love Rhys. You can't just walk away without even trying because you want some perfect story-book relationship. It's not like that, Thea. Sophie is always going to be part of Rhys. He wouldn't be the man he is without her, and she comes as part of the package. At least you like her and she likes you—that's a huge thing.'

'What about Lynda?' Thea had been so sure that walking away had been the sensible thing to do, and she had expected the ever-practical Nell to support her, not make her doubt that she had taken the right decision.

'She probably will be a bit difficult sometimes, but you can deal with that. You should feel sorry for her, not resent her.'

'*Sorry* for her? Why?'

'She's Rhys's past. You had a chance to be his future. I know which one I'd rather be.'

Thea knew what she wanted to be too, but she was terribly afraid that she had thrown away the one chance that she had, and as September slid into October and the leaves began to turn, she began to lose the little hope she had that Rhys would find that he missed her enough to try again.

She did her best to be cheerful, but it wasn't easy with this nagging ache inside her, this dullness lying on her heart, this dismal sense that however much effort she made the future stretched bleakly and interminably empty without him.

Nell worried about her. 'Why don't you ring him?'

'I can't. I've thought about it so many times. I even get

as far as picking up the phone sometimes, but what would I say? ''I didn't really mean it when I said I was just pretending to be in love with you? Oh, and by the way, is that invitation to dinner still on?'''

'You could start by saying hello, and see where you went from there.'

'Nell, he's never said anything about loving me. Not once. We've never even kissed for real. It's always been part of some pretence. What if I'm just building up some relationship that doesn't really exist in my mind? If there *had* been something there, Rhys could have contacted me.'

'He probably thinks you aren't interested after you brushed him off about the restaurant,' Nell pointed out.

'I've decided to be fatalistic about it,' said Thea. 'If it's meant to be, it'll be. And if it's not, it'll probably be because Lynda's right. I mean, we *don't* have anything in common.'

Apart from a sense of humour. And memories of those starlit nights in Crete. And lips that seemed made for each other.

'No, Rhys needs to decide what he wants. If it's me, he'll get in touch. If it isn't… Well, I'll just have to get on with my life, won't I?'

She turned her head as the front door banged, glad of the excuse to change the subject. 'Is this Clara?'

'Yes, Simon said he'd bring her back. She's been bowling with Sophie, I think.'

Clara leapt on Thea when she saw her. 'I haven't seen you for ages and ages!'

'No, not for at least a week,' said Thea, hugging her before she added, super-casual, 'How's Sophie?'

'She's fine.'

Thea longed to ask about Rhys, but what would Clara know? She would just say that he was fine too, and Thea didn't want to know that. She wanted to know that he was thinking about her, that he was missing her, that his nights were as miserable and empty as hers.

Clara was helping herself to a biscuit from the tin on the table. 'Thea?' she said in a wheedling tone.

'Yes?' she said cautiously, wondering what was coming.

'Will you take me skating? There's a brilliant new ice rink and I need someone to help me. Dad won't do it, and Mum can't because of her ankle.'

'I haven't been skating for years, and even then I was useless,' said Thea. 'I could hardly stand upright. I don't think I'd be much help.'

'Oh, *please*,' begged Clara. 'It would be fun if you came.'

What else did she have to do? 'Oh, all right then. We'll go next weekend if you like.'

Clara was determined that she wouldn't forget her promise. She rang Thea twice during the week to make sure that she had remembered she was to pick her up on Saturday afternoon. 'Then we can get there about two-thirty, can't we?'

'I suppose so,' said Thea, puzzled. 'They won't close before then, surely?'

'No, but we want plenty of time,' said Clara vaguely.

'I'm a bit nervous,' Thea confessed to her sister when she turned up obediently on Saturday afternoon. 'I'm sure I'll never be able to stand up, and I don't want to break *my* ankle.'

There was an air of suppressed excitement about Nell, she realised belatedly, and looked at her sister more closely. 'What's up?'

'Nothing,' said Nell quickly. 'Ah, here's Clara. Are you ready?'

'As ready as I'll ever be,' said Thea, getting up. 'Wish me luck!'

To her surprise, Nell put her arms round her and hugged her tightly. 'Good luck, Thea.'

'Hey, I was just joking!'

Nell smiled mistily. 'Good luck, anyway.'

Thea forgot about her sister's odd behaviour when they got to the rink. She eyed the crowded ice dubiously as she put on her boots. 'I hope I can remember how to do this.' Glancing up, she saw that Clara was scanning the rink. 'Looking for someone?'

'No,' said Clara airily. 'Just...watching.'

They had rather a wobbly start, and Thea wasn't sure who was hanging on to who, but after a while she began to get the hang of it. It would have been easier if they didn't have to keep going round the other nervous skaters who were hugging the edge equally assiduously.

'Let's go over there, where there's more space,' said Clara suddenly, and before Thea could protest had towed her out into the centre.

'Clara, I don't think this is a good id—' Thea broke off as she saw the two figures heading straight towards them.

Rhys and Sophie.

Unprepared for the great lurch of her heart, Thea's legs gave way, and she fell smack on her bottom, taking Clara with her.

The two girls promptly dissolved into helpless giggles, which left Rhys to lean down a hand.

'I'm not sure I'm very steady myself,' he confessed, 'but I'll do my best.'

Clara had already scrambled up, and between them they got Thea upright, although her legs were trembling so much she didn't think they would stay that way for very long.

She couldn't take her eyes off Rhys. Paralysed by the fear that this would turn out to be a dream, she just stared and wondered what on earth she could say to keep him there. Then she remembered what Nell had said about simply saying hello and seeing where it took them.

'Hello,' she said shakily.

Rhys smiled at her. 'Hello.'

'Dad, Clara and I can skate together now,' said Sophie artlessly, 'so you and Thea can sit down if you want.'

'Thank God for that,' said Rhys, watching the two girls skate off, miraculously restored to competence. 'Well?' he said to Thea, who had hardly noticed they were gone. 'Do you think we can make it back to the side?'

'I might need to hang on to you,' she managed to say huskily, and Rhys took her firmly by the hand.

'If you hang on to me and I hang on to you, I think we'll make it,' he said.

Thea felt in a curious state of limbo as she took off her boots, still hardly able to believe what was happening. For a while she just sat there by his side, reliving that feeling of his hand closed firmly around hers, the blissful security of knowing that he was strong enough and steady enough to stop her falling.

It was almost as if the touch of his hand had said everything that needed to be said. As if everything had been explained and understood without saying a word. Thea could feel herself filling up with a warm and wonderful sense of certainty.

'Did Clara set this up?' she asked at last.

'I believe it was a joint effort. Sophie certainly chose the venue.' Rhys glanced around the echoing hall, at the crowded ice rink and the hard green plastic seats. 'I'm not sure she's quite got the hang of romance yet.'

'So you knew all about it?'

'Not until yesterday. I guessed something was up when I went to pick Sophie up from Clara's. I met your sister. She's nice, isn't she?'

'*Nell* knew?'

Thea remembered the brilliance of Nell's eyes earlier, the way she had hugged her and whispered, 'Good luck'. Of course she had known.

'She hadn't known long. The girls worked it all out themselves,' said Rhys. 'They were sure that we were both unhappy and they decided to do something about it.'

'*Have* you been unhappy?' asked Thea.

'Yes,' he said simply, looking into her eyes, his own very light and clear. 'I've missed you, Thea. I've missed you more than I would have thought possible.'

'I've missed you too,' she said and, when he held out his hand, she took it and held it tightly as the awful tightness around her heart began to ease.

'I'm in love with you,' said Rhys in the same direct way. 'I think I've been in love with you since you sat on our terrace that morning. You took that deep breath to smell the coffee, and you smiled at me, and I was lost.'

'Why didn't you say anything?'

'I didn't want to admit it, not even to myself. I didn't want to fall in love. I'd made up my mind that I was going to devote myself to Sophie, and I felt guilty about thinking about anyone except her, but it was so hard not to when you were there, smiling, talking, so easy to be with. I clung to the idea that it was all a pretence, and that it didn't really mean anything when I kissed you, but it got harder and harder to remember that it wasn't real.'

'I know,' said Thea with feeling, curling her fingers around his.

'Do you?' he asked seriously, and she nodded.

'Yes, I do, Rhys. I know exactly what it's like to fall in love with someone when you least expect to, when you don't really want to. When you think they're just pretending to be in love with you.'

'I didn't think you could love me.' Rhys sounded uncertain for the first time. 'I thought you were just pretending.'

A smile was tugging at the corners of Thea's mouth, and she ran her free hand up to his shoulder.

'I'm not pretending now.'

He kissed her then, a long sweet kiss on the hard plastic seats with the hissing ice and the shrieking children in the background, and Thea wound her arms around his neck and kissed him back as her heart swelled with happiness and joy spilt in a dizzying rush along her veins.

They were roused by the sound of clapping. Sophie and Clara were leaning on the edge of the rink, beaming with self-satisfaction. 'Can we be bridesmaids?'

Rhys sighed. 'Go away,' he said, without taking his arms from around Thea. 'I haven't asked her to marry me yet.'

'Oh, Dad, what have you been *doing*?' Sophie rolled her eyes. 'You will, won't you, Thea?'

Thea started to laugh. 'Who's making the proposal here?'

'Well, you did say you would prefer being proposed to in public rather than in a boring candlelit restaurant,' Rhys reminded her. He made to get up. 'Would you like me to find a microphone and everybody can watch?'

'No!' Half laughing, half horrified, Thea caught at his sleeve and pulled him back down beside her. 'No, it's quite public enough here with just the four of us!'

'All right then. Will you marry me, Thea?'

'Say yes,' hissed Clara.

'Yes,' said Thea obediently.

'And now will you go away?' Rhys said to the two girls. 'It would be nice to kiss Thea without an audience for once.'

'Ooh,' chorused the girls, but they waggled their hands and skated away, their mission accomplished.

'Don't forget the ring, Dad,' Sophie shouted over her shoulder.

'What ring?' mumbled Thea a few minutes later as she emerged from his kiss. 'You must have been very sure of me!'

'No,' said Rhys, suddenly serious. 'I was just very hopeful. Anyway, it's just this old thing.' He pulled out a familiar box and took the sapphire ring out to slip it back on to Thea's finger. 'I'm not whether Lynda would have noticed if you were wearing it or not that evening. That was just an excuse. I just wanted to see you wearing my ring. When you gave it back that night it felt like a slap in the face.'

'I'm sorry,' said Thea, kissing him to make up for it. 'I won't give it back again.'

They sat on, oblivious to the cold, while Sophie and Clara whizzed around the ice rink, well pleased with their afternoon's work. Thea snuggled into Rhys's side.

'We've wasted so much time!' she said with a sigh. 'Why didn't you tell me how you felt in Crete?'

'I thought you were still in love with Harry,' he pointed out. 'You'd been very honest about him, and it seemed as if you were just being nice about taking part in the pretence. I didn't feel as if I could tell you, and anyway, I wasn't even that sure how I *did* feel then. I kept telling myself that it was just a holiday romance and that I'd get over it when I got home, but I didn't. I couldn't get you out of my mind, so when Lynda asked to meet you I jumped at the excuse to see you again.

'When I did, I realised it wasn't just Crete,' he said, laying his palm against her cheek and turning her head so that he could look into her glowing grey eyes. 'It was you. It'll always be you.'

He kissed her softly, sealing the promise.

'You could have said something then,' said Thea when she had kissed him back.

'I was going to. I thought it would be best if I tried to start again, like a proper relationship, so I suggested dinner, and I thought it was all going to be OK, especially when I met you at the tube. But then you backed off after meeting Lynda.'

She had, Thea remembered guiltily. 'Is that why you seemed so angry?'

'I was angry. I was angry with her for interfering, angry with you for letting her put you off, and angriest with myself for getting in such a mess and handling it all so badly. You were still preoccupied with Harry, or at least that's what you made me think, so I decided I should just leave things for the time being and concentrate on Sophie.

'The trouble was that I couldn't concentrate properly when Sophie kept talking about you. She was always asking when we would see you again, if we could go on holiday again... She kept saying how much she liked you and how much fun it had been when we were engaged, until I couldn't bear it any longer. I told her that you were in love with someone else and hadn't got over it, so that was the end of it.'

'Poor Sophie.'

Rhys snorted. 'Poor Sophie wasn't about to accept that it was the end of it at all. She reported everything back to Clara, who had apparently decided that you and I were both being very silly and that if we'd had any sense we would have made the engagement a real one while we were still in Crete.'

'I hate the way Clara's always right,' said Thea, resting her face against his shoulder.

'Anyway, Clara told Sophie that you weren't in love with Harry any more at all.'

'*I* told you that too!'

'You didn't tell me that Harry had wanted to get back

together with you and that you'd said no. I was under the impression that you were still nursing a broken heart, but when Sophie told me that I began to wonder why you hadn't taken him back when you had the chance. And then it wasn't a very big step to hoping that you'd discovered that you didn't really love him at all.'

'I didn't,' said Thea, nuzzling his throat. 'I was far too much in love with you by then.'

She felt Rhys smile into her hair and then bend his head to kiss her again, another long, long kiss that left her breathless and dizzy with happiness.

'Are you sure?' he asked. 'I don't want you to feel that you were bullied into marrying me by those girls.'

Thea thought about the reasons she had decided to walk away at the tube station that day, and then she thought about what Nell had said, about not letting true love slip through her fingers because she wasn't prepared for some hard times. Nell had told her that she had to make a choice, and Thea was making it now. She wanted to be Rhys's future, not his past.

'Yes, I'm sure,' she said. 'Are you?'

'Absolutely.'

'What about Sophie?' she persevered a little hesitantly. 'I don't want you to feel torn between us.'

'You saw how keen Sophie was for us to get married,' said Rhys. 'I don't think she's going to feel left out, and she won't be. I thought I would feel guilty about that, but I had a long talk with your sister when I picked Sophie up yesterday, and she said a very wise thing.'

'What was that?'

'She said that the best thing I could do for Sophie was to give her the example of a loving relationship. She said Sophie needed to see that adults could live together and laugh together and love together. How else would she learn to do that herself when she was grown up?'

Good old Nell.

'You said once that we didn't have anything in common,' Rhys went on. 'It's true that you don't know much about rocks and I don't know much about shoes, but I can't imagine living and laughing and loving with anyone but you, Thea. If we've got that in common, we don't need anything else, do we?'

'No,' said Thea, pulling his head down for another kiss, 'we don't.'

Thea stood in the panelled room and watched the children running around, thoroughly over-excited after the wedding ceremony and wilder still at the prospect of hanging up their stockings when they got home.

The hotel had been beautifully decorated for Christmas. A great fire burned at one end of the room, the leaping flames casting jumping shadows over the gleam of gold on her finger, while a spectacular Christmas tree stood at the other, spangled with lights and hung with gold and silver baubles.

She stepped back as a gaggle of flushed and giggling children ran past, Sophie and Clara in the thick of it all as usual. Both girls were wearing bridesmaids' dresses in a deep, warm green colour that suited their vivid personalities much better than a pastel shade would have done.

Thea had imagined them each wearing a simple Christmas rose in their hair, but their hearts had been set on the little tiaras they had spotted in the wedding shop, and in the end she had given in. It was hard to resist when she was constantly being reminded that if hadn't been for them she wouldn't be getting married at all.

She herself was wearing a suit of ivory shot silk, but the

unaccustomed elegance ended there. Defying even the hair-dresser's ministrations, her hair rioted about her face as normal, but she had decided to opt for the natural look. On a day like this, even her hair didn't matter.

Oops! Thea nearly spilt her glass of champagne as Damian—or was it Hugo?—cannoned into her, in hot pursuit of the others.

'We've got to invite Kate,' she had said to Rhys. 'If it hadn't been for her, we might never have thought of a Christmas wedding.'

They might never have pretended to fall in love.

They might never have done it for real.

And she might not be standing here now, with a brand new ring on her finger, and a brand new husband talking to her father a few feet away.

Thea could see Kate and Nick talking to Nell now. Kate had been gracious, if a little disapproving at the speed with which the wedding had been arranged.

'Two months!' she had exclaimed. 'I wonder you found anywhere—and on Christmas Eve too!'

'We were lucky the hotel had a cancellation.'

'Very lucky,' Kate had said, so obviously torn between satisfaction at getting another couple of singletons married off and a certain irritation that they had managed to arrange everything perfectly without her advice, that Thea had had to suppress a smile.

'What are you smiling about?' Rhys slipped an arm around his bride and she kissed him.

'I was just thinking about luck,' she said.

'That's funny, *I* was just thinking what luck it was that you're standing right where you are.'

'Standing…?' Puzzled, Thea followed his glance upwards to where a huge bunch of mistletoe hung from the chandelier. Several guests had stopped and were watching, smiling as they realised his intent too, and she laughed.

'Don't you think that just once, Rhys, you could kiss me in private, without an audience?' she said with mock severity.

Rhys smiled as he drew her into his arms. 'Later,' he promised.

A SURPRISE CHRISTMAS PROPOSAL

by

Liz Fielding

Liz Fielding was born with itchy feet. She made it to Zambia before her twenty-first birthday and, gathering her own special hero and a couple of children on the way, lived in Botswana, Kenya and Bahrain – with pauses for sightseeing pretty much everywhere in between. She finally came to a full stop in a tiny Welsh village cradled by misty hills and these days mostly leaves her pen to do the travelling. When she's not sorting out the lives and loves of her characters, she potters in the garden, reads her favourite authors and spends a lot of time wondering…"What if…?"

For news of upcoming books – and to sign up for her occasional newsletter – visit Liz's website at www.lizfielding.com

Don't miss Liz Fielding's exciting new novel, *The Sheikh's Unsuitable Bride,* out in January 2008 from Mills & Boon® Romance.

CHAPTER ONE

'WHAT kind of job are you looking for, Miss Harrington?'

'Please, call me Sophie. Peter always does.'

And where was Peter when I needed him? I'd been bringing my untapped potential to this employment agency for the last five years. Dropping in whenever I got bored. Or when an employer decided that I wasn't quite what he was looking for and encouraged me to widen my horizons. As far away from him as possible. Or when he decided that I was exactly what he was looking for and wouldn't take no for an answer...

Actually, on this occasion I'd quickly realised that I was never going to be what my present employer was looking for, so, although it wasn't a good time for me to be out of work, I'd taken pity on him and done it for him. Now, confronted by the frosty-faced female on the business side of the desk, I was beginning to wonder if I'd been a bit hasty.

'Anything,' I said, finally cracking in the face of her silent refusal to pick up my invitation to engage in social interaction. Get some kind of relationship going. 'I'm not fussy. So long as it doesn't involve heavyweight typing or computers. I've had computers up to here.'

I touched my forehead with the tips of my fingers

to emphasise just how far 'up to here' with them I was.

Then I smiled to show that, computers apart, I wasn't going to be difficult. I couldn't afford to be difficult...

Like my expensive manicure, it was totally wasted on this woman. Unmoved, she said, 'That's a pity. Your experience at Mallory's would seem to be your most promising asset. What kind of reference would they give you?'

That was a tricky one. My interview technique had involved nothing more taxing than flirting at a party with a software boffin who had, apparently, been in search of a secretary. I'd never actually been a secretary—and I'd told him that—but I'd been prepared to give it my best shot. And he, sweet man, had been prepared to let me. Now, there was a man who appreciated well applied nail-polish...

Unfortunately perfectly painted nails and good eyelash technique, even when coupled with the ability to make a perfect cup of coffee, hadn't entirely compensated for my inability to type with more than two fingers. Especially since, attractive though he undoubtedly was, flirting had been as far as I was prepared to go.

To be brutally honest, I'd only held onto the job for so long because his boss, Richard Mallory, had been about to marry my best friend. I'd brought them together through some seriously clever matchmaking and Rich hadn't quite been able to bring himself to invite me to take my skills elsewhere—which was why I'd made everyone promise to keep my resignation a secret until they'd left on their honeymoon.

He'd found out somehow, but I'd kept well out of his way during this last week before the wedding. Right now I needed a job—really needed a job—but not so badly that I'd watch a grown man break into a sweat as he tried to persuade me to stay. And I wouldn't be asking him for a reference for much the same reason.

I'd given it my best shot, but I'd missed the target by a mile. I was never going to be secretary material.

'I tend to do better in jobs where social skills are more important than the ability to type,' I admitted, avoiding a direct answer to her question. 'I've done reception work,' I offered helpfully, indicating the thick file that lay in front of her. It was all there. Every job I'd ever had.

'Presumably in the kind of reception area that doesn't involve the use of a computer,' she replied, signally unimpressed.

'Unfortunately they're few and far between these days,' I said, and tried the smile again. In the face of her total lack of encouragement it wasn't easy; this would have been so much less difficult if I were talking to a man—men, simple souls, took one look and tended to forget about tedious things like computers and typing speeds. But I wasn't sexist. If she'd just give me a chance I was prepared to work with her on this. Really. 'I worked in an art gallery once. I enjoyed that.'

Well, I had—until the gallery owner cornered me in the tiny kitchen and I'd had to choose between unemployment and taking my work home with me. That had come as something of a shock, actually. I'd been fooled by his fondness for velvet trousers and satin waistcoats into believing I was quite safe...

'Lots of opportunities to meet wealthy art collectors, no doubt. We're not running a dating agency, Miss Harrington.'

If only she knew how far she was from the truth.

'I don't need a dating agency,' I said, possibly a little more sharply than was wise under the circumstances. But I was rapidly losing any desire for interaction of any kind with this woman.

I didn't have any trouble attracting men. It was convincing them that I wasn't in the business of making all their dreams come true that was the problem. The ones who worked it out and still wanted to know me became friends. The others became history. Dates I could manage for myself. What I needed was a job. Now.

'I usually see Peter,' I said, offering her a way out. 'If he's in? He understands what I can do.'

The look I got suggested that she understood, too. Only too well. 'Peter is on holiday. If you want to see him you'll have to come back next month. But I doubt if even he would be able to help you. Companies are looking for function rather than adornment in their staff these days.' The woman indicated the file in front of her. 'You've had a lot of jobs, Miss Harrington, but you don't appear to be actually *qualified* for anything. Do you...did you ever...have a career plan?'

'A career plan?'

For heaven's sake, did this woman think I was a total fool? Of *course* I'd had a career plan. It had involved an excessive quantity of white lace, two rings and a large marquee in the garden of my parents' home. I'd started working on it from the moment I first set eyes on Perry Fotheringay in a pair of skin-tight jodhpurs at some horsey charity do my mother had organised.

I was going to get engaged on my nineteenth birthday, married on my twentieth. I was going to have four children—with a Norland nanny to do all the yucky stuff—breed prize-winning Irish setters and live happily ever after in a small Elizabethan manor house in Berkshire.

Perfect.

Unfortunately Peregrine Charles Fotheringay, a man of smouldering good looks and heir to the manor house in question, had had a career plan of his own. One that did not include me. At least, not in connection with the white lace, rings and marquee.

And when that plan fell apart I just hadn't had the heart to start again from scratch.

Probably because I didn't have a heart. I'd given it away. It was gathering dust somewhere, along with my career plan, in PCF's trophy cabinet.

My big mistake had been to believe, when he'd said he loved me, that marriage would follow. An even bigger mistake had been to fall totally, helplessly, hopelessly in love with him. I had discovered, too late, that men like him didn't marry for love, but for advantage. And, having taken full and frequent advantage of my stupidity—admittedly with my whole-hearted co-operation—he'd married the heiress to a fortune large enough to fund the expensive upkeep of the said Elizabethan manor and keep him in the kind of luxury to which he felt entitled. As his father had done before him, apparently.

As Perry had explained when I confronted him with a copy of *The Times* in which his name was linked with the said heiress under the heading 'Forthcoming Weddings', it was in the nature of a family business: Fotheringay men didn't work for their money; they married it.

The heiress was short-changed. For that kind of money she really should have got a title as well.

Anyway.

Here I was, spending my twenty-fifth birthday at an employment agency when I should have been organising a spur-of-the-moment frivolous celebratory bash for my friends. The kind that takes weeks to plan. I just hadn't got the heart. What was there to celebrate? I was twenty-five, for heaven's sake—that was a quarter of a century—and to make things worse my father had persuaded the trustees of my grandmother's trust fund to put a stop on my monthly allowance so that I would have to get a serious job and stand on my own two feet.

That would teach me to tell little white lies.

Three months ago, in a spectacularly successful attempt to toss my shy best friend into the path of a billionaire playboy, I'd made up a story about having to hang onto my job because my father was threatening to stop my allowance. Something he did on a fairly regular basis, but which we both knew was nothing but bluff and bluster.

But now he'd actually done it.

It was for my own good, he had assured me.

Oh, sure.

I might not be clever, like my sister Kate, but I wasn't stupid. I could see the way his mind was working. He thought that if I was short of money I'd have no choice but to return to the family nest and play housekeeper to him: a singularly unattractive prospect that offered all the undesirable aspects of marriage without any of the fun. Which was presumably why my mother had legged it with the first man to pay her a compliment since she'd walked down the aisle as Mrs Harrington.

'Well?'

Miss Frosty was getting impatient.

'Not a career plan as such,' I said. Even I could see that she wasn't going to be impressed with my romantic notions of connubial bliss. With the twenty-twenty vision of hindsight even I could see that it wasn't so much a career plan as total fantasy... 'I was never what you could describe as academic. My strengths are in what my mother described as "home skills".'

'Home skills?' She didn't actually get as far as smiling, but she did brighten considerably. 'What kind of home skills?'

'You know...flower arranging—that sort of stuff. I can do wonders with an armful of Rose Bay Willow Herb and Cow Parsley.'

'I see.' There was a significant pause. 'And do you have a City and Guilds qualification for this?' she asked finally. 'Something I can offer an employer as proof of your capabilities?'

I was forced to admit that I hadn't. 'But the Ladies' Home Union were jolly impressed when I stood in for my mother at the church flower festival at such short notice.' Well, they'd been polite anyway. No one had so much as breathed the word 'weeds'. Not within my hearing, anyway. Which, considering they'd been expecting the best blooms from my mother's garden, had been generous of them.

Unfortunately, when she'd decided she'd had enough of tweeds and dogs and jumble sales and departed for South Africa with the muscular professional from the golf club, my father had driven a tractor through her prize-winning roses. Then, when there was nothing left to flatten, he'd repeated this pointless act of vandalism by doing the same thing to her immaculate herbaceous borders.

Now, that *was* stupid. She wasn't there to have her heart broken over the destruction of all her hard work. She didn't even know he'd done it, for goodness' sake. And he was the one who had to live with the mess.

But after that Willow Herb and Cow Parsley had been all that I could lay my hands on in any quantity at such short notice.

'Anything else?'

'What? Oh...' I was beginning to get irritated by this woman. Just because I couldn't type a squillion words a minute, or do much more than send e-mails on my laptop, it didn't mean I was worthless.

Did it?

No. Of course not. There were all kinds of things I could do. And with a sudden rush of inspiration I said, 'I have organisational skills.'

I could organise great parties, for a start. That took skill. One look at Miss Frosty Face, however, warned me that party organising might not actually be considered much of an asset in the job market. Frivolity in the workplace was definitely a thing of the past.

But there were other things.

'I can organise a fundraiser for the Brownies, or a cricket club tea, or a church whist drive.' In theory, anyway. I'd never done any of those things single-handedly but, unlike my clever older sister, who had been too busy studying to get involved, I'd enjoyed helping my mother do all those things. It had been a heck of a lot more fun than revising for boring old exams, and it wasn't as if I'd had any intention of going to university. I'd been going to follow in my mother's footsteps—marry landed gentry and spend the rest of my life oiling the community wheels of village life.

Of course Kate had never had any trouble getting— or keeping—a job. And now she had a totally gorgeous barrister husband who adored her, too.

Maybe I should have paid more attention at school.

'I can produce fairy cakes in vast quantities, ditto scones and sandwiches at the drop of a hat.' I hadn't done it since I'd left home at eighteen—to avoid running into PCF in the village, driving his new Ferrari, a wedding present from his bride—but it was like riding a bicycle. Probably. 'And I can speak French, too,' I said, getting a bit carried away.

'Well?'

When I hesitated between lying through my teeth and a realistic appraisal of my linguistic skills she reeled off something double-quick in French. Too fast for me to understand, but I could tell it was a question because of the intonation. And I could make a good guess at what she was asking...

Show-off.

'And play the piano.' Before she could ask me the difference between a crotchet and a quaver I added, 'And I know how to address anyone, from a Duke to an Archbishop—'

'Then you appear to have missed your vocation,' she said, cutting me off before I made a total idiot of myself. Or maybe not. Her expression suggested that I was way beyond that point. 'You were clearly destined to marry one of the minor royals.'

I began to laugh. Too late I discovered I was on my own. This was not, apparently, her idea of a little light-hearted banter.

It occurred to me that this woman did not—unlike the much missed Peter—have a sense of humour. And, unlike him, she did not look upon a lack of formal qualifications as a challenge to her ingenuity; she just thought I was a total waste of space, a spoilt 'princess' who had some kind of nerve taking up her valuable time and expecting to be taken seriously.

It occurred to me, somewhat belatedly, that she might have a point, and that maybe I should consider a totally serious reappraisal of my entire life. And I would. Just as soon as I was in gainful employment.

'Look, I don't need a job that pays a fortune,' I told her. 'I just need to be able to pay the bills.' And treat myself to a new lipstick now and then. Not a fortune, but not exactly peanuts, either. At least I had the luxury of living rent-free, thanks to Aunt Cora, who preferred the guaranteed warmth of her villa in the south of France to the London apartment that had been part of her lucrative divorce settlement. I only hoped my mother had been taking notes... 'I'll consider anything. Really.'

'I see. Well, since your skills appear to be of the domestic variety, Miss Harrington, maybe you could put them to good use. I don't have much call for free-form flower arrangers just now, but how are you at cleaning?'

Cleaning? 'Cleaning what?'

'Anything that people will pay good money to someone else to clean for them rather than do it themselves. Cookers come top of the list, but kitchen floors and bathrooms are popular, too.'

She had got to be joking! The only cleaning fluid I'd handled recently came in small, expensive bottles from the cosmetic department at Claibourne & Farraday.

'I don't have any real experience in that direction,' I admitted.

Aunt Cora's flat came equipped with a lady who appeared three times a week and did anything that required the use of rubber gloves. She charged the earth on an hourly basis for her services, but I'd planned on sub-letting my sister's old room in order to pay her. And to cover some of the monthly maintenance charges. Just as soon as it was vacant. Unfortunately Aunt Cora had taken advantage of Kate's departure to offer her room to 'some very dear friends who need somewhere to stay in London while they're looking for a place of their own.'

I was hardly in a position to say that it wasn't convenient. Actually, at the time it had been fine, but that had been months ago and there was still no sign of them finding anywhere else. And, staying rent-free—

and, unlike me, expenses-free—in London, why would they be in any great hurry?

'Well, that's a pity. We can always find work for someone with the ability to apply themselves to a scrubbing brush. ' She gave a dismissive little shrug. 'But clearly that's an ''anything'' too far for you.' With that, Miss Frosty stood up to signal that as far as she was concerned the interview was over. But just to ram the point home she said, 'Should I be offered anything in your particular niche in the job market, I'll give you a call.'

She managed to make the prospect sound about as likely as a cold day in hell. That I could live with. It was the smirk she couldn't quite hide that brought an unexpectedly reckless 'I'll show her...' genie bubbling right out of the bottle.

'I said I was short of experience. I didn't say I wasn't prepared to give it a try.'

Even as I heard myself say the words I knew I'd regret it, but at least I had the satisfaction of surprising that look of superiority right off Miss Frosty's face. I hoped it would be sufficient comfort when I was on my knees with my head inside some bloke's greasy oven.

'Well, that's the spirit,' she said, finally managing a smile. It was a smug, self-satisfied little smile, and I had the strongest feeling that she couldn't wait to get stuck into the 'domestic' files and search for the nastiest, dirtiest job she could find. 'I've got your telephone number. I'll be in touch. Very soon.'

'Great,' I said, looking her straight in the eyes.

In the meantime I'd treat myself to the best pair of

rubber gloves money could buy. It was, after all, my birthday.

It would be fine, I told myself as I reached the pavement and, on automatic, raised my hand to hail a passing taxi. Then thought better of it and stood back to let someone else take it.

It would be fine. Peter would be back from his holiday in a week or two, he'd find me something to do, and life would return to normal—more or less. But in the meantime my expenses had doubled and my income had just become non-existent.

It wouldn't hurt to start economising and take a bus.

It wouldn't hurt to buy a newspaper and check out the job prospects for myself, either. The only possible excuse for not taking whatever revolting job Miss Frosty dug up for me—and I had no doubt that it would be revolting—would be that I was already gainfully employed.

The prospect of telling her so cheered me up considerably. It wasn't as if I was unemployable, or even lazy. I'd had *loads* of jobs. But the unappealing prospect of becoming unpaid housekeeper to my manipulative and thoroughly bad-tempered father was all the incentive I needed to stay seriously focussed. I was in the mood to show him, too.

Okay, so I'd majored in having fun for the last few years. I mean, what was there to be serious about? But I'd had a wake-up call, a reminder that I couldn't carry on like this indefinitely.

Apparently I was supposed to get serious now I'd turned twenty-five. Get a career plan.

Let's face it. I didn't even have a life plan.

It occurred to me that if I wasn't jolly careful another twenty-five years would drift by and I wouldn't have had a life.

Yes, it was definitely time to get serious.

I stopped at the corner shop to stock up on cat food, and while I was there picked up the evening paper. I scanned the ads while I was waiting for the girl behind the counter to stop flirting with a man buying a motorcycle magazine and discovered to my delight that I could job hunt on the internet, thus bypassing the doubtful pleasure of being made to feel totally useless on a face to face basis.

I also bought a notebook—one with a kitten on the cover and its own matching pen. I'd need a notebook if I was going to do all this planning. And, feeling virtuous, I circled all the likely job prospects in the paper while I was on the bus, jumping off at my stop fired up with enthusiasm and raring to go.

'*Big Issue*, miss?'

Saving money or not, I wasn't homeless like the man standing on this freezing corner selling copies of a magazine for a living.

'Hi, Paul. How's it going? Found anywhere to live yet?'

'It's looking good for after Christmas.'

'Great.' I handed over the money for the magazine and then bent down to make a fuss of the black and white mongrel pup sitting patiently at his side.

'Hello, boy.' He responded happily to a scratch behind the ear and I gave him a pound, too, which more or less cancelled out my economy with the taxi. 'Buy yourself a bone on me.'

I went in through the back entrance to the flats so that I could feed the little stripey cat who'd made a home there. She appeared at the first sound of kibble rattling in the dish. She was so predictable. Then I walked through to the lifts, grateful that my 'guests' were away for an entire week and determined to make a serious start on the job hunting front.

There were distractions waiting for me in the lobby, however.

I might be trying to ignore my birthday, but nobody else was taking the hint. The porter had a pile of cards for me, as well as a parcel from my sister—who was away visiting her in-laws for a family celebration—and some totally knockout flowers.

There was a whopping big bunch of sunflowers—my absolute favourite, and heaven alone knew where the florist had managed to get them this late in the year—from Ginny and Rich. I felt a lump forming in my throat. I was practically certain that it was a rule of being on honeymoon that you were supposed to be totally self-centred and forget that the rest of the world existed. I touched the bright petals. Not Ginny…

There was an orchid in a pot from Philly, too. I hadn't seen my here-today-gone-tomorrow next door neighbour in ages. She and Cal were always flitting off to some corner of a foreign field, or jungle, or mountain range to film exotic fauna. Neither of them had allowed the arrival of their baby daughter to slow them down, but just carried her along with them, papoose-style, wherever they went.

I'd have been okay if the arrangement of pale pink roses hadn't been from my mother.

I sniffed. Loudly. I refused to cry. I did not cry—I'd used up all the tears I was ever going to shed over Perry Fotheringay—but it was a close-run thing. Everyone in the world I loved was married, or away on an adventure, or busy getting a life. Not that I begrudged any of them one bit of happiness or success. I was just a little bit tired of endlessly playing the dizzy bridesmaid and doing my best to avoid catching the bouquet tossed so carefully in my direction before waving them off on their new lives. That was all.

I opened the package from my sister. Nestling inside the layers of tissue paper, I found a pot of industrial strength anti-wrinkle cream, support stockings and a pair of 'big knickers'. The card—'Over the hill? What hill? I didn't see any hill…'—that went with it contained a voucher for a day of total pampering with all the extras at a luxury spa. It was exactly what I needed.

A laugh and a bit of luxury.

I was still grinning when the phone began to ring. I picked it up, expecting to hear a raucous chorus of 'Happy Birthday to you' from one of the gang I hung around with.

'Sophie Harrington—single, sexy and celebrating—'

'Miss Harrington?' Miss Frosty's voice froze the smile on my face. 'How are you with dogs?'

'Dogs?'

She wanted me to wash dogs?

'One of our clients needs a dog-walker, and it occurred to me that this might be something you could do.'

Oh, very funny.

If this was her idea of 'changing my life' she could keep it. I'd go somewhere else. I cleared my throat, about to tell her what she could do with her dog-walking job; I just about managed to stop myself from saying it.

I'd said 'anything'. If this was a test I wasn't about to fail it just because I was too proud to walk some-one's dog for money. Not when I'd probably have done it for nothing, if asked nicely. Who was I kidding? Not *probably*—I'd have volunteered like a shot. I loved dogs. They were always the same. Up-front and honest. They had no hidden agendas, no secrets. They never let you down.

'How much an hour?' I asked. Since I hadn't been asked nicely, I might as well be businesslike about it.

She told me.

A dog-walker didn't rate as much per hour as a secretary, but if I was totally honest I had to admit that I could walk a lot better than I could type. And I couldn't afford to be choosy.

'Two hours a day—first thing in the morning and again in the evening,' she continued. 'It will leave you ample time to fit in other jobs during the day.'

'Great,' I said, the spectre of greasy ovens looming large. But it occurred to me that not only would I have a little money coming in—and I wasn't in any position to turn that down—I'd also have plenty of time to work on my career plan. Look for a proper job. 'When do I start?'

'This afternoon. It's a bit of a crisis situation.'

Naturally. Some idle bloke couldn't be bothered to walk his own dogs and it was a crisis.

'That's not a problem, is it?'

'Well, it is my birthday,' I replied sweetly. 'But I can take an hour out from the endless round of fun to walk a dog.'

'Two dogs.'

'Do I get paid per dog?' I asked. 'Or was the rate quoted for both of them?' I was learning 'business-like' fast.

'You're being paid for an hour of your time, Miss Harrington, not per dog.'

'So I'd be paid the same if I was walking one dog?'

I thought it was a fair question, but she didn't bother to answer. All she said was, 'The client's name is York. Gabriel York. If you've got a pen handy, I'll give you the address.'

I grabbed my new kitty notebook, with its matching pen, and wrote it down. Then, since the ability to put one foot in front of the other without falling over was the only potential of mine that Miss Frosty-Face was prepared to tap, I registered with a couple of online agencies who might ignore me but at least wouldn't be rude to my face.

CHAPTER TWO

I WAS late. It wasn't my fault, okay? People had kept phoning me to see what I was doing to celebrate my birthday. No one had believed me when I'd said nothing. They'd just laughed and said, 'No, really—what are you doing?' and in the end I'd relented and promised I'd meet Tony down the pub at nine o'clock.

Then my mother had phoned from South Africa, wanting to tell me about everything she'd been doing—well, obviously not *everything*—and I could hardly say I had more important things to do, could I?

Anyway, it was hardly a matter of life or death. Dogs couldn't tell the time and I didn't have to rush off anywhere else. They'd get their hour. Start twenty minutes late; finish twenty minutes late. Sorted.

Gabriel York's address proved to be a tall, elegant, terraced house in a quiet cul-de-sac untroubled by through traffic. Its glossy black front door was flanked by a pair of perfectly clipped bay trees which stood in reproduction Versailles boxes; no one in their right mind would leave the genuine lead antiques on their doorstep, even if it would take a crane to lift them. The brass door furniture had the well-worn look that only came from generations of domestics applying serious elbow grease—a fate, I reminded myself, that awaited me unless I gave some serious thought to my future.

The whole effect was just too depressingly perfect for words. Like something out of a costume drama, where no one was interested in the reality of the mud or the smell of nineteenth-century London.

This was a street made for designer chic and high, high heels, and I felt about as out of place as a lily on the proverbial dung heap.

My own fault, entirely.

I'd stupidly forgotten to ask what kind of dogs Mr York owned, and since there was no way I was going to call back and ask Miss Frosty to enlighten me I'd gone for the worst-case scenario, assuming something large and muscular, times two, and dressing accordingly. At home that would have meant one of the ancient waxed jackets that had been hanging in the mud room for as long as I could remember and a pair of equally venerable boots. The kind of clothes that my mother lived in.

Had lived in.

These days, as she'd told me at length, she was to be found stretched out poolside in a pair of shorts, a halter neck top and factor sixty sunblock. I didn't blame her; she was undoubtedly entitled to a bit of fun after a lifetime of waiting hand, foot and finger on my father for no reward other than an occasional grunt.

I just didn't want to be reminded of the difference between her life and my own, that was all.

Here in London it was doing something seasonal in the way of freezing drizzle, and although I'd stuffed my hair into a pull-on hat I hadn't been able to find a pair of gloves; my fingers were beginning to feel decidedly numb.

Anyway, without the luxury of a help-yourself selection of old clothes to choose from, I'd had to make do with my least favourite jeans, a faux-fur jacket—a worn-once fashion disaster that I'd been meaning to take to the nearest charity shop—and a pair of old shoes that my sister had overlooked when she moved out. They were a bit on the big side, but with the help of a pair of socks they'd do. They'd have to. I wasn't wearing my good boots to plough through the undergrowth of Battersea Park.

Now I realised that I looked a total mess for no good reason. I needn't even have bothered to change my shoes. I only had to take one look at those pom-pom bay trees to know that Mr York's dogs would be a couple of pampered, shaved miniature poodles, with pom-pom tails to match. They'd undoubtedly consider a brisk trot as far as Sloane Square a serious workout.

So, I asked myself as I mounted the steps to his glossy front door, what kind of man would live in a house like this? My imagination, given free reign, decided that Mr York would be sleek and exquisitely barbered, with small white hands. He'd have a tiny beard, wear a bow tie and do something important in 'the arts'. I admit to letting my prejudices run away with me here. I have a totally irrational dislike of clipped bay trees—and clipped poodles.

Poor things.

I rang the doorbell and waited to see just how well my imagination and reality coincided.

The dogs responded instantly to the doorbell—one with an excited bark, the other with a howl like a timber wolf in some old movie. One of them hurled itself at the door, hitting it with a thump so emphatic that it echoed distantly from the interior of the house and suggested I might have been a bit hasty in leaping to a judgement based on nothing more substantial than a prejudice against clipped bay trees.

If they were poodles they were the great big ones, with voices to match.

Unfortunately, the dogs were the only ones responding to the bell. The door remained firmly shut, with no human voice to command silence. No human footsteps to suggest that the door was about to be flung open.

Under normal circumstances I would have rung the bell a second time, but considering the racket the dogs were making my presence could hardly have gone unnoticed. So I waited.

And waited.

After a few moments the dog nearest the door stopped barking and the howl died down to a whimper, but apart from a scrabbling, scratching noise from the other side of the door as one of them tried to get at me that was it.

Seriously irritated—I wasn't *that* late and the dogs still needed to be walked—I raised my hand to the bell to ring again, but then drew back at the last minute, my outstretched fingers curling back into my palm as annoyance was replaced by a faint stirring of unease.

'Hello?' I said, feeling pretty stupid talking to a dog through a door. The scrabbling grew more anxious and I bent down, pushed open the letterbox and found myself peering into a pair of liquid brown eyes set below the expressive brows of a cream silky hound.

'Hello,' I repeated, with rather more enthusiasm. 'What's your name?'

He twitched his brows and whined sorrowfully.

Okay, I admit it was a stupid question.

'Is there anyone home besides you dogs?' I asked, trying to see past him into the hallway.

The intelligent creature backed away from the door, giving me a better look at his sleek short coat, feathery ears and slender body, then he gave a short bark and looked behind him, as if to say, 'Don't look at me, you fool, look over there...' And that was when I saw Gabriel York and realised I'd got it all wrong.

Twice over.

His dogs were not poodles and he wasn't some dapper little gallery owner in a bow tie.

Gabriel York was six foot plus of dark-haired, muscular male. And the reason he hadn't answered the door when I rang was because he was lying on the hall floor. Still. Unmoving.

I remembered the echoing thump. Had that been him, hitting the deck?

The second hound, lying at his side, lifted his head and looked at me for a long moment, before pushing his long nose against his master's chin with an anxious little whine, as if trying to wake him up. When that didn't have any effect he looked at me again, and the message he was sending came over loud and clear.

Do something!

Oh, crumbs. Yes. Absolutely. Right away.

I dug in my pocket, flipped open my cellphone and with shaking fingers punched in the number for the emergency services. I couldn't believe how much information they wanted—none of which I had. Apart from the address and the fact that I had an unconscious man on the other side of the door.

How did I know if he'd hit his head? And what difference would it make if I told them? It wasn't as if they could do anything about it until they got here...

Maybe I sounded a touch hysterical, because the woman in the control centre, in the same calming voice more commonly used to talk to skittish horses, over-excited dogs and total idiots, told me to stay right where I was. Someone would be with me directly.

The minute I hung up, of course, I realised that I should have told her the one thing I *did* know. That they wouldn't be able to get in. I looked around in the vain hope that a passing knight errant—and I'd have been quite happy to pass on the gleaming armour and white horse—might leap to my rescue and offer to pick the lock, or break a window, or do some other totally clever thing that had completely eluded me and climb in.

The street—and the way my day was going I was not surprised by this—was deserted.

Actually, on second thoughts, maybe that was just as well. I wasn't sure that anyone who could pick a lock at the drop of a hat would be a knight errant. Not unless he was a bona fide locksmith, anyway.

I looked through the letterbox again, hoping, in the way that you do, that Gabriel York had miraculously recovered while I'd been panicking on his doorstep.

There was no discernible change. Was he actually breathing?

'Mr York?' It came out as little more than a whisper. 'Mr York!' I repeated more sharply.

The only response was from the dogs, who reprised the bark/howl chorus, presumably in the hope of rousing someone more useful.

Oh, help! I had to do *something*. But what? I didn't have any hairpins about my person, and even if I had I couldn't pick a lock to save my life. His life.

I looked over the railing down into the semi-basement. The only window down there was not just shut, it had security bars, too, so breaking it wouldn't be much use.

I took a step back and looked up at the house. The ground-floor windows were all firmly fastened, but, blinking the drizzle out of my eyes, I could see that one of the sash cord windows on the floor above street level was open just a crack. It wasn't that far, and there was a useful downpipe within easy reach. Well, easyish reach, anyway.

I stowed my phone and, catching hold of the iron railing that guarded the steps, pulled myself up. Then, from the vantage point of this precious perch, I grabbed the downpipe and hitched myself up until I was clinging, monkey-like, with my hands and feet. I didn't pause to gather my breath. I was very much afraid that if I paused to do *anything* I'd lose my nerve. Instead I clung with my knees, reached up with my hands, pushed with my feet. The cast iron was cold, damp and slippery—and a lot harder to climb than I'd anticipated.

I hadn't got very far when the muscles in my upper

arms began to burn, reminding me that I hadn't been to the gym in a while. Actually, I really should make the most of it before my membership expired, I thought, and slipped, banging my chin and biting my lip in the process.

Concentrate, you silly cow…

Quite. I gritted my teeth and, telling myself not to be such a wimp, hauled myself up. Things didn't improve when I finally got level with the window, which was rather further from the pipe than it had looked from the ground. Just a bit more of a stretch. Excellent from a security point of view, but an unnervingly sickening distance to span from mine.

It was perhaps fortunate that the biggest spider I'd ever seen decided to investigate the bipedal blundering that had disturbed whatever it was that spiders do when they lurk behind downpipes—and frankly I'd rather not know—thus confirming the fact that I would rather risk the fall into a stone basement area than endure a face-to-face encounter with eight horribly long though undoubtedly harmless legs.

Idiotic, no doubt, but as a force for overcoming inertia arachnophobia takes some beating.

Have you ever wished you hadn't started something? Just wished you'd never got out of bed that morning?

It was my birthday. I was twenty-five years old and everyone was telling me that it was time to grow up. As if I hadn't done that the day I'd realised that love was no competition for money.

But, clinging to Gabriel York's windowsill by my fingernails, I had a moment of truth. Reality. Let me live through this, I promised whatever unfortunate de-

ity had been given the task of looking after total idiots, and I will embrace maturity. I'll even get to grips
with my dislike of technology and sign up for a computer course.

In the meantime I dug in and hauled myself up,
trying not to think about my expensive manicure—
probably the last one I'd ever be able to afford—as
my nails grated against stone and, with my knee on
the sill, I managed to grab hold of the window and
push it upwards.

Someone must have been listening to my plea for
help because, unlike the sash cord windows of my
family home, which stuck like glue in damp weather,
Mr York kept his well oiled and perfectly balanced.
In response to a shove with the full force of my body-
weight behind it the window shot up and I fell in,
landing in a painful heap on a polished oak floor,
closely followed by a spindly table and something
fragile that shattered noisily very close to my ear.

Make that half listening. Bumped chin, bitten lip,
wrecked nails, and now I had a throbbing shoulder to
add to the tally. And my knees hurt. This job definitely came under the heading 'life-changing'.
Whether I'd survive it was yet to be proved.

I opened my eyes and was confronted by the ruin
of what might have been a Dresden shepherdess. And
something told me that this wasn't a replica. It was
the real thing.

I blamed its total destruction on the latest craze for
ripping up carpets and polishing original wooden
floors. If there had been a draught-stopping fitted carpet, with a thick cushion underlay, the shepherdess
would have still been in one piece and I wouldn't

have bruised my knees. And, of the two, it was my knees I was more bothered about. The shepherdess would undoubtedly be insured for replacement value. My knees were unique.

Not that I had any time to lie there and feel sorry for myself. Somewhere in the distance I could hear the sound of a siren—hopefully that of the ambulance I'd summoned. I had to get to the front door and let in the paramedics...

I got up and pulled down the window, leaving grubby fingermarks. I rubbed my hands down the front of my jeans before I left them on anything else, and headed for the door. Not before noting that the room, like the Dresden shepherdess, did not quite fit the glimpse I'd got of Gabriel York. It was a thoroughly feminine room. Presumably the territory of Mrs York. I blamed her for the bay trees while I was at it.

And where was she when her husband needed her to walk his dogs? Pick him up off the floor? Call an ambulance...?

The nearest dog—clearly an adolescent—leapt on me in his excitement as I ran down the stairs, nearly knocking me off my feet again.

'Get off, you stupid hound,' I said, pushing him away, trying not to look too closely at my employer as I stepped over him—if he'd fallen downstairs and broken his neck I'd rather not know—and went to open the door.

I looked out. No ambulance... Well, it was building up to the rush hour, so it would undoubtedly have to battle its way through the traffic, like the rest of London.

It was down to me, then. I left the door ajar, so that they could get in when they arrived, and turned back to face the man who lay supine and unmoving, taking up most of the floor.

And I got a reprise of the 'do something' look from the dog lying protectively at his side.

Deep breath, Sophie. You can do this…

'Mr York…' I knelt down beside him and it didn't take a genius to see that even when he was on his feet Gabriel York wasn't going to look terribly well. His skin had a yellowish pallor and his face was drawn-out and haggard with the sharply attenuated features of someone who's lost a great deal of weight without any of the tiresome bother of going on a diet. He was wearing a black dressing gown over a pair of cotton pyjama pants—which, considering it was late afternoon, suggested that it wasn't simply idleness that had stopped him from walking his dogs.

He might, of course, have slipped on the stairs—his feet were bare—as he'd come down to answer the door. Or one of the dogs might have got underfoot in its excitement and unbalanced him.

But, looking at him, I would have gambled that he'd just passed out. At least I hoped that was all he'd done; I gingerly touched his throat, seeking a pulse.

I couldn't find one.

The hound who'd been guarding him, but who had shifted slightly to let me get closer, licked my hand encouragingly. I patted him absently, swallowing as I attempted to dislodge a great big rock that suddenly seemed to be stuck in my throat.

How long had he been lying there? Was it too late for the kiss of life?

How long had it been since I'd rung the bell and heard that distant thump that I was now certain had been Gabriel York hitting the floor? He was still warm to the touch, but then my own hands were freezing. I rubbed them together, trying to get the feeling back into them.

I'd never actually given anyone the kiss the life, but I'd seen a demonstration once, years ago in the village hall, at a first aid course organised by my mother. You covered the victim's mouth and blew. No, there was more to it than that. Think, think... I put my hand beneath his neck and tilted it back to clear the airway. I remembered that much.

As I looked down into his face, forcing myself to take steady, even breaths—I hadn't realised until then that my heart was beating rather too fast for comfort—it occurred to me that even in extremis Gabriel York had an austere beauty, that his wide, sensual mouth was the kind a girl might enjoy kissing under less trying circumstances. At least she would if she was into kissing and all the messy stuff that inevitably followed.

Heartbreak, pain...

I forced myself to concentrate, cupping his chin in my hand and placing my lips over his to seal off the air.

His unshaven chin was bristly against my palm, my fingers. His mouth was cool, but not cold...

I forced myself to concentrate and blew steadily into his mouth.

At this point I nearly passed out myself from lack

of oxygen. I'd been concentrating so hard on remembering what to do that I'd missed out the vital step of taking a breath first. Okay. I'd got it now. Breath in, mouth to mouth, blow. And again.

How long was I supposed to keep this up? As if in answer, I heard that long-ago demonstrator sternly warning that once you began CPR you had to continue until relieved...

How much longer was the ambulance going to be?

I paused for another breath, and this time when I looked at him he seemed to have regained a little colour. Encouraged, I tried again.

There was a definite change—the kind of response that if I didn't know better would have given me the distinct impression that I was being—well, kissed back. No, definitely kissed back...

Oh, sugar...

I opened my eyes—that level of concentration had required my eyes to be tightly shut—and discovered that I was not imagining things. Clearly I had this kiss of life thing down to a fine art, because Gabriel York had his eyes open, too. Black, glittering behind quite scandalously thick lashes, and dangerously over-heated. Quite suddenly, I was the one in need of mouth-to-mouth resuscitation.

Rapidly recovering my wits—I had a highly developed sense of self-preservation where thick dark lashes were concerned—I decided it was time to put a safe distance between us. He was having none of that; his arm was around my waist before the message from my brain reached my limbs, holding me with rather more strength than anyone who'd been unconscious just moments before should have been able to summon up.

'Who the devil are you?' he demanded.

Huh? Whatever happened to, Thank you for saving my life?

Charitably putting his brusqueness down to disorientation—and bearing in mind that my electricity bill was in his hands—I didn't say the first thing that leapt into my mind. Instead I replied—somewhat breathlessly, it's true—'I'm Sophie Harrington.' All my spare breath had been pumping up his lungs, okay? I would have offered him my hand at this point, and said the obligatory How d'you do?, but one of my hands was already busy cradling his chin, while the other was doing something Florence Nightingaleish in the vicinity of his brow. I immediately stopped that nonsense and, in the absence of any other bright conversation ideas, said, 'I've sent for an ambulance. It should be here any minute.'

'What the hell did you do that for?' he demanded, with a lack of gratitude that I found just a bit galling, considering all I'd been through.

'Because you were unconscious—'

'Rubbish!'

'You had your eyes closed, you didn't respond to the doorbell and...and I couldn't find a pulse.'

'Where did you look?' I stopped cradling his chin and pressed my fingers against his Adam's apple. He moved my hand to the right and pushed it firmly beneath his chin. 'Try there.'

'Oh...' He definitely had a pulse. His heart was beating almost as fast as mine.

He made a move to sit up, but, hoping to retrieve

some credibility in the first aid department, I said,
'Look, you were out cold. I think you should roll over
into the recovery position and wait for the paramedics.' He made no attempt to obey instructions and he
was too big for me to push him—at least he was if
he didn't want to be pushed—so I said, 'In your own
time.'

I added a smile, just so he'd know he was in safe
hands.

All I got for my pains was a scowl, but at least he
was alive and talking. Whether he was quite making
sense only time would tell. Whatever. I'd done my
bit, and at this point I should have been safe in assuming that nothing worse could happen. Indeed, that
when he'd recovered sufficiently to realise that I'd
risked my life to save his he would be transformed
into Mr Congeniality and I would be showered with
thanks for bravery above and beyond the call of dog-
walking duties. Possibly. I could wait.

Instead, still frowning, he said, 'Why were you
kissing me?' From his tone, I didn't get the impression it was an experience he would wish to repeat any
time soon.

Well, snap.

'I wasn't kissing you,' I replied, losing the smile.
What did he think I was? Some crazy woman who
leapt on unconscious men? I wanted to make sure he
understood that I did not kiss men I didn't know, and
even if I did I certainly wouldn't have to wait until
they were unconscious. 'I was giving you the kiss of
life.'

He barked out something that might have been a
laugh. The dismissive kind that lacked any kind of

humour or warmth. 'That had about as much in common with CPR as—'

I was spared whatever unflattering comparison he
had in mind as a couple of uniformed policemen, taking advantage of the fact that I'd left the door ajar
for the paramedics, burst into the hall. One of them
grabbed me by the arm and without so much as a by-
your-leave hauled me to my feet with an, 'All right,
young lady...'

With that, pandemonium broke out as the older of
the two dogs—the one that had been keeping watch
over Gabriel York—leapt up, pushing himself between me and the policemen. From somewhere deep
in his throat he produced a low, threatening growl that
he might well have learned from his master.

The other dog immediately stopped dancing excitedly about the new arrivals and joined in. My heroes.

'Percy! Joe! Down.'

Percy, still baring his teeth but lowering the growl
until it was scarcely audible, obeyed his master's
voice in his own good time, his haunches almost but
not quite in contact with the floor, ready to spring to
my defence at the slightest provocation. Joe followed
his example. The policeman, taking heed of this canine warning that any injudicious move would be met
with extreme prejudice, let go of my arm and took a
step back.

'Would someone like to tell me what the hell is
going on?'

Gabriel York had taken advantage of the distraction
to sit up and now, grabbing hold of the stairpost, he
hauled himself to his feet.

'No...' I began. He glared at me for apparently

daring to defy him. More gently, I said, 'You really should sit down, Mr York.'

He gave me a look that suggested he would deal with me later, before ignoring my advice and turning to the nearest policeman. 'You,' he said. 'What are you doing here?'

'One of your neighbours called us, sir. She saw this young woman—' he unwisely gestured in my direction, got a warning reprise of the growl from Percy for his trouble and immediately lowered his arm '—er, apparently breaking in through an upstairs window and called the local station.'

Gabriel York turned back to look at me. Sweat had broken out on his upper lip and he looked as if he was about to pass out again at any minute. But not, apparently, before he'd got some answers. 'Is that right? You climbed in through an upstairs window?'

'I had to do something!' I was absolutely livid. I'd been out there, hanging on by my fingernails, risking my life, and instead of coming to help me his nosy neighbour had sat behind her curtains and called the police. Actually, my own legs felt suddenly less than solid as I had a quick flashback of the risks I'd taken. 'I couldn't just leave you lying there.'

'How did you know I was—' he made a gesture in the direction of the floor '—lying there?'

'Look, my name is Sophie Harrington,' I said, turning to the nearest policeman. 'I was sent here by the Garland Agency. They'll vouch for me. When no one answered the doorbell I looked through the letterbox and saw Mr York lying unconscious—' he snorted dismissively at this '—lying unconscious,' I repeated, 'on the floor at the foot of the stairs, so I climbed up the downpipe and in through the window.'

The policeman turned to Gabriel York for a response to this. This time he didn't snort. After a few moments' silent contemplation he nodded, then winced, then said, 'My neighbour undoubtedly did the correct thing, but Miss Harrington is right—' well, hallelujah '—she's here to walk my dogs.'

'Lifesaving is all part of the service,' I volunteered, earning myself another black look.

'I'm sorry you've been bothered, gentlemen,' he added, clearly hoping they'd leave so that he could collapse quietly. To be honest, he looked so grim that I had to force myself to stay put and not rush over to him and make him sit down before he collapsed in a heap at the foot of the stairs. Something warned me that it would not be a good idea.

Fortunately I did have one ace up my sleeve. I turned to the policemen. 'They're not the only ones who've been bothered, I'm afraid. Before I climbed in through the upstairs window and applied the kiss of life—'

'I was not dead!'

No. He certainly wasn't that. Even in extremis he'd managed a fairly good impression of being very much alive.

'—I called for an ambulance,' I finished, as if I had not been interrupted, hoping that I sounded as if I didn't care one way or another if it ever arrived.

'Then you can ring them again and call them off.'

The effort of talking was exhausting him, but his eyes held mine with an inner power. They were full of anger at his own weakness, hating me for having seen him that way, and I knew that there was no way I was going to be keeping this job—which was, I suppose, why I shrugged and said, 'If you can make it to the phone, Mr York, you can call them off yourself. Otherwise you're stuck with them.' I smiled at the younger of the two policemen. He looked barely old enough to shave. Blissfully, he blushed. 'You'll stay until the paramedics arrive, gentlemen? These poor dogs really have to do what a dog has to do.'

They raised no objection.

The dogs' leads were looped over a chair, along with—oh, joy—a pooper-scooper and some plastic bags. I picked them up, fastened the leads to the dogs' collars and, leaving my employer in the capable care of two strapping policemen, said, 'Okay, boys. Walkies.'

Joe needed no second bidding, leaping to his paws, his feathered tail whirling, his slender cream body quivering with excitement beneath his short silky coat. Percy looked to his master.

Gabriel York never took his eyes off me, and I found myself reliving the moment when the kiss of life had become something much more personal, remembering exactly how his lips had felt beneath mine, how his dark hair had felt beneath my hand as I'd brushed it back from his forehead. The strength of his jaw as I'd cradled it...

Then, with the slightest movement of his hand, he gave his dogs permission to go, and with a jerk on my aching shoulder I found myself being towed through the door, down the steps and into the street.

An ambulance turned the corner as we headed in the direction of Battersea Park and I grinned.

Obviously he hadn't got to the phone in time.

It was only when I reached the park and set the dogs loose that I wondered what on earth I was going to do with them if the paramedics carted him off to hospital.

CHAPTER THREE

THE alarm was like a chainsaw chewing through my brain. That was the trouble with surprise parties. They took you by surprise and you didn't have time to re-mind yourself of the golden rule about not drinking on an empty stomach. More particularly the platinum, diamond-encrusted rule about not drinking too many margaritas on an empty stomach.

Since I'd been expecting nothing more than a quiet drink with a mate, I hadn't made a huge effort with my appearance either, going for comfort rather than glamour. I'd taken a long hot shower, to remove what seemed like half of Battersea Park, filed down the ruins of my nails and decided to forgo the doubtful pleasure of spending hours with a brush and hairdryer in an effort to return my hair to sleek perfection, and gone for the rumpled, dragged-through-a-hedge-backwards look instead.

Well, it had come close.

A dab of concealer on the nicely developing bruise, a pair of favourite—if past their fashion statement days—trousers, a baggy shirt and a pair of boots and I'd been all set.

Then I'd walked into the bar.

Everyone else had been dressed to kill, of course. I'd been the only one actually in the mood to perform the deed.

Tony, a bloke a girl could usually rely on not to

do anything clever, had ignored my 'I do not want to even think about this birthday, let alone celebrate it' response to his query about a party. He'd assumed that I was joking—I said he wasn't clever—and pulled out all the stops.

But—and these are probably the three most damning words in the English language—he'd meant well. To be honest, after the second margarita what I was wearing hadn't seemed to matter that much, and I'd surprised myself by having a great time. Cleverer than I thought, perhaps...

I groped for the clock, turned it off and fell out of bed while I was still awake. A walk—a long walk with two very lively dogs—would undoubtedly be good for me. Always assuming I could remember how to put one foot in front of another. Always assuming I still had a job.

On my return to Gabriel York's house yesterday I had been met by a frosty-faced Mrs York, who had wordlessly handed me a large towel at arm's length and watched from a safe distance while I'd removed all traces of mud from the dogs. Then, with the minimum of words, she'd indicated I should take them downstairs to the utility room and give them some water. After I'd removed my shoes. Clearly she didn't 'do' dogs.

Actually, I sympathised. She'd been wearing a charcoal grey business suit that had clearly cost a mint and in her place I wouldn't have wanted two excitable and muddy hounds near me. Honesty compels me to admit that it had been a mistake not to clip their leads back on before we reached the lake. It was asking for trouble and, as usual, I got it. They'd instantly spotted a couple of ducks so far away that I hadn't noticed them and plunged right in, proving to be selectively deaf when I'd called them to heel.

They'd heard 'walkies', no problem.

Anyway, I'd mopped up the resulting mess under her chilling gaze, and in an effort to break the ice—and because I had a stake in his health, besides really wanting to know—enquired after Mr York. All the time I'd been out with the dogs I'd wondered whether he'd been hauled off in an ambulance, undoubtedly protesting that it wasn't in the least bit necessary, and what I was going to do if he had.

No worries. There'd been lights on all over the place when I returned. Great. And Mrs York was there to answer the door. Not so great.

In reply to my query, she had informed me that he was 'as well as could be expected under the circumstances'—which told me precisely nothing. I mean, I'd have liked to know if he was suffering from a bad bout of something flulike so that I could stock up on painkillers and tissues. One look at her had suggested it might not be advisable to explain about my 'kiss of life'. She hadn't looked as if she'd appreciate my sacrifice.

What she had done, was leave me with the unsettling impression that the 'circumstances' had everything to do with me.

Tempted as I'd been to point out that I'd actually saved his life—probably—I had restrained myself. A fair number of silky cream dog hairs, disturbed by my brisk towelling of Joe's coat, had floated in her direction and attached themselves to her skirt; I hadn't wanted to be around when she noticed them.

She hadn't mentioned the shattered figurine in her sitting room. It had occurred to me, however, that it could be the reason for the below-zero welcome. I have to say that I wouldn't be in the least bit surprised if she and Miss Frosty-Face were closely related. It was hardly any wonder that Gabriel York was such a grouch.

I had half expected to find a message from my least favourite job-finder on the answering machine when I got home, informing me smugly that I'd failed at even this undemanding task and my services were no longer required.

No message. Maybe dog-walkers were in short supply. Maybe I could name my own price. More likely she'd known she wouldn't be able to get anyone else to take my place by eight o'clock the next morning and I'd simply been granted a temporary reprieve until she found a more competent replacement.

It occurred to me that once I'd taken Gabriel York's dogs for a run I'd be well advised to check my e-mail and see if the internet employment agency I'd contacted had lived up to its promise and sent me a load of jobs that would suit me perfectly. Since that seemed unlikely, I'd also follow up a number of possibilities I'd circled in the newspaper. The 'working from home' one hadn't mentioned computers...

I used industrial quantities of one of those wake-you-up shower gels on my unwilling limbs, reminding myself that in the meantime the dog-walking would just about keep the wolf from the door. Today, I told the brown stripey cat as I went out, I would be on time if it killed me.

She was sympathetic, rubbing against my legs as I

gave her a handful of kibbles while keeping an eye out for the porter, who strongly disapproved of me giving her any encouragement to stay. I would have taken her in if pets were allowed at Chandler's Reach. No cats. No dogs. Nothing that couldn't be safely confined to a cage.

My experience with the little white lie about my allowance should really have taught me not to tempt fate.

Okay, so the journey to work hadn't killed me. I'd arrived on Gabriel York's doorstep in one piece, but it was no thanks to London Underground. The escalator hadn't been working when I arrived at my stop and I'd had two choices. Wait for it to be fixed or walk up to street level.

It was about a million steps, and whilst any other day I would have breezed the climb, my over-indulgence in margaritas meant that I'd arrived at street level dry-mouthed, panting and gasping for water.

By the time I'd queued at the kiosk, bought a bottle, swallowed enough of the stuff to ensure that I'd live and was once again bracketed by the mop-head bay trees, I was—and you will already have guessed this—late again.

It was as if some dark force didn't want me to have this job, and to be brutally frank I wasn't that keen on ringing the doorbell. Nothing good had come from it yet. Putting if off wasn't likely to improve matters, though. But, whatever happened in the next few minutes, I vowed that I would not be climbing up that downpipe again.

Having cheered myself up with that promise, I finally rang the bell. Somewhere a long way off I heard Percy and Joe barking in joyous expectation and the cheering up process was complete. It was, I decided, highly probable that I liked dogs better than I did people. Some people anyway.

Then Gabriel York, scowling for the Olympics, opened the door. And I knew I did.

I hadn't, even when over-indulging in the party spirit, quite been able to get him out of my mind. I kept recalling that moment when I opened my eyes and saw him looking at me. And the moment when my attempt at mouth-to-mouth resuscitation had become something else...

If I hadn't already been rather pink in the face from my exertions, I might have blushed.

Totally ridiculous.

Actually, he did look marginally better than he had moments before I'd been dragged through the door by his hounds. He'd shaved, and he was dressed in well-worn grey sweats—the kind you pull on when your skin can't stand the chafing of anything more demanding—but it occurred to me that he didn't go with the bay trees. Unlike his designer-perfect wife.

'Miss Harrington,' he said wearily. 'Are you always half an hour late for work? Or are you just doing your best to kill me?'

'Definitely trying to kill you,' I replied. I could do sarcasm without any prompting from him, but it always helped to have someone worthy of one's best efforts. You'll have worked out for yourself by this time that I was my own worst enemy. Then, because he was leaning rather heavily on the door for support—and as if I hadn't tempted providence enough for one day—I added, 'Should you be out of bed?'

'Not according to anyone with an opinion on the matter,' he conceded, apparently caught offside by my counter-attack. This didn't look like a man who was used to admitting he was wrong—ever. About anything. He stood back to let me inside without bothering to check my footwear for mud. 'But since I'd just about given up on you I didn't seem to have a choice.'

'And?' I prompted, wiping my feet really thoroughly. I thought he had enough problems without me leaving muddy footprints all over the hall floor.

'I'm sorry?'

I had the distinct feeling they weren't two words he used often—at least not as an apology. Along with those other special words—thank you. For risking life and limb to save his. Life.

But then he wasn't apologising. He was simply prompting me to elaborate.

'Are you telling me that you've risen from your bed of pain to take Percy and Joe for a nice long rootle around the park yourself?' I enquired, sweetness itself. Clearly Mrs York wasn't going to do it for him. Where was his wife anyway? He shouldn't be left on his own. He should be tucked up in bed with someone to bring him warm drinks and hot water bottles and home-made chicken soup.

My smart mouth earned me another scowl, probably—no, definitely—deserved. Even if I was not to blame I was still horribly late.

'Regrettably not. If I was capable of walking anywhere further than the bathroom I wouldn't need you.'

He was frank, too.

'I was going to let them out into my sister-in-law's immaculate garden and earn myself two black marks. Not that she deserves any better.'

She was his sister-in-law? Not his wife? My heart leapt in the most ridiculous manner. This man was favourite for the Grouch of the Month award, for heaven's sake. Maybe of the year. Why would my heart be interested?

'Two black marks?'

'One for getting up and slowing down my recovery, thus prolonging my imposition on her busy life. One for letting the dogs do—'

'Right,' I said. I'd got the picture.

She wasn't his wife, and she not only disliked his dogs she didn't much care for him, either.

And? What possible interest was that to me?

He sketched a shrug. 'I would, of course, have blamed you.' The thought appeared to cheer him slightly. '*Are* you always late?' he repeated.

'Certainly not.' I was outraged at the suggestion. No matter how near the truth it might be. 'I started out in plenty of time—' as indeed I had; it was simply that events had conspired against me '—unfortunately there was a problem on the—'

He held up his hand to stop me. It was a big, square hand, with long, sexy fingers, attached to a thick wrist, a strong arm...

Maybe I was staring at it rather too obviously—hands are so important in a man—because somewhat self-consciously he clenched it into a fist, then dropped it back to his side. 'Spare me the details,' he said. I was clearly wearing what little patience he possessed so thin that it was practically transparent. 'I just thought that if it was standard I'd book you for half an hour earlier in the hope that you might arrive before Percy and Joe had chewed the door off the utility room in desperation.'

The corners of his eyes crinkled promisingly in what might have been the beginning of a smile before he remembered that he was being irritable and thought better of it. I didn't care. He wasn't going to phone Miss Frosty-Face and ask for a replacement!

Quite suddenly I wanted to hug him. Well, not that suddenly, really. The thought had been there all the time, just looking for an excuse—just as an experiment. To see if yesterday's surprising response was a one-off.

I mean, for heaven's sake, he'd looked as if he was at death's door. Hardly love's young dream. But then I'd already tried that with PCF.

Remembering him made it so much easier to restrain myself.

I wasn't in the market for dreams of any kind. But especially not the romantic variety.

'Really, it isn't necessary,' I said, doing a rather good job of keeping the desire to grin from breaking out all over my face, too. My job was apparently safe, but this was just two hours a day walking dogs, not personal assistant to some movie star. Or anyone the slightest bit interesting who didn't expect me to be clever with computers. 'I may be reduced to dog-walking to earn a living, but I can tell the time,' I said, perhaps a little more briskly than was entirely justified. I was late for the second day running. And I'd only been doing the job for two days. Then, 'Maybe I should get started,' I said. 'Joe and Percy are beginning to sound hysterical.'

'After yesterday they've been confined to the utility room,' he said, and with that any chance of a smile receded into the far distance. 'It's downstairs. Take them out through the rear—there's a gate leading to the mews at the back.' He reached out and took my hand, placed a key, warm from his pocket, into my palm, and then closed my fingers about it, holding them closed for a moment. 'It's kept locked.' And this time his dark eyes did warm, momentarily. 'To keep out burglars.'

An hour with Percy and Joe was a spirit-lifting adventure. They were so overjoyed to be free that it was impossible not to respond to their excitement as they rootled through the woods, exploring all the wildest bits of the park before doing a reprise of their duck-hunting in the lake.

They moved like greased lightning, and Percy returned with the tail feathers of a mallard, fat and lazy from the easy living in a London park, clenched between his teeth. These dogs were clearly bred to hunt rather than live in designer chic in Belgravia. They needed space and should be living out in the country.

Under other circumstances I might have volunteered to take them home. That was dog paradise. No one there had ever made a fuss about scuff marks on the doors or mud on the carpet.

My mother, when she'd phoned, hadn't enquired about the man she'd been married to for best part of thirty years. But she had asked about her old spaniel. He was getting on, poor love, and would be missing her dreadfully.

I blinked, surprised by a tear.

I totally lost track of time, but, mud-splattered and happy, we eventually arrived back at the York homestead.

The happiness did not last.

Gabriel York met me at the back door with a face that would curdle milk. 'Where the hell have you been?' he demanded. 'I thought you'd—'

'What? Lost them?'

He drew in a sharp, annoyed breath—whether he was annoyed with himself or with me I couldn't say—dragged his fingers distractedly through his thick dark hair and said, 'You're back in one piece; that's all that matters. But if they're too much for you to handle—'

'No. I'm sorry if you were worried, but we were just having too much fun to stop. Although to be honest—' I dug around in my pocket, found the duck feathers and put them on the nearest work surface '—I'm not too sure about the legal position on duck-hunting in London parks. This one got away, but it was a near thing. I rely on you to bail me out if necessary. What kind of dogs are they?'

'Salukis. Persian greyhounds. They're sight-hunters. I'm sorry, I should have warned you that they'll see stuff long before you do.'

'You weren't in much of a state to do anything that useful,' I reminded him. 'You still look pretty ropey, actually. If you don't mind me saying.' Ignoring the way his mouth tightened as he resisted the urge to tell me that he minded very much, I said, 'I'll bring you a cup of tea when I've rubbed these two down.'

'You will?' He looked as if he really didn't want to ask the next question. But he just couldn't help himself. 'Where will I be?'

'Lying down.' He really did look out on his feet, gaunt and a bit grey around the mouth, and whilst I had no serious objection to giving him the kiss of life again I didn't want to seem too eager; he might get the wrong idea. Or maybe it was the right one; much worse. 'In bed. Before you fall down,' I added, in my bossiest nanny-type voice. It hadn't worked on the dogs, but I had an ace up my sleeve. 'I warn you, Mr York, if I have to call an ambulance again I'll stay and make sure they take you away in it this time.'

'Do that,' he warned, 'and the dogs will have to go into boarding kennels. And you'll be out of a job.'

'No!'

'Cristabel is only putting up with them because she thinks having them around is good for me,' he replied. 'She's only putting up with me because I was released from hospital on the sole understanding that I was not going to be on my own.' He shrugged. 'As you've noticed, I get dizzy spells.'

'Is that what you're calling it? I'd have said you passed out cold, myself.' Which was rather unkind since, gratifyingly, he hadn't mistaken my horror for selfishness but concern on behalf of the dogs.

'She's really being very generous,' he continued, ignoring my interruption, 'but I suspect that broken figurine in her sitting room is trying her patience practically beyond endurance.'

Oh, right. Ace up sleeve fielded and neatly returned.

'That wasn't the dogs,' I said, owning up. 'But you already know that…'

Creases at the corners of his eyes fanned unexpectedly into a wry smile. 'I know that. The dogs know that. But I've given her a hard enough time already without putting her in the position of having to explain to her insurance company how easily you managed to climb in through an upstairs window—'

'It wasn't *easy*. I've got the broken fingernails to prove it.' I displayed them for his inspection and, quite unexpectedly, he took my hands, holding them as he looked at the shortened version of what had only yesterday been long, well-manicured perfection. Then, after what seemed liked hours, a sudden tremor seized him and he dropped them.

'Even so,' he said, abruptly, 'a burglar wouldn't have worried about his nails, and I suspect they'd take exception to the lack of security and raise her premiums.'

'It's fortunate the window was open. A piece of china can be replaced—'

'Possibly,' he snapped, before I could suggest that he couldn't be. He stuffed his hands into his pants pockets and lost the smile. 'But she'd still blame the dogs. If they hadn't been here you wouldn't have had to climb in through the window.'

'Someone should have been here to let me in.'

'If you'd been on time my brother would have been. He was supposed to walk them himself, but there's been some sort of crisis…' He stopped, shrugged. 'He waited for as long as he could. I'd just about given up on you and was on my way down to let them out into the garden.'

Oh, knickers. That was what he'd meant by me trying to kill him. He should have been in bed last night. And undoubtedly I'd messed up the system again this morning. And then I'd spent ages longer than my allocated hour in the park.

He should be there right now. Which made me feel bad. But one thing was clear: he wasn't staying in this horrible house out of choice. And that cheered me up enormously. Ridiculous, but there it was. Not that he seemed to be getting too much in the way of TLC from his busy family. Considering he wasn't supposed to be left on his own.

I kept the questions to myself and said, 'In that case I suggest you go back to bed, Mr York, before you collapse and the situation is taken out of both our hands.'

'Gabriel,' he said. 'Or Gabe, if you find that a bit of a mouthful.'

'Gabriel is fine,' I said, without having to think about it. 'I'm Sophie. If you ever call me Soph you'll be walking your own dogs.'

'Sophie.' He regarded me steadily for a long moment. 'I won't forget.'

'Good. And I'll make an effort to be on time in future.' How, I wasn't sure, but I'd think of something. 'Just go back to bed, Gabriel.'

It felt oddly intimate—exchanging names, ordering him to bed as if I'd known him for ever instead of being total strangers. Feeling unexpectedly self-conscious, I busied myself getting out of the hideous

faux-fur, pulled off the close-fitting hat that kept my
ears warm.

'You're blonde,' he said, in an 'I should have
known' voice, as my hair fell down around my neck.

'I know that,' I assured him, rapidly losing the
smile and setting to work rubbing the dogs down with
a pile of old towels left for the purpose. I knew my
limitations. Blonde jokes I could do without. 'Is that
a problem?'

He didn't answer, or move for what seemed like
for ever, then he said, 'Second floor, first door on the
right.'

'Gabriel?' He paused in the doorway, half turned.
'Can I make you some toast or something?'

'Will you take any notice if I say no?'

'Probably not.'

'Then, providing you don't mind wasting your
time, I won't waste my breath.' Wisely, he chose not
to hang around for an argument.

So much for intimacy. And he hadn't smiled back.

'That's us women,' I said to Percy as I carefully
cleaned his paws. 'Tiresome creatures who always
think we know what's best for a man.' Unlike men,
who never did. 'Although, come to think of it, that
sounded suspiciously like a roundabout way of saying
yes, don't you think?' Being a man, he couldn't just
come out and say it.

Percy, bless him, licked my neck, which I knew
meant he agreed with me. I gave him and Joe a hug
and promised I'd be back later. Then I went through
into the kind of kitchen that I'd only ever seen fea-
tured in lifestyle magazines. The kind that looked as
if it had never seen a frying pan in action.

The fridge, however, was well stocked with the kind of expensive organic stuff that a food-conscious hostess would offer her guests. Maybe I was letting my prejudices get out of hand. Gabriel York's sister-in-law was probably a very nice woman when she wasn't burdened with unwanted guests. Especially when two of them were very lively dogs.

I knew from experience exactly what kind of mess two dogs could make.

I filled the kettle with filtered water, sliced stone-ground organic bread and placed it in the toaster. I found a tray and set out a glass of freshly squeezed orange juice—could it be freshly squeezed from a plastic bottle?—and added French butter and English marmalade. I did consider boiling one of the fat brown organic free-range eggs nestling in what looked like genuine straw, but decided that was just asking for abuse. Tomorrow, I promised myself as I poured the tea. I'd advance to an egg tomorrow.

I carried the tray up three flights of stairs and congratulated myself on the fact that I could save money on gym membership. I wasn't going to need to belong to a gym if I kept this up.

Gabriel York had, fortunately, left the door open, so I didn't have to use my foot to knock. Nevertheless, I thought it wise to advertise my presence before I went barging in.

'Gabriel?'

No reply. I put my head around the door and saw why. He'd flopped on top of the bed and fallen asleep. I put the tray down on a table by the window, then quietly cleared the night table so I could leave it close to hand for him when he woke. At least the orange juice would still be okay...

'What are you doing?'

I jumped, and a book slid on the floor. 'Trying not to wake you,' I offered as I bent to pick it up. Scarcely a little light sick room reading. It was a text book. Tropical medicine. Good grief, what on earth had he got?

'Then you failed.'

I put the book back and said, 'You know, it's a good job you're sick, or people might just tell you that you've got a serious problem with your inter-personal skills.'

He glowered at me. 'Is that right?'

'They might even say you're a bad-tempered grouch.'

'But only if I wasn't sick?'

'Very sick,' I amended, thoroughly fed up with his irritability. He might be having a hard time, but he didn't have to take it out on me. 'Fatal would just about cover it,' I added, under my breath.

'Not this time,' he replied. Clearly his hearing wasn't impaired. 'Although malaria is tricky. It will kill a fit man in days if it goes to the brain.'

'Malaria?' Good grief, I hadn't meant it. He looked bad, but not that bad... 'I thought you could take something to prevent that.'

'You can. It isn't infallible. Especially if you don't take it. This is a serious case of physician heal thy-self...' He finally managed something approaching a smile. It was worth the effort. The lines carved into his cheeks turned from haggard to rugged and it lit up his incredibly dark eyes in a way that more than made up for the sallow complexion.

I finished clearing a space for the tray and placed it beside him. 'You're a doctor?' I asked. 'I'm sure the agency said mister.'

'They would. I'm a surgeon.'

'Oh.' Which explained the bedtime reading. 'Why?'

'Why am I a surgeon?'

'No. Why is it mister? For surgeons? They don't do that in the US, do they?'

'You've lived there?'

'No, but I've watched *ER* on the television and...' I stopped, realising just how stupid that must sound.

'You know how the British like to be different,' he said, pushing himself up against the headboard. 'You may have noticed, while you were watching television, that we drive on the wrong side of the road, too.' My foolishness had at least raised another of those rare smiles. Even if it was at my expense, it was worth it. 'Are you going to give me that cup of tea, or is it just for decoration?'

'Oh, sorry.' I handed him the cup and saucer. He took the cup and I spooned sugar in until he told me to stop. My instincts were all urging me to say that so much sugar was not good for him. Luckily my will-power roused itself sufficiently to suggest that, since he was a doctor, he almost certainly knew that, and I kept quiet.

'Toast?' I didn't wait for a reply, but applied butter and marmalade, cut the slice of toast neatly in two, handed him one half and bit into the other half myself. I thought he'd be more likely to eat if he had company. Actually, all that organic stuff tasted pretty good. I just wished I'd brought up my tea, too. 'It's a long time since breakfast,' I said in response to a slightly ironic look. I didn't add that I hadn't actually eaten any breakfast. I didn't want any of that 'most important meal of the day' stuff. I was the one doing disapproving here.

'Help yourself. But sit down and take your time or you'll get indigestion.' He moved his long legs over to make room for me. Maybe I hesitated, feeling just the teeniest bit self-conscious about sitting on the bed of a man I scarcely knew—at least while he was in occupation—because somewhat irritably he added, 'That's my professional opinion. I won't charge you. This time.'

I sat.

CHAPTER FOUR

'WHERE did you get malaria?' I asked, in an attempt to distract myself. Which was ridiculous. I was twenty-five, for heaven's sake. And a day. It wasn't as if he was naked. Apart from his feet. He had excellent feet. Big without being excessive. And long sexy toes. They matched the long sexy fingers which were curled tightly around the cup.

He was, however, in no state to jump me. And he couldn't have made it any plainer that he didn't want to. Which was good.

I didn't want to be responsible for setting back his recovery.

'I mean, it isn't like the common cold,' I said, reverting to the distraction of malaria. 'You aren't likely to pick it up in Belgravia, are you?'

'I don't live in Belgravia.' He shrugged when I refused to be distracted into asking him where he did live. I'd get to that later. 'I was in West Africa, working with a medical charity. I spend a couple of weeks every year with them, doing cataract ops.' He was an eye surgeon, then... 'Did.'

'You don't think they'll let you do it again? Not even if you promise to be good and take your medicine?'

He finished the piece of toast he'd been holding for ever. I got the distinct feeling that he found it easier to eat than answer my question.

'So,' I said, buttering a second piece of toast and delaying the moment when, inevitably, I would put my head on the block. I cut it in two, but didn't hand him his share. I knew better than to try to force-feed invalids. I was hoping he'd take it just to be awkward. Being a man. 'Why didn't you take the stuff that would have protected you from getting it? Malaria?'

'The side effects were making it difficult to work, and the truth of the matter is that you just never think it will happen to you.'

I opened my mouth to say that he, if anyone, should have known better. And that there had to have been an alternative. Which he would have known a lot more about than me.

'Men are so useless. You need a wife to take care of you,' I said. Then, well aware that I was overstepping my dog-walker role, bit down on the toast. He wouldn't throw me out while I was eating. I'd definitely get indigestion...

He gave me an old-fashioned look. Well, it was a pretty old-fashioned idea.

'That's a somewhat un-PC notion. Are you volunteering?' he asked.

'Well, that would solve a lot of my problems,' I replied. I could get control of my trust fund and give up dog-walking as a career. On the other hand... 'But it would also present me with a whole new set.'

'All of them man-sized?'

'Quite. It's yet another example of the inequality of the sexes. Women don't actually need husbands, you see. We know how to take care of ourselves. Although I must admit I've heard a few career women remark that they could do with a wife of their own to handle all the tedious details of life. But men need wives. Take you, for instance.'

'I promise you, I'm managing well enough without one.'

'Oh, I don't mean just for sex,' I said, irritated that he was reducing my beautiful theory to the basics, then found myself blushing.

'Oddly enough, neither did I,' he replied, having to put a real effort into not showing his amusement. Which was not the same as smiling.

'I only meant,' I said, 'that if you'd had a wife she'd have made sure you took your anti-malaria drugs.' He was about to object, but I hadn't finished. 'And if they'd had side effects that bothered you she'd have made it her business to find something else that didn't.' Then, well into my stride, I added, 'And if she couldn't find anything suitable she'd have made sure she lost your passport.'

He concentrated on his tea. 'There's a flaw in your argument. That kind of wife has gone out of fashion.'

'How do you know? Have you been looking?'

'No. The last thing on earth I need is a wife. A marriage needs to be worked at. Requires serious emotional input.'

'So? It's not exactly hard labour.'

'No,' he said. 'But one in three marriages end in divorce.' Heavy on the irony, there. 'Of course my family is doing its best to buck the national average.'

He was divorced?

'Oh…sugar.' Me and my big mouth. He was sick, and instead of cheering him up I was adding to his depression. 'I'm sorry. I didn't mean… I should go.' I made a move, but he caught my arm, stopped me.

'Don't apologise, Sophie. It's scarcely your fault. It's just something of a family failing.' His hand lingered longer than was strictly necessary, and as if he couldn't think what else to do with it he finally reached out and took the other triangle of toast. 'Stay and finish your breakfast,' he said.

'What about your brother?' I said, gesturing at the house around us. I took the view that since he'd asked me to stay I had been given tacit permission to continue with the conversation. 'He's married.'

He looked at me with something close to exasperation. 'Tell me why we're having this conversation.'

'Unlike you,' I informed him, 'I have excellent inter-personal skills—a fact you might mention to that woman from the agency if she asks if I did a good job. People talk to me. You were telling me about your brother?' I prompted, before doing as I was told and taking another bite of toast.

He surrendered without a fight. Well, he was sick, poor man. 'Michael and Crissie live detached lives. They share a house, a bed, but precious little else. As a family we tend to be single-minded in our pursuit of a goal. And it's not just the men. The women are as bad. The people who make the mistake of loving us tend to get brushed aside by the slip-stream. Crissie only survives because she's like us. Totally single-minded in pursuit of her objective.'

On the point of allowing myself to be side-tracked with a Which is…?, I stopped myself. I wasn't interested in his sister-in-law. I wanted to know about him. 'You have sisters?'

'One. She's a politician.'

'Really? Would I have heard of her?' His expression suggested I think for a moment, and when my brain ran its memory program it didn't have to work too hard to come up with Jessica York. The woman everyone was watching as she rose to the top faster than Jersey cream. 'Jessica York is your sister?'

'My *divorced* sister.'

'I didn't know she was ever married.'

'She wasn't for long. Her husband caught her very young. She rapidly outgrew him.'

'Oh.'

'My mother is a lawyer,' he said, without waiting for me to ask. 'She led a campaign for equal rights for women in the workplace. Now she's a member of a government think-tank on women's issues. And, incidentally, also divorced.'

'I'm almost afraid to ask what your father does.'

'Irons his own shirts?' he offered. Then shook his head. 'No, of course he doesn't. He has a housekeeper to take care of the boring details and a series of charming lady-friends to take care of his other needs. He's a heart surgeon.'

'You take after him?'

'I've chosen to leave out the broken marriage.'

He *wasn't* divorced...

'Can you do that?' I asked. 'What happens when you fall in love?'

'I don't. It isn't compulsory.'

'I didn't realise there was a choice.' Then, in case he decided this was an invitation to switch the conversation to my own romantic attachments, or lack of them, I said, 'You're making a big mistake, you know. Married men live longer than bachelors simply because they have someone who cares enough to sweat the small stuff for them.'

'Is that right?'

'There are statistics,' I assured him.

My father had never had to give one thought to the details in his entire married life. How long would he manage before he started going downhill without my mother to take care of him? Or me.

Not wanting to go on that particular guilt trip, I offered Gabriel the last piece of toast, but as he reached to take it he lost control of the cup in his other hand and it tilted, spilling warm tea into his lap.

He let rip with one short but telling word, then flung himself off the bed and began to rip off the soaked bottoms.

I had one glimpse of long, hairy legs before I busied myself retrieving the cup, pulling off the cover before the tea soaked through to the sheets. I dashed downstairs with it, and by the time I'd stuffed it in the washing machine, found the soap and worked out the right program, he'd followed me down and added his tracksuit bottoms to the machine.

'I don't think that should go in with something white,' I protested.

His only response was to hit the 'on' switch.

'I'll, um, go and get the tray, shall I?'

'Leave it.'

'Right. Well, I'd better go,' I said, not really wanting to leave Gabriel alone. Hoping that he'd ask me to stick around. 'Will you be all right on your own?'

'I have a feeling that I'll be a lot safer that way. You are not good for my health.' I thought that was unfair, but didn't argue. Clearly my expression had other ideas. 'You're here to walk the dogs, Sophie, not fuss around me.'

Someone should. 'I thought the point of you staying here was to have someone on hand.'

'Then you thought wrong. It was to get me out of hospital. I don't need anyone mopping my fevered brow.'

I'd been that obvious?

'Go and do whatever you do with the rest of your day. Crissie's daily will be here any minute, and my brother will look in at lunchtime to ensure that the dogs don't wreck the designer garden while they have a comfort break.'

'Well, that's something, I suppose.' There was a pen and a notepad beside the kitchen phone. I wrote down my phone number, tore off the sheet and gave it to him. He took it, and I saw that he was shivering. 'You should put something on your feet.' He stuffed the paper into his pocket. 'If he can't make it, call me, okay? Don't go falling downstairs or passing out again.' I didn't wait for him to tell me he was perfectly able to manage, but headed for the door. 'I'll be back this evening.' I looked back, still reluctant to go. 'Is there anything I can bring you?'

I got a raised eyebrow for my trouble. 'Such as?'

'I don't know. A little light reading, perhaps? Medical text books are notoriously bad for your health. What about the latest Clancy or Grisham?' He didn't look impressed. Tired of putting myself out constantly for someone who couldn't be bothered to say thank you, even if it was coupled with no, I said, 'Maybe you'd prefer something off the top shelf? I won't tell your sister-in-law...'

He opened his mouth as if to say something. Then, no doubt deciding that discretion was probably the better part of whatever, paused before saying, 'No. Thank you.'

Even grouches could be brought to good manners with a little shove in the right direction.

'What about a video? Something to make you laugh.'

'Crissie doesn't have a television.'

'Oh.' His brother and sister-in-law might be very nice people—I was reserving judgement on that one—but they wouldn't be my choice of convalescent heaven.

Obviously he didn't have a choice.

'I've got a little portable set I could spare,' I offered.

'No, thank you. I'll survive.'

'A radio? A CD-player?' I was on a roll, going for the thank-you hat-trick. 'That's my final offer...'

'Just bring yourself,' he growled. 'And try to get here on time.'

'You can count on me.'

'I won't hold my breath.'

The internet agency was as good as its word. It had flooded my inbox with job opportunities, each one more unspeakably depressing than the one before. It was possible that by the time I'd worked to the end of them the first job would, in contrast, suddenly become so appealing that I'd beg for an interview. Maybe that was the plan.

I called the 'work at home' ad, hoping for something more exciting, but it turned out to be a scheme where I sent them money for a start-up kit of stuff to put together. Whilst I might not be a genius, it did occur to me that this was not the way it was supposed to work. I thanked them politely, but declined this fabulous opportunity to make them richer at my expense. And afterwards I reported them to the Trading Standards Office. There had to be a law…

I was trying to decide whether I'd rather be 'bright and articulate' in telesales—which was apparently the only growth industry at the moment—or if I wanted to embrace a career selling mobile phones, when my own phone rang.

'Sophie Harrington?' Miss Frosty. I felt the chill emanating from the earpiece of my phone. 'Lucy Cartwright.'

'Miss Cartwright.' All other contacts I'd had with agencies had been on a matey first-name basis. I just couldn't imagine ever calling this woman Lucy. 'Good morning.' One has to observe the civilities even when 'good' is a blatant exaggeration.

'I've got another little part-time job which might suit you. Bloomers need someone immediately, and remembering your enthusiasm for flower-arranging I naturally thought of you.'

'Oh!' Golly. *Bloomers!* They were the most seriously upmarket florists in London. My birthday sunflowers and roses had come from there. It seemed that I'd totally misjudged the woman. 'How kind of you.'

'Not at all. You'll have to work after the shop has closed, of course. Will that be a problem?'

'Er, no…'

'It's only temporary,' she warned. 'While their cleaner is off for some minor op. You start at six this evening. Someone will be there to show you what's required.' Maybe my underwhelmed silence warned her that suddenly I wasn't as totally thrilled, because she said, 'Of course, if you're too busy just say…'

This woman had a way of leaving me speechless that I was beginning to find extremely annoying. Since I was fairly sure that was her intention, I confined my response to a polite, 'Not at all.'

I took down the details, writing them beneath the dog-walking job. They were, at least, within easy walking distance of each other.

Dog-walker and cleaner. As a career plan it didn't exactly sparkle with prospects. But it could be worse. I was building a portfolio of jobs. I might not earn much, but I was going to be very fit.

The doorbell rang. Since no one had buzzed up from the entrance I assumed it was my 'guests' returning early from their country break only to discover that they'd forgotten their key.

It wasn't them. It was Aunt Cora, my mother's flighty younger sister; although, considering my mother's recent behaviour, maybe they were more alike than I'd imagined. It had just taken Mum longer to get going.

'Cora, what a lovely surprise!' I gave her a huge hug. Everyone needs an aunt like Cora. Generous, outrageous, full of fun. I adored her. 'Why didn't you call? How long are you staying?'

'It's a flying visit, darling. I've booked us a table for lunch at Giovanni's.' She regarded my sloppy attire with the critical eye of a woman who'd never been seen outside her own bathroom without a full make-up job. 'Did you know you've got a dirty mark on your chin?'

I rubbed at it, then wished I hadn't. 'Actually, it's a bruise.' She gave me a look that suggested no woman in control of her life would ever get a bruise on her chin. 'It's a long story—'

'Then save it for over lunch. I've got a taxi waiting.'

I didn't have time to do anything fancy with my hair, so I just brushed it and, since the curls were beginning to corkscrew wildly, fastened it back in a big ebony clasp. I dabbed concealer on my chin, to cover the bruise, and confined my make-up to a quick pass with mascara and lipstick, then slipped into a simple grey trouser suit and a pair of slender heels. Ten minutes later we were on our way.

'So? Flying visit?' I prompted.

She pressed a small jeweller's box into my hand. 'Happy birthday for yesterday.'

Did I say she was generous? The box contained an exquisite Victorian pendant set with amethysts and pearls. 'This is so lovely, Cora.'

'It belonged to your great-grandmother. She gave it to me when I got married.' She shrugged. 'The first time.'

And I found myself thinking of Gabriel. Committed never to marrying rather than risk failure, pain, heartache. Even if it was someone else's. I'd suggested that he was wrong, but I was no better...

'I was planning on giving it to you on your wedding day, but hardly anyone seems to bother with the formalities these days. Such a shame. There are pitifully few good excuses left for being totally extravagant with a hat.'

'I'm sorry to be such a disappointment,' I said, having to hunt for a smile. 'But thank you for a gorgeous present.'

'Oh, I haven't given up on you entirely. One of these days you'll meet someone else.'

'Someone else?'

'And stop pining over that Fotheringay boy.'

Which dealt with my smile. How could she possibly know? 'I'm not—' But she stopped me, patting my hand.

'Don't worry. I'm the only one who connected the fact that you left home when his engagement was announced. Or notices that you have a lot of boyfriends but no one who gets close enough to touch.' And, as if she hadn't just dropped a small bombshell, she went on, 'So, in the meantime, rather than let this moulder in a box I decided to give it to you now.'

'Well, thank you. I'll treasure it.'

'Just so long as you don't treat it like the crown jewels and keep it for state occasions. Make the most of it while your neck is still in good shape.'

All of a sudden I had the feeling that this wasn't going to be such a fun treat after all, but I told her about Kate's pot of anti-wrinkle cream and that made her laugh. Then we arrived at Giovanni's and conversation was put on hold while we decided what to eat.

'So,' I said, when we'd ordered and Cora seemed unusually quiet. 'What's the occasion? Adorable though you are, I can't believe you flew from the South of France for the day simply to give me a birthday present that you could just as easily have sent by courier.'

'No.' She sighed. 'Look, there's no easy way to say this, Sophie. My investments haven't been doing so well lately. I'm going to have to use the flat to top up my income.'

My mouth dried. What was it I'd been saying about things not getting worse?

'You want to let it?' I asked. 'At the market rate?' Wondering how on earth I could raise that kind of money.

She didn't answer immediately. All around us the restaurant hummed with people having a good time, leaving our table a little bubble of silence.

Heart sinking, I continued, 'You've already let it?'

'Actually, darling, I've sold it. Nigel and Amber just fell in love with it, you see. They've been looking everywhere for something that would come close, but you know how it is when you've seen somewhere perfect. Nothing else will do.'

I understood the concept very well. Perry Fotheringay had been perfect. I'd tried looking for someone else who would come close, too. But it was more than just his good looks. It was chemistry. A kind of recognition...

Without warning Gabriel York's glowering face was filling my head. His irritable growl as he pushed away help. Nothing could be further from Perry's soft teasing laughter, sparkling come-and-get-me eyes, yet my pulse-rate lifted until it was thudding through my ears as if I was still breathing my own life into his body.

'They've been pushing me and pushing me for

weeks.' Cora's voice broke through, bringing me back to reality. 'I imagine they think I've just been waiting for a bigger offer, but honestly until last week I wasn't interested. A meeting with my accountant has put a different complexion on things.'

'Oh, Cora, I'm so sorry.'

She put on a brave smile. 'A little temporary difficulty, that's all. Anyway, I'm here to sign the contracts. The completion date is down to you.'

She wanted to know how quickly I could move out. Clearly, for her sake, the sooner the better. 'It'll take me a day or two to pack. The weekend?'

'So soon? That would be wonderful.'

I sat back, momentarily winded. By the weekend I was going to be homeless. I could scarcely believe it. My house guests—who'd conveniently gone away for a week so they wouldn't be around when Cora broke the news—had bought my home from under me.

'It's not as if you could afford to stay there by yourself, Sophie,' Cora pointed out gently. 'Not now your father has suspended your trust income.' And how did she know about that? 'You haven't even got a job at the moment.'

'No, but—' About to tell her about my plans to sub-let Kate's room, I stopped myself. Cora had generously let us use her flat for years, asking nothing more than that we covered all the running costs. Now she needed the money, and the least I could do was make this as painless as possible for her. 'But that's just a little temporary difficulty,' I replied, echoing her own sentiments and managing to find a smile from somewhere. 'I'm more concerned about you.'

'No, no. You mustn't worry. I'll just have to be a

little less extravagant for a while.' Then, 'Why don't you go home for a while, Sophie?' This was beginning to sound like a conspiracy. Except Cora would never do that to me. She sounded genuinely concerned as she said, 'Your father really needs you. He's falling apart without your mother.'

Of course he was. He'd never once in all his married life reached for a clean shirt and not found one ready and waiting. She'd run the house, the church social committee, the community council, the whole village, for heaven's sake, practically single-handed. She'd given and given and given, until one day she'd found herself on the receiving end of a little attention for a change. It had gone to her head. And would undoubtedly end in tears.

'He's not the only one who misses her,' I said. 'Maybe instead of sitting at home feeling sorry for himself Dad should break the habit of a lifetime and go after her—tell her how much she means to him. Show her how much he needs her.'

'That's a no, I take it?'

I stifled a sigh. It would be so easy. No worries about a job. No worries about where to live. Just while I got my act together. The career plan. The life plan.

Too easy. And not just for me.

'I can't replace my mother. And I won't be doing Dad any favours by offering him a crutch to lean on. He needs to face up to what's happened and move on. We all do.' Cora winced at my thoughtless choice of words and, feeling guilty, I said, 'Don't worry. It isn't a problem. I can bunk with a mate while I look for somewhere more within my means. You can tell

Nigel and Amber that it's safe to come back. One way or another, I'll be gone by Saturday.' I stood up, suddenly oppressed by the noise of the restaurant, needing to get some air. 'Look, I'm going to have to run.'

Cora hugged me. 'Thank you for being so sweet about this.'

'No, thank *you*. You've been brilliant and we've taken you horribly for granted. If I can do anything, any time, you only have to ask.'

'In that case, do you really have to rush off? I'm not leaving until this evening. We could go shopping,' she said, totally incorrigible. So much for being less extravagant.

'Haven't you got to see your lawyer? Sign contracts?' I reminded her, resisting temptation without too much difficulty. One of us had to be responsible. Since the older generation seemed to have lost the plot, it was down to me.

'Ten minutes, tops,' she promised.

'I'm really sorry, Cora. I'd love to keep you company, but I've got a date with a couple of hounds who'll chew the legs off the kitchen table unless I'm on time to take them for a run.' Keeping it light—not wanting her to feel that I was avoiding her company—I said, 'Of course, if you're really stuck for something to do, you're very welcome to join me.'

'Er, thanks, but I think I'll pass on that treat.'

'You don't know what you're missing.'

'Mud, mud, and more mud?' she offered. 'I'm not dressed for it.'

'Neither am I, which means I really have to dash or I'll be late again.'

And to think I'd been congratulating myself that things couldn't get worse. I really must learn to curb my optimism.

At least I wasn't late.

It was just as well. My arrival coincided with that of a taxi. I beat the driver to the bell and the door was immediately flung open by Gabriel York. He was wearing a long dark overcoat and looked as if he'd been pacing the hall, scarcely able to contain his impatience.

Pacing was clearly an exaggeration—he didn't look as if being on his feet was that bright an idea. But feverish energy radiated from him, and the small overnight bag at his feet suggested he had more than pacing in mind.

Percy and Joe were sitting—just—with their leads ready clipped to their collars, in keen anticipation of an outing. He handed me their leads without a word, then picked up the bag.

'Where on earth do you think you're going?' I demanded.

I hadn't had a good day so far, and I certainly wasn't taking any nonsense from a man who looked as if a puff of wind would blow him over.

'Home,' he said.

'Excuse me?'

'I'm going home,' he repeated slowly, as if I was dim.

This, I was sure, was not a great idea. Did his family know? 'Have you outworn your welcome?' I asked. 'What happened? Did Crissie find out about the bedcover? Did one of the dogs leave hair on the hall carpet? Eat the organic chicken?'

'Quite possibly all three.' He might have smiled, but he needed all his energy to keep on his feet. Anyone with a thimbleful of sense could see that he should be in bed, not moving house. 'But that's not the reason I'm going. My brother's flown to New York this afternoon. Some crisis at the UN that only he can handle, apparently. He didn't even have time to come home and fetch a toothbrush.'

'So?'

'Crissie's packing now so that she can follow him with his stuff.'

'Why? Don't they sell toothbrushes in New York?'

He stopped, finally looked at me. Since I was blocking his way, he didn't have a lot of choice about this. 'I'm sure they do, Sophie, but he's going to be away for at least a month and he'll need more than a toothbrush,' he explained, wearily patient. From somewhere inside the house I heard the rattle of coat hangers in freefall, followed by the exasperated scream of a woman at the end of her tether. 'As you can hear, she's got quite enough to cope with without having to worry about me.'

'Someone needs to,' I declared, absolutely twitching as every feminine instinct urged me to reach out, put my arm around him, take his weight on my shoulder and put him straight back to bed, where it was warm. Every feminine instinct also warned me that it was the worst thing I could possibly do.

'I can look after myself.'

'Oh, right.' I injected a certain amount of disbelief into my voice.

As if to prove my scepticism, he took a step towards the door and swayed noticeably. Oh, to hell with it. He wasn't in any shape to argue. I stepped up to him and tucked myself beneath his arm, keeping tight hold of the dogs with the other hand.

'You need to sit down,' I said.

'In the taxi,' he said, with grim determination, and while he didn't exactly push me away there was only one direction he was going to allow me to take him in.

'You should have phoned me,' I said, when he was sitting inside the cab. 'I could have been here earlier.'

'I tried. Your phone was switched off.' He made it sound as if I'd done this deliberately, just to thwart him.

'It most certainly was not,' I declared, and fished it out of my pocket just to prove it. I was right. It wasn't switched off. But the battery was dead. 'Oh, knickers.'

'I left a message on your voice-mail,' he said, manfully resisting the temptation to say what was clearly at the forefront of his mind.

'It's rapidly turning into that sort of week,' I said. 'There are probably dozens of people trying to phone me and offer me jobs right now...'

'Really?'

'No. Just wishful thinking.' I put the phone away and looked at him. 'Are you sure you should be doing this? You look terrible.'

'I feel terrible. Talking to you isn't helping.' He held out a piece of paper with an address and phone number written on it. 'Take the dogs for their run and then bring them home. This is the address.'

'Only if you promise me you'll go straight to bed when you get there. Leave the door on the latch and I'll let myself in.'

He looked as if he was about to argue, but contented himself with muttering, 'Bossy cow.'

'Technically, that would be heifer,' I replied, closing the door before giving the driver the address.

CHAPTER FIVE

I WAITED until the taxi was out of sight, then went back up the steps to shut the front door. But before I could do that Cristabel York appeared at the foot of the stairs.

'Has he gone?' She looked surprised. 'Damn the man. He didn't even bother to say goodbye.'

'I think he decided you had other things on your mind.'

'You don't have to make excuses for him. He wouldn't bother to do it for himself, believe me.' She brushed her sleek hair back from her face, leaving it ruffled and untidy, and quite suddenly she looked human. Vulnerable. Exhausted. 'This is a nightmare. York men individually are difficult to live with, but two of them under one roof are more than flesh and blood can stand.'

Technically, right now she didn't have any. But I kept that thought to myself. I thought I'd probably gone about as far I could safely travel on the technical front.

'They must have some good points,' I offered. I felt honour-bound to defend Gabriel; he was my employer, after all. Although since she was married to his brother she presumably knew what she was talking about.

'Oh, they're absolute bristling with good points,' she agreed. 'They're forceful, dynamic, totally irresistible forces of nature who, once they've set their minds on a goal, are unstoppable in its pursuit. That's why I'm married to one of them. That's what makes them totally impossible to live with. I have a career. I have a business to run. But does that count for anything? No, I have to drop everything to fit in with Michael's personal mission to save the world. At least Gabe has had the decency not to inflict himself on a wife...' Perhaps she realised that she was running on in front of a complete stranger and she let it go. 'Sorry. You don't want to hear this. But, really, I'm not the uncaring bitch my brother-in-law would have you believe. He not only doesn't want anyone to care, he positively discourages any hint of concern.'

I'd noticed, but I just said, 'I can quite see that with a couple of dogs in tow he doesn't make the ideal house guest.'

'If he'd just stayed put in hospital until he was fit enough to be left on his own...' She threw up her hands. 'Not him. He couldn't be that reasonable. But then doctors notoriously make the worst patients. As for the dogs...I thought bringing them here would help him settle, feel at home.'

She'd brought them?

'Where were they? While he was away?'

'Staying with a colleague. A nurse. The ideal solution would have been for him to move in with her, but of course that would have been too simple. He wouldn't hear of it.'

He'd lied about the kennels...

She shook her head. 'I'm being too hard on him. He was so depressed he couldn't think straight. It's one of the after effects of malaria, apparently. Did he tell you he'd had malaria?'

I nodded.

'Well, as I said, I thought it would help.'

'I'm sure it has.'

'Do you think so?' That seemed to cheer her momentarily. Then, 'Now he insists on going home. Wretched, stubborn man. He could have stayed here. My cleaner would have come in every day to check up on him. Make sure he had something to eat. He really shouldn't be on his own.'

'No.' We were in total agreement on that one.

'Well, at least he'll have you popping in twice a day to make sure he hasn't passed out again.' She grabbed a pen from the table by the telephone and jotted something on a notepad. 'Look, this is our number in New York,' she said, tearing off a sheet of paper and offering it to me. 'If there's a problem, ring me—okay?'

I had the feeling I was getting deeper into this than I wanted to go. Risking more than life and limb... *Limbs* mended.

'Look, I'm just the dog-walker,' I said, as self-preservation asserted itself. I was about to suggest that Mrs York's cleaner could still pop in to see him every day—he was only down the road in Pimlico—when the dogs, alerted by this reference to walks, began to make encouraging little yelps and tug impatiently on their leads.

'That's why you're the perfect person to keep an eye on him,' Crissie York said, seizing the initiative. 'Those wretched dogs are the only things he cares about and he can't take them out himself.' Gabriel was right—it wasn't only the York men who were unstoppable in the pursuit of what they wanted. 'If he's rude, just remember that and tell him to get lost.'

'If?' I enquired, finding myself warming to the woman, despite her attempt to entangle me in her personal crisis.

'Don't worry, I'll sort it out with the agency. Pay for any extra time.'

'No. Don't do that.' I was reluctant to get that closely involved. I had, as Cora had suggested, built a protective wall about myself. The minute I'd started worrying about Gabriel York I'd felt the foundations being undermined. 'Isn't there anyone else?'

She ignored my obvious desperation, just continued to hold out the piece of paper. Unstoppable in her persistence. And if there had been anyone else she wouldn't have asked a total stranger, would she?

It wasn't so much the responsibility that bothered me, but I was supposed to be job-hunting. Flat-hunting. Moving.

'Please?'

I was a sucker for a please. And what else could I do? I had to go there twice a day to take the dogs out, anyway. How much more work would it be to check up on him? Make sure he had something for breakfast. Get him a ready-meal from the supermarket to stick in the microwave for supper, perhaps.

I took the piece of paper, tucked it into my kitty notebook and pushed it into my pocket.

'I'll do what I can.'

'Great.' She opened her purse and thrust some money into my hand. 'This will cover any expenses. If it comes to more I'll pay you when I get back.'

'No...' This wasn't a job like dog-walking or cleaning. It would be completely wrong to take money for doing what a good neighbour would do. But the phone began to ring and she reached for it, waving her thanks as she kicked the door shut.

Percy and Joe had a somewhat curtailed gallop in the grounds of the Royal Hospital, Chelsea—which confusingly wasn't a hospital at all, but a retirement home for old soldiers. I had to find Gabriel's place in Pimlico—he'd only given me the address, no directions—and I didn't want to leave it too long. Heaven alone knew what state he'd be in when I got there.

Then I had to get to Bloomers for six o'clock and put in a couple of hours of cleaning before going home to start packing.

Gabriel lived in a mews cottage—whitewashed on the outside and the door painted black, but long enough ago to have lost the gloss, with brass fittings that hadn't seen metal polish in living memory. He didn't go in for tortured greenery on the doorstep, either. There was a stone pot, but whatever had been planted in it had long since died. He had remembered to leave the door on the latch, however, and the dogs, thrilled to be home, raced through the rooms, turning dizzy circles with excitement.

'Gabriel?' I had at the most twenty minutes in which to give the dogs some water and make sure he hadn't collapsed before I had to leave in time to make it to Bloomers.

I turned on the cold tap to let the water run for a minute while I looked around. Amazingly the place had a little garden at the rear, and the dogs had an electronic flap triggered by a device on their collars to let themselves in and out. Hardly the same as living in the country, but a lot better than being shut up in someone else's utility room.

I filled the bowls, set them down and, since I'd had no response from the boss, went to look for him.

It was a totally masculine cottage, with the whole of the ground floor given over to the kind of kitchen that was a genuine comfort zone, with a couple of armchairs and an ancient sofa covered by a throw. The dogs flung themselves onto it.

I found Gabriel in the rear bedroom.

He must have been feeling bad, because for once in his life he'd done exactly what he'd been told and put himself to bed. Well, no. That was a bit of an exaggeration. What he'd actually done was kick off his shoes, wrap himself in a duvet and fallen asleep still wearing his coat.

I didn't think it was a good idea to leave him that way but, checking my watch, realised I didn't have time to do anything about it right then. I'd have to come back.

I shrugged. I was always going to have to come back. Make sure he was okay. In the meantime I had to get to Bloomers. If I ran all the way I might just make it.

I paused just long enough to scribble a note in my kitty notebook, tear it out and leave it propped up by the bedside lamp.

I'll be back.

As I let myself out, leaving the door on the latch and relying on the dogs to deter unwelcome visitors, it occurred to me that it had sounded more like a threat than a promise.

The ladies at Bloomers were totally brilliant.

I didn't realise they'd still be working so late—to be honest I didn't know what to expect, having never done anything like this before—but there were three of them, bundled up in coats against the chill, hands red from close contact with cold water as they plucked flowers from the surrounding buckets.

They took one look at me, flushed of face, bent practically double as, clutching my midriff, I gasped out my apology for being three minutes late, and immediately took me under their collective wing.

'You sit there and get your breath back. I dare say we could all do with a tea break. Greta, put that kettle on.'

'I'm sorry, really. I don't want to keep you waiting…'

'It's not a problem. We're going to be here half the night preparing everything for this wedding, anyway. So long as the shop gets cleaned it doesn't matter whether it's at six o'clock or seven, does it?'

'It doesn't?'

Actually, now I'd recovered sufficiently to concentrate on something other than the simple act of breathing, I could see what they meant. The floor of the preparation room behind the shop was all but hidden by buckets of flowers, and one of the girls was putting together those beribboned posies for the pewends of a church at a speed that made me blink.

'Wow. Who's getting married? Royalty?'

'No, just some TFB. I don't know how much the

whole affair is costing, but I do know how much
we're charging for the flowers and, believe me, I'm
not complaining at having to work late.'

'TFB?'

'Trust Fund Babe,' the one called Greta replied
with a grin as she placed a mug of tea in my hand.
'The kind of girl who's never going to have to turn
out on a chilly late-November evening to mop floors
for a living. Do you want sugar in that?'

I shook my head. A TFB.

That's what I was.

Without the TF.

I felt guilty sitting there, drinking the tea they'd
made me, being made a fuss of as if I was one of
them. A worker, rather than someone who'd taken her
education, her advantages, totally for granted.

What on earth had I been doing with my life?

Flitting from job to job without a thought for the
future, like some brainless butterfly.

Suddenly I saw myself through Miss Frosty's eyes
and knew why she'd been so hard on me. She could
have been a lot harder. This, as cleaning jobs went,
wasn't that bad. In fact, having watched Greta and
the rest of the girls, their hands red from cold, I decided that my job was pretty cushy in comparison and
put my back into it.

They were still at it when I left, clutching a deli-
ciously scented posy of trimmings. I'd been invited
to help myself; it was one of the perks of the job,
apparently. I could scarcely tell them that I already
had two gorgeous arrangements they'd delivered to
me the day before. They'd probably think I was some

privileged idiot, slumming it for a bet or something, and despise me.

I'd put my hands up to the privileged idiot, but they were great women and I didn't want them to despise me, so I thanked them and took the flowers.

What I did need, though, was to find a bed before the weekend, and so far all I'd done was leave a message for Tony on his voice-mail. Even if he had called back, my cellphone battery was flatter than one of my mother's banqueting cloths. And I had to pack, too. But I couldn't even start to think about that until I'd checked on Gabriel.

I walked back to Pimlico, feeling a bit light-headed from the scent of so many lilies. Or maybe it was from lack of sleep. My feet didn't seem to be quite my own, and the pavement had a disconcerting tendency to come up to meet me. It was a relief to let myself back into the cottage, even though I didn't dare sit down. It was all I could do to push away the dogs, who'd rushed out of the kitchen to see whether they should eat me or love me. They decided to love me, presumably in the hope that I could be fooled into feeding them again.

I stuck the colourful posy in a jug, yawning widely as I headed for the stairs to see how Gabriel was doing. Definitely lack of sleep. I'd had a late night followed by an early morning and been on the go ever since.

His bedroom was cold—at some point he must have woken up, thrown open the window and taken off his coat—but he was restless and muttering incoherently. I laid my hand on his forehead and discovered that he was hot to the touch. Feverish.

I shut the window. While getting him cooled down was undoubtedly a priority, I was pretty sure he wouldn't appreciate a case of double pneumonia to add to his woes.

After that I set about prising the duvet from his grasp so that I could get him properly undressed. He was tangled up in it, and by the time I'd managed to get it free he wasn't the only one feeling the heat. Maybe the effort had exhausted him, too, though, because he was quieter after that, giving me a chance to unfasten the waistband of his trousers and ease them down his legs. Not that it was particularly easy. He was a dead weight. And they were long legs.

Eventually, though, I was done, and I left him stretched out on his back, wearing just his shirt and pair of clinging grey boxers that—well, clung. To a pair of undeniably sexy hips.

Not that I was in the slightest bit interested in his hips.

I dragged my gaze away from them and went back downstairs in search of something for him to drink. The fridge, inevitably, was empty, so he was going to have to make do with tap water.

Then, because there was no hot water in the tank, I had to heat some in a kettle to sponge him down with—just enough to take the chill off. My legs wobbling with fatigue, I finally climbed back up the stairs, feeling a bit like some poor relation out of a Victorian melodrama, delegated to sit by the invalid's bed and mop his forehead, waiting for the fever to break..

Too late. By the time I made it back to his bedside Gabriel had cooled down. More than cooled down. He was shivering uncontrollably.

Maybe at this point I should have given up and called an ambulance.

Maybe I should at least have *looked* for a hot water bottle, but frankly I didn't believe he would own such a thing. Besides, the thought of facing those stairs again was enough to make my legs buckle.

I don't know how many miles they'd walked—and run—that day, but believe me they'd done more than enough. If I went downstairs I wasn't sure I'd ever make it back up again.

Added to that, my back and arms ached from the unaccustomed wielding of an industrial-sized mop. As for my head...

Okay, you've got the picture.

It was warmth he needed. Right now. And I was warm.

And in desperate need of a lie-down.

Two birds with a single whatever.

I stripped off my trousers and sweater and fell into bed beside him, pulling the duvet up under his chin to warm him with my own body. I must have been paying more attention to those first aid lectures than I'd realised, because I remembered some stuff about heat transfer. Good for hypothermia. In an emergency.

Well, this was an emergency. And, lying sideways so that my cheek was pressed against his shoulder and my body was pressed firmly along the length of his, I pulled the quilt over us both and cradled him. It shouldn't take long. As soon as he stopped shivering I'd get up and go home.

*   *   *

'Tell me, did I miss something?'

I opened my eyes and found myself face to face with Gabriel York. He seemed bemused. Not bothered, you understand, but those dark eyes definitely betrayed a man who was in the throes of bemusement.

I could understand that. I struggled with bemusement myself for a moment or two while I mentally disentangled the events that had led to me to the point where I'd fallen into his bed, his arms.

By the time I remembered he'd got his expression under control, and that cool, slightly guarded look was firmly back in place. But I could have sworn that, just for a moment, he'd been smiling. Well, maybe not quite smiling, but there had been a slight softening of his mouth, something about the eyes that suggested he was definitely thinking about it.

And why not? He had every reason to smile.

It wasn't just my face that was—well, face to face with him. My entire body seemed to be pressed very firmly against his. Chest to chest. Thigh to thigh. Hip to, um, hip. And, well, *hellooo*. He was clearly feeling a lot better this morning. Because it was morning. And not particularly early, judging by the daylight pouring in through the windows. We'd slept through the entire night, wrapped close as lovers, as innocent as babes, in each other's arms.

Reality intruded. He was aroused, as any man might be if he woke and found a strange woman in his bed. That my own body, released from a long cold purdah, should respond with a similar heat, real physical desire, was considerably less expected. Breath-stoppingly unexpected. Shockingly so. No, worse than shocking, because not only wasn't I making any move to distance myself from him, I didn't *want* to move. I wanted to be even closer...

'You, um, had a fever,' I said, in an attempt to distract myself. Well, I had to say something. 'You were shivering.'

'Is that right? And is this some new treatment that hasn't made it into the text books?'

There was a hint of something teasing in his voice, but like the smile it was buried deep. I was prepared to dig...

'It was an emergency,' I pointed out. 'This seemed like the most energy-efficient way of dealing with the situation.'

'Energy-efficient?'

That one had nearly got him. He was having to work at not smiling now. Encouraged, I said, 'It's called heat transfer.'

'I thought that was something to do with plumbing.'

Close...

'You're thinking of heat exchange.'

'I am?' He sounded surprised that I would know the difference. Well, heck, I was a blonde...

'I worked as a receptionist at a heating and ventilation company for a while.' A very short while. One of the directors had been very keen to explain all about heat exchange one night. After the office had closed.

'Oh, please, don't misunderstand me. I'm not complaining. This is much more, um, efficacious than being manhandled into an ambulance by a couple of burly paramedics and carted off to hospital.'

Efficacious?

Oh, no. I wasn't going to smile until he did. Close thing, though.

I cleared my throat, giving myself a moment to get my face under control. 'Actually, I did think about calling them.' Well, I had. Momentarily. Until I'd realised I'd have to go downstairs to use the phone. 'But since you'd undoubtedly refuse to go with them, for the second time in as many days, I decided I'd just get arrested for serially time-wasting the emergency services' overstretched resources. And I'm much too busy for that.'

'Doing what?'

He sounded genuinely interested. I suspected he was applying the same distraction technique…

'Finding a proper job—' as opposed to an improper one, where I ended up lying in bed with my boss '—preferably in the next twenty-four hours. Finding somewhere to live, ditto. Then there's walking your dogs twice a day. Oh, and cleaning a flower shop in the evening.'

'Busy schedule. And you've still found time to make it your personal responsibility to be my guardian angel.'

I didn't feel like an angel, but clearly it would not be in my best interests to tell him that. Probably. But with a name like Gabriel he would know more about it than me. 'Someone needs to be,' I said.

'Well, I'm glad it was you. You seem to have a natural gift for one-to-one caring.'

'Oh, it's not a gift. I did a first aid course. That's where I learned how to do CPR—'

'Believe me, you did *not* learn how to do CPR.'

'—and all about heat transfer.'

His smile hovered again. His face didn't change. There were none of those sexy crinkles that men do so beautifully—the kind that on women would just be crow's feet—but somewhere behind his eyes there was a warmth that betrayed him.

'Are you sure you learned this at first aid?' he enquired, with the barest suggestion of innuendo.

I swallowed. 'Absolutely. There was a section on improvisation. You know. If you're lost up a mountain, or something...'

'You cuddle together to keep warm. You seem to have grasped the principle with extraordinary enthusiasm.'

'No,' I said firmly. 'If someone falls, succumbs to hypothermia...' It occurred to me that, while I was probably talking utter nonsense, he was a professional and knew exactly what I was getting at.

It also occurred to me that the treatment had worked extremely well. He was looking and sounding a whole lot better this morning.

And maybe I should make a move.

'So, let's recap,' he said, clearly not done with teasing me.

No! Please don't let's recap!

'First there was your interesting version of mouth-to-mouth resuscitation. More commonly called the kiss of life...'

I let out a gasp that might have been of outrage as he bent without warning and brushed his dry lips over mine. The unexpected touch sent shock waves of warmth spreading through me and my body responded like the motor of a very expensive car, purring so quietly that you could hardly hear it, but ready to leap into action the moment pressure was applied to the accelerator...

'Did that work?'

Work? My heart, dormant and neglected, was pounding away like a jackhammer.

'You're a doctor. You have an unfair advantage.'

'Oh, I think we're about evens on that one. But the heat transfer is more difficult...' His arm, which was beneath me, with his hand spread over my back, tightened slightly. His other hand, which I belatedly realised was cupping my bottom, did the same.

It had not seemed possible that we could be any closer. But the difference was breathtaking.

Well, I was finding it hard to breathe anyway.

'I think perhaps we're both already warmer than is absolutely wise,' I managed.

Since I was the one who'd tucked up against him I realised I was in no position to complain. But enough was enough. Even if he was just teasing...

Teasing? The dour and grouchy doctor?

How likely was that?

Since the only alternative was that he was putting a move on me, I decided to bank on it. And stay put. Clearly any abrupt move to put some distance between us it would make altogether too much of it. But it was time to call a halt.

'In fact that's more than enough,' I said. Which was not true. I was fairly sure that I could take this kind of close encounter all day.

'Enough?'

'Dosage is critical,' I explained, with what I can only describe as admirable cool under the circumstances. The knee to breast contact. His warm breath tickling against my ear. The pulsing beat of his heart in counterpoint to mine... Even so, I was forced to swallow again before I said, 'Overdoing it will almost certainly lead to a relapse. Possibly even a return of the fever.'

I was not prepared to gamble on which of us would overheat, reach boiling point first.

'I suspect you're right.' He didn't move a muscle. Well, maybe just one... 'But it's almost worth having a relapse to see just how far you'd take this interesting therapy.'

'This is the end of the treatment session, Doctor.'

For a moment he held me hard up against him, his dark eyes unreadable, his face expressionless, any hint of warmth, a smile, long gone. My top had ridden up in the night, as had his shirt, and my bare stomach was pressed against his midriff, my thighs languorously soft against the hairy masculinity of his legs. Warm skin against warm skin. It felt dangerously thrilling, like balancing on the edge of a precipice. I just knew that one wrong move would lead to disaster.

Never had disaster seemed such an attractive proposition. All I had to do was lift my mouth to his, run my tongue along his sensuous lower lip and...

And he let me go.

I was lying in his bed, locked in his arms, letting my imagination run away with me, and he just...let me go.

He didn't move. He simply took his hands away in one clean movement, without allowing the one to trail enticingly down my leg or the other to ruffle against my hair.

My leg deeply regretted the omission.

My hair was already so ruffled that a little more wouldn't have made the slightest bit of difference.

My head, having taken due note of all of the above, appeared to have gone with the 'disaster' scenario. Or maybe it was too busy drowning in the forgotten sensory pleasure of a man's hard body against mine to send the 'move' signals to the rest of my body.

'It's nearly eight o'clock, Sophie. You do realise that you're going to be late for work again?'

Oh, well, that did it. Like a basinful of ice-cold water, it brought my head, my thighs, all those other wayward bits of me that hadn't been behaving for the last five minutes, right back into line, and I was out of his bed—and dearly wishing I was the kind of girl who kept a pair of clean knickers and a spare toothbrush in her bag—before you could say Jack Robinson.

'You'll find my wallet in my coat,' he said. 'Take some money for a taxi home. The dogs can wait an hour.'

'You read minds?' I demanded.

'It's hardly mind-reading. When I've been working all night the only thing on my mind is to get home, take a shower—'

'Working?' I was outraged. 'I stopped working the minute I brought your dogs home, Mr York. This was… This was…'

I couldn't for the life of me think *what* it was, but I was damn certain it wasn't anything to do with work.

'Therapy?' he prompted. 'You'd better take my

keys, too,' he said, since I was clearly lost for words. 'So that you can let yourself back in.'

I was hopping on one leg as I tried to get the other one into the tangled mess of my jeans as quickly as possible. Sitting on the bed would have made it easier, but I wasn't going back there. Not until I'd given myself a refresher course in common sense.

And taken a shower. A cold one seemed like a sensible move.

But what he'd said about taking keys finally filtered through to my brain 'You're not planning on going out?' I demanded.

That shouldn't have been a question, I realised, so I rephrased it.

'You're *not* going out. You *are* staying in bed.'

My mind, clearly out on a limb and sawing off the branch behind it, chimed in with, Oh, right. And how are you going to make him do that?

Fortunately it was on its own. Or maybe Gabriel had decided to let me off the hook—however unlikely that seemed. Anyway, completely ignoring my concern for his health, he said, 'I'll find you the spare key later.'

That made me mad. I kept saving this man's life, for heaven's sake. I had every right to demand he took better care of it.

'I don't need a key. You are not—'

'No, Sophie. I'm not going out. I'm going to do exactly what the ministering angel ordered and stay put for a while. But you said you needed somewhere to stay temporarily and I've got a spare room. So use it.' He rolled over onto his back and closed his eyes, as if that was an end to the matter. Not quite. He added, 'That way you won't have any excuse to be late for work this evening. Or tomorrow.'

Did I say I'd been lost for words?

Wrong. They were positively tumbling over themselves to get off my tongue. Once I'd made up my mind between telling him what he could do with his spare room. Or possibly throwing my arms around his neck and thanking him.

I compromised. 'Are you hungry?'

'No. My appetite is zero. A side effect of malaria.' Along with depression. I reminded myself to look it up on the internet and see what else I could look forward to. 'Although if you're feeling in a ministering mood you could bring me another glass of water before you go.'

Reaching for the glass at his bedside, I realised it was empty. 'Oh, good, you found it—' I began. Then stopped. The glass was empty and there was a bottle of pills beside it that hadn't been there last night. Which meant that at some time in the night he'd woken up, got up and found his pills, and then got right back into bed, put his arm around me and gone back to sleep.

Perhaps he'd thought he was hallucinating…

'You can trust me,' he said, doing the mind-reading thing again.

'I know. You're a doctor…' I snapped.

'And you needn't worry that I'm looking for a nurse on the cheap.'

'Oh, well, fine. You're not getting one.' I fetched him a fresh glass of water, put it by the bed. 'I won't be long.'

He'd burrowed beneath the covers. 'Just feed the

dogs before you go, will you?' he muttered from the depths of his quilt.

Oh, crumbs. He was feeling rotten and I was giving him a hard time. I hovered for a minute, wondering what to do for the best, until he opened his eyes and said, 'Are you still here?'

'No,' I snapped, 'I'm just a figment of your imagination.'

He looked, for just a moment, as if he might take issue with me on that. But he must have decided it was too much effort and closed them again.

I took his keys and a twenty-pound note. I couldn't afford to be stupid about it and I really didn't see why his sister-in-law should subsidise his care in the community. Then I went downstairs, fed Percy and Joe and, since time was short, used the taxi ride to put in some work on a realistic assessment of my immediate choices.

I could sleep on Tony's sofa until I found somewhere within my budget—sound of hollow laughter here—which would no doubt please Tony.

I could go home. Which would certainly please my father. As well as my sister, my aunt and probably my mother. Everyone, in fact, I cared about.

I could take up Gabriel York's offer and use his spare room. Which would please no one.

CHAPTER SIX

THE first option was going to be uncomfortable, and might rekindle any hopes Tony had of getting me into his bed. It wouldn't be kind.

The second was just going to be admitting defeat. I'd rather take my chances on Tony's sofa. Besides, I'd meant what I'd said to Cora. It would allow Dad to put off confronting some pretty painful choices. He needed to get on with it. As I'd been forced to do.

That left the third option which was, no doubt about it, utterly stupid.

I didn't know anything about Gabriel York beyond the fact that he was an eye surgeon, had a brother called Michael who was intent on saving the world, a sister-in-law called Crissie who cared for him a lot more than she'd ever admit, and two of the nicest dogs I'd ever met. Oh, and he'd turned me on for the first time since Perry Fotheringay had so carelessly turned me off.

In other words he was a man to be avoided at all costs, because I certainly wasn't going to fall for that 'trust me...I'm a doctor' routine. He was a man, wasn't he? I'd had ample evidence of that while I'd been up close and personal. His mind was willing. It was just my good fortune that he was too weak to do anything much about it at the moment.

He'd recover.

But then he was taking a pretty big chance on me,

too. He knew even less about me than I did about him. He certainly didn't know I was a TFB—temporarily without the TF, it was true, but nevertheless well endowed with my own income. All I had to do was convince my father that he couldn't use it to control me. Or get married. Or wait until I was thirty.

I could be a crook for all he knew and, having gained his confidence with my ministering angel routine, I could empty his house while he was asleep. Run off with his credit cards. Perpetrate fraud of all kinds.

I could even be a *dognapper*, for heaven's sake. I'd heard of that. People stealing precious pets and holding them to ransom...

Now *I* was the one hallucinating. Lost in the realms of fantasy. Or more likely just putting off the inevitable.

He was the one who was sick, and I knew I was going to worry about him every minute of the day while he was out of my sight. I did that. Worried about helpless things.

I mean, who was going to give the stripey cat kibbles now I was leaving Chandler's Reach? Who was going to give her that stuff that stopped fleas and all the other nasties?

No one. That was who.

But I could ensure that Gabriel York was taken care of. That he had something to eat. That someone would be around if he had another dizzy spell.

I could even phone Crissie and put her mind at ease.

Having convinced myself that I was doing the right thing, I didn't waste too much time packing. I just flung everything I was likely to need in the next couple of weeks into a suitcase, including my hot water bottle. Just in case Gabriel got the shivers again; I didn't think a repeat of the heat transfer treatment would be good for my peace of mind.

Then, because his fridge was bare, I filled a carrier with the contents of my own fridge. Flung in a few other essentials.

Finally I left a note, asking Nigel and Amber to pack up the rest of the stuff in my room and send it home to Berkshire. And the bill to my father. It was the least they could do under the circumstances. The least he could do. I finished by wishing them good luck in their new home. I meant it, too. My predicament wasn't their fault, after all.

I left my keys on the kitchen worktop, so that if I lost my nerve between Chelsea Harbour and Pimlico there could be no turning back. And Gabriel York's address with the porter so that he could forward my mail.

The taxi was halfway to Pimlico when I made the driver turn around and go back. The cat was pleased to see me, although she wasn't quite so happy about the taxi ride. She remembered the last time she'd been in one, probably. When she'd cut her paw and I'd taken her to the vet.

But I found a few kibbles in my pocket to distract her and I made it without too many scratches.

I dumped my bags and the cat in the spare bedroom, before fetching her a saucer of milk and finding her an old jumper to curl up on when she was finished—just so that she'd know she was in clover. Then I plugged in my mobile to recharge and, making sure to shut the door so that she couldn't escape, went to check on Gabriel.

He was fast asleep. He didn't seem to be feverish, but I made a hot water bottle just in case, and slipped it under the quilt at the bottom of the bed, then held my breath as he turned over. I didn't want to have to confess to the cat just yet. I needed time to think of a really good reason why I hadn't mentioned her before. When he'd suggested I move in.

I didn't want it to be *that* temporary.

Then I took the dogs out.

They didn't want to go. They wanted to go upstairs and investigate the interesting new scent of cat. But I was firm and they were obedient, mostly. Or maybe they knew the cat would keep until they got back.

I decided it might be a good idea to wear them out and gave them a real workout, telling them that I was making up for their curtailed exercise the night before.

It gave me more time to work on my cat story.

There wasn't enough time in the world, I decided. As it happened, I didn't have to beat about the bush when I owned up. When I got back, Gabriel was stretched out in one of the kitchen armchairs.

The cat was on his knee.

Mayhem ensued.

The dogs, keen to fling themselves on Gabriel, were stopped in their tracks by the cat who, panicked into action, dug her claws into his leg, bringing him to his feet, cursing inventively and clutching at his knee.

I made a grab for her but she backed off, arching her back and hissing furiously, and when Joe—

younger and stupider than Percy—decided to investigate, and stuck his nose too close for her liking, she slashed at him with claws fully extended.

He yelped and leaped back, banging against the table, sending the jug of flowers flying.

The cat, having made her feelings well and truly felt, dived beneath the armchair.

For a moment all that could be heard was the gentle trickle of water as it ran over the edge of the table and splashed onto the quarry tiled floor.

I cleared my throat.

'Hi,' I said brightly, and, going for the obvious, 'You're awake.'

I got a look that would have curdled milk. 'Your cat objected to being shut in. Loudly.'

'Did she?' All innocence. 'In clover' hadn't worked, then. 'I'm really sorry. She's not used to being shut up.'

'That would be why she was trying to claw her way through the door, I expect.'

Pure sarcasm. This was definitely not the moment to reveal that she wasn't used to being inside, let alone shut up. 'Oh, your poor leg!' I exclaimed, hoping to distract him with the trickle of blood that had appeared beneath the hem of his bathrobe. 'You should put something on it. Have you got any antiseptic?'

Gabriel gave me a look that warned me he knew exactly what I was doing and he hadn't finished with the subject, but for the moment he left it. 'There might be some in the cupboard under the sink.'

There was. I poured some into a bowl and diluted it, then, lacking cotton wool, I further demonstrated my ability for improvisation by dipping the end of my T-shirt into the bowl.

As I turned to demonstrate, yet again, that I was a dab hand at first aid, he said, 'You can't use that!'

'Don't make such a fuss. It's clean.'

'But is it sterilised?'

'Have you got an unopened pack of cotton wool?' I demanded. His only response was to glare at me. 'No, I thought not.' He might be a doctor, but I was in no mood to take any namby-pamby nonsense from Gabriel York. 'Just sit down and let me clean you up.'

Maybe he recognised that argument was futile. Or maybe he wasn't feeling strong enough to follow through. Whatever, he subsided into the armchair and, since I had no wish to renew my acquaintance with his sexy underwear—assuming he was still wearing underwear—I carefully lifted aside his bathrobe and blotted his knee.

'Will I live?' he enquired, sounding as if he didn't much care one way or the other.

'I can't guarantee it,' I said, concentrating on cleaning up the rest of his leg. 'Not unless you eat something very soon. An egg would be good.' If I was going to browbeat him into eating some breakfast I might as well make it worth my while. There was no immediate response to this and I looked up. 'Any time in the next half an hour,' I prompted.

'I told you that I'm not looking for a nurse,' he said, not in the least bit amused. Clearly he was having second thoughts about his rash invitation for me to move in. 'I seem to recall receiving an assurance that I wasn't getting one.' Okay, third thoughts. Or possibly even fourth ones.

'You did,' I assured him, equally straight-faced. 'I lied.'

I was hoping that might raise the promise of a smile, but in case it didn't I got quickly to my feet and crossed to where the dogs had prudently retreated, to the safety of the far side of the kitchen, and repeated my first aid on poor Joe's nose. That sensible creature raised no objections to my T-shirt. Just whimpered for a cuddle.

He got one. As did Percy.

'I don't recall you mentioning a cat, either,' Gabriel said, interrupting this canine love-in. 'Didn't it occur to you that she might not want to share a kitchen with two dogs?'

'She hasn't got a choice. It's their kitchen.' I finally turned to face him. 'I couldn't leave her behind, Gabriel.'

'I didn't suggest you could. But you should have told me. Have you any idea of the noise that creature was making?'

I considered, briefly, what it must have been like waking up to the yowling of a desperate cat; I was well aware of how much noise she could make. I was rather more concerned at the kind of mess she'd made...

'Yes, I should. I'm sorry. I hoped she'd settle down and sleep for an hour while I walked the dogs. If you want to withdraw your invitation, I'll quite understand.'

'Where would you go?'

Damn! He wasn't supposed to say that! He was

supposed to say that of course he wouldn't do any such thing. That they'd quickly sort out territorial boundaries and settle down. Which they would. Probably.

On the other hand, I could sympathise with his point of view. Bringing the cat was undoubtedly taking advantage of his generosity.

'I suppose I'd have to give in and go home,' I said.

Choice one—Tony—was now a complete non-starter. He was allergic to cats. And I'd left the keys behind to prevent a bolt back to safety. Maybe my subconscious had been busily burning all bridges behind me when it had prompted me to go back for her. I wanted to stay here…

'Where's home?'

'What? Oh, Berkshire. It's a bit too far to come and walk your dogs twice a day.' When he didn't respond to that prompt, I added, 'I'm afraid I'd have to charge travelling expenses.'

Oh, oh…nearly got him with that one.

'That's a consideration,' he said carefully. Damn it, smile! It won't kill you… 'And then, of course, there's your job at the flower shop. There'd be no one to clean that.'

'Well, quite.'

There was a long moment when he appeared to be considering it, before he did something with his shoulders that was very nearly a shrug. Something with his mouth that was very nearly a smile.

'Why don't you show me how good you are with scrambled eggs?' he finally invited. 'Then I'll decide.'

Which effectively took my mind off the problem

of the cat. Of all the egg dishes in all the world he had to choose to have his scrambled…

Not good.

But not bad either.

From beneath his armchair I could hear the cat purring contentedly, and, to be honest, I felt a bit like purring myself.

Gabriel had more or less promised to eat something nourishing. And I had somewhere to live while I sorted myself out.

All I had to do was scramble an egg without burning it.

There was a first time for everything.

'I'll, um, just go and wash my hands.'

'Don't be long.'

I must have looked as surprised as I felt. I hadn't got any real feeling that he was panting for breakfast.

'You said I had half an hour,' he reminded me.

'Yes, but I was only—'

'Joking?'

Don't you just hate men who can keep a poker-straight face even when they're teasing?

'Only offering a rough estimate,' I countered. 'Who knows? You may have as long as an hour.' If I didn't kill him first. I was beginning to see where Crissie was coming from…

I tugged off my soggy, antiseptic-soaked top and gave my hands a scrub—I didn't anticipate that he'd have any real appetite for my scrambled eggs, but if they tasted of antiseptic it was quite possible that he'd never eat again.

I dug around in my suitcase, found a fresh T-shirt, then picked up my mobile and switched it on. It beeped to let me know I had messages. I turned it back off. They would have to keep. Right now I had something more important on my mind.

Scrambled eggs.

The last thing I needed was Miss Frosty phoning me and disturbing my concentration. I already had one brooding presence in the corner to do that.

'Okay. To work,' I said brightly, looking around the kitchen in an attempt to get my bearings. It wasn't exactly the kind of kitchen that would have lifestyle magazines clamouring for a photo-shoot, but it had possibilities.

There was a terrific butler sink. A huge old Welsh dresser minus the fancy china—just piled up with books and papers, all of them coated with a fine film of dust. I was overcome with an unexpected urge to find a duster and do something about it.

I managed to restrain myself.

One of the walls was completely filled with fitted cupboards and drawers, as if someone had embarked on a Shaker-style upgrade but had lost interest before completing the job. No self-respecting Shaker would allow that disreputable old sofa, and the mismatched armchairs in her kitchen.

Then there was the big wooden table, the only work surface, dominating the business end of the room. I mopped up the spilt water and topped up the jug.

'Are they perks of the job?' Gabriel asked. 'The flowers?'

'Pretty, aren't they?' I set the jug on the windows-ill, tidied the dishevelled posy. 'They were up to their armpits at Bloomers last night, working on big wed-ding.' I straightened the posy, touched a blushing pink rosebud. The bride would be awake now, too excited to sleep, too nervous for breakfast, her designer gown waiting under its covers. The man of her dreams ready to commit himself for the rest of his life...

'These were just a few discarded scraps.'

'And the roses and orchids and sunflowers?'

'What?' I turned to look at him. 'Oh, those.' I'd put them in my bedroom. He must have seen them when he'd let the cat out. 'No. They aren't perks of the job. It was my birthday a couple of days ago.'

'And you got flowers? Isn't that a bit like sending coal to Newcastle?'

'I only started at the flower shop yesterday.' I didn't want to discuss my lack of a career plan with Gabriel York, so I opened the nearest cupboard and found not bowls, or pans, or anything seriously useful, just a stack of medical journals. Great. 'Look, if I'm working against the clock, you're going to have to help me out here. I need a bowl. I need a whisk. I need a saucepan. A non-stick saucepan,' I added hastily. Then I gestured at the array of cupboards. 'Would you care to give me a clue?'

'Sorry, I haven't any idea where things are kept.'

Of course not. He was a man. He sat back and let someone else cook for him.

Who? Someone he'd hurt as she'd been brushed aside in the slip-stream? The nurse who'd cared for his dogs...?

I felt a totally unexpected, unlooked-for riffle of jealousy sweep through me at the thought of some unknown woman in his kitchen. Cooking. And wished I'd spent a little of the past twenty-five years learning how to cook proper food.

A man couldn't live on fairy cakes and scones...

'In that case,' I said, 'this may take some time.'

'I have no pressing engagements.'

There was something in his voice that made me turn. His hands were caught in tight fists, his expression bleak, and I had the feeling that he'd been making an effort just for me.

As if aware that he'd betrayed himself in some way, he forced a rictus smile that chilled my heart.

That was *so* not the kind of smile of I'd hoped for.

'That makes two of us,' I said, pretending that I hadn't noticed anything odd. I began to work my way through the cupboards, finally running to earth everything I needed, then made a start on unpacking the groceries I'd brought with me, putting them away in the fridge. Apart from the eggs. I'd need them. The box seemed a bit light and I opened it to discover that it contained only two eggs. Thank you, Nigel and Amber. I hope you enjoyed your breakfast before you left...

But the bread was okay for toast and the butter was fresh.

It had seemed to take for ever to assemble the equipment, but finally I was done. Then I looked for a toaster. There wasn't one. Great. That meant I was going to have to watch the toast *and* the eggs. At the same time.

The tension between the livestock didn't exactly help. Joe had recovered his courage and was inching across the floor on all fours towards the armchair. I had the uneasy feeling that total warfare was going to break out the moment I took my eye off him.

'Joe! Stay.' I turned as Gabriel warned the dog. Joe

sat up, a big daft smile on his face. All innocence. Gabriel placed his hand on the dog's head to reward his obedience and I had a flash image of a prince sitting on his throne, faithful hound at his side.

I needed to get more sleep.

'Shall I turn up the heating?' He didn't answer. 'You're shivering, Gabriel. Is it the fever...?'

I was looking at his hands, and he clenched them to stop the tremor. 'No. It's not the fever. It's nothing heat will cure.'

And then I was the one with a streak of ice racing down my spine. He was a surgeon. An eye surgeon. With a tremor. And I thought I had problems.

I wanted to put my arms around him and hold him and tell him it would be all right. That it was only temporary. His expression warned me that I couldn't promise that. That the perfect steadiness of the hand, once lost, might never be regained...

'You need to eat,' I said, sounding exactly like my mother faced with a crisis. 'It won't be long.' And I began to beat the eggs furiously.

I put the bread under the grill and the eggs on a low heat, but it was a slow business. I had to take them off the heat while I looked at the toast. And I didn't dare leave the toast. I had to get this right. It was important.

'Here, let me do that.'

The grill pan hit the floor as he placed his hand on my shoulder. The dogs flew onto the sofa, flattening their long, elegant heads as close to the cushions as possible. The cat's tail lashed angrily from beneath the chair.

'Damn it!' I turned on him. 'You made me jump!'

'Sorry.' He picked up the grill pan and slid it back under the heat. 'It's just that you looked a little stressed.'

'That could be the understatement of the year. This domestic goddess stuff is all new to me.'

'I had noticed.'

'No, Gabriel, you're supposed to say that since I'm a goddess you can manage without the domesticity,' I snapped. Then, realising I'd overreacted just a little bit, 'However, you're sick, so I'll forgive you. This time.'

'You're a goddess?' He sounded sceptical. 'Is that the kind of response you usually evoke in the male breast?'

I reached up and put my hand on his forehead. 'Cool, dry... Extraordinary. I thought you must be running a raging temperature to have asked a fool question like that.' Then, suddenly self-conscious as I realised what I'd done, I took my hand away, curling my fingers against my palm. 'Of course, you haven't seen me at my best.'

'No?' He smiled. He actually smiled. 'I thought you were pretty amazing, actually. Not a goddess, but pretty amazing nonetheless. But if there's more...'

Oh, good grief. I could see why he didn't do it often. The smile. I'd always known it was going to be special, but that was understatement on a grand scale. It should have a health warning attached.

Danger: this smile is bad for your heart...

Mine responded by putting in a couple of little skips that threw it completely out of sync. And left me totally speechless.

'Shall I keep an eye on the toast?' he asked finally.

'Um...'

My brain had seized up, too.

'One of us should, or it'll burn...'

I went to snatch it from the heat, but he beat me to it. Turned it over.

'Why don't you take care of the eggs?' he suggested.

'Right,' I said. 'Good plan.'

Maybe in the end it was a good thing it had taken such an age to prepare. That I was so useless that he'd had to get involved. There was nothing like the scent of warm toast to tempt a jaded appetite. Nothing like waiting to make you long to sink your teeth into it. And Gabriel ate every scrap of the meagre spoonful of egg—which was absolutely perfect, even if I do say so myself—resting on the single slice of lightly buttered toast. Equally perfect.

We made a good team.

I would have given him all of the egg, but I knew that if I didn't have anything he'd make a fuss. I wasn't about to give him any excuse to duck out of eating what I'd sweated over, and I knew it would be better to leave him wanting more than pushing away what he couldn't eat.

Of course he might just have made the effort to eat because it had obviously been such an effort for me to prepare the food. I didn't care. He'd eaten something that I'd cooked for him and I felt triumphant. Ready to tackle chicken soup—although I knew better than to say so.

And first I'd need a recipe.

I was still starving, of course.

'Would you like some tea?' I offered as I gathered

the plates to cover the sound of my stomach rumbling.
There was cottage cheese in the fridge, but that wasn't
going to help. This wasn't a cottage cheese sort of
week. I'd grab a burger when I was out; I was burning
up calories by the thousand, okay? And possibly some
fries. 'I've got some Earl Grey.' I would have preferred coffee—a double espresso would have been
about perfect—but I can't stand coffee when I'm off-
colour. Even the smell…

'No. Thanks. I'll stick to water.'

'Look, maybe you should go back to bed,' I suggested. Good food and sleep. Nature's cure… I
blinked. If my mother didn't come back soon I was
going to turn into her.

'What are you going to do now?'

'Wash up?' I suggested.

'You said you had to look for a job.'

And somewhere to live, hint, hint.

'Wash up and then check my laptop and mobile to
see what fabulous offers have been pouring in overnight,' I advanced, hoping he'd get the message that
I wouldn't be under his feet for long.

'Why don't you work in the kitchen? It's warmer.'
He got up and headed for the stairs.

'Gabriel…' He glanced back. 'Thank you.' I made
a vague gesture that encompassed the cottage. 'This
is a life-saver.'

'Then we're quits.'

I wasn't looking for any settling of imagined debts,
simply grateful for the breathing space he'd given me
to sort myself out, but I let it go. I waited until he'd
used the bathroom and settled himself back in bed

before I went upstairs to collect my laptop. I listened to my messages while I waited for it to boot up.

There were a lot of messages. Some of the people who'd been at my party, just to say 'great party' and 'what are we doing this weekend?'. Maybe it was reaching the advanced age of twenty-five, but suddenly filling the weekend with entertainment didn't feel like the most important thing in the world.

There was a message from my sister, who wanted to talk about Dad. In other words, when was I going to go home and take care of him…?

Three eager messages from Tony, offering me sanctuary, each one more fulsomely than the one before. I got the feeling that if I hung on long enough he'd offer to move out and let me have his apartment.

It occurred to me that I needed to take a step back. Give him a chance to meet someone who'd return his affection with more than—well, affection.

And finally there was one from Miss Frosty.

She had a job for me doing some shopping for an elderly lady. I checked in, took the details. I didn't, I noticed, get any sarcasm from her this time. Things were looking up.

The internet agency wanted to know if I wanted a job as a waitress in a pub. Now that I could do. From the age of twelve Kate and I had earned extra pocket money by laying the table and acting as waitresses at dinner parties for Mum.

I called the number and they wanted me *now*. Black trousers, white shirt; they'd provide the apron.

I tapped on Gabriel's door and he shouted for me to come in. He was propped up against the pillows, reading something weighty. He looked up as I stuck my head around the door.

'I've got a couple of jobs. I'm just going to get Tigger—' I'd thought a name might give the cat a little probity, but didn't have time to get inventive '—some kitty litter, then I'll be gone until about four-thirty. Have you got your mobile?' He indicated the bedside table. 'If you need me ring, okay? I don't want to come back to another crisis.'

'No, ma'am.'

'Don't mock. Are you warm enough? Do you want a fresh hot water bottle?'

'Stop clucking about me like some mother hen. I've had breakfast. Your good deed is done for the day.'

His phone lay on the bedside table and, ignoring this rapid reversion to bear-with-sore-head mode—for all I knew, he had a sore head—I said, 'You've still got my number?'

He picked it up and I thought for a moment that he was going to throw it at me. Instead he said, 'Remind me. I'll program it in.'

'Under G for goddess?'

'Under N for nag. There. Happy?' he asked when I'd refreshed his memory.

'Delirious,' I said.

'For all the good it will do me.'

'I'm fully charged,' I informed him. 'All you have to do is call.'

I was halfway down the mews when my phone rang. 'Sophie Harrington, universal aunt. No job too small,' I said.

'This hot water bottle…'

His voice, low, slightly gravelly, totally unexpected, brought a warm rush of some forgotten youthful joy surging through my body. I made a belated effort to dam it up, but without success. He'd got to me. And I couldn't even blame the smile. He'd got to me the minute I set eyes on him.

'What about the hot water bottle?' I enquired, cool as a cucumber. I might have lost all control of my emotions, but I was still in charge of my voice.

'It looks like a sheep.'

All street-cred blown, I confessed as much. 'His name is Sean.'

'Sean the Sheep?' Yes, that was disbelief in his gravelly voice.

'He's cuddly. And he's comforting.'

In other words, about as unlike Gabriel York as it was possible to get.

'If I need to be cuddled or comforted, I'll let you know. And in the meantime please take note that if I need emergency warming I don't want this sheep as a stand-in. I want the heat transfer method.'

Maybe his tremor was catching, because without warning I was standing in the middle of the cobbled mews and my whole body was trembling. But, since it would be total madness to do what it was telling me to do—rush back and jump right in beside him— I said, 'C-call a plumber.'

The stutter undermined my throw-away attempt to make light of it. But that was okay. He didn't hear me.

I was already listening to the dialling tone.

CHAPTER SEVEN

'Sophie?'

'Oh, hi, Kate. I didn't think you were back until tomorrow. How was Scotland?'

'Forget Scotland. How are *you*?'

'Me? I'm fine.' More than fine. Great.

'More to the point, where are you? I just called round to the flat to see you and Amber told me they've bought the flat. That you've moved out.'

'I was going to call you.' Tomorrow... 'Cora needed the money.'

'And she asked you to move out without any notice? How could she do that?'

'With great embarrassment. She's been good to us, Kate. I didn't want to make it any tougher for her. Don't worry; I've got somewhere to stay while I sort myself out.'

'With Tony? Is that wise? You know how he dotes on you—'

'Not Tony. It's no one you know. But if you hear of anything—'

'For heaven's sake, Sophie, why don't you just do us all a favour and go home for a while?'

I stared at the phone.

'Dad called last night. I'm sure he'd been drinking. I tried talking to Mum, but she refused to discuss it. Please, Sophie. I can't take any more time off work.'

And I didn't have a job. Not a proper one. She

wouldn't be impressed with the dog-walking, or shopping for the housebound, or cleaning, or the late-night shelf stacking at the toy store.

'And Simon needs me,' she added.

Or a life.

'I can't right now. I have commitments, too.'

She made a dismissive little noise that I found distinctly annoying. My commitments might not pay as much as hers, but they were no less important—and Christmas was getting closer. Even those of us without a life still had cards and gifts to buy…

'Couldn't you at least go down at the weekend?' she said.

'I don't have a car, Kate.'

Gabriel did, though. A big silver Range Rover with plenty of room for two dogs in the back. He'd been convalescing for nearly two weeks now. A walk in the country would do him good.

'The problem with a portfolio career—' and I was building up an impressive portfolio of 'little' jobs '—is that it doesn't leave a lot of time for flat-hunting.'

'You don't have a career, Sophie,' Gabriel said from behind the Sunday newspaper. 'You're just a general dogsbody, gofer and dog-walker.'

'I'm fulfilling a need.' I applied a little more beeswax to the dresser. 'Take Mrs Andrews, for instance.'

'Must I?'

'She's the lady I shop for each morning.'

'I imagine she pays you handsomely for the service?'

'Yes, of course she does.' Then, 'Well, not handsomely, but probably more than she can afford. I could do it once a week, and clearly it would be a lot cheaper for her, but that's my point. It isn't shopping she needs; it's someone to talk to. She's always got a pot of coffee waiting when I get back, and some little treat. In fact I think she just buys the biscuits and cake especially for me. What do I do? Say, Sorry, too busy…?' Encouraged by the lack of a reply, I continued, 'We have coffee and cake and she tells me all about her life. She was a musician. A violinist. She travelled all over the world with her orchestra, met some amazing people.'

'You're not supposed to stay and chat, Sophie. You don't get paid for that.'

'You're totally heartless.'

'That, as you must know, is a physiological impossibility.'

'I was speaking figuratively, Doctor,' I replied, gallantly resisting this open invitation to inform him that he was a miserable pedant. 'Your heart is nothing more than an emotionally sterile pump. It beats, but it doesn't…*feel*.'

'Doctors can't afford to be emotional. Neither can a girl who hasn't got a proper job.'

'She's lonely, Gabriel.'

'She should get a cat.' He glanced over the top of the newspaper. 'Why don't you give her yours?'

'Very funny.'

'I was perfectly serious. This woman—'

'She has a name.'

'—is keeping you from earning a living.' He didn't say…and finding somewhere to live. He didn't have to.

'It's not her fault.'

I'd been staying with Gabriel for nearly two weeks and so far hadn't done a thing about finding somewhere else. I was attempting to explain why. It wasn't that I didn't intend looking. Every day I set out with the best of intentions. I just never seemed to have the time to do anything about them.

'Every minute of my day seems to be taken up with rushing from one job to the next.'

'I'd have thought it would give you more freedom,' he said, manfully resisting the open invitation to remind me that I could have spent the time I was wasting chatting to Mrs Andrews rather more usefully in the pursuit of suitable accommodation.

'Theoretically,' I admitted, 'it does. In practice it just doesn't seem to work out that way.' Especially since I was going out of my way to call back at the mews two or three times a day to make sure he was okay. 'I've asked everyone I know to keep an eye out for me, though,' I said, rubbing at a particularly stubborn mark.

'Good. Let's hope they have twenty-twenty vision.'

'I just didn't want you to think I'm taking advantage of your good nature.'

'I don't have a good nature. Ask anyone who knows me.'

'I know you, and I'm telling you that your nature is perfectly good. You took me in when I was pretty desperate—'

He finally gave up trying to read the paper. 'What the hell are you doing?'

It was a classic diversionary tactic, but I let him get away with it. For now. 'Getting rid of some dust,' I said.

The dark wood of the Welsh dresser gleamed in the low winter sunlight that had finally reappeared after days of drizzle and gloom. It was the sunlight that had driven me into action, showing up the layers of dust, every mark and smear.

'Stirring it up and moving it around, more like,' he said. 'It'll get in your bronchial tubes and irritate them. Worse, it'll get in mine.'

'You don't need dust to irritate you. It's your natural state.'

'Proving my point that I don't have a good nature and that you're living dangerously—'

'I've been doing that since I knocked on your door,' I reminded him. I'd started out determined to keep my cool—I had an ulterior motive for this conversation—but I was only human and my own irritability quotient was ratcheting up with every exchange.

There was a momentary pause before he said, 'A little dust, left undisturbed, won't harm you. Best leave well alone.'

Easier said than done.

'This from the man who objected to the fact that my T-shirt hadn't been sterilised when I cleaned up a scratch on his knee?'

He responded with something that sounded distinctly nineteenth century. 'Pshaw', perhaps. Or maybe it was nearer 'harrumph'. Or it might have been altogether less polite. And retreated behind the newspaper.

'How is it now? Your knee?' I enquired, with saccharine sweetness. 'Any sign of infection?' He muttered something unintelligible. 'Sorry? I didn't quite catch that.'

'It's fine. What's for breakfast?'

I wasn't fooled by this sudden change of subject. I was doing my very limited best to produce the kind of light but tasty food to tempt his appetite, but he wasn't eating enough to keep a bird alive. That was, I fully admit, probably as much to do with my cooking as his lack of interest in food. The scrambled eggs had been a high point that I hadn't managed to repeat.

And, like his appetite, his temper was deteriorating with every passing day.

The promising moment of closeness, of teasing intimacy, as he'd invited me to be his personal body-warmer hadn't lasted beyond the telephone call. Maybe I should have turned around and gone back then. By the time I'd shopped for Mrs Andrews and spent two hours waiting on lunchtime tables—they'd been really desperate at the pub, so my interview had involved tying on an apron and getting on with it— he'd been back to high-octane grouch mode.

He hadn't wanted to eat; he hadn't wanted anything except to be left alone. And he hadn't cavilled at telling me so.

In fact he couldn't have made it plainer that he was sorry he'd invited me and my cat to stay.

Well, just me. He hadn't invited the cat, obviously.

Tough. He was stuck with us until he was well enough to be left on his own or until I could find somewhere I could afford. Of the two, the former was more important. But I didn't tell him that. Or that I was ringing Crissie every day to keep her up to date with his progress.

Nil.

Not that he was malingering in bed. Making a performance out of being an invalid. I wished he *would* stay in bed, instead of pacing feverishly, reading great tomes of text books. He needed to rest.

I'd only suggested it once, and had my head bitten off for my trouble. So, since I was tired of asking him what he'd like to eat and being told to leave him in peace, that if he wanted anything from me he'd say so, I'd made him a cup of tea and left him to his newspaper while I got on with cleaning the dresser. Right now he was using it as a barrier between us, holding it up so that I couldn't see his face. As I stood there it began to shiver like an aspen leaf, and with an exclamation of annoyance he tossed it aside.

'I don't know why I waste my time reading this rubbish,' he declared furiously, standing up as if he wanted to run and run…but knew there was nowhere to hide. He looked thinner, paler, his dark eyes hot and angry at his helplessness. And my heart, my poor heart that had never been disturbed by anyone since Perry Fotheringay had broken it, was hit by a shock-wave of an emotion so strong that I was rocked to my heels. Had to clutch at the dresser for support.

I yearned to reach out, take his shaking hand in mine and hold it to my breast, heal him with my warmth. Even as I moved to make the thought the deed I was repelled by the force field of keep-your-distance anger with which he'd surrounded himself; I suspected that it was the only thing holding him together. I recognised the symptoms. I'd been there.

Oh, I hadn't used anger to hide my hurt. I'd used careless gaiety—cut myself off from all risk of emotional attachment with an endless round of parties and shopping and meaningless jobs.

How shallow it was. How stupid. What overweening self-pity and pride to think that my eighteen-year-old heart was worth so much.

What was a broken heart compared to the prospect of never being able to use his hands to repair, heal, restore the precious gift of sight…?

Nothing.

I would have done anything to spare him that. Anything to ease the pain just a little. Given him the one gift a woman could offer to help a man forget everything, lose himself for just a few moments. But I knew he'd see it as an act of pity and loathe the weakness in himself that had evoked it. Loathe me for seeing him so reduced.

I wasn't sure whether the keep-your-distance snapping was to prevent me from getting close enough to hold him in the simple act of comfort or to prevent himself from reaching out and accepting it.

I'd thought I was good at concealing my feelings, but perhaps the feelings were too strong to hide and my face betrayed me, because he turned the anger on me. 'Well?' he demanded. 'What does a man have to do around here to get some breakfast?'

Good move. Great distraction. I wasn't falling for it.

'Ask nicely?' I suggested. If I couldn't use desire to promote a little temporary amnesia, I'd use whatever emotion came to hand. 'Or get it himself.'

His response was to cross to the fridge and take out a new carton of orange juice. I knew from experience that they were a pig to open, but knew better than to offer to do it for him. By the time he'd managed to tear an opening his hand was shaking so badly that he spilled more than he poured into the glass. He stared at the mess for a moment, then picked up the glass and threw it hard at the nearest wall. I flinched as it smashed in a shower of splintered glass and juice.

No emotion, huh?

Into the ghastly silence, during which the juice—it was the thick kind, full of pulp—slithered down the wall, I said, 'There is a third alternative.'

He turned a ferocious glare on me, taking a step towards me as if he wanted to take me by the shoulders and shake me. I bet he'd reduced junior doctors and nervous young nurses to jelly with that performance. I stood my ground. If he wanted to do that to me, he was using the wrong technique. He should try the smile...

'Well, don't keep me in suspense,' he snapped, belatedly remembering to keep his distance. I didn't want him to remember. I wanted him to forget. Everything. Once he'd touched me, once I had him in my arms, anything might be possible...

'You could take me to that little Italian place on the corner.'

His eyes flared. 'Why should I do that?'

'Because I've walked your dogs and polished your dresser and now I'm hungry.'

'I pay you to walk my dogs. Extra on Sundays,' he reminded me, and I couldn't fault him. 'And I didn't ask you to polish anything.' He seemed impregnable, but he wasn't. I knew he felt something. Knew he wanted to touch me, wanted to hold me. I'd been there in his bed...

'It's breakfast, for heaven's sake, not dinner at the Ritz. I'm hungry, I don't feel like cooking, and...and I hate going into strange places on my own.' Maybe that was a step too far. 'Also,' I declared, 'you could do with some fresh air—'

'It's not fresh; it's freezing. I'll get pneumonia.'

'Wimp,' I said. 'The sun's shining, for heaven's sake. It'll give you an appetite. And the food will be edible.'

'Well, that's a plus,' he conceded. With sarcasm like that, I decided, he didn't need a scalpel.

'Also, you've been a Grade A grouch all week,' I continued, on a roll. I knew I should clear up the glass before one of the dogs decided that it was safe to get down off the sofa and investigate, but Gabriel was talking, reacting—angrily, but reacting—and I wasn't going to give up while there was a chance that he'd crack, just a little... 'I deserve a break.'

'Grouch? I'm not a grouch. I've been the very soul of patience,' he ground out. 'Tolerant beyond belief, considering I haven't had a moment's peace with you rushing in and out all day. Your phone ringing non-stop. Considering,' he added, getting into his stride, 'that you introduced a cat into my household without so much as a—'

'And,' I said, cutting him off in full flow. We were discussing his failings, not mine. 'I've been so busy working that I haven't had time to shop, so there's no bread.'

'You couldn't fit it in during your daily shopping trips for Mrs Andrews?' he enquired.

'She was paying for my time,' I reminded him, doing my best to try his patience and tolerance to the limit. 'You weren't.'

I could keep this up as long as he could.

'Are you saying that I have to buy an hour of your time to get some breakfast?' he demanded, taking another step towards me. I noticed the shaking had stopped.

'No. I'm saying you should wrap up warm and take me out to breakfast. I could murder a toasted muffin. One that isn't burnt.'

He didn't appear to have an answer to that one. Another minute and he'd remember he wasn't really hungry, that he was just mad at me, and retreat back into his shell of misery, so I did the big sigh thing, threw up my hands and said, '*Okay.* If you're going to be cheap, I'll split the bill with you. But that's the best offer you're going to get, so you'd—'

'Sophie...' Suddenly he was a lot closer.

'—better take it—'

He grabbed my shoulders. 'Sophie, shut up.'

'—while you—'

His mouth came down on mine, hard and hot. As kisses went, it certainly wasn't out of the fairytale school of romance, but what it lacked in tender finesse it more than made up for in fierce, breath-stopping intensity, and my crushed lips sizzled beneath his, the heat spreading in an arc of fire that threatened to consume my entire body.

It was swift, shocking, and all but overwhelming. I slammed my eyes shut and held on, doing my best to ignore the racketing demands of a hot, insane desire that seized me by the throat. It didn't mean any-

thing, I told myself. I'd pushed him over the edge—
it had been my firm intention to push him over the
edge—and I'd succeeded beyond my wildest dreams.
All I had to do was hang on to that thought and it
would be over in a moment...

Then his mouth softened.

Without warning his desperation to shut me up,
stop me nagging at him, had turned to something
quite different and I was in trouble.

His grip on my shoulders shifted, his fingers
spreading across my back, setting up ripples of sensual excitement that escalated all the need to be held,
loved, that I'd kept locked tightly away for so long.
I'd forgotten how it could take and possess you.

My body yielded to the demands of his mouth. My
lips parted, my tongue invited deeper exploration of
possibilities that for years my heart had denied. My
legs buckled and I swayed towards him, wanting to
feel his body against mine, the urgency of his need...

And then, just as suddenly, it was over.

'Is that it?' Gabriel demanded, his eyes hot, obsid-
ian-black. I would have taken a step back, except that
his fingers were still digging into my shoulders. 'Are
you quite finished?'

If I'd wanted to speak, I couldn't.

I swallowed, trying to recapture the flippant, dare-
you provocation that he'd cut off so effectively with
his mouth.

I'd provoked and, finally, he'd dared.

Good job, Sophie. Terrific job...

Except I'd been so determined to get through to
him I hadn't seen the danger. That in applying the

blowtorch to his emotional freeze-up I would, inevitably, be caught in the flame.

I hadn't been kissed like that since...

No. Forget 'since'. I'd never been kissed like that. Never felt like that. Shaken, stirred, to the very tips of my toes.

'Don't tell me I've finally managed to shut you up?'

I had to speak. Now. Had to act as if that was all he'd done. But it took every ounce of will-power to resist the desperate need to swallow before I said, 'That depends.'

I heard the words: sharp, couldn't-care-less. It didn't sound like my voice. And why, when I was shaking everywhere else, was my voice steady as a rock?

'Are you determined to stay here and mope, Gabriel? Or are you going to admit defeat? Prove that you can walk a hundred yards without falling flat on your face?'

His grip on my shoulders relaxed and then he let go. I felt adrift, alone.

'Will I get any peace until I agree?' he asked.

'What do you think?'

'I think a dose of fresh air suddenly seems very attractive. I'll get my coat.'

He turned and walked quickly away from me, and as I heard his feet pounding up the stairs I finally slumped against the dresser. Who knows how long I'd have stayed there if Joe—stupid, adorable Joe—hadn't slithered off the sofa, in that belly-to-the-ground way that dogs have when they hope not to be noticed, quite unable to resist the lure of the orange juice?

I called him off, sent him back to the sofa and, by the time Gabriel returned with his coat, I'd cleaned up glass and was back in control. Almost.

The chill put some colour into Gabriel's cheeks. I'd had a momentary qualm about dragging him out against his will, but eased my conscience by reminding myself that I was doing it for his own good, tucking my arm through his as if it was the most natural thing in the world. If he suspected it was just in case the effort was too much for him he didn't say so, but took my hand and eased my arm more firmly in place, so that I was close enough to feel his warmth.

He stopped and I looked up at him. 'Are you okay?'

'Yes. No. You engineered that, didn't you?'

'What?'

'Don't pull that stupid blonde stuff on me, Sophie. I've shared a house with you for nearly two weeks. You engineered that row—pushed me until I did what I've been wanting to do since you gave me the kiss of life.'

'Excuse me? I thought you said…' I stopped. That searing kiss? He'd been holding onto that for the best part of two weeks? But that meant…that meant… Actually, I wasn't sure what it meant. He fancied me rotten but didn't like me enough to bother getting involved? He fancied me rotten but liked me too much to risk getting involved, considering his family's apparent genetic inability to make an emotional commitment? He just fancied me… 'Um, you said…'

'I know what I said and I was right. It wasn't CPR, but I know how it made me feel. Alive.'

'Well…good.'

Except that it wasn't good. Not from his point of view. He didn't do relationships.

We were standing facing each other, our arms still linked, my hand on the soft cloth of his overcoat, my cheek almost brushing his lapel.

'Do you have a problem with that, Gabriel?' I asked, pushing for an answer. 'Feeling alive?'

He reached out, as if to touch my cheek, but thought better of it, curling his fingers back into his palm. Then he said, 'Good grief, is that a Christmas tree?'

What?

He was glaring at a window, ablaze with coloured lights, as if it was a personal affront. 'It's nowhere near Christmas.

He'd seized the first distraction that came to him— anything rather than confront the question. Discussion over. Change subject before it could get messy…

Too late. Life is messy, but it's the only one we have, and while you're trying to avoid pain—or trying avoid causing it—time doesn't stop. He'd lowered his guard, given me a taste of the passion he had battened down for fear of hurting someone in his driven need to be the best. Well, I was ready to take that risk, but for the moment I was happy to drop the subject. Just for now.

'Of course it's a Christmas tree. Where have you been for the last month?' I asked him as we resumed our stroll towards the coffee shop. Then, realising what I'd said, I apologised, 'Sorry, Gabriel, please forget I asked that question, but it *is* the middle of December. There are only eight shopping days to Christmas. We're rushed off our feet doing Christmas lunches for office parties at the pub. Turkey, mince pies and seasonal indiscretion—all to the accompaniment of "White Christmas" non-stop on the sound system.'

'That sounds like something to be missed.'

'Don't be such a misery. It's great to see people enjoying themselves. And the tips are great.'

'By the time Christmas arrives you'll be heartily sick of the whole thing,' he warned me, seizing this opportunity to steer the conversation well away from dangerous emotional currents.

'No. I love Christmas. It's always the same. The decorations, the cheesy songs on the radio, choosing the perfect presents.'

Even as I was saying the words I realised that this year nothing would be the same. Not keen to dwell on exactly what Christmas would be like this year, I turned and looked up at him. 'What about you? Have you got any plans? Will your brother and his wife be home by then? Or do you spend it with your parents?'

I was fishing, of course. What I really meant was, Will you be spending it with the nurse? I hadn't seen anyone special, but that didn't mean there wasn't someone. I wasn't there all the time. A bowl of fruit had materialised one day while I was out. He'd said the woman who'd taken care of his dogs had called round with it.

My brain assured me that she'd be some solid retired nurse, who made a little money taking care of people's animals while they were away.

But my imagination offered an alternative reality in which she was sexy and gorgeous, a thoroughly modern woman who, like him, preferred to keep relationships on a strictly physical level. Who knew what treats she dropped in with while I was busy rushing around serving turkey and all the trimmings between twelve and two every day?

'I usually work through the holiday,' he said, not answering any of those questions. Or perhaps giving me more of an answer than he'd intended. 'I suppose you'll be at home in the bosom of your family?'

'Not this year.'

The big family Christmas wasn't going to happen without my mother to organise it. She masterminded the whole thing—cutting the tree, everyone going to church at midnight, rounding up anyone from the village with no one to share the holiday with, Dad carving the turkey, the stupid games…

Even Kate had said she wouldn't be there. I understood. She'd want to start making her own family traditions. But it just made the huge empty gap in the family harder to paper over.

'My parents split up a few months ago,' I said. 'My mother is spending Christmas in the sun with her toy boy. As you can imagine, it's put a bit of a dampener on the whole ho-ho-ho thing.'

'You could always spend the day with Mrs Andrews, listening to her stories.'

I knew I could rely on him not be 'sympathetic'.

'I'm sure it would be a lot more fun than rattling around the house while my father drowns his sorrows in Scotch. I wonder if she's going to be on her own?' I said as we reached the coffee bar.

'Since she pays you to do her shopping just so that she has someone to talk to, I imagine the chances of that are quite high.'

Pretty much my own thought. 'Maybe I should do something about that.'

'Maybe you should.' He unhooked his arm from mine and reached over my head to push open the door.

'Hey, Doc! We missed you. Where've you been?' The man behind the vast chrome espresso machine hurried out, beaming a welcome that immediately turned to concern as he shook Gabriel's hand. 'Nowhere that did you any good,' he said, without waiting for an answer. 'Sit, sit. I'll get Maria to make you one of her special *zabaglione*. It'll put you right back on your feet.'

Zabaglione? With eggs so lightly cooked they might be considered raw? This should be interesting…

'Thank you, Marco.' *Huh?* 'Ask her to leave out the alcohol, though. I'm on all kinds of medication.'

'Sure, Doc, you leave it to me.' He turned to me, his expression including me in his broad smile. 'And for your friend?'

'Marco, this is Sophie. She's taking care of the dogs until I'm fit.'

'Just the dogs?' With one lift of his expressive eyebrows he conveyed whole paragraphs of meaning. 'And who's taking care of you?'

'She's doing her best to do that, too. But, as she's just pointed out most forcefully, I'm not being terribly receptive.'

'The British reputation for understatement is safe in his hands,' I said.

'The Doc only cares about other people, eh, Sophie?' Marco said, as if we alone understood him. 'So, what would you like?'

'A toasted muffin, please. And a large cappuccino.'

'Make that two cappuccinos,' Gabriel said.

Marco brought us our coffee and lingered to invite us to join his family at the local church to see his daughter in the Nativity play on the Friday before Christmas.

'We'd be honoured to come,' Gabriel said. And, actually, I wasn't as surprised as I believe he'd meant me to be.

His presence demanded 'pronto' by his wife, Marco left us with the promise that our food would be with us in '*un momento*'.

'The Grinch at a Nativity play?' I teased.

'Will you come with me?' he asked.

'Thanks. I wouldn't miss it for the world.'

'Don't thank me. I'm not being kind. I'm being selfish,' he said, and sounded thoroughly disgusted with himself. But he didn't withdraw the invitation.

My turn to change the subject, I decided.

'I get the feeling you eat here on a regular basis. You're almost part of the family.'

Gabriel shrugged. 'I work long hours and I can't be bothered to cook.'

A young girl brought my muffin and some butter. Then she fetched Gabriel's *zabaglione*, shyly placing it in front of him. Gabriel said something to her in Italian and she giggled, then, after glancing at me, whispered something back to him.

He spoke Italian?

How…how…*un-English*.

How wonderful.

How shaming. What had I been doing all my life that I couldn't speak another language properly? I hadn't even bothered to enrol in a computer course, despite all those big promises I'd made to myself…

'Lucia has heard we're going to see her play. She wants to know if that means you're my girlfriend,' Gabriel said, distracting me. And without warning that errant smile was simmering just beneath the surface. Just the promise of it made my cheeks feel warm. My heart beat a little faster than usual. My lips heated up with the memory of his kiss.

I knew that feeling. I'd felt that way when Perry Fotheringay had looked at me. Dazzled, reckless, excited. And I knew all the other feelings that went with it. Misery when he hadn't called. Heartache when he'd betrayed me.

The ice-cold feeling inside as I'd pretended that it didn't matter. That I'd never taken him seriously.

I stared into the trap I'd set for myself. And fallen right into.

Just because he didn't flirt, or smile too easily, and guarded his emotions, I'd thought I was safe, but I wasn't. I was going to get hurt again, but at least this time I knew the score. And if I could show Gabriel that he was wrong, that emotional commitment had nothing to do with genetics and everything to do with heart… For that, I'd risk any amount of pain.

'I'm your friend,' I said lightly. 'The fact that I'm a girl makes no difference.'

He said something to her and she laughed, clearly

not taken in by this sleight of language, before skipping happily back to her papa.

Gabriel said nothing to me until I bit into the muffin, and when I had my mouth safely full he said, 'It does make a difference, you know.'

What made a difference? With my mouth full, all I could do was raise my eyebrows at him.

'Being a girl.' He took his time, tasted the sweet egg dish. 'If you'd been a man, driving me insane with your endless nagging, Sophie, I wouldn't have kissed you to shut you up.'

There's only one way to deal with a man who's scored a cheap point.

I took my time about finishing the piece of muffin, wiped my fingers on the napkin, finished my cappuccino.

Only then did I sit back and say, 'Gabriel?'

'Yes?'

'Can I borrow your car this afternoon?'

CHAPTER EIGHT

GABRIEL YORK had to be a lot sicker than I'd realised. He didn't even flinch. His only response to this outrageous request was to glance at me and ask, 'Do you have insurance?'

'Er, yes.' I was covered for everything, from a tractor to my father's BMW and anything else I drove, by the estate motor policy. Not that I had ever actually wanted to drive the tractor—well, not since I was about ten anyway—or was likely to be allowed to drive his precious saloon, despite my Advanced Driver's Certificate. This was something my father insisted on for everyone who drove his vehicles since it kept the insurance premiums down.

'Then help yourself. Just be careful how you reverse out of the garage; it's a bit tight.'

He wasn't even going to insist on doing that bit himself? What kind of man was he?

'I'll try not to do too much damage.'

'Since you're insured I'm not sweating.'

'Right.' Well, that had fallen flat. Tony had practically gibbered when I'd asked if I could borrow *his* car. Of course it was a hand-built Morgan; he'd been on a waiting list for three years before it was finally delivered. And I'd only been teasing. Only a fool would drive in London if she didn't have to. 'Don't you want to know where I'm going?'

'So long as you're back to walk the dogs, that's your business.'

'Actually, it's yours, too. I thought I might take Joe and Percy out into the country for a good run.'

'Where?'

Now he was interested. Obviously he cared more about his dogs than his car. He was a man with his priorities, if not his heart, in the right place. 'Home. I can check up on my father at the same time.'

'And with the excuse of the dogs and getting my car back he won't be able to talk you into staying to look after him?'

'Smart, aren't you?' I said, embarrassed to have been so obvious.

'He can't make you stay if you don't want to, Sophie.'

'Oh, he won't say a word. But he'll be *so* pathetic. He won't have shaved for a week, the fridge will be bare, he'll have no clean clothes...'

'Oh, I see.' He didn't even bother to hide his smile. 'It's that soft heart of yours that you don't trust.'

'Nothing of the kind,' I declared hotly. 'My heart is as tough as old boots. Kate—my big sister—has been nagging me about it, that's all.'

'I didn't know you had a sister. Does she live in London, too?'

'Yes, but she's been away.'

'Well, if she's back there's no reason why she shouldn't go and make sure he's all right. If she's so worried about him.'

Implying that I wasn't.

'I suggested that,' I said, doing my best to live up to the 'tough as old boots' boast. 'Unfortunately she has a cast-iron excuse. Unlike me, she applied herself to her lessons, went to university and graduated with an impressive degree in law, as a result of which she now has an equally impressive job.' I threw in a careless shrug. 'The rewards of hard work are never having to go home and pick up the pieces when your parents' marriage falls apart...'

The careless shrug didn't work, and I found myself in urgent need of a sniff.

Oh, sugar!

If I wasn't jolly careful I was going to cry. I hadn't cried in years. But, while I was prepared to accept that my mother needed a break, some excitement, I really, really wished she'd come home now—I searched my pocket for a tissue and blew my nose—and not just because my father was being such a pain in the *gluteus maximus*...

'It's Sunday. Most of the lawyers I know take Sunday off,' Gabriel said, ignoring my pathetic sniffle.

'That's true. But because she's not only clever, but seriously beautiful, she now has a totally fabulous husband to complete the set. Sunday is their one day together.'

'Is that just a touch of an inferiority complex showing?' Gabriel said, sounding a touch bored. And why wouldn't he? Who wanted to listen to a poor little rich girl whining on about her problems? Not that he knew I was rich. Well, I wasn't now, and wouldn't be until I reached the age of thirty or married—whichever came sooner.

'Actually, no,' I said, making a good attempt at

matching his boredom with the subject and topping it. 'I never wanted the degree or the fancy job.'

'What did you want?'

That was the problem with going over the top; it led you into dangerous conversational waters and suddenly there you were, way out of your depth and sinking fast.

Frantically treading water, I edged back from emotional exposure, got a grip and painted a smile on my face. 'To have fun. What else?' I asked brightly.

He did not look impressed by that, either, and, put baldly that way, I could see that it wasn't an impressive ambition.

'You consider walking dogs, cleaning, waiting on tables in a pub to earn a crust, *fun*?'

'To tell you the truth, it's a big improvement on some of the jobs I've had in the past. And I'm getting to meet some really extraordinary people. Greta, for instance, at the florist. She's bringing up two children single-handed after their father died. It must be so tough for her, but I've never heard her utter a word of complaint. And Alan at the toy store. He was a ''special needs'' kid and he was put into care because his parents didn't want him, but now he's working his way through university—'

'I'm sure they're all wonderful people. But it's not something you'll want to be doing in five or ten years' time, is it?'

'Having fun?' I asked, wilfully choosing to misunderstand.

'Swabbing floors in a flower shop,' he replied, as selectively deaf as his dogs, apparently, when it came to taking a hint and dropping a subject. 'I may be wrong, but it doesn't quite seem to go with the top-of-the-range laptop and cellphone, the designer label clothes—'

I opened my mouth to protest.

'Cutting out the labels doesn't change what they are, Sophie.'

He'd noticed?

'It makes me feel better about wearing them to work. But you're right, of course,' I said. 'I won't be doing that.' I gave him just long enough to look smug before I said, 'It's just temporary cover while the lady who normally does it is recuperating from minor surgery. I'll have to find something else after the holiday.'

'I'm almost afraid to ask what.'

'Well, I was thinking of enrolling on a computer course.'

This time he did flinch. 'No. Don't do that, Sophie.'

'Why not?'

'I've seen the trouble you get into just sending e-mails. The thought of you doing something that really mattered would keep me awake at nights.'

'That sound you just heard was my self-esteem hitting the floor.'

Making no attempt to retrieve it, soothe it, hand it back to me, he said, 'If you really need a job—'

'You think I'm doing this for fun...?'

Oops.

Actually, it was worth having my feet chopped from under me—metaphorically speaking—just to see him smile. It was a good job I was sitting down on all counts.

'There must be something else you can do?'

'Must there?' I asked. Smile time was over and we were back to the career plan. 'I had this conversation with a woman at my employment agency very recently. She's the person who offered me the job walking your dogs.'

Which left him with nowhere to go.

'I think what you need, Sophie, is a husband,' he said. And there was absolutely no doubt in my mind that he remembered me telling him something very similar and was enjoying the opportunity to return the lecture.

'I can't cook,' I reminded him.

'A rich husband,' he amended.

'Too bad the one I had picked out had other plans.' Oh, fiddle-di-dee. I *sooo* had not meant to say that. Or maybe I had. I'd never had any trouble keeping my failed career plan from anyone else. 'Anyway,' I said, quickly returning to the original subject of this conversation, 'I need to go home this afternoon and check that my father is at least going through the motions of daily life.'

'But you don't intend to linger, and if you take my dogs and car you'll have all the excuse you need to get away again?'

'You think I'm being mean?'

'Only you can answer that one. Are you?'

'He's been doing some serious arm-twisting to get me to go home and take care of things until my mother comes to her senses.' I didn't voice the fear that was at the back of my mind. That she might never come to her senses...

'You mean he's cut off your allowance? That's what this is all about? No money, nowhere to live...'

'Actually, the flat that I'd been staying in wasn't anything to do with him.' Or was it? Was it possible that Cora and my Dad were in cahoots? Using me to try and get my mother to see sense and come home? I shook my head in an effort to clear it. 'I'm not about to let him get away with emotional blackmail,' I said.

'And if he asked you nicely?'

'Thankfully there's no danger of that. Why do you think my mother's lying by a swimming pool in Cape Town instead of at home organising the Christmas festivities, making sure no one in the village is alone on the big day, that everyone is having a good time?'

'Maybe she thinks it's someone else's turn.'

'Thanks. Add selfish daughter to selfish husband and it's obvious why she left home.'

'I'm not criticising you, Sophie. He's an adult. Responsible for his own life. It's just that you don't seem particularly happy—'

'Yes, well, you can tell yourself that what you're doing is right, for the best, but when it comes right down to it...' I was avoiding looking at Gabriel '...well, he's still my dad.' I painted a smile on my face and looked up. 'I suppose you don't fancy coming with me?' I asked brightly, now that he'd given me the opening I'd been hoping for. 'It'll get you out of the house for a few hours.'

'You suppose correctly.'

I didn't push it. 'Okay, but if I'm not home by the dogs' bedtime you'd better send out a rescue party,' I said, hanging onto the smile by the skin of my teeth.

I couldn't believe how miserable I was that he'd turned me down.

'I'll ring you on that expensive cellphone at a pre-arranged time and get heavy about needing the car, if you like,' he offered.

'That's the best you can do?'

'I'd need a lot more to tempt me out than an hour's drive along the motorway followed by an uncomfortable confrontation with your father.'

'We could take the dogs for a walk in the woods. You should start getting some exercise.'

'Thanks for the consultation, Doctor,' he said. 'Don't call me, I'll call you.' Then he shrugged, 'Of course, if you'd care to enliven the journey with the story of the man that got away, I might reconsider...'

Enliven? For a glimpse of that rare smile I'd have promised anything, even laying my heart bare for his amusement, but there was no smile.

'There's nothing to tell. He wanted a rich wife so he married someone else. His mistake.'

I know, I know. Just minutes ago I'd all but issued him with a gold-edged invitation to get nosey. Now, when he'd accepted, I'd totally blown it.

I didn't really know what I was saying.

All I knew was that I so much didn't want to own up to being such a pathetic creature for the last seven years, that the lump in my throat was back and my eyes were stinging. Also I needed to blow my nose again.

'Are you starting a cold?' Gabriel asked.

'You're the doctor.'

'Runny nose, watery eyes. There are only two possibilities. You have a cold. Or you're crying.'

'Why would I be crying?' I snapped.

There was a momentary pause when he looked as if he might say something—well, *kind*. Offer me his broad shoulder in time-honoured fashion so that I could let myself go. Get it all off my chest. But he just did something with his eyebrows and said, 'It must be a cold, then.'

'Right. And what do you recommend—in your professional capacity—to alleviate the symptoms?'

'Plenty of fluids. Go to bed. Keep warm—'

'And would that be with a hot water bottle? Or are you offering the heat transfer method so recently pioneered by—'

Deep in his eyes heat flared in the darkness, for a moment burned so bright that it stopped my words. Stopped my breath.

Then he spoiled it all by saying, 'Professionally speaking—'

'No, Doctor, I want your personal opinion on that one.'

He took way too long to respond. If he'd known how unique such an invitation was from me, how many men had hoped and been disappointed, he might have been a little more excited. The hot flare in those eyes had given me hope, but in the meantime he was left hunting for some kind way to let me down. So that he wouldn't hurt me.

I'd been there so many times myself that I could read his mind as he struggled for the words. I could write the script for him. You said... Sorry, I like you, but I don't want to go to bed with you...

For that, only love would do.

I saved him the bother of hunting for the right

words. If the answer wasn't yes, I didn't want to hear it, and, checking my watch so that I could look away without being obvious about it, I said, 'If I'm going to make the most of the daylight I need to get on my way.'

'Sophie—'

But he'd waited too long, and when, finally, he managed my name it was with that apologetic hesitation that boded absolutely nothing but embarrassment for both of us. I didn't want that, so I stood up. When, like the gentleman he was, he automatically made to do the same, I shook my head, waved him back to his seat.

'No. Stay and finish your breakfast. I know where the car keys are kept.'

I didn't wait for him to offer an argument but fled the heat of the coffee bar, grateful for the frosty cold to clear my head, even if it did make my eyes sting.

I quickly loaded the dogs into the caged area at the back of the Range Rover, not wanting to be there when he returned, taking only a moment to familiarise myself with the vehicle before starting it up and backing slowly out of the garage. But my 'cold' seemed to be getting worse. The lump in my throat had grown so big that I could scarcely swallow and my eyes were swimmy. Perhaps that was why I misjudged the distance and clipped the garage door as I reversed out into the mews.

Or maybe it was because, as I checked the rearview mirror, I saw the tall, dark figure of Gabriel York, backlit by the fragile winter sunlight as he walked towards me. Or a combination of both. Whatever. My foot wobbled on the clutch, there was a loud rending of metal against wood, and for a moment I completely lost control.

Which explained why I reversed into the stone urn with the dead foliage. It hit the cobbles with a crash. The dogs yelped in fright. Then the car stalled.

The door beside me opened and Gabriel said, 'I should have guessed that your driving would be on a par with your computer skills.'

'N-no!' I protested. 'I'm a perfectly c-competent driver.' It wasn't just my foot that was shaking. My hands, hanging onto the wheel in a vice-like grip, were perfectly still but the rest of me was shivering uncontrollably. 'I've been driving since my feet c-could reach the pedals,' I said, in an attempt to convince him that, useless as I was in other directions, this incident was an aberration. 'I've n-never so much as scratched the paintwork.'

He just looked at me.

'It's true!' I yelled. And then, for absolutely no good reason, I burst into tears.

Before I could find a tissue he had his arms around me and my tears were soaking into the soft cashmere of his coat.

'No...no...' I fought the yearning to cling to him. I didn't cry. I didn't cling. Not even when Perry had explained the situation to me in words of one syllable so that even a stupid girl could understand that what I'd thought was undying love was no more than a bit of fun. The pride that had kept me dry-eyed through that nightmare had stood me in good stead ever since... 'I should make sure the dogs are okay,' I mumbled into his solid chest.

'They're fine,' he said, holding me close, not letting me go, and I gave up to the need to be held, reassured, loved...

'I'm so s-sorry, Gabriel. I don't do this...'

The words were muffled, but the sentiment must have been clear because he stroked my head. 'I know. It's just shock...'

Shock. Of course. That was all right, then.

My cheek was nestled into the hollow of his shoulder; his fingers were threaded through my hair, holding me there. Close against his heart. And then his lips brushed my forehead. It felt perfect. I'd never felt so safe and I didn't want to move. Ever. Which made it absolutely vital that I did so. Immediately. I pulled away and he made no attempt to stop me.

I slumped back into the seat and mopped up the tears, blew my nose. He left me to gather myself while he walked around the vehicle to check the damage.

'Is it bad?' I asked when he returned.

'Just a couple of dents in the bumpers. Nothing vital. No damage to the lights. Nothing to prevent your journey.' Then, 'Move over.'

'W-what?'

'Move over. You're in no fit state to drive.'

'I'm fine...' My voice wobbled a bit on 'fine'.

'No, you're not. You're worried to death about your parents, added to which you've been overdoing it with all these crazy jobs you've taken on and still finding time to rush back and check on me two or three times a day.'

'No...' Then, because he continued to look at me in a way that suggested I was wasting my breath, 'Why would I do that?'

'You do a very convincing scatterbrained blonde, Sophie, but even you couldn't have forgotten so many absolutely vital things in the last couple of weeks. Could you?' he insisted, when I didn't answer.

'I guess not. I didn't think you'd noticed.'

'It's malaria I've been suffering from, not myopia,' he said. 'You've been kind, Sophie, but it really does have to stop.'

Stop? I didn't want it to stop. Ever. Apparently I was on my own there. I'd been making a fool of myself and embarrassing him, which was why I said, '*Kind*? Oh, *please*. I'm sorry to disillusion you, but you're just another of my "crazy jobs". Your sister-in-law is *paying* me to keep an eye on you.' Not a total fib. She had offered. I just hadn't accepted. 'Make sure you don't have a relapse. Provide the occasional meal.' And, remembering my attack on the dresser with beeswax, I added, 'Do a little light dusting…'

I wanted to snatch the words back as, with his face expressionless, he voice offering not the slightest hint as to his reaction to this disclosure that my 'concern' was apparently being paid for by the hour, he said, 'Well, you give good value for money, Sophie. If you're as conscientious with all your employers it's scarcely any wonder you're exhausted. Now, move over.'

'You c-can't drive, Gabriel, you're not well.'

'On the contrary, I had the all-clear from the quack several days ago. I'm afraid you're going to have to find another job to fill the gaps in your day.'

'You didn't tell me.'

'No. He came at lunchtime, when I could be certain

you would be too busy serving food to the hungry hordes to dash home.'

'Oh, but...' But if he'd worked out that my dashes back to the mews were on his behalf, why hadn't he said anything?

'Not that it makes any difference whether I have a clean bill of health...'

Of course not. He might have recovered from the fever, but there was no way he could return to work. He couldn't do anything. No wonder he was so angry...

'...I could drive better than you when I was unconscious.'

This was clearly rubbish, but presumably meant to deal with any sympathetic feelings. He didn't want my sympathy. After that stupid outburst he wouldn't want anything from me.

But, on the point of protesting this calumny, it occurred to me that I'd got exactly what I'd been angling for back in the coffee bar. His company. So that the yawning gaps at home wouldn't seem so noticeable.

His company.

And at least he'd be getting some exercise, doing something to take his mind off his own problems instead of staring at the four walls of his kitchen and wondering if his career was over.

He climbed up beside me, handed me a pack of tissues from the door ledge and said, 'Fasten your seat belt.'

In view of the way I'd felt as he held me and comforted me, it was way too late for that, but there are times when it's wise to keep quiet and just do as you're told.

He bunched and stretched his hands a couple of times, then reached for the key and restarted the engine. With it ticking over he laid his hands lightly on the wheel. There was just the faintest tremor before he gripped it hard and hung on for a moment. Then he engaged gear and moved off. 'I take it we're heading for the M4?' he said abruptly, as he took the road west out of London.

I hadn't realised I'd been holding my breath until I tried to speak. He glanced at me.

'Yes,' I said quickly. 'The Windsor junction.'

Knightsbridge was ablaze with Christmas decorations sparkling against the pale blue sky and the thin winter sunlight. The tinsel looked out of place, wrong, somehow, needing winter darkness and snow to provide a proper seasonal setting.

'What will you do?' Gabriel's voice recalled me from an inner emptiness and I glanced at him. 'What will you do this Christmas?'

I shook my head. 'I don't want to think about it.'

'You're running out of time. You don't have friends you can go to? What about your sister?'

'Kate and Simon want to be on their own. It's their first Christmas together. And Tony, who I've always been able to rely on, has finally met the girl of his dreams and they're going to spend the holiday in the Maldives…' He'd phoned me and told me about her. He'd sounded—well, as if he didn't know what had hit him, to be honest.

'Is he the rich guy that got away?'

'Tony?' That, at least, made me smile. 'No, bless

him. Well, he's not poor, but to tell you the truth it
was a bit like Buttons telling Cinderella he's fallen in
love with someone else. Unexpected, but something
of a relief that I don't have to feel responsible for him
any more.' Then, 'But it's a good job I got a better
offer and wasn't forced to camp out on his sofa.
Dream girls tend to take a dim view of that.'

'You should know.'

'Me? Hell, no, I've never been anyone's dream girl,
Gabriel.'

That earned me another glance—a frankly disbelieving one, which I suppose should have been flattering. Except it was the truth. 'I may have been an
object of desire, or more probably lust, but I've never
been the girl of any man's dreams. The one person
who could put the world right with just a touch of her
hand...'

My mother had done that for Dad. Just reached out,
touched his arm or his cheek, and suddenly the storm
clouds would lift and he'd be smiling. How could he
have been so careless with such treasure? How could
she have walked out on her life for a man with easy
charm and a trim waist?

Maybe it wasn't just Dad. Maybe we'd all taken
her for granted for too long.

'What will you do this Christmas, Gabriel? I don't
suppose you'll be working?'

'No, I won't be working,' he said. 'I'll just take
the dogs for a walk, defrost a ready-meal...'

'Not exactly festive.'

'I've never had a traditional family Christmas, and
what you've never had you don't miss.'

'Life-saving surgery, rights for women and world peace took priority in the York household, huh?'

'It has a seasonal theme, wouldn't you say?'

'But you do that all the year. It's definitely time to give yourself a treat and indulge in some serious celebrations.'

'I wouldn't know where to start.'

'With lists. At the beginning of September,' I replied. 'Then you make the puddings and the cake. You order the free-range organic turkey and the ham. You choose the Christmas cards...'

I stopped. It was way too late to worry about any of that.

'What then?'

'After you've hit the shops and burned up your credit card buying presents for absolutely everyone you know? You have to go and find the biggest, bushiest tree that will fit in your living room and abandon all sense of taste as you load it with anything that sparkles.'

He laughed. 'Is the lack of taste essential?'

'Totally,' I began. 'No colour co-ordination allowed...'

He *laughed*! I turned to stare at him, completely knocked out by the unexpectedness of the sound. Stared at him, knocked out at the difference a few creases in a man's cheeks can make.

My silence must have warned him he'd done something odd. He glanced at me and the laughter died.

'Okay,' he said. 'Well, nothing too painful so far.'

'Don't get complacent. That's just the beginning...'

As the big four-wheel drive ate up the miles I set about entertaining Gabriel with all the hair-curling

stories—long embroidered in the years of retelling—
that made the season so memorable. I'd made him
laugh once and I'd do it again.

I gave him the one when we'd had a power cut and
had to cook, and eat, by candlelight. Very Dickensian.
Very picturesque. Very hard work.

The one where my perfect sister had over-indulged
in the pre-lunch drinks and fallen asleep with her face
in the pudding: my particular favourite.

The one when Aunt Cora had caught husband number two *in flagrante* with her best friend during a
game of Sardines on Boxing Day.

And last year, when Kate and Simon had announced they were getting married and everything
had seemed so absolutely perfect that nothing could
ever top it...

'Is this is our junction coming up?' I asked. It
wasn't, but quite suddenly I didn't feel like laughing.
And I didn't want to talk about Christmas any more.

CHAPTER NINE

GABRIEL, perhaps sensing my change of mood, put some music on the sound system and didn't speak again, except to ask for directions, until we approached the village and he was forced to stop as the congregation from the late-morning family service spilled into the street.

I was instantly spotted by the village postmistress. The last person, in fact, in the entire that world I wanted to talk to. But before I could say, Let's get out of here, and just wave back as we passed, Gabriel lowered the window.

'Sophie, dear. You're quite a stranger.' She glanced curiously at Gabriel. 'Home for Sunday lunch with your father? He's quite a stranger, too, these days.'

'Not lunch. I've just taken pity on a couple of London dogs and brought them home for a run in the country. This is their owner, Gabriel York. Gabriel, Vera runs the post office and general store. She keeps us all up to date with the news.' I hoped he'd get this code for 'village gossip'.

'Charmed,' Vera said, then, 'Have you heard from your dear mother? Is she feeling any better? Getting plenty of rest in the sun, I hope.'

Better? My father was telling people she'd gone away for her health? That wouldn't fool anyone...

'It must be so hard for your poor father, not able

to get away from the estate to be with her. Such a busy time of year.'

Or maybe all those years of good works had ring-fenced her reputation. 'Yes,' I said. 'It is.'

'We've all missed her so much. She'll be home for Christmas, I hope. She so embodies the spirit of the season, with her kindness, the way she includes everyone in her family celebrations.' She offered a hopeful smile. 'We all quite understand that she won't be able to cope this year, of course...'

Gabriel, as if he could feel me floundering, lost for words, reached across and took my hand, and, as I felt his strength pouring into me, I found myself saying, 'Of course this year it's more important than ever to make the effort. Tell everyone that we're expecting them. That they're all to join us, just as usual, won't you?'

'Really?' Her face lit up and I realised just how much they did all rely on my mother to cover the yawning emotional gaps that appeared in everyone's lives at this time of year. 'But how—?'

'I'll take care of everything.' Then self-preservation made me add, 'Actually, I could do with a little help. I'm working right through until Christmas Eve.'

'Anything, dear. We'll all be more than happy to pitch in. We never liked to offer before...' Behind us someone hooted impatiently, anxious to get home to Sunday lunch, and Vera reached out, touched my arm. 'Ring me in the week. Just tell me what you want and I'll organise everyone. Good to meet you, Gabriel.'

As we moved on I said, 'What have I done? I can't cook a turkey…'

'You can read. There are cookery books.'

'You think that's all I need do? Read a cookery book? If that's all it took we'd all be cordon bleu cooks.'

'Every journey starts with a single step.'

'Not Christmas. It starts in September and it's a route march. There are no puddings made. Or cake…'

'You can leave those to me.'

My heart leapt, but I didn't dare look at him. 'You're going to come for Christmas?'

'You looked after me. Now it's my turn.' He paused at a junction. 'We'll negotiate my hourly rate later.' Then, 'Which way?'

'Right…' I'd hoped he might have forgotten my bruising remark about taking care of him at my usual hourly rate, but clearly he hadn't. Lies, even the well-intentioned ones, came back to haunt you, and the ones that were meant to hurt deservedly came back tenfold. I vowed at that moment that I would never tell another, no matter how well intentioned, how severely provoked, and then, forcing a grin to my lips, a lightness to my voice that I was far from feeling, I said, 'Okay, but I'm not paying you as much as I earn. You can't cook.'

'Neither can you,' he reminded me. 'But I know a woman who can.' He glanced across at me. 'Of course, you'll have to find another place at your table for her.'

Forget tenfold. This was beyond numbers. 'The more the merrier,' I said, the grin—if possible—even broader, and my voice filled with all the lightness and substance of a meringue. Then, 'Turn in here.'

Dad wasn't at home, nor were the dogs.

'I expect he's taken them out,' Gabriel said, presumably putting my sudden disinclination for conversation down to unease.

'Maybe. Maybe we'll meet him out in the woods. It'll be muddy,' I said, looking doubtfully at Gabriel's town shoes. 'You'd better find a pair of boots that fit. I waved at the row of Wellingtons that lived in the mud room and, without waiting to see if he was taking my advice, kicked off my shoes and pulled on a pair that looked about my size. 'And you might want to take a waxed jacket. Brambles are hell on cashmere.'

I picked up a thumb stick and let the dogs out of the Range Rover as Gabriel joined me, looking about as far from the saturnine surgeon as it was possible to imagine in his hard-worn country clothes. He looked exactly like the man I'd always expected to spend my life with. Too bad I'd left it so long to work out that it wasn't the trappings that made the man, but the man himself.

'Let's go,' I said, and headed towards the woods, throwing sticks to distract the dogs from the pheasants which flew up in a panic at their approach.

'Tell me about the estate,' Gabriel said. 'What does your father do here?'

'Arable farming, deer, some rough shooting...' This was easier. 'He's been growing willow as a renewable energy source.' I found myself telling him about the complex issue of balancing the needs of the environment with modern farming methods—I'd been listening to my father for years, and knew a heck of a lot more than I'd thought I did—the decline of the songbird population—anything, in fact, but what I wanted to say.

That my heart was breaking.

I knew it was because it had happened to me before. But why on earth would he be interested?

And it was all right. I'd survived then and I'd survive now. But it was going to be tougher this time. Apparently it hurt more when you were older...

I slashed at a bramble blocking the path and it rebounded and caught my hand, bringing my endless chatter to an abrupt halt. Gabriel carefully disentangled me, blotted the scratch with a clean handkerchief and then looked up. 'How does that feel?'

'It stings a bit, but—'

He leaned forward and kissed me, soft and tender, on the mouth.

His lips were cold against mine, but like ice they burned, and the heat rippled through me like a volcano in the long seconds before he pulled back.

A million words flooded into my brain. Not a million different words. The same one. Again. A million times.

'How does it feel now?' he asked.

'What?' Then, 'Oh, my hand.' I'd forgotten all about my hand. 'Better...'

'Wrong answer,' he said.

'Sorry?'

'Think about it.' He took my good hand and headed back to the house. The wrong answer? Then it hit me. If I'd been on my toes, kissing it better

could have been a slow, delicious, drawn-out affair.
But he'd taken me by surprise...

Maybe I could have a relapse...

No. No pretence. No games. He clearly had someone else who fulfilled all his needs. Dog-carer, cook,
buyer of fancy baskets of fruit. I needed to know it
all. Now.

I could always have a relapse later...

'That's a very effective anaesthetic, Gabriel. Maybe you should patent it.'

'Kissing it better is as old as time.'

Not like that, it wasn't...

'Let's get back and get that cleaned up properly. If
your hand gets infected you won't be much use on
the twenty-fifth.'

Okay, we were back to Christmas. Exactly the
opening I'd been looking for. 'Tell me about this cook
of yours,' I demanded.

He glanced at me. Well, maybe I had been a bit
fierce. 'June?'

'Yes,' I said, before I could lose my nerve. 'Tell
me about June.'

'She was a theatre nurse.'

Of course. All that eye contact over the operating
table...

'More than that—' *No!* 'A great theatre nurse.
Unfortunately she was hurt in a car accident and had
to give up work.'

Oh, great. I couldn't even hate her...

'That's tough,' I said.

'Yes, but she's a fighter, and she's always loved to
cook. She doesn't need the money—she received sub-

stantial compensation—but she likes to keep busy, so
she set up a small catering business.'

'And she takes care of your dogs when you go
away as a little sideline?'

He stopped, blocking the path. 'Jealous?'

About to do the whole 'Excuse me and why on
earth would I be jealous of her taking care of your
dogs?' bit, I remembered my vow. No more pretence.
No more lies.

'Jealous as hell,' I said.

'Good.' And then he kissed me again, taking his
time about it. He tilted my chin up with the edge of
his thumb, his cold fingers stroking against my neck
as he looked at me with those bottomless eyes for
what seemed like a century. 'I'm really glad about
that,' he said, his voice low and husky and thick with
need as he slowly lowered his mouth to mine.

He'd kissed me before. Hot and hard. Cold and
sweet.

This was different. I'd never been kissed like this
before. It was as if he was giving me a part of him
that he hadn't even known existed, and something so
deep inside me that I'd forgotten it was there responded and answered him with everything I had to
offer.

It was as if I'd been living in glass box for years.
I could see everything that was happening around me
but I was detached, apart. Nothing had been able to
touch me until now, without warning, the glass had
been shattered and noise and colour and life were
rushing in, bludgeoning my heightened senses.

The touch of Gabriel's hands as they held my face,
his thumbs brushing my cheeks, cold-on-cold. Leaves

rustled around our feet as the wind stirred them. The scent of his skin, touched by the clean wind.

This went way beyond kissing me better.

He had told me he'd show me how to give the kiss of life. And this was it.

It left me clinging to him. Weak, trembling from head to toe, but undoubtedly alive.

And then there was a clatter of pheasants' wings and the dogs, stupid things, came careering out of the woods, expecting to be told how brilliant they were.

Gabriel held me for a moment, face as grave as it had ever been. Then he smiled and said, 'You'll like June.'

I thought he was being overly optimistic, frankly, but I loved him, so I left him with his illusions and said, 'Of course I will.' Then, because I didn't want to tempt fate, I added, 'I'll do my best, anyway. But right now I think we'd better leave these birds in peace.'

I set off briskly for the house as Gabriel whistled the dogs to heel, but he caught me, took my arm, tucked it beneath his. Then, as we passed the tree nursery, he stopped. 'What's this?'

'The Christmas tree farm.'

'This is where you pick the biggest, bushiest tree you can find?'

'The very place.'

'Well, hadn't we'd better go pick out a Christmas tree?'

'I think we need to get back. I'm worried about Dad.' Then, because even from the road I could see the one I'd pick, I said, 'Okay. That one.'

*   *   *

Dad still wasn't there when we got back, and I went upstairs and stuck a dressing on my hand while Gabriel gave the dogs some water. It wasn't that I didn't want a repeat of the kissing it better thing. I just needed to concentrate on one problem at a time.

Returning to the kitchen, I opened the fridge, checking to see what was there, making sure that he was eating. It was worse than I'd thought. There was nothing, not even milk.

'I was going to ask if you're hungry,' I said to Gabriel as he joined me, putting his hand on my shoulder as he looked over my head.

'Actually, I'm famished, but it looks as if I'm going to have to buy you lunch as well as breakfast.'

'It's too late. The pub stops serving lunch at two.'

'The motorway services never close,' he pointed out.

In reply, I opened a cupboard and found a couple of cans of soup. He took them from me and opened them while I dug around in the freezer for some of my mother's home-made bread rolls. I stuck some in the Aga and within minutes the kitchen smelled enough like home to make me wish I'd taken the motorway services option.

'How many people are we going to be catering for?'

'What?' I dragged myself back to the present. To reality. Trying not to let my heart get in a giddy state about that 'we'. This was a man who'd spent his life avoiding hurting other people by refusing to get in-volved. Mr No Commitment. He'd never lied. Never pretended. He was straight down the line. Absolutely serious. And I was going to have to let him go without a backward glance. But I would have Christmas. I would be his gift from me. He would be my gift to myself.

'Guests? For Christmas Day?' he prompted, while my mind was freewheeling.

'Oh, right. Well, usually about twenty. But Mum won't be here, and I don't suppose Aunt Cora will come unless she wants to take the opportunity to glare at Dad. Kate and Simon won't be here, nor will Tony, but you and your lady cook will fill a couple of gaps.'

'Sophie—'

'What?'

'I heard a car.'

It was Dad. He had his Labradors at his heels and he was carrying Flossie, my mother's old spaniel, in his arms. Percy and Joe sat respectfully, keeping their distance. He didn't evoke any surprise at seeing me. Just said, 'I took her to the vet. There's nothing he can do. She's pining for your mother.'

All the anger, all the rage I'd been feeling for weeks, just washed away from me and I went and put my arms around him. 'Go and find her, Dad. Tell her how much you need her.'

'But I can't leave. The farm…'

'You've got a manager to take care of the day-to-day running of the place.'

'The dogs…'

He was afraid, I realised. Scared she wouldn't come.

'We'll take care of them,' Gabriel said without hesitation.

It said much for Dad's state of mind that he didn't

even query this offer from a total stranger. He just looked at me and said, 'Do you think she'll listen?'

'You'll never know unless you try.'

I packed him a bag while Gabriel booked him a flight. He came upstairs to find me and give me the details.

'I've booked him on a flight leaving this evening,' he began.

'Gabriel, it's impossible. We can't take all these dogs back to London. I'll have to stay here,' I said, desperate because I couldn't let all those other people down, either. Desperate because I didn't want to leave him.

'No, Sophie. Take your father to the airport. I'll stay here. Keep an eye on things. I'll take good care of Flossie, I promise.'

'Well, that deals with one of the desperates,' I said, under my breath. 'There's plenty of transport—you'll find all the keys in the office. And you'll be looked after. I'll phone Mrs Marsh, the daily, to warn her you'll be here. She'll cook for you.' Then, 'Unless, of course, you'd rather have...' I found I couldn't bring myself to say June '...someone else.'

'I'll be fine,' he said, and held me briefly. Which didn't exactly answer the unasked question. 'Now, you'd better go or your father will miss his flight. Call me when you get home.'

The thing about Christmas is that once you open up and decide to enjoy it, it seems to take on a life of its own. I asked Mrs Andrews, of course, and since it was obvious that Alan from the toy store was going to be on his own I asked him to join us, too. There was plenty of room in the Range Rover.

And when I found Greta breaking her heart because she didn't have the money to give her girls everything she wanted, I thought, What the heck? The more the merrier. We could all squeeze in somehow, and what was Christmas without children?

Then, when I called in at the agency to sort out a few things, and asked Miss Frosty—Lucy—what she was doing for the holiday, instead of snapping at me she burst into tears and told me all about how she'd split up with the man she'd been living with for years. Fortunately she had her own car, because the Range Rover was getting to be a bit of a squeeze.

Gabriel drove up for the Nativity play. As we sat together in church and watched the story unfold, heard the children sing the carols, my eyes filled with tears.

I hoped he hadn't seen, but he took my hand and held it. He didn't need to say anything. Afterwards we had supper with Lucia and her family, and then walked back to the mews cottage.

With his fingers laced through mine, I felt emboldened enough to turn and say to him, 'Please don't drive back tonight.' He couldn't possibly have mistaken my meaning.

'I have to. I left Vera babysitting Flossie.' He kissed my cheek. 'I'll be back on Christmas Eve, to help transport your waifs and strays.'

'Drive carefully,' I said, letting him go. Please drive carefully...

* * *

On Christmas Eve, after I'd served my last portion of turkey at the pub, I made a detour to see Paul, the homeless guy with the little dog, who sold the *Big Issue* near the underground station. I hadn't seen him for a couple of weeks, and I wanted to deliver a couple of tins of food for the pup's Christmas dinner.

'Have you heard anything about a flat,' I asked, as I made a fuss of the little mongrel.

'New job, new flat,' he said, pleased as punch. 'Right after Christmas.'

After Christmas.

Well, I knew what my mother would do. Not that it mattered. I invited him to spend Christmas with us because it was what *I* would do, and took him back to the mews and introduced him to Gabriel, who'd already arrived and, having got Tigger crated up, was busy packing the stuff I'd left out to take home with me into the rear of the Rover.

'I've missed you,' he said quietly, after I'd introduced him to Paul. And he briefly took my hand. His eyes said how much. Or maybe it was just a reflection of my own need.

'You look a lot better,' I said.

'I feel better. Walking the dogs has helped. And I've made some decisions about my future.' He had that ready-for-action look of a man with his sights set on a distance horizon and I was seized with fear. 'I'll tell you later,' he said.

'Any news from Dad?' I asked, hoping to disguise the fact that 'later' seemed like for ever.

'There's still time.'

'How's Flossie?'

'Holding on.'

*   *   *

Mrs Marsh and Vera had done us proud. The house was gleaming, the fridge and freezer were loaded, and there was a note on the kitchen table to tell me that they'd be arriving early to start vegetable duty the following morning.

Only the decorations were missing. And my parents.

'Where are they, Gabriel? I phoned; I sent a text...' No one was answering.

He opened his arms and I went into them. Just for a moment. Then I took a deep breath, found a smile, and said, 'Okay. I can do this.'

'Of course you can.'

He left me organising supper for everyone while he lit the fire in the drawing room and then organised for the other men to bring in the luggage and boxes from the cars, sorted out the bedrooms. By the time everyone had finished, and Gabriel had opened a bottle of something old, warming and festive from a hamper he'd brought with him, the kitchen was filled with the scent of potatoes baking to go with the ham.

'Relax, your dad won't let you down,' he said, as he handed me a glass.

'No.' I sounded more convinced than I was, but the festive cheer was trickling down to warm all the chilly corners of my heart and it was beginning to feel a little bit more like Christmas. Then another car arrived. Lucy or June?

Gabriel went out to help with the bags while I went back to rolling pastry for little fruit tarts. And when I looked again it was to see Gabriel with his arms enfolding a small woman who was completely hidden.

Was I jealous?

Too right.

It stabbed through me, sharp and poisonous, and then Gabriel straightened, turned, and said, 'Sophie, I'd like you to meet June.'

June was a slight, elegant woman in tight jeans and a floppy sweatshirt, with short, spiky silver hair. And she was sixty if she was a day. Gabriel caught my jaw-drop moment as introduced her, smiling at me over her head.

Bastard! He knew exactly what I'd been thinking and he'd let me go on thinking it…

It was perhaps as well for him that, having welcomed my guest with an enthusiasm that she might have found a little bit over the top, I was distracted by the arrival of Lucy. And then Greta's little girls, apprehensive and shy in a strange house full of people they didn't know, came downstairs from their bedroom, clinging to their mother's skirt. I loaded them up with the box of decorations I'd asked Gabriel to bring down from attic and despatched them with their mother and Alan to blitz the house with tinsel, then, while Gabriel showed June to her room, Lucy and I laid out supper in the kitchen.

'You were right,' she said, as I checked the potatoes and hoped I'd done enough. 'You do have domestic skills.'

I was saved from having to respond to this unlikely compliment by a rush of cold air as the back door was flung open, and I turned to see Gabriel with the thickest, bushiest bunch of mistletoe I'd ever seen.

'I thought you were taking it easy with June,' I said meaningfully. Then, 'Where did you get that?'

'I saw it when we were in the woods last week. I meant to get it earlier, but Vera arrived...'

For a moment I was speechless. 'You went out there in the dark?' I was furious. 'You could have fallen. Been hurt. No one would have known where you were—'

'I eat plenty of carrots,' he said, grinning as he cut me off in full vent, and I realised that I'd totally betrayed myself. That I was emotionally naked... 'Where do you want it?' he asked.

'Just hold it right there for the moment.'

'Here?' He looked up, as if expecting to see a beam above him.

'That's it. Maybe a little higher...higher... Perfect.' And then I kissed him. Once you were emotionally naked there was no point in playing it cool. Actually, I'd meant just to touch his lips with mine, but the mistletoe magic must have been particularly strong because the kiss seemed to go on and on, an unbreakable enchantment that enfolded us, isolated us—

'Hey, don't keep that gorgeous stuff to yourselves, you two!'

I pulled away to the laughter of a kitchen full of the people I'd gathered together. 'I've missed you,' I said, so that only he could hear. Then, louder, '*Excellent* mistletoe...'

And into those two words I put everything else I wanted to say to him but couldn't right there in the kitchen, with everyone looking on, which was probably a good thing. It would be absolutely fatal to risk letting slip those three little words 'I love you' to a man who'd apparently erased 'commitment' from his dictionary. He'd probably run a mile.

As it was, he simply put out a cold hand, touched my cheek. 'Ten out of ten,' he agreed.

It was all it took to make the world seem like a magic place as the air filled with the warm scent of spiced wine, baking potatoes and warm bread.

'All we need now,' I said, 'is snow.'

We got the next best thing. Aunt Cora.

Supper was a riot. Too much food, too much everything. And, at the far end of the table, Gabriel. A man with his future all decided. Was there going to be any part in it for me?

'What are you doing?'

It was late. I'd had to wait for everyone to settle down before I could hang up the stockings along the mantel. One for everyone, each with an orange, some nuts, chocolate money, a sherbet dab, a pocket diary and a bath fizzer, plus all the other silly little gifts that had been a part of our family Christmas for as long as I could remember. It was the first time I'd done them and I discovered it was as much fun as— no, more fun than getting one.

'Playing Santa Claus. You are supposed to be in bed,' I said.

'And this?' He picked up the gift I'd wrapped for him. I'd stuck on a big label that said *'Not to be opened until Christmas'*.

He ignored it, pulling at the ribbon.

'Hey! You can't do that!' I said, pointing at the label.

'I've got news for you, my love,' he said, as the clock on the mantel began to chime, and, grinning like a big kid, he tore the paper. 'It is Christmas...' The words faltered as a silk négligée slipped from the paper. Palest oyster silk. Size eight. 'I think there's been some mistake, here,' he said.

'No. No mistake.' I took it from him. I'd meant this for tomorrow night, but all evening I'd been melting with desire, wishing we were on our own... 'Come on, I'll show you how it works.'

I took his hand and led him up the stairs to my bedroom, and, leaving him standing in the middle of the room, said, 'Wait there. I'll be right back.'

It was entirely possible that by now he'd got the idea. But when I opened the bathroom door, wearing nothing but the négligée and Chanel No 5, I realised with delight that for once he was the one rendered speechless. So I put my arms around his neck and said, 'Happy Christmas, Gabriel.'

'I don't know what to say.'

'You don't have to say anything. All you have to do is open your present.' And then I kissed him and he pulled me into his arms. I could tell he wasn't going to need any further encouragement.

I was woken by a shattering noise, but as I disentangled myself from Gabriel's arms and grabbed for the alarm clock I realised that the sound was coming from downstairs.

I flung back the covers, grabbed a wrap, and with Gabriel hard on my heels rushed into the drawing room. The girls were there. One of them was screaming. The other was motionless, not breathing, her face swollen.

'Peanuts,' he said, spotting an open packet raided from the cupboard as he scooped her up and carried her through to the kitchen. 'She's gone into anaphylactic shock. I need a sharp knife and a ballpoint pen or a straw.'

'What's happening? What's wrong?' Greta shrieked as she came flying down the stairs to join us.

'Go and start the car, please, Greta,' Gabriel said, ice-cool, and when she would have ignored him, to rush to her little girl, I grabbed the Range Rover keys from the dresser and thrust them into her hand.

'He's a doctor. Go and get the car started. Use the phone to call the local hospital and tell them we're coming in with her.' And, when she still hesitated, 'Now!'

She fled. And I turned in time to see Gabriel plunge a small sharp knife into the child's windpipe. 'Take the refill out of that pen,' he said, without looking up. My hands were shaking so much that the simple task seemed beyond me, but it came free and he used the plastic tube to keep the incision open so that he could blow air into the child's lungs...

There was a nightmare drive to the cottage hospital, and a nightmare wait for the swelling to reduce in response to the antihistamine. Then she was cleaned up, stitched and put to bed.

And I was *still* shaking.

Gabriel was like a rock.

'You said you'd show me how to give the kiss of life. That was a bit closer than I ever want to come again,' I said, trying to hold onto the cup of tea someone had given me without spilling it.

'You don't need lessons, Sophie. Just being in your company is enough to breathe life into the most moribund of hearts.' He reached out, took the cup from me and held my face between his hands. 'Tell Lucy to take you off her books,' he said. 'I'm employing you for the rest of your life. I may not need a wife, but I sure as hell need you.'

What? *No-o-o.* It took me a moment to reply— *employing* me! 'You've already had me. Unlike a puppy, I'm just for Christmas.' What else could I say to a man of no commitment?

But then, with perfect timing, Greta walked in. 'Gabriel, Sophie… How can I ever thank you both?' She looked flattened, shell-shocked. 'I had no idea…'

Gabriel, who, I'm happy to say, looked a touch shell-shocked himself, tore his gaze from my face and said, 'These things sometimes flare up without any warning. The hospital will give her a special device to keep with her at all times. Show her how to use it. Explain how to live with the allergy. They'll probably let her out in an hour or two. Just as soon as they're sure she's stable.'

'We'll get someone to come over with some clothes for you and bring you back,' I said through a sort of creeping numbness. My mind wasn't really on the conversation at hand, but on one a lot more personal to me—and Gabriel. *How could he say that?* How was I going to get through the rest of the day? Somehow… 'But I have to get back. If I don't get the turkey on soon no one is going eat before nightfall…'

Gabriel butted in. 'Stuff the turkey! I've got something to say to you and it's more important than any turkey—'

He grabbed my hand and, ignoring Greta, a couple of nurses who'd gathered by the drinks machine and a number of sorry-looking patients waiting to be seen by the doctor, dragged me into the nearest cubicle. 'What the hell do you mean "just for Christmas"?'

There was no way on earth this conversation wasn't being shared with everyone on the other side of the curtain.

'Gabriel,' I said, as quietly as I could. 'You don't do commitment. You just said it. You don't need a wife—'

'I was wrong. I didn't mean… Sophie, I'm going back to Africa—'

Wrong?

'Oh, I see,' I said, cutting him off. 'You need me to sort out the details, is that it? Find you a compatible anti-malaria drug? Make sure you take it—'

Okay, I was beginning to get the picture. He *needed* me. Well, he'd got me—even if it was going to be in Africa—but first he was going to have to pay for that 'employing you for the rest of your life'. That had *not* been romantic…

'No!' He ran his fingers through his uncombed hair and said, 'No, damn it. I need you. Just to be there to come home to. Just to be there to reach out and touch when the world seems a dark place. Just to hold…'

He stopped, struggling to put exactly what he was feeling into words.

'Gabriel, it's okay…'

That was romantic enough. I wanted to get to the rest of our lives now...

'No, it's not okay. I have to tell you this. You thought you'd given me the kiss of life, Sophie? Well, I'm telling you that you've turned my heart from an efficient pump into something that beats faster whenever I think of you. And I think of you constantly. You've warmed my heart and my spirit and the simple truth is that I cannot imagine living without you,' he said.

'What are you saying, Gabriel?'

He reached out then, cradled my cheek in the palm of his hand. 'I'm saying that I love you, Sophie.'

From beyond the curtain a cheer went up.

He glanced briefly towards the commotion, then smiled. 'I love you, and despite the fact that you've already told me that you don't need a husband I'd like you to give some serious consideration to the idea. Not because I need someone to take care of me, or even because you need someone to take care of you, but because together we will be so much greater than the sum of our two parts. Marry me, Sophie.'

Now I was the one struggling for words. 'You shouldn't say things like that on the spur of the moment,' I said. 'I might take you seriously.'

He reached into the pocket of the trousers he'd pulled on even as he'd plunged down the stairs back at the house. 'Not the spur of the moment.' And he produced a small box. 'I bought this when I came up to London last week. I know it fits because I borrowed one of your rings...' He opened the box, slid the ring onto my finger. 'A diamond is for ever, Sophie, and whatever else I do in my life I want you beside me that long. For ever.'

'This is all part of the macho York thing, isn't it? When you go for something, you don't quit.' *Please.* 'There's absolutely no point in me playing hard to get, is there?'

The smile deepened. 'Well, you can try,' he offered. 'But after last night I'd have said it was a bit late—'

'Shh! Everyone's listening.'

'Then you'd better hurry up and say yes, or I'll tell them exactly how you seduced me...'

I'd already had a master class in how to shut someone up. I put it to good use and kissed him, long and hard.

After what seemed like an age, I pulled away. 'I have a confession to make,' I said, fighting to get my breath back. 'But I'll tell you in the car.' I'd eventually remembered the turkey and had to get back to the house. Pronto.

'Confess away,' he said, once we'd settled ourselves into the car.

'Crissie did give me some money to look after you—told Lucy to pay me for the hours I worked. I wouldn't let her. I put the cash in an envelope and put it back through her letterbox.'

'Tell me something I don't know.'

'But—'

'I notice when bills don't arrive and I called the agency. Lucy told me you'd paid the dog-walking account yourself.'

'Why didn't you say?'

'I thought you'd tell me yourself, eventually. And I was right.'

'Know-it-all. I knew you wouldn't take rent from me, but I couldn't deprive the agency of their fee.'

'You are something else, Sophie.' He pulled into the drive, reached across and took my hand, spreading out my fingers beneath his. 'Something very special.'

'Of course I am. It takes a special woman to ride the slip-stream and hold on long enough to catch a York man.' I moved my hand so that the diamond flashed in the low, slanting rays of the sun. And then I realised something. 'The tremor. It's gone!'

'Days ago. The minute I realised that it wouldn't actually be the end of my life if I couldn't be a surgeon. I'm not just a surgeon, I'm a doctor, and I still have something useful to offer. That's when I asked the medical charity if they'd take me on permanently. It's time to put something back, Sophie. You do understand?' He grasped my hand, held it tight. 'It won't be easy. I know I'm being selfish, taking you with me.'

'Just try and leave without me.' I lifted his hand to my lips and kissed it. 'But right now I have a house full of guests to feed.'

Except I didn't.

At home, Vera was in charge of the vegetables, Mrs Andrews was in charge of the sherry, and my mother was in her rightful place—in charge of the turkey. It seemed so right, her being there, that I almost forgot she'd been away.

She finished basting the bird, closed the cooker door and came and gave me a hug that didn't need words. It said, Well done. And I'm proud of you. And

I'm happy to be home. No words needed. Well, maybe just a few—

'Mum, this is Gabriel York. He's been looking after Flossie for you.' Flossie looked up at the sound of her name and wagged her tail. 'We're getting married and going to work in Africa. Together.'

'That sounds exciting,' she said. And gave him a hug, too.

We went in search of Dad and found Kate and Simon in the dining room, laying the table. 'She forgot to defrost the turkey,' Simon said with a grin, and got a slap with a cracker for his cheek.

Dad was in the drawing room, looking a bit jet-lagged, but he roused himself to say, 'I got it all wrong about the golfer, you know. She just wanted to get away. Have some time to herself.'

'Take care of her, okay. And give her a hand putting the garden back together.'

'Absolutely. Anything she wants.'

'I think we're surplus to requirements here,' Gabriel murmured in my ear. 'Let's go and take a shower. I've got a little Christmas present for you…'

It was a ticket to St Lucia; he'd bought one for himself, too. 'And then I want to have another look at my Christmas present from you…'

The wedding wasn't the way I'd planned it all those years ago. We didn't have time to wait while all that stuff was organised. Besides, my mother was too busy rebuilding her garden and she was doing enough looking after Percy, Joe and Tigger while we were away.

We just had a quiet service in the village church,

with Ginny as my 'best woman' and a party at home for our friends and family.

Of course the flowers were spectacular...totally in keeping with my TFB status. But that was my only concession to fantasy. This marriage had nothing to do with fantasy. It was solid, based on truth, honour and the kind of love that isn't about staring into one another's eyes across a candlelit table but facing in the same direction, moving forward together.

Besides, I had much better things to do with the money my father had saved on a fancy marquee and a thousand guests. A new medical centre with my mother's name on it in an African village, for a start.

It was just the beginning.

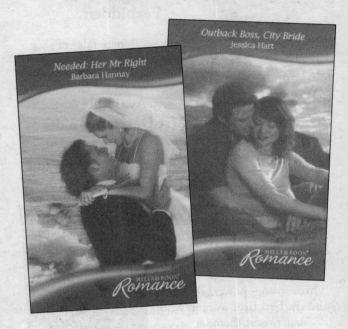

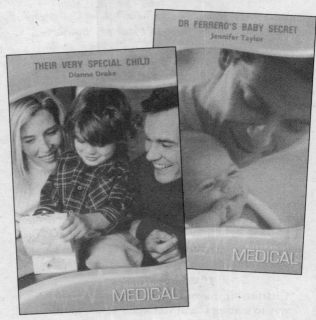

MILLS & BOON®
MEDICAL™

Proudly presents

Brides of Penhally Bay

*A pulse-raising collection of emotional,
tempting romances and heart-warming stories by
bestselling Mills & Boon Medical™ authors.*

January 2008
The Italian's New-Year Marriage Wish
by Sarah Morgan

Enjoy some much-needed winter warmth with
gorgeous Italian doctor Marcus Avanti.

February 2008
The Doctor's Bride By Sunrise
by Josie Metcalfe

Then join Adam and Maggie on a 24-hour rescue mission
where romance begins to blossom as the sun starts to set.

March 2008
The Surgeon's Fatherhood Surprise
by Jennifer Taylor

Single dad Jack Tremayne finds a mother for his
little boy – and a bride for himself.

*Let us whisk you away to an idyllic Cornish town –
a place where hearts are made whole*

COLLECT ALL 12 BOOKS!

100 Reasons to Celebrate

2008 is a very special year as we celebrate Mills and Boon's Centenary.

Each month throughout the year there will be something new and exciting to mark the centenary, so watch for your favourite authors, captivating new stories, special limited edition collections...and more!

www.millsandboon.co.uk